SHADOW OF THE VOID

D1506927

Also by Nathan Garrison

Veiled Empire

SHADOW OF THE VOID

Book Two of the Sundered World Trilogy

NATHAN GARRISON

HARPER

VOYAGER

IMPULSE

An Imprint of HarperCollins Publishers

This is a work of fiction. Names, characters, places, and incidents are products of the author's imagination or are used fictitiously and are not to be construed as real. Any resemblance to actual events, locales, organizations, or persons, living or dead, is entirely coincidental.

EPub Edition MAY 2016 ISBN: 9780062451996

Print Edition ISBN: 9780062452924

10 9 8 7 6 5 4 3 2 1

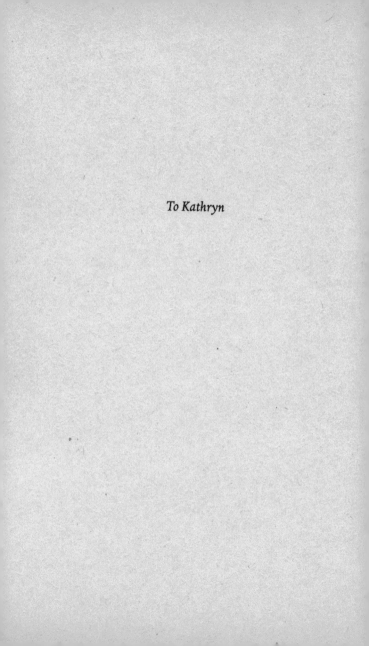

To Kathryn

A page from *History of the Veiled Empire*, Chapter 9
Uva Thress, Imperial Historian
11,748 A.S.

The end of the Mierothi Civil War came in 11,712 with the assault of Mecrithos by Vashodia's puppet rebellion, and the subsequent defeat of Emperor Rekaj and all[1] high-ranking members of his regime. Though seeming of little importance when compared to future events, this occasion is worth noting because of a few key points of interest.

Firstly, it set the groundwork for future peace between mierothi and valynkar. Draevenus, brother of Vashodia, and Gilshamed,[2] once-leader of the revolution, were reported to have met in the ruins of the Imperial Palace and found a way to put aside the ancient enmity between their races. One can surmise that it likely had to do with the return of the long-

---

1   High Regnosist Lekrigar was rumored to have escaped the destruction at both the palace and the fields outside Mecrithos. Though not confirmed, he was never seen or heard from within the empire again.

2   See: Chapter 8: The False Revolution, Section 2a: Key Figures

imprisoned valynkar, including Voren the Redeemed and Lashriel, life-mate of Gilshamed. This fact became crucial during the Non-Battle for Humanity.[3]

Secondly, it marks the only occasion in all of history where the winners of a civil war did not ascend into positions of power. Vashodia, the undisputed mastermind behind all these events, ordered the surviving mierothi into exile, leaving the rule of the Veiled Empire (what is now called the Free States of Ragremos) in the hands of her favored lackey, Yandumar Daere.[2] His son, Mevon,[2] who was personally responsible for Rekaj's demise, faked his own death for reasons unknown, though many speculate that he would not have done so had he known that the great sorceress Jasside,[2] Vashodia's apprentice at the time, had still been alive.

Lastly, Vashodia's final act in the Veiled Empire was to destroy the Shroud, which separated the continent from the rest of the world. This, more than anything else, led directly to what colloquially came to be known as the Chaos War.[4]

---

3   See: Chapter 11: The Rise of Chaos, Section 4: The Great Blindness and the Non-Battle for Humanity

4   See: Chapter 13: The Fall of Chaos

PROLOGUE

Two figures stood on a hillside in the shade of a willow tree, watching the inevitable come to pass.

The valley below them, a field called Trelnizor, was packed with humanity. Men and women in the thousands clustered around a series of enormous tents, the flags of their respective nations fluttering atop them in the breeze. Though there were many soldiers among them, they had not come to make war.

A fact, the two figures knew, that would soon change.

To the north sat the largest of the tents. Stark compared to all its neighbors, the flag it flew bore the image of a bear over a background of colored stripes: brown for the soil they tended and grey for the metal they mined.

Sceptre. A country still foolishly calling itself an empire.

To the south, nestled in the elbow of a creek, lay a pavilion whose magnificence seemed in defiance of Sceptre's grim shelter. A bird that appeared as if on fire flew across its flag's brilliant white background, its edges adorned by golden tassels.

Panisahldron. The jewel of the world.

Next to them, small but never insignificant, flew the white-halo-and-stars-on-black of the valynkar.

Every nation was gathered together in peace for the first time in centuries, to discuss an event that concerned them all. Everyone had felt it, even those without a drop of sorcerous blood in their veins. The world had *shaken*. Everywhere at once. And the source of this monumental disturbance appeared to be, by all accounts, a land long forgotten.

A land known only as the Veiled Empire.

That news was monumental, to say the least. The problem was, though, that opinions were divided as to what they were all going to do about it.

But the figures on the hillside beneath the willow tree cared naught for the deliberations. They knew that the energy released by the shattering of the Shroud had reached far beyond this mere realm. Someone else had felt it. Despite the unshakable mien the two figures affected, they both flinched as long-forgotten enemies made their opening moves in a war both new and mythologically old.

The pavilion belonging to the fair nation of Panisahldron burst into flames.

It did not spread like a normal fire. Rather, the entirety of the canvas ignited at once, trapping hundreds of Panisian citizens inside it: servants, soldiers, and, most importantly, the royal family.

Not one could have escaped the blaze alive.

A dozen men and women scampered away from the scene, wearing the brown-and-grey armor of Sceptre. No less than a hundred people from four different nations saw them and gave chase. The dozen fled, but not towards the Sceptrine encampment. They came straight for the hill occupied by the two figures. They were nimble and quick, and soon outpaced their pursuers. They gathered behind a thick copse of trees and discarded both their strange weapons and their soldiers' garb, throwing them all into a pile. One of them snapped fingers, and a spark of green light flashed. When it diminished, the pile had turned into ash.

The dozen changed into simple clothes in a variety of styles and stole away individually. They disappeared, one each, into the crowds of every represented nation.

The two figures looked towards each other for the first time since they had both appeared on the hillside. One of them was dressed in a fine suit, white as pearls, and was leaning on a golden cane. The other wore a simple black robe.

"And so," said the one in white, "this is how it begins."

"No," said the one in black. "This is how it ends."

"Feeling dour tonight, are we?" The one in white chuckled. "How typically pessimistic of you."

"I always considered myself more of a realist," said the one in black. "Practicality, as history has proven, ever triumphs over ideology."

The one in white twirled his cane once, then pointed it towards the burning tent. "And look where your practicality has led us. After all, it was *your* child that plunged us down this road, ill prepared as we are."

"She is no child of mine. Not anymore. I don't think she ever was."

The one in white laughed again, louder this time. "So you finally see the truth, do you? Took you long enough."

"Yes." The one in black furrowed his brow. "How long has it been since we last spoke?"

"You don't remember?"

"No."

"Then your time grows short indeed."

"Just answer the question, please."

The one in white sighed. "Eighteen hundred and forty-four revolutions. You seemed in . . . better shape back then."

The one in black nodded, closing his eyes.

Neither of them spoke for some time, each electing silence instead as they watched the chaos in the valley below wither and die. Chaos that they both knew had only just begun.

At long last, the one in black cringed. "It has taken great effort to come here. Too great. Have you given any thought as to how you will proceed?"

"Yes," said the one in white, smiling sadly. "I will do

the last thing our children would wish of us. Which, of course, happens to be the very thing they need."

"Intervention."

"Indeed."

The one in black sighed. "It may be too late for that."

"There's that pessimism again."

"No. It's just . . . like you said . . . our children have outgrown us. My own efforts, which far outweigh yours by the way—"

"Not fair."

"—may still fall short of what is needed to prepare them. To *protect* them."

"Well, then, we'll just have to do what we always do."

"What? Pray for a miracle?"

"Of course. What little faith you have!"

The one in black finally cracked a smile.

The one in white twirled his cane again, then peered into the darkening sky. "Alas, I must prepare for my nightly appearance. Until next time, Ruulan."

"If there is one, Durelos."

A swarm of brightwisps fled in one direction, and a swarm of darkwisps in the other. Of the two figures, nothing could be seen.

PART I

CHAPTER 1

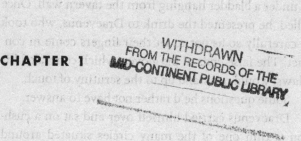

Dead leaves swirled at his feet as Draevenus swept into the tavern, such as it was. The door, which consisted of goat's hide stretched over a frame of sticks, slammed shut in the wind, causing all those inside to turn their eyes towards him. The moment was brief, however, as Draevenus marched with confidence towards what passed for a barkeep in these parts.

He acknowledged the man with a slight nod. "Kefir, please," Draevenus said, giving his order.

"One saphy."

Draevenus fished around in his purse until his fingers grasped onto something blue. He pulled out an uncut sapphire and placed it on the keeper's small, square table. In most parts of the empire, such a gem would be enough to buy an entire shipment of liquor, but here, where the things practically sprouted up like weeds, it barely procured a single drink.

The keeper swept the sapphire into a pocket of his apron, then grabbed a round, wooden bowl and held it under a bladder hanging from the tavern wall. Once filled, he presented the drink to Draevenus, who took it carefully so as not to let their fingers come in contact. The false ends of his gloves, which concealed his claws, would not stand up to the scrutiny of touch.

Some questions he'd rather not have to answer.

Draevenus carried himself over and sat on a cushion within one of the many circles situated around the room. Nine other men were seated there as well, facing inwards and talking quietly. Most smoked from narrow pipes, filling the place with a haze that stained the round, mud walls before escaping through a hole at the center of the roof. They wore clothes with colorful, zigzagging patterns and sported straight black hair with various gems and beads woven in.

Draevenus had donned similar costumery though the wig he sported was empty of jewelry. Some complicated system determined the meaning behind the inclusion and placement of the beads, and even after a year among these people, he had still not quite solved the riddle. It was fine, though; most other travelers kept their hair plain as he did.

He took a sip of his kefir, a kind of fermented goat's milk that he'd come to enjoy. When the only alternative was rice wine, it wasn't hard to find it pleasant. He remained silent, and after some prescribed length of time, the men around him finally acknowledged his presence.

He'd barely exchanged greetings with his neighbors when the door slammed open again. Everyone turned to stare. But unlike the cursory inspection they'd given Draevenus, every eye lingered longer—and wider—on the giant of a man who had just walked in.

Mevon Daere tended to have that effect on people.

Remember the plan, Mevon, Draevenus thought, *and at least try to be subtle about it.*

"By the night mother's breath . . ."

Draevenus turned to the man next to him, who had uttered the words like a curse. It was exactly the opening he had hoped for. "Night mother?"

The men within his circle broke off their gazes from Mevon, locking them on him instead. "What do you mean?" asked the man Draevenus had addressed.

"That's actually what *I'm* asking. I'm a traveler, as you can see. From far up the Shelf to the north. I have never heard of this 'night mother' before."

Behind him, Mevon slapped a handful of sapphires down, rattling the keeper's table. "I'm a thirsty man. Is this enough to keep me quenched all night?"

This breach of etiquette again drew the entire tavern's attention. Men began shifting nervously, whispering to each other. The keeper's face turned red and puffy. Draevenus knew that, at the moment, the locals probably thought of him as family compared to this bumbling barbarian in their midst. He almost had to bite his lip to hide his smile but thought better of it; revealing his shark-sharp teeth never turned out well.

Good start, Mevon. Just don't overdo it . . .

. . . like you have all the other times.

He wondered why he still held on to the hope that things would go smoothly for once. Mevon had come a long way in the past year but was still uncomfortable in any situation that couldn't be solved best by a blade.

Draevenus canted his head towards his neighbor. "Well? Who is she?"

His attention clearly divided, Draevenus was surprised when the man actually answered. "She is the darkness that chases away the sun every evening. Her breath rises from the abyss to drive fear into our hearts and madness into our herds. Crops fail at her cold touch. The wombs of our wives wither at the sound of her wailing laughter. She is the night mother. How can you not know her?"

Draevenus had to struggle to keep his excitement in check. "It seems I *do* know her, but where I come from, there are as many names for her as there are waves upon the sea."

But Draevenus needed only one.

Ruul.

He could forgive these isolated villagers for getting the gender wrong. Abyss, he could forgive them just about *anything* right now. This was the strongest lead they'd gotten so far, after a frustrating and fruitless search. Most villages would shut down or grow belligerent at even the slightest probing of their mythology. Tricking them into talking was the best he and Mevon could manage.

Draevenus peeked over his shoulder. The Hardohl had settled in a circle across the room and arranged half a dozen bowls of rice wine—Mevon's poison of choice—in front of him. He immediately began chatting up his neighbors. Loudly. The other men tried to both ignore Mevon and shame him into silence at the same time.

It didn't work.

Draevenus took several gulps from his kefir to cover his grin at their futile efforts, savoring the creamy burn before turning back to the man at his side. "I will admit, though," he said, "that part about her breath rising from the abyss is not something I've ever heard before. Are there places nearby where her darkness actually seeps from the ground?"

The man at his side stiffened up, and Draevenus knew immediately that the question had gone too far. *And here I am, blaming Mevon for his lack of subtlety.*

"Why do you wish to know such a thing?" the man asked.

Draevenus sighed. *No use in backing out now.* "Because," he said, "sometimes I wonder what it would be like pay her a visit and make her answer for all the terrible things she's done."

Stunned silence descended on his circle, holding them all in shock for four long beats. Then the man jumped to his feet.

"You will bring curses upon us all with such talk." He withdrew a bone dagger from his belt. "Begone!"

The other men in the circle rose, brandishing similar weapons. "Begone," they intoned as one.

Draevenus sprang to his feet and leapt backwards to the center of the tavern. He raised his hands. The men with daggers shuffled toward him. Other circles were also rising to their feet, weapons coming out and waving his way.

"Time to go," Draevenus called.

Mevon was at his side in an instant, draining the last drops from a bowl before tossing it towards the startled barkeep. "So soon?" he asked, smiling. "I was just getting to know my new friends. What happened?"

"I asked the wrong kind of questions. People pointed sharp objects at me. You know how it goes."

Mevon chuckled. "I'm just glad it wasn't my fault this time."

"Well, there's a first time for everything."

"Hey, I've been trying. You know this isn't my style. Did you at least get *something* out of it?"

"Yes," Draevenus said, feeling the corners of his lips twitch upwards. "More than we ever have before."

"That isn't saying much."

"True enough. I guess the only question left is— what do we do about them?"

During their rather casual exchange, every other man in the room had encircled them, faces sneering and blades bared. They edged closer with every passing beat.

"The same thing we always do." Mevon crouched

into a fighting stance. The crowd flinched back. "Give them something they'll never forget."

Draevenus sighed and began energizing. "If we must." Dark lightning crackled from his fingertips.

Eyes widened on every face, and whispers of *"night mother"* cascaded through the tavern. The daggers, once held firmly, began shaking. Draevenus gathered more dark energy to himself as Mevon cracked his knuckles.

Someone in the crowd let loose a whimper. Draevenus released his spell.

Curtains of pure darkness sprang up around—but not touching—both him and Mevon, leading out towards the tavern's entrance. The once-Hardohl, careful not to contact the sorcerous conjuration, lest his innate talent render the spell void, leapt out the door. Sighing, Draevenus followed.

He cast one last glance at the bewildered villagers, who had just seen two mysterious men vanish before their very eyes. He and Mevon couldn't help but laugh as they ventured out onto the rocky slopes beyond the small collection of yurts, dead leaves swirling in their wake.

Vashodia strolled along the edge of the new mierothi settlement, admiring her impeccable handiwork.

Over seven hundred freestanding houses, one for each of her kin, dotted a hillside strewn with boulders and clumps of red grass. The hill curved in a bowl-like manner, with the western quadrant open and spilling down the mountainside into Weskara. On the ridges ringing the valley, two hundred large tenements sat in a protective ring, home to nearly ten thousand daeloth who had followed the better half of their blood out of the Veiled Empire.

After a year of traveling, their migrant nation had been more than ready to settle down. Vashodia had happily obliged. Leading massive caster circles, she had slaved for days crafting every last building. Her apprentice had helped, too. Clever girl that she was, Jasside had picked up the method of shaping solid stone structures out of thin air after seeing it done only once.

This one shows promise. I may have to keep her.

Vashodia swept her eyes over the hillside in search of Jasside's house. She'd set the girl to a task, and Vashodia intended to check her progress. *There.* The place stood out. While most of the mierothi had elected to paint their homes in, at most, three different colors, her apprentice had chosen a much more radiant collage. Black and white dominated the faces, with purple and gold intertwining around the edges. Red bloomed from each sharp corner. Vashodia began threading her way towards it.

A chill gust of wind fluttered her black robes, reminding Vashodia of the altitude. Their exodus had led her people to occupy this territory high in the Nether Mountains, which, though technically unclaimed, bordered regions controlled by three separate nations. Sceptre and Fasheshe hadn't yet made their intentions known, but the Weskarans seemed almost rabid in their opposition to the sudden mierothi proximity. She'd been trying to avoid their emissary for the better part of two days, but as she passed a group of mierothi women carving personalized sigils and protective wards into the walls of their homes, the man nearly bumped into her.

"There you are," the emissary said. "I've had to search your entire village thrice over to find you. Did you think you could just—"

"Yes," Vashodia said, smiling.

The emissary clenched his jaw, face turning red. His yellow tunic quivered through no fault of the wind. "Insolent wench! I represent King Reimos of Weskara, and he is no man to be trifled with by a mere child. I've given you ample time to contemplate our terms, but we must now discuss the relocation of your people from our border."

Vashodia raised an eyebrow at the man. Then she started giggling.

"You find something funny?" he demanded.

"Oh, nothing," Vashodia said. "Just wondering whether or not you'd have time to scream before I turned your bones to ash."

The emissary stepped back, fumbling for the sword at his waist as a choking sound emanated from his throat. Vashodia sighed and brushed past him. She had more important matters to attend to.

She ignored his stuttering denouncements, which grew fainter with each step she took away from him.

Boorish man. Why can't you see that you simply don't matter at all?

Vashodia marched up to Jasside's abode and strode in unannounced.

She found the girl seated cross-legged in the center of her main chamber, dressed in lacy black attire that shrouded every bit of flesh below her neck. Long time spent in the sun during the journey to this place had tanned her skin and lightened her hair to the purest blond.

A flower in a clay pot rested before her, bathing in a ray of sunlight, which streamed through a high window. Vashodia could see the filaments of dark energy reaching from Jasside's brown eyes to the plant, stroking petal to root with delicate brushes. The girl was seeing truly, on a scale so small, most people couldn't even fathom it.

And her face was full of wonder.

"Marvelous, isn't it?" Vashodia said.

"Yes, mistress," replied Jasside. "An incredible feat, this method of crafting sustenance from light and soil."

Vashodia sat down in a cushioned chair. Energizing, she latched onto a bottle of wine left on a table across the room and floated it over to herself. She didn't see any glasses, so she decided to make her own. Sparks of stray energy shot out from her hand as she manipulated the atoms into the proper arrangement and shape. A beat later, a perfect wineglass rested in her palm. She poured from the bottle and took a sip.

Jasside grinned. "I see you've made yourself at home."

"Naturally. Especially as there were no more homes to make."

"The settlement is finished, then?"

"Just this morning."

"Ah, good. Sorry I couldn't shoulder more of that particular burden. You did, after all, keep me busy with other matters." Jasside waved towards the flower.

"So I did. And how much progress have you made?"

Jasside laughed, a sound made purely of joy. The kind Vashodia herself didn't quite know how to conjure. "Oh, I finished last night. Angla organized the daeloth, and they've already begun planting. The first harvest should be in a week, so long as they use the crop artifices I gave them correctly. Now, I'm just working on speeding up the cycle."

Though she let no outward sign of it show, Vashodia was quite impressed by the results. She'd expected Jasside to be at it for a day or two more. And one week from seed to harvest? Unheard of.

Even I struggle to produce such drastic results. It may be time to arrange for another dose of humility to come your way, Jasside.

We can't be letting your head get too big, now can we?

Vashodia smiled, already pondering possible scenarios. "Good," she said, standing. "Then perhaps you have time to accompany me to the binding?"

Jasside's eyes flashed with both worry and excitement. "You're doing it today?"

"Right now, actually. But if you are busy . . ."

"No." Jasside jumped to her feet. "I'll come."

Together, they strolled out of the house and down the hill to the very center of the settlement. There, a dark obelisk shot up from the ground. Smooth stone rose the height of fifty men, facing each cardinal direction. Right now it was just a tower, but soon . . .

. . . it will be so much more.

A crowd was already gathered at its base, having answered Vashodia's summons. Among them was Angla, who turned at their approach. "Good afternoon, Mother dearest," Vashodia said. "Is everything ready?"

"Daughter dearest," spat Angla. Her eyes shifted over to Jasside. She hesitated a beat longer before adding, "Granddaughter."

Jasside inclined her head. A measure of respect that made Angla twitch. "Grandmother."

Vashodia giggled, remembering when that little revelation had dawned on them both. It had been just after their makeshift fleet of rafts had crossed the straits from the empire, landing in the desert region of their soon-to-be-neighbors, the area called the Weskaran Wastes. Both women had been shocked, but Angla had taken the news the hardest. She still didn't like being reminded of the countless daeloth children she'd had over the centuries. Having one of *their* offspring constantly nearby, then—someone unquestionably of her own bloodline—must have felt like a sharp pebble in her shoe.

Vashodia relished having Angla irritated whenever Jasside acknowledged their relation. But when it came to herself, she had forbidden Jasside to call her "aunt." "Half-aunt" would be a more proper form of address, but that sounded too awkward to fathom. "Mistress" would have to do.

"Yes," Angla said at last. "Everything is in order. The darkwisps have been arranged and the . . . volunteer . . . knows what is expected of him."

"Excellent." Vashodia turned to Jasside. "Now, I just want you to observe. These things aren't built every day. I don't know when you'll get a chance to see it next."

"Are we planning on building many more?"

Vashodia shrugged. "You never know."

"That's not much of an answer."

"True. But the process is difficult, even for enlightened persons such as ourselves. What would it do for my reputation if you muck up some *theoretical* future attempt?"

"I see your point," Jasside said. "I won't miss a thing."

Vashodia turned from her apprentice and trotted up the hillside, where the crowd stirred in anticipation. A quick glance across the settlement confirmed that more and more people were converging on the scene, perhaps the entirety of their burgeoning little nation. Daeloth made up the majority of them, but nearly eight hundred mierothi were there as well. Almost all that was left of their species. Most of them were women, and of the three hundred who had been held captive with her mother, not one was without a human male at her side. "Bodyguards" Draevenus had called them. Most, however, had become so much more.

The assembly reached a threshold, and all began to mill about. More glances than not were fixed straight at Vashodia.

Time for the show. It seems they all know that I never disappoint.

"Clear the grounds around the tower, please," Vashodia said.

Her mother nodded, then shouted out the command. The loiterers dispersed. Angla strode next to her companion, the ever-endearing Harridan Chant, who slipped a familiar arm around her waist. Vashodia found herself alone with but one other soul. She walked up to him, smiling.

"You are prepared?" she asked.

The aging daeloth nodded. "I've had a good life. But the little hurts keep adding up, and no amount of healing can make it any better. Don't want to end my days making messes in my pants and forgetting my own name."

"Well, you won't have to worry about such trifles anymore. Your days may not ever end at all."

"Ruul willing."

Vashodia snorted out laughter at this.

Before he could change his mind, Vashodia began energizing, pulling in the very limit of her capacity. She wrapped tendrils of power around the daeloth and began lifting him into the air. Higher and higher he rose, until at last he dangled over the pinnacle of the obelisk. She manipulated another strand of energy and split open the stone at the top.

Angry buzzing filled the valley as a thousand dark-wisps stirred to life within the tower.

The floating daeloth energized, forcing the ancient creatures into harmonization, even as their snapping strands of power began shredding him to pieces. Vashodia lowered his bleeding body into the mouth of stone.

The sound of his screams echoed throughout the settlement as he disappeared into the obelisk, and Vashodia resealed its stone summit. Silence descended in its wake.

For a mark, nothing happened. The crowd held its breath, Vashodia among them, straining forward for any sign, any motion.

Then a single tremor shook the whole mountain.

The new voltensus had awakened.

Queen Arivana Celandaris of Panisahldron sat among the violet rhododendrons in her palace gardens, plucking out a complicated melody on her harp. Gilding traced vine-like patterns up and down the instrument, with rubies and diamonds that glimmered in the late-afternoon sunlight interspersed throughout. She thought the thing was monstrously large for her adolescent hands but wouldn't replace it for the world. Her mother had given it to her.

And you don't throw away gifts from the dead.

Her fingers slipped at the thought, mangling a chord, which drew a hiss from her instructor. Today it was Mariun Trelent . . . or maybe it was Leruna Trelent? Arivana couldn't distinguish them. Both ladies, from that dull but prestigious household, tended to wear prim, elegant dresses and kept their greying hair tied up in buns.

Whichever one she was, Arivana avoided eye contact, trudging through the rest of the song with as much queenly grace as she could muster.

Which isn't saying much.

When the final notes had stilled, she pushed the harp forward, handing it off to her handmaiden, Flumere, before standing and taking a bow.

Her instructor clapped only once. "Your technique has come a long way, your majesty."

"Thank you." Arivana angled her lips and exhaled, blowing a strand of orange hair out of her face.

"But you lack focus and feeling."

Arivana's shoulders slumped. "Sorry."

"Nonsense," said her instructor. "You are the queen, not some merchant's daughter. Do not say you are sorry. Say you will do better next time. Say you will be perfect!"

"But perfection is so *hard*."

"The people look to you for inspiration. You cannot afford to be anything less."

Arivana sighed. "Yes, madam . . ." *Abyss!* She still wasn't sure. " . . . Mariun?"

The woman squeaked indignantly.

"Oh, stop being so hard on the girl, Leruna."

Arivana turned towards the newcomer, stiffening up out of habit. "Minister Pashams!" she said. "I wasn't expecting you. I am honored." She curtsied, spreading the hem of her pink-silk skirts.

The Minister of Gardens bowed. His ornate robes, in official white, red, and gold, swayed with utmost grace as he straightened. The crest of his station, a blooming tree, adorned his left breast. "It is I who am honored, your majesty. And please, call me Tior. You are a princess no longer."

Oh, how I wish I still were. Arivana fought to hold on to her smile. It was difficult to keep up appearances when she was reminded of how she had come, quite unexpectedly, to be queen at the age of thirteen.

Leruna placed her hands on her hips. "You can't seriously advise leniency on her, Minister. The girl is far behind on her arts."

"Not leniency," Tior said. "Just a drop or two of patience. It's been barely a year since the assassinations. With three healthy, older siblings, our lovely Arivana couldn't possibly have foreseen herself being crowned." He turned his slightly wrinkled but still handsome face down towards her, giving a grandfatherly smile. "Isn't that right, my dear?"

Arivana nodded. He had the right of it, but she didn't trust her own voice at the moment. *Has it already been a year? When am I supposed to stop stumbling through grief?*

"Besides," continued Tior, "a few mistakes are nothing to get upset about. Flaws are what make life interesting."

Both Arivana and Leruna gasped at this pronouncement. Among the Panisians, such talk bordered on blasphemy.

Tior stepped closer and gently patted Arivana's shoulder. "Come, your majesty. Your lessons are done for the day. There is something I wish to discuss with you."

Unable to refuse him anything after all the unflinching support he'd given her this past year, she let herself be guided away. She checked over her shoulder to make sure that Flumere was following. The handmaiden remained at a respectful distance, however, so as to avoid the appearance of eavesdropping. Arivana actually wouldn't have minded if she were closer but knew it wasn't proper. Still, the queen couldn't say why, but she was comforted by the woman's constant presence.

They strolled in silence for a time. Arivana listened to the twitter of birds and the hum of a breeze, which snaked through the sculpted bushes and trees of the royal gardens. She inhaled the scents of blooming fruits and flowers in a thousand delectable varieties. Multicolor lightglobes sprang to life as evening took hold, spreading their luminescence through branches and vines before landing on the marble walkway at their feet.

The combined effects of the garden soothed her,

as Tior must have known they would—his family had been cultivating it for more than a thousand years, after all—and she was finally able to summon a smile again without having to force it.

Minister Pashams at last cleared his throat. "You've done well in your duties. You know, for your age and . . . circumstances."

Is that a compliment? I'm not sure. "Thank you?"

Tior laughed. "The Jeweled Throne has never been an easy place to sit. Our people look to it for guidance, for a true measure of the beauty and artistry that has ever been our nation's greatest asset." He waved towards her head. "You have your mother's perfect facial structure and your father's striking eyes, and are already the envy of half the women in the world. With time, your skills will flourish, and the other half will fall in line as well."

Arivana felt heat rushing to her cheeks—those were *definitely* compliments. "That is most gracious of you . . . Tior. I will do my best to continue improving."

"I have every confidence that you will. Now, however, there is another, more serious matter I wish to discuss with you." He gestured towards a nearby bench. "Please."

She plopped down, spreading her skirts over her knees, and Tior sat next to her. His lips curled into a smile, but his eyes seemed strained. She knew the look. It always came right before adults started talking about a difficult subject. "We need to talk about the war," he said.

Arivana swallowed hard, shivering despite the warmth seeping up from the artifices built into the bench. "Has something gone wrong?"

"Not at all. The coalition forces continue to secure new ground in Sceptre with each passing week, and our losses remain low." He lifted a hand and conjured three orbs of yellow fire, spinning them in a blazing dance. "They have few casters of their own and cannot hope to contend with our sorcery or our enchanted weaponry."

Arivana stared at the flames until Tior clenched his hand, extinguishing them. She always did love to see magic in action. "I see. What is the problem, then?"

"The problem is our allies—a term I use loosely. Some have begun grumbling that the war is unjust and have threatened to pull their troops from the front lines."

"Unjust!" Arivana gripped the arm of the bench with a shaking hand. "How can they possibly say that? They were all there at the summit when the Sceptrine assassins . . ."

She couldn't even finish. Tears fell from her eyes, unbidden, and sobs began wracking her chest. She buried her face in her hands.

Tior wrapped an arm over her shoulder, pulling her close. "It is all right, my queen."

She cried into his chest for half a mark, staining his robes with her tears. Suddenly embarrassed at the whole situation, she pulled back and scooted as far from him as she could, wiping the moisture from her face. "I'm sorry, Minister," she said. "It's just . . ." *I miss my family. So very, very much.* She cleared her throat. "What can I do about our allies? How can I help?"

"You need not do anything, Arivana. I merely wished to bring it to your attention lest you start hearing whispers from . . . other sources." His eyes flicked past her, and he frowned. "I have the situation well in hand."

Arivana turned around to follow his gaze. A cloaked figure was walking down the garden's path towards them. She wore a skintight blouse and leggings, both purple with edges of coppery lace, and had on riding boots and gloves. Arivana recognized her immediately.

"Aunt Claris!"

She sprang up and bounded over to the smiling woman, who pulled back her hood to reveal black hair edged by hints of grey. Both of them spread their arms, then wrapped them around each other as Arivana crossed the last two paces with a jump.

Arivana laughed and cried, feeling the woman's arms squeeze out the last frozen drops of sorrow and filling her instead with blessed warmth of joy. *You're the only family I've got, Aunt Claris. I'm never letting go!*

After their mutual fit of giggles had passed, her aunt set her down, mussing her hair. "And how is my favorite little queen doing?"

"Much better now that you're here. How was your trip? I didn't even know you were coming back today!"

"Yes," Tior said, coming up behind Arivana. "Neither did I."

Arivana, inspecting both their faces, found that neither of them looked particularly surprised to see the other. Most casters she knew were like that, though. And yet, there was something else in their looks, something she couldn't quite put her finger on.

"Minister Pashams," her aunt said, with only the slightest nod.

He returned the gesture in kind. "Minister Baudone."

Arivana stepped back, trying to remove the girlish grin from her face. Claris Baudone was the Minister of Dance, and though not related to her by blood, she had grown up fast friends with Arivana's mother. That bond had carried over to the former queen's children, all of whom had never called her anything but "aunt."

"To answer your question," Claris said, "I cut the trip short because my mission was complete. Fasheshish peasants took to my instructions on blade dancing with surprising aplomb. Those few who have mastered the techniques are more than capable of finishing the training in my place."

"That is . . . good to hear," Tior said. Arivana was pretty sure, though, he thought it was anything but.

Why?

"Yes," Claris said. "It's so grand that we send the poorest people from the poorest countries to fight and die on our behalf."

"The treaties are clear on the matter, Claris. It is not

up to us which of their citizens our allies choose to fill the required troop tributes. They should be grateful for the chance to receive such high-quality training. It will serve them well in Sceptre."

"How altruistic of me."

Tior sighed, and Claris busied herself removing her gloves one finger at a time. Arivana had the feeling this was the continuation of an old argument between them, but the specifics of it seemed far above her understanding.

Right now she didn't care. Her aunt was back, the only family she had left, and that was reason enough for celebration.

Tassariel twisted in flight, her body and wings alike canting sideways as she swooped between a pair of greatvines beneath Halumyr Domicile. The plants were thicker than three valynkar standing on top of each other and connected each section of their city to the cloud-touched mountains far below. But they left little room between them. Tassariel didn't even have to look to know that her pursuers hadn't followed.

"You can't go in there!" Eluhar called, still safely outside the vines. "It's too dangerous!"

"Only if you don't know what you're doing!" Tassariel replied.

She tucked her wings in, free-falling into a dive below two greatvines that had knotted together. Once clear, she spread them fully and banked into a long arc around another twisted trio.

"Yes," Eluhar said, "but I'm pretty sure it's out of bounds."

Tassariel glanced down at the Serpent cradled in her elbow. Her team had already located the abyss ring, now she just needed to deliver the prize. *Victory is so close, I can taste it!* "I'm trying to lose our opponents, El. But the longer you talk to me, the harder that will be!"

"Oh. Sorry."

"Shut it!"

"Right."

Tassariel growled, canting upwards to lose velocity. When she had come to a stop, she grabbed onto an arm-length thorn sticking out of the nearest greatvine, then turned to look behind her. Belying her earlier assessment, two members of the opposing team had entered the vine forest in pursuit.

Abyss, they're persistent! She could understand why, though. Her team had won the last six contests. Today, she meant to make it seven.

Tassariel looked up towards the silverstone belly of Halumyr. A plan formed in her mind, and she put it into action immediately. She dismissed her wings. Their lavender glow—a hue that matched her short hair braided over each shoulder—winked out, leaving her in shadow. She climbed from thorn to thorn, until she was on the opposite side of the greatvine, and waited.

Ten beats later, her opponents flew by, oblivious to her presence. They headed deeper into the vine forest. Tassariel smiled, waiting until she could no longer see the red and green auras of their respective wingspans. She then tucked the Serpent into the belt of her midthigh breeches and began climbing upwards, swinging between thorns when they were close enough and leaping when they weren't.

She soon reached the very bowels of the domicile. From there, it was simply a matter of locating a suspended walkway and strolling out towards the playing space.

Loranmyr Domicile shone like mirrors in the midday sun across a league of empty sky, while Fanilmyr and Gormatismyr lay to the south in a distant haze. The other domiciles couldn't be seen. Somewhere far below her, beneath the perpetual fog, rested the mountain peaks of the Phelupar Islands, to which each section of the valynkar homeland was connected by the greatvines.

Tassariel enjoyed the sight, as she had for the last ninety-nine years. But with her century mark approaching, the opportunity for freedom beckoned, and she had no intention of ignoring that lure.

It's about time I had an adventure.

Eluhar's pale yellow wings glimmered in her peripheral vision, reminding Tassariel of her present task.

An adventure, she thought once more, *greater even than the game.*

She did a quick tactical scan of the playing field. It

was obvious their opponents knew the location of the abyss ring. They flew in a ragged circle around its invisible location, swiping viciously at her teammates when they drew too near and forcing them to fall away. But with two of their members stuck wandering the vine forest, her team now had the advantage in numbers.

Tassariel loved punishing her opponents for their mistakes.

She withdrew the Serpent and took aim. "Hey, Eluhar!" she said. "Feel like winning the match for us today?"

He turned and she chucked the Serpent at him. The twisted black snake bounced off his chest and over his head. It took him a few frantic moments, but he finally managed to get a solid grasp on it.

A look of terror crossed his face.

To find the Serpent, teams had to follow the clues left in a unique set of symbols created by the arbiters specifically for each contest. Everyone knew that Eluhar was the best among their peers at deciphering the messages. Opponents had even taken to following him instead of solving the riddles themselves, thinking to dart in at the last moment to claim the prize.

But Tassariel always came with him. *And no one is quicker than I.*

Six members of the opposing team now swept towards Eluhar like vultures, sensing his weakness and hoping for an easy reclamation of the Serpent. Tassariel smiled. *So predictable.* She leapt off the end of the walkway, unfurling her wings.

Eluhar took one glance at the half dozen other valynkar streaking towards him and blanched. "Not today, Tass." He drew back his arm and flung the Serpent at her.

Tassariel caught it one-handed and began picking up speed. A gap had been left by those overzealous players, and she had an almost unobstructed path to the abyss ring. Her teammates around the perimeter dove towards their respective opponents, grappling with them in midair so they couldn't impede her path, and it became a race between her and the six who had chased after Eluhar.

Four of her allies darted to intercept them. But the six formed a tight wedge and drove them all off, losing only two in the exchange.

Tassariel wasn't worried. She flapped her wings faster and faster, ascending towards the ring. She could feel it now. It had to be close. Those chasing her couldn't match her speed, and she even heard one of them cry out in frustration.

That same one started energizing.

She dared glance back. A whip of light energy lashed out from the rearmost one's hand, wrapping around her foot and jerking her backwards with a burst of pain.

It vanished almost instantly. A crackle of lightning struck her assailant, and he plummeted groundwards. *Thank Elos for those arbiters.* Casting was strictly forbidden during a match, and one of the game arbiters, floating nearby unseen, had penalized the offender. Safety artifices activated, catching him in a net of light.

It didn't matter, though. The pull of his whip had stopped all of Tassariel's momentum. She hovered, unmoving, as the other three converged.

Three at once. Difficult, but not impossible. I just need a little . . . distraction.

Tassariel held out the Serpent in a gesture of defeat. "Looks like you finally broke our streak."

They didn't even hesitate, barreling forward with victorious grins.

"Or maybe not." Tassariel laughed and tossed the Serpent high above them.

Their heads all jerked up . . . just as they came within arm's reach.

She jabbed forward and broke the nose of the middle one, a female. Blood sprayed as the woman's head snapped backwards.

The males on both sides tried sweeping up past her, intent on the Serpent. Tassariel drove her elbows into their sternums, doubling them over with twin grunts. She grabbed a collar in each hand and yanked with all her strength. Their skulls cracked together with a thud.

The males fell, and the female flapped blindly, clutching her bleeding face. Tassariel, almost lazily, stretched out a hand. The Serpent plopped into her palm.

Four beats of her wings later, she penetrated the concealing spell around the abyss ring and dropped the Serpent inside.

"VANQUISHMENT!"

The pronouncement boomed from each of the half dozen arbiters at once, who were now dropping their spells of light bending. The game was over.

Her team converged on the tiered viewing stands, where friends and family had gathered to observe and show their support. Tassariel didn't have anyone there for her, but she was more than used to that. After several rounds of everyone's congratulating each other—and healing the small injuries inevitably sustained during these games—she pushed Eluhar towards the path that led to their quadrant of the Halumyr Domicile.

"You were magnificent as always, Tass," Eluhar said after the walk had allowed them to cool down.

"Thanks," Tassariel said. "It's too bad this was my last game."

"Shade of Elos, you're right—"

"Hey, watch your language!"

"Sorry. It's just that I had forgotten your hundredth birthday was only one month away."

"Thirty two days," she corrected. "But it's not like I'm counting down or anything."

Eluhar chuckled softly. "I take that to mean you're looking forward to finally becoming an adult?"

"Who wouldn't? Sure, the games are fun, but if giving them up means I finally get to escape this dull place and see the world?" She sighed. "Don't expect me to cry over their loss."

"Oh. I see."

Tassariel glanced at his pathetic-looking face. "Hey, cheer up, El. You've only got three years left before it's your turn. Think of all the places you could go? The people you could see?"

"I don't know. Traveling doesn't seem like a very worthy use of one's time."

Tassariel went silent, unable to think of anything to say in reply.

The path before them split, curving both ways around a public garden ringed by hedges. Tassariel's mirth vanished when she saw who was there. She stopped in her tracks.

Eluhar took two more steps before realizing she wasn't at his side. He turned. "Tass? Is something wrong?"

"I . . ." she gulped. ". . . I wasn't expecting to see them here."

He joined her gaze as they looked upon the two figures in the garden. A woman lay on her side, sniffing flowers and twirling her fingers around in the dirt. Violet hair spilled down from her head in a tangled mess. Like the other thirty-nine of the returned, she had reverted to infancy, and even after a year of treatments, the woman still hadn't retained any sense of herself. And the golden-haired man standing over her . . . well, there wasn't a valynkar alive who could fail to recognize the great prodigal avenger.

Lashriel and Gilshamed.

Eluhar's eyes widened. "Isn't that . . . ?"

"Yes," Tassariel said. "My aunt and uncle."

She turned away, unable to bear the scene one beat longer. "Please, I need to be by myself right now."

Tassariel walked the rest of the way home alone, struggling to fight off tears.

Elos, she prayed, *please show mercy to your suffering children. Help them find their way out of darkness and back into the light.*

CHAPTER 2

Mevon stared straight down at a drop of over three-quarters of a league. His feet dangled over the edge of the Shelf, which was far higher on this westernmost edge than elsewhere in the empire, as he tore off another bite of dried goat meat. The ocean waves were too small to make out individually at this distance, merging into pockets of sparkling brilliance wherever sunlight peeked through the overcast sky.

It was, he decided, a beautiful sight. Such things had become much easier to recognize.

Mevon held out a hand. Draevenus, seated next to him, dropped their shared waterskin into his grasp. Mevon quenched his thirst with the cold liquid, glacial runoff they'd procured just that morning, and thrust it back at his companion. He felt, more than saw, Draevenus hesitate as he held apart the edges of their food sack. Mevon gave the barest shake of his head, and the mierothi began packing up their lunch.

They both stood, and Mevon hefted the larger of two travel packs onto his shoulders. He didn't mind the burden at all. Draevenus would have to cast blessings on himself just to be able to carry an equivalent weight. And besides, carrying 90 percent of their combined load allowed his companion to scout ahead, as was often necessary, and helped Mevon stay strong.

Killing had always been his primary form of exercise before. *Now, I must look for alternatives anywhere I can find them.*

They set off to the south in silence, picking their way across the rocky strip of land between the Shelf and the snowy summits of the Andean Mountains, which seemed like points of white spears thrusting up to pierce the void itself. They avoided what little trail could be found. It often became lost among fields of boulders and tough tufts of grass, or veered into hidden draws among the foothills that would leave them backtracking for tolls. They stuck close to the cliff's edge instead.

It's truly wondrous how little needs to be said between us anymore. After a year of being constantly on the trail together, all the routine things, the little wants and needs, could be expressed more easily by simple gestures and motions. Now, they primarily used their voices for three things: planning their next move, discussing pertinent matters or events from their pasts, and telling jokes.

Mevon used to have no desire to engage in this

latter form of communication, thinking it banal and immature. But the past year had taught him differently. The ability to make someone smile or laugh, to impart joy upon his soul, had become the greatest of treasures he'd obtained from this journey. He almost viewed the pastime as sacred, holy even.

The gods alone know I've had little enough joy in my life.

"You did well back there, Mevon," Draevenus said, breaking the long silence. "You should be proud."

"Proud?" Mevon said reflexively, shaking off his reverie. "What do you mean?"

"I know it's still hard for you to walk away from a fight. Last night, in that tavern, you made it look like you'd been doing it your whole life."

Mevon shrugged. "Those people were just scared."

"Yes, but there were at least fifty of them. With weapons bared. Surrounding us on all sides."

"Simple folk with simple superstitions. It wasn't difficult to see they just wanted us gone."

"Some of the best people I know are 'simple folk.' I'm beginning to think they're better off for it."

"Is that so?" Mevon said. "It sounds like you're implying that knowledge is a thing to be avoided. If it's so dangerous, perhaps we should give up this quest while we still have a chance?"

"But we've finally confirmed we're going in the right direction!"

"All the more reason we should turn back now."

Mevon glared at Draevenus. The mierothi glared right back.

Both of them burst into laughter.

"Seriously though, Mevon," Draevenus said after they had composed themselves, "you've come a long way in the time we've been together. I mean, do you even remember those first few villages we went to up north?"

Mevon cringed. "I've been trying to forget."

"A dozen men with broken bones and egos aren't likely to."

"Can you go back to the part about my having 'come a long way' please?"

"Oh, come now. We can't very well expect ourselves to grow if we try to bury our mistakes. We must acknowledge them. Embrace them. Learn from them what we can. And, you know, try not to make the same ones again."

Mevon flashed a brief smile but felt his mirth melting away. *But I've made so many. Can such a debt of sin ever be overcome?*

Draevenus sighed, "I know what you're thinking—"

"Of course you do."

"—you're thinking you can never right all your wrongs. Never atone. Never make up for all the pain and death you caused in your ignorance."

"Ignorance?" Mevon shook his head. "I knew what I was doing."

"You knew about your *actions*, sure, but not about the motives behind them. You were born into a system designed to turn you into a monster. They taught you to justify, and rationalize, and push off the blame onto others. Onto duty, and loyalty, and justice. You had no choice but to shield yourself from the horror of your own existence by willful stupidity."

"How is that better exactly?"

"It's not. But now you've decided to take responsibility for your actions. And that is the *only* way healing can begin."

Mevon grunted, grinding his jaw in thought. *Healing? I don't know if I deserve that. Not after losing so much.*

Losing her . . .

"The only thing I know," Mevon said, running from his own thoughts, "is the same thing I came to realize back in Mecrithos."

He recalled standing there with a mountain of molten stone falling down on him, Justice at his feet, an open door at his back, and a question that had plagued him since he'd first joined the revolution.

Draevenus raised an eyebrow. "And what's that?"

Mevon smiled. "I'm not ready to give up. Not yet."

The mierothi laughed and clapped Mevon on the shoulder, flinching as all casters did when they made contact with his magic-deadening skin. Flinching, but not shying away—accepting him. *Trusting* him. "That's good to hear, my friend."

"We're friends now, are we? Just a year ago, I was at war with your people."

"And almost two *thousand* years ago, I helped my people enslave yours. We'd be small men if we let such trivialities define us."

"It was no trivial thing, the death we caused, the violence we let consume us. The blood . . ." Mevon hung his head. *And I enjoyed every drop of it.* He took a deep breath before continuing. "How did you ever get over it?"

"Get over what?"

"The bloodthirst. By all accounts, you personally caused more death during the mierothi rise to power than any of your kin. Yet, as you've told me, you somehow turned away from violence completely in favor of a life of peace. And you did so for centuries. How were you able to accomplish such a complete turnaround?"

Draevenus looked skyward, contemplating—and accessing ancient memories, no doubt—for an entire mark before answering. "At the beginning, our conquest wasn't going well. I saw a way to shift the momentum in our favor, so I started doing it. Turns out, I was pretty good at it."

"Assassination."

Draevenus nodded. "But I'm not like you, Mevon. I never *craved* violence. I wasn't born to it. It was simply a necessity. I'm afraid I'll be a poor mentor if you're seeking my wisdom to help you change your ways."

"Perhaps you're right," Mevon said. "But you've already helped me come so far. I haven't killed anyone in over a year, a feat I could never have done on my own. Even if our pasts aren't quite the same, I'll always be grateful for what you've taught me. And more importantly, what you've shown."

Draevenus let his gaze drift, seemingly unsure

what to make of the praise. He stared off towards the horizon and became silent.

Mevon hiked at the mierothi's side, peering down the sides of the Shelf at flocks of seagulls that nested in the cliffs. He watch as an osprey swooped down among them and lost sight of it just as it brought its talons to bear. When it came back into view, Mevon was surprised to find those talons still empty and a pair of seagulls pecking at the osprey as it retreated.

Mevon chuckled under his breath, hoping to share the amusing moment with Draevenus, but when he looked at his companion, he noticed a storm cloud of despondency surrounding the other man.

"Is something the matter, Draevenus?"

The mierothi clinched his eyes and lips shut for a few beats, sighing. "I think you were right about those villagers."

"How so?"

"They were just scared and superstitious and defensive. Not *truly* a threat at all. It's just . . . I don't think your newfound resolve of peace has been tested yet. Not really."

"I . . . see." Mevon couldn't help but feel ashamed. He had been so proud of his accomplishments. But a year without blood on his hands didn't make him a good person, or even a better one. *I've been given a second chance, and what have I done with it?* He shook his head. *Nothing of worth.* "You don't think I'm ready for a life free from violence, do you?"

"Perhaps. Perhaps not. I don't rightly know. I think

you're the only one who will ever be able to answer that question. I wasn't lying when I said I'd be a poor mentor, Mevon. But I want you to know that when your trials *do* come, I'll be here, at your side, ready to pull you back from the abyss should you need it."

Mevon closed his eyes. In his mind he replayed the words just spoken, paying close attention to the meaning *behind* the words, and realized, at last, just what Draevenus was getting at.

"You had no one," said Mevon. "No companion or teacher. Nobody to help you or keep you accountable."

Draevenus slowly shook his head.

"Not even your sister?"

Draevenus stared at him in horror for three straight beats. Then he belted out a single peal of laughter. "Vashodia is many things, Mevon. But a shoulder to lean on is not one of them. She thinks that she alone carries the fate of the world on her back. For her, there's no time for . . . distractions."

Mevon smiled. "Well I, for one, welcome them." He pointed. A league distant, and barely visible around the curving rim of this section of the Shelf, a thin haze of smoke rose from a cluster of dwellings. "Care for a race?"

Draevenus returned the grin. "Terms?"

"Same as before. Only this time I present you with a challenge."

"Oh? Let's hear it."

"You are allowed to cast all you want, but . . ."

Mevon shrugged out of his pack, dropping it to the ground with a thump, ". . . *you* have to carry *this*."

Draevenus energized, casting what Mevon could only assume was a temporary self-blessing to increase his strength and speed. The mierothi picked up the pack, which nearly dwarfed him, and shoved his arms through the straps. "Challenge . . . accepted."

Jasside blew on her tea, sending rivulets of steam towards the ceiling as she peered over the rim of her cup at Angla. The mierothi woman knelt on a floor cushion opposite her, hoisting her own drink to her lips and taking short sips. Jasside followed suit. The tea nearly burned her tongue and throat, but she was glad for the warmth on this chill day, not to mention the soothing effect it had on her body.

A kettle not much larger than her fist lay suspended over a fire between them. Real wood, real flames. That, plus the archaic style of both kettle and cups, made Jasside raise an eyebrow as she inspected them.

"Old ways," Angla said, noticing the gesture. "Sometimes they are best."

"Only sometimes?" Jasside said, unable to keep the amusement from her face.

"Bah. Only fools cling to useless traditions when better, more practical solutions come along." Angla raised a clawed finger. "But it does no good to forget where you came from. A fire built from logs your own hand chopped, and vessels formed from your own labors—such small things serve well to help you remember who you are."

Jasside bowed her head. "I thank you for sharing."

Her time as Vashodia's apprentice had taught her many things, *knowledge* chief among them. But as far as *wisdom* went, there were few sources so inexhaustible as her recently discovered grandmother.

Once we overcame the awkwardness anyway.

"And I," Angla said, "thank you for coming early."

"It's a pleasure," Jasside said, truthfully. "I'll always try to make time for what little family I have left."

"Family . . ." Angla closed her eyes, lowering her teacup to her lap and turning away. "It always seems such a . . . tricky business."

"None trickier."

Angla grimaced. After a long moment, she cleared her throat. "It is nice to finally be settled down somewhere. I enjoy a good journey every now and then, but a year on the road is a bit much. Even Harridan is glad for a repose."

"Glad to hear it."

"I suppose I have you to thank for the new dwellings?"

Jasside sipped, flipping one wrist dismissively. "I only helped a little. The construction was mostly your daughter's doing. If you feel so inclined, you can save your thanks for when the new crops come in."

"Oh, I certainly shall. Still, it never ceases to amaze me what the two of you can accomplish." She waved an arm around to indicate her home.

Jasside let her eyes wander, examining her surroundings more completely now that pleasantries allowed. A rug decorated one wall, freshly woven and dyed in swirling patterns of yellow and orange that made it seem a sea of flame. Another wall held a trio of paintings, all landscapes, depicting the broken string of islands they had crossed to reach this new continent, each spaced in intervals with a pair of tall windows so one appeared to be looking out on two different worlds. Four sculptures sat atop clay pedestals, the largest no bigger than her head, each an abstraction, a depiction of a dream she would have liked to share.

The mierothi, it seemed, were rediscovering talents they had all but forgotten. Jasside thought it was a sign that things might turn out all right for them. If, that is, they could conquer a few lingering issues.

"I suppose," said Angla, "that you are wondering why I asked you here, ahead of the others."

Jasside set down her cup. She had been expecting this for some time. "You wish to speak of the daeloth."

Angla nodded.

Jasside felt a tremor rising in her right hand and had to grasp it with her left to stifle it. "Yes. They are . . . a problem."

And that isn't even close to a mere understatement.

Jasside fought off the memories, which always made her feel like a helpless child again. The rare visits from her daeloth father. The beatings that ensued each time, for both herself and her mother, when his insane expectations inevitably failed to be met. His hands around mother's throat. The mierothi who had given the order, laughing as the life left her mother's bulging eyes.

Two different days, with two different daggers, when Jasside had made each of them pay for the crime.

What a fool I was to think I would feel better when it was done. Safer, maybe. Not better. Her father had been a cruel man, but he had been born to a life where kindness and compassion were laughed away as weaknesses and he had been forced to choose between murder or death. He'd taken the coward's path. Jasside's thirteen-year-old self had been unable to comprehend the semantics.

But she'd had plenty of time since then to contemplate.

"What is it you wish?" Jasside asked.

"I wish," Angla said, "to no longer feel shame when I look at them." She wrapped her arms around herself, moisture forming in her eyes. "I wish to no longer feel so small."

Jasside swallowed hard, not knowing what to say.

"Why?" Angla continued, a tear now staining each cheek. "Why did Ruul have to make us this way? Why couldn't he let us continue to bear children as we always had?"

Jasside brought her cup to her lips once more and drained the rest of her tea in a single gulp. "I can't speak for Ruul. But as far as I'm concerned, it's ludicrous to make children suffer for *any* reason, especially because of the circumstances of their conception."

Angla nearly gasped at this. "Could it be so simple as that?"

"Nothing is ever simple, but maybe holding this truth in our minds will help make it start being a little easier."

"Perhaps." Angla nodded to herself, eventually forming a weak smile. "Perhaps."

Jasside reached across, laying a firm but gentle hand on her grandmother's forearm. "We'll find a way through it, somehow. Together."

The sound of a whistled tune, in perfect pitch, of course, gave them warning as to figures approaching the house. A moment later, three knocks sounded on the door. Angla wiped her pale face dry. "Come in."

Harridan Chant pushed open the door and poked his head in. "You were expecting this one, love?" he asked, jerking a thumb over his shoulder.

Angla peered past him, sighing. "Yes. Send him in."

"I'll just be outside if you need me then." Chant winked, conspiratorially, then withdrew. He wisely left the two women to handle matters themselves.

The emissary from Weskara tiptoed in, scanning the room with a wary look on his face as Harridan closed the door behind him. "Is the child here?" he asked.

Jasside raised an eyebrow. "Child? Do you really not know?"

"Know what?"

She laughed, looking towards Angla. "I think you'd better explain it to him."

Angla glared up at the man. "For all intents and purposes, we mierothi are immortal. My daughter, the one you insist upon calling 'child,' is more than nineteen hundred years old."

The emissary's jaw threatened to attack the floor. "But . . . how is that possible? Not even valynkar age so slowly!"

"A fact you can take up with our god should you ever be unfortunate enough to meet him."

The man shook, as if insulted, and dropped a hand to the sword at his side. Jasside energized on reflex. Though not a muscle budged, she readied four different flavors of obliteration to the point where even a relaxing of her will would activate them if the man posed the slightest threat.

Angla gestured towards a cushion at her side. "Please have a seat. I'm sure Vashodia will be here shortly."

The man grunted, looking askance at the choice of furnishings. But he sat all the same.

As he did so, the mierothi woman shot Jasside a questioning glance. She knew Angla couldn't help but feel the virulent energy pulsing within her, but Jasside wondered at the strength of her own reaction. Surely, the man posed no threat. He was here to negotiate, not threaten. Why did she feel the need to so casually prepare his annihilation?

Power begs to be used. This power of mine demands it.

Jasside cringed at the thought. She exhaled slowly, bleeding off the energy she had gathered.

Angla was just finishing pouring tea for the emissary when Vashodia burst in. Vashodia snatched the cup meant for him from her mother's hands and began sipping even as she sat down opposite the man.

He sighed, shaking his head. "I don't understand you people. You two . . ." he pointed to both Angla and Jasside, " . . . are at least civilized and reasonable. Why do you let this one speak for you?"

Vashodia smiled, staying silent.

"Because," Jasside said, "my mistress knows things you've never even dreamed of. And none of us would be here at all if she hadn't allowed it."

The man stared, blank-faced, seemingly unable to comprehend her words. After a while, he waved a hand dismissively. "Fine. As long as you all abide by the agreements we make here, the king will be satisfied."

"Oh, do please tell us your demands," Vashodia said. "I'm dying to hear them. I'm in need of a good laugh."

The emissary fumed but took a deep breath and went on. "Very well. Our first and most vital stipulation is that you relocate your settlement immediately."

"And why should we do that?" Vashodia asked.

"The First Law of Weskara states that no persons with sorcerous blood in their veins may dwell within our borders."

"Then there you go."

"Excuse me?"

"We're not within your borders. We both know your nation hasn't made claim to this ground in thousands of years."

"It matters not. Our treaties with the other nations—"

"Make no mention of us."

The man shook in frustration. "Will you not even hear me out on this?"

Vashodia giggled. "No. We've traveled such a long way and have become quite attached to this little plot of soil. Relocation will not happen." She sipped her tea, as if the matter was settled.

Jasside knew that it already was. She wondered if the man had figured that out yet.

The emissary cleared his throat before continuing. "Our second demand is this: You shall not travel within our borders, for any reason, without a writ of passage signed by an ambassadorial authority, and without an escort from our border patrol of no less than double the number of your party."

"Agreed," Vashodia said.

The man's eyes flashed wide. "No challenge?"

Vashodia shrugged. "They are perfectly reasonable terms. Don't get snippy and make me reconsider. Next."

"I see. Then our last demand is that you put an end to all hostile activity along our southeastern trade routes."

Jasside tilted her head, furrowing her brow. "Hostile activity?"

The man sneered at her. "Don't pretend like you don't know. Our caravans and tradesmen began disappearing from that region eight months ago. About the time your people began marching across the foothills on our eastern border. Denying the connection is a waste of both of our times."

Jasside opened her mouth to refute the man but shut her lips when Vashodia raised a single finger.

"Done," Vashodia said.

Angla turned a furious gaze at her daughter. "What do you mean? You know very well we have noth—"

"I know what I am doing, Mother." She turned to the emissary. "Are we agreed then?"

He pursed his lips. "As long as you abide by the latter two terms, I will bring the matter of your refusal to relocate to King Reimos for consideration. I would not suggest testing the bounds of our newfound peace if I were you, though."

"I wouldn't dream of it." Vashodia stood. Jasside followed suit, as did both Angla and the emissary. "Now then, I expect your escort to be ready in two days' time. Fifty soldiers should be sufficient to cover our party."

The man jerked his head back. "Wh-what are you talking about?"

"Just abiding by our new terms," Vashodia said.

"I don't understand."

Jasside didn't either. She glanced to her grandmother, but Angla merely shrugged, looking just as confused as the emissary.

"By your own words," Vashodia began, "you wish us to 'put an end to all hostile activity' in the forests to the south. How are we to do that without going there in force?"

"In force?"

Vashodia laughed again. "You were right to say there was no use denying the connection. Now, we're not *at fault*, so to speak, but a connection exists nonetheless. If we're to correct this atrocity, we must take an armed force into your land and put an end to this nasty business.

"And, as you've stipulated, all parties traveling in your borders require an escort. Two to one you said, right? Fifty should do. Two days. Now, as I'm not fond of repeating myself, I suggest you get out of my sight before my quota of civility for the day runs out."

The man was out the door before Jasside could blink. She turned to Vashodia. "You know, very little of that was actually necessary."

"Perhaps not," Vashodia said, giggling. "But it sure was fun!"

Arivana smiled into the wind, letting it whip around her unbound hair as she leaned over the railing of the skyship. The palace docks retreated below her as the magical artifices built into her yacht lifted them higher and higher. The Hundred Towers of Panisahldron filled her view.

Round or square, bulbous or lithe, the buildings pierced the sky in a circle around the center of the city, growing higher like stairs as they drew nearer the palace. They all glowed by the light of a hundred thousand sorcerous globes, festooned in and around each tower in twinkling arrays. Atop them all, like crowns, sat crystal statues carved in the likeness of the families who owned them.

Arivana thought they were all beautiful, but none could compare to the seven at Panisahldron's focal point.

There was one for each of the six great houses: Pashams, Baudone, Trelent, Merune, Vandulisar, and Faer. Each of them soared twice as high as even the tallest of the lesser houses, but were as perfectly equal to each other as could be. Arivana thought that the original builders must have been so thoroughly satisfied at outdoing the surrounding towers that they felt no need to try to top their peers.

But the tower at the center managed to outshine them anyway. *Her* tower. Equal in height to the others but for the great phoenix statue at its apex, which seemed to writhe and burn as sunlight bounced around inside it. The seat of House Celandaris, who had ruled for five thousand unbroken years.

Arivana shivered when she realized just how thin the line had truly become. *Five millennia of tradition and rule all resting on my shoulders.* She began leaning farther over the edge of the railing. *Look how easily it could all be washed away.*

A hand clamped down on her shoulder, pulling her back. "My lady!" cried Flumere. "You mustn't lean so precariously. You might fall!"

Arivana sighed, letting herself be manhandled

by her handmaiden. "Relax, Flumere. My dance instructors say I have very good balance. Besides, the wardnets would catch me even if I *do* fall."

"But it would be most improper for the queen to be seen in such a manner."

Arivana raised her arms and twirled around. "Who's there to see? It's just us and the pilot."

"Don't forget me," Claris said, marching up from belowdecks.

"I could never do that!" Arivana rushed over and grabbed her aunt's hand, pulling her towards the bow. "I'm so glad you could make it. Come on, the best view is up here."

Claris laughed airily. "I'm sure the best view is wherever you're looking, Arivana."

Arivana smiled. "That's so kind of you to say. And so true. Look!"

She pointed off in the distance. As the city faded behind them to the north, the land rose before them, forming an immense plateau. A river wound its way from the mountains and across the flat terrain, cascading down the plateau's edge in a waterfall a thousand paces wide. The water raged onwards, carving a lush valley on its long journey out to the Endless Sea.

"Do you remember?" Arivana asked.

"Yes. It will be good to see this place again. It has been too long since we came here." Claris turned. "But perhaps we should give your handmaiden some assistance."

Arivana looked behind her and saw Flumere struggling up the stairs with three enormous baskets laden with their goods for this outing. She and her aunt shuffled over to the woman.

"Nonsense, my ladies," Flumere said, huffing. "I cannot in good conscience let you carry a thing."

Claris laughed. "Oh, nothing so scandalous as that." She raised a hand and, after a moment, formed a magical sheet of light. She gestured at it, and Flumere set the baskets on top. Claris pulled out a bit of string and fastened it to two corners of the hovering sheet with little rings of light, fashioning a makeshift handle. The handmaiden tugged on it, now able to tow her cargo with ease.

Flumere bowed and gave Claris a smile. "Thank you, my lady."

The pilot maneuvered the skyship into a private moorage halfway up the cliff next to the waterfall. The three of them stepped off and began treading through a tunnel carved into the plateau. Softly glowing lightglobes, despite having lain dormant for over a year, came awake to guide their steps.

A few marks later, they came to the cave. Arivana couldn't hold in her excitement any longer. She let loose a high-pitched squeal and sprinted towards the pool. *Abyss, I've been needing this!* More lightglobes sprang to life to illuminate the chamber, setting the natural crystal formations around the walls and roof to sparkling. The crystals in the pool itself, appearing like clusters of colored bubbles trapped forever on the water's floor, had been rounded off ages ago to prevent cuts on any swimmers.

As Flumere fussed over readying the picnic, Claris

joined Arivana by the pool. They kicked off their shoes and tugged off their dresses to reveal the swimming attire they had both put on underneath.

"Ready?" Claris asked.

Arivana dipped a toe in, then shrieked and yanked it back. "It's a little cold."

"Is it?" Claris bent down and reached for the water with her hand.

Arivana pushed her in.

She giggled uncontrollably as her aunt came splashing back to the surface, a look of pure indignation plastered on her wet face. "How dare you, young lady! Such behavior is not fit for a queen."

"Well, I wasn't queen last time I came here. How was I supposed to know the rules have changed?"

Claris smirked. "I guess I'll just have to teach you." She lifted a hand out of the water.

Arivana felt strands of sorcery wrap around her body. She became weightless, floating to the center of the pool. Claris dropped her hand. The strands holding Arivana vanished.

She tucked her legs beneath her as she plunged into the water.

Arivana splashed and laughed, dove deep to try counting the crystals, floated on her back, and tried to see how long she could hold her breath. Claris entertained her with a water dance, climbing at times onto a surface hardened by her magic and kicking up great sprays of water like a choreographed fountain.

After a toll, they both became tired. They dried off,

then lay on a blanket and began nibbling on the lunch Flumere had prepared. As they relaxed, Arivana felt like something was missing. She'd been feeling it since she first stepped foot inside this place. It took a while, though, to realize what it was.

It's too quiet.

She squeezed her eyes shut.

Father and Mother, Beckara, Lisabet, and Tomil . . . why aren't you here? Why did you have to leave me?

Though she tried her best to stifle it, a little sniffle escaped from her throat, and a tear leaked from the corner of her eye.

Flumere knelt at her side in an instant. "What is the matter, my queen?"

"It's nothing." Arivana turned away, trying to hide her face. But she only succeeded in facing her aunt.

And the woman had always been able to read her like a book.

"You miss them," Claris stated.

Arivana nodded.

Her aunt scooted over and pulled Arivana against her breast, stroking her hair and sighing. "So do I, my love. So do I."

"You speak of your . . . family?" Flumere asked, intruding on the moment.

Claris tried to *shush* the handmaiden, but Arivana pushed away gently and turned to Flumere. *If I'm to be queen, I need to stop acting like a child all the time.* She took a deep breath, composing herself, and gazed up at her handmaiden. "My family used to come here all the time, but that was before you came to be in my service. Before they were . . ." Arivana gulped, " . . . murdered."

Flumere nodded. "And that is why we make war."

Claris scoffed. "So they say."

"Everyone's told me that it was very clear what happened," Arivana said. "Do you know something different?"

Claris shrugged. "Oh, I'm sure it happened the way everyone claims."

"But I thought you were there?"

"I was."

"Then . . . what?" Arivana rubbed her eyes in confusion. "Didn't you see it happen? Where *were* you?"

Claris stood suddenly, tense like someone preparing for combat. Flumere edged in close and put her hands on Arivana's shoulders, as if to protect her. Arivana hadn't ever thought she'd need someone to guard her against her own aunt, but right now she's wasn't so sure.

"Who put you up to this?" Claris said. "Was it Tior? It was, wasn't it?"

Arivana crossed her arms. "I don't know what you're talking about."

"Don't you dare defend him!"

"Why wouldn't I? He's been looking after me since my family died. Where have *you* been?"

"Off fighting a pointless war. Or do you actually imagine it's justified?"

Arivana gasped, lowering her eyes. *I can't even look at you right now!* "Tior warned me about this. About dissenters. It always seemed like you and my mother were as close as sisters. I never thought you'd spit on her memory so easily."

Claris let out a breath that seemed to go on forever, releasing her tension. It was replaced by something else, though. Something that didn't make Arivana feel any better.

Resignation.

"You're a simple girl, Arivana, and you still see the world in simple terms. But the world is complex. Messy. Truths and lies, hopes and fears . . . the line between them often blurs." Claris snatched up her clothes and began dressing. "You've much growing up to do before you'll be ready to comprehend it."

Without another glance, her aunt stormed out of the cave.

What did I say?

Arivana winced, grunting in pain. Her handmaiden's hands had tightened into a death grip. She stared up at the woman. "Please let go."

Flumere started, releasing her immediately. "Apologies, my queen."

They packed up together and returned to the royal yacht. Claris remained belowdecks for the entire trip home.

Tassariel hung inverted from her meditation bar, hands pressed together in repose, when the chimes sounded outside her door.

"Coming," she called.

She grasped the bar, released her legs, and flipped over backwards, landing like feathers on the balls of her feet. She padded across her one-room home, naked toes gripping the faux-grass carpet.

Tassariel came to a halt by her door. "Open," she said. The silverstone panels slid apart at the command.

Sunlight beamed down on the narrow path outside, which wound like a brook through this section of Halumyr Domicile. Eluhar stood beneath the shadow of her awning. Though she was delighted to see him, as always, it was the package tucked under his arm that drew her smile.

"Praise Elos, it came!" She snatched the rectangular object from him and twirled away, already ripping into the paper pouch.

"Ummm . . . you're welcome?" Eluhar said, stepping inside.

"What? Oh, yes. Thank you." She finished destroying the wrapper, then held her prize up in triumph. "Finally!" She nestled down into one of the two chairs she owned and flipped open the book.

Eluhar plopped down opposite her. "I was just at the post picking up some bolts of silk for my father's loomery when I saw you had a new delivery in. They were kind enough to let me bring it to you."

"Of course they were. You're practically a brother to me."

She noticed him wince over the rim of the book. *Probably not what he wants to hear, but at least it's not a lie.*

He picked up the shipping note from among the debris she had left on the floor. "Sender is listed as a Lerathus. Point of origin is Panisahldron. Is he from the consulate there?"

"Mm-hmm."

"Is he a . . . friend?"

Tassariel nodded. "He's one of their archivists. Been helping me track down rare books for decades. I'm sure I've told you about him before."

Eluhar shook his head, running a hand through his short blond hair. "What's this one?"

"The rarest yet." She held up the front cover towards him: *An Interactive Primer on Yusanese Martial Techniques, 10th Level.*

"Interactive?"

She shuffled until she found an appropriate page. "Here, watch this."

A series of diagrams were drawn on the paper showing a pair of people in the midst of various fighting moves. Tassariel pressed a finger to one them, and said, "Show me."

The diagram instantly started glowing, then sprang off the page to hover in midair. The flat image popped, becoming rounded from all angles. Then the figures started to move.

Tassariel watched with fascination as the figures weaved through the demonstration. She tapped on another and watched that, too. Then, soon after, all the rest.

"This is impressive," Eluhar said. "But I don't understand. I thought you were finished with your first Calling. Why are you still studying it?"

"Why?" She laughed, standing, then pointed to the fourth corner of her home—an area set aside specifically to practice her Calling. "Let me show you *why*."

He sighed. "Will I need healing afterward?"

"Not if I do it right. The artists from Yusan specialize in disarming and subduing techniques. I promise there won't be a repeat of when I was studying the Fasheshish schools."

"Fine. At least let me dress for the occasion, as you already are." He tilted his head towards her.

She looked down at her black breeches and shift, both tight yet flexible, like a second skin. Practical attire for what she had in mind. Eluhar stood and removed his ornate outer robe, revealing the white tunic and trousers he wore beneath.

"Did your father make that one?" she asked, pointing at the robe as he laid it over a chair.

"No, actually." Eluhar blushed. "*I* made it."

"You? Only ninety-seven, and you're already starting on your second Calling. Did you grow bored with astronomy so quickly?"

He shrugged. "I don't know if forty-seven years can be called 'quick,' but yes, I think I may have. Few other valynkar maintain any interest in it, and there's not much going on up in the void that we can make sense of. I'd rather turn my focus to more practical matters. You know, keep my feet planted on the ground."

Tassariel pointed towards her square practice mat. "Well, you can start by planting them *there*."

As he shuffled to the spot, she bounced over to the weapons rack against the wall. She selected a dagger and handed it to him. "We'll start simple. Now, attack me."

To his credit, he didn't hesitate at all. She'd taught him, over the hundreds of times they'd sparred, that she was a master and he a novice. She could tell he no longer feared harming her.

With the blade in his right hand, tip forward, he lunged.

She stepped left in a slight crouch. The dagger swept past her shoulder. She surged up and in, twisting her hips to generate force, and rammed her fist into his solar plexus.

The air escaped his lungs, and he stumbled to his knees, the dagger falling from limp fingers. He clutched his belly with both arms and collapsed onto his side.

It was almost half a mark before he sucked in another breath.

After his wheezing had come under control, he glared up at her. "I thought you were practicing disarming techniques?"

Tassariel grasped the dagger with her toes and flipped it up into her hand. "You dropped it, didn't you?"

"I . . . yes."

"Best way to disarm someone is to render him incapable of holding on to anything. Just be glad I didn't go for your throat."

His eyes widened. "But you promised!"

"So I did." She reached down and helped him to his feet. She returned to the weapons rack and slid the dagger back in its place, yanking out an axe this time. "Now, on to bigger things. I swear, though, only takeaways from now on."

He groaned but assumed a fighting stance. "Chop or slash?"

Tassariel grinned. "Surprise me."

Over the next toll, they fought through her entire arsenal. Tassariel set the book open at her side and studied the new techniques before attempting each one. Her hands grew numb from all the gripping and twisting, and they both worked up a slick sheen of sweat. The closest she ever came to breaking her promise was when she executed a counter on a sword thrust by chopping at Eluhar's fingers. She'd already swept his arm down, and the tip of the sword struck the ground, snapping the blade off at the hilt. The metal flew straight up, bounced off the ceiling, and spun towards Eluhar's face. Tassariel managed to snatch it out of the air a few finger widths from his eye, getting a bloody thumb for her bravery.

The last weapon was a spear, which he now began thrusting at her. She backed away, kicking to avoid the point until he finally overextended. She then twirled, tucking herself inside his reach, and used his own momentum to flip him over. She pounced on his chest, pinching the nerves on his inner arms with her knees, then plucked the spear from his twitching fingers.

Her chest heaved, aching for breath, as she tossed the weapon aside. "I win at last."

"So soon?" Eluhar paused, wheezing. "I thought we were just getting warmed up?" He brought his hands down on her hips and began rubbing in small circles. "Right?"

"Uh . . . no." Tassariel hopped up, annoyed, and strode towards her balcony. She grabbed a towel off the edge of her bathing pod and wiped the sweat from her face and neck as she stepped outside.

The afternoon sun sparkled across the silverstone roofs of a thousand other singles' homes just like hers, all stacked in a steep, sloping terrace. Less than a third of them were occupied. Wind cooled the flush from her skin—not all of which had come from the exercise. She leaned her elbows over the railing, where long troughs full of soil clung like leeches. Most other valynkar grew flowers or herbs in them, but Tassariel had never been good at keeping plants alive naturally. And using magic to do it felt like cheating. Her little gardens remained empty.

Tassariel heard the slow shuffle of feet behind her, which came to a stop less than a pace away. She didn't turn.

"I'm sorry," Eluhar said. "That was . . . in poor taste."

"Abyss right it was. You should know better than to joke about things like that with me."

"Joke. Right. Just a joke."

Tassariel turned to face him. "My mother died giving birth to me. And my father?" She scoffed. "He'd rather be off chasing the skirts of human women than bear to even look at me. I thought I'd made it clear that this is a not a subject I wish to discuss."

"I know. Please . . . forgive me."

She sighed, releasing some of the tension that she hadn't even known was gripping her chest. *Elos, grant me the patience to show grace to others as you have shown grace to me.* "Oh, El . . . Of *course* I forgive you."

They gave each other a hug, as they always did upon parting, though this time it was mutually kept short. Eluhar retreated to her doorway, asking if it would be okay if he joined her table at dinner. She replied that it would be fine.

Lost in nebulous thought, she watched the sun circle the sky for tolls until it began throwing deep shadows across her home district, and the wind grew cold.

My hundredth birthday can't come soon enough. Perhaps then, Elos will finally be able to answer my questions.

CHAPTER 3

Within the realm of the casters, the endless white of commune surrounded Draevenus as he waited, broken only by the cluster of dark stars hovering before him. Farther off, perhaps a day's march away—though distances were tricky in this place—he saw thousands upon thousands of tiny black pinpricks, a massive well of power surpassed only, he suspected, by the valynkar themselves.

Must be the new mierothi settlement. My sister should be proud. It's not easy to get so many of our kind so close together without everyone's trying to kill each other.

He thought back to the formation of the Veiled Empire and how almost everyone was in favor of mierothi dispersion. They all *said* it was to address the practical concerns of ruling an entire continent, but Draevenus knew the truth: With no more war to fight, it was hard keeping their claws from each other's throats.

Even from this distance, one of the dark stars drew him. Ten thousand of them were what he considered middling in size and could only belong to daeloth, while another six hundred were triple their strength or better. Mierothi for sure. The one he focused on was nearly equal in power to his own. Draevenus knew the feel of it well.

He had, after all, started a war just to free her.

"Good to see you, Mother," he said. Though he communed with her from time to time, today he had other matters to attend to.

Turning towards those closest to him, he spied a score of daeloth surrounding another, stronger pair. The last two stars could only be Vashodia and her mysterious apprentice. Though so close in power to each other that Draevenus could not tell which had the edge, they made all others he knew seem like mere pebbles among twin boulders. Only the first two mierothi emperors could have laid claim to greater strength in their day, and that only by a slim margin.

As always, Vashodia tested his patience, but at last her star began pulsing and drawing in on itself, collapsing to a point. It disappeared, and, a beat later, his sister stood beside him in commune.

"Good morning, dear brother," she said.

"Good evening, dear sister," he replied.

She yawned, stretching, as if the body she conjured for this place had any need for such things. "It was difficult enough coordinating our schedules when we were separated by half a continent. Being half a *world* away will quickly grow tiresome."

"Ah, but back then we were plotting the downfall of an empire. No such need drives our meetings now." He fixed her with a piercing gaze. "Right?"

"Worry not. We're just getting settled in. Making friends with our new neighbors and whatnot."

Draevenus groaned. "Please tell me you haven't started any wars yet."

"Why would you even ask such a thing?" She placed hands on her hips and lifted her chin. "Have you no faith in me?"

"Faith? That's rich, coming from you."

"But unwarranted?"

Draevenus shrugged. "Fine, then. I have faith in you, Vash. All the faith in the world."

"Thank you."

"Faith," he continued, "that you'll manipulate all those around you into doing your bidding, whether they want to or not. Abyss, whether they're even aware of it!"

Vashodia giggled.

Draevenus sighed, smiling. "Just like old times, eh?"

"Indeed."

"But what's this about settling in? It looks like you've left the colony." He pointed towards the thousands of dark stars grouped a distance away.

"Oh, just taking a little trip. Some old cobwebs to clear to help keep peace with the Weskarans."

"Cobwebs?"

"Nothing to concern yourself over."

He frowned. "But I *am* concerned. This isn't exactly your style."

"What isn't?"

"You know. *Peace*."

"I may not look it, dear brother, but I'm an old woman now. Maybe I've decided to change. To calm my ways. Ruffling feathers just doesn't have the same appeal it used to."

"Right. I'm sure that's why you've taken on an apprentice who could lay waste to half a nation by herself."

She held up a finger, wagging it back and forth. "A valiant attempt, but you can stop fishing now. I'll tell you about her when I'm good and ready."

"And when will that be, exactly?"

Vashodia smiled. "When I decide if I'm going to keep her."

Draevenus could only shake his head.

"Speaking of apprentices," Vashodia said, "how is that dear deceased Hardohl of yours doing?"

Draevenus stiffened. "You haven't told anyone about him, have you? That he's still alive?"

"Of course not. If nothing else, I *do* know how to keep secrets."

"Good. Thank you."

"I am curious, though. Has he said yet why he wishes to remain lost, even to those he loves?"

Draevenus closed his eyes, pondering all that had

happened in the last year. Trying to draw conclusions from what little insight he could glean from Mevon's actions and words. "I think," he said, "that *lost* is an appropriate description. He searches for something. For himself. For a reason to justify his existence. He carries his sins on his shoulders, buried beneath the weight of all those souls who wrongly felt his justice. For some reason, he thinks that I can help him."

"Can't you?"

"I don't know." Draevenus turned away, staring into the endless white. "I need something that will give him hope. Have you heard from Orbrahn recently?"

"I have."

"And?"

"And the new ruler of the Veiled Empire is doing well. Although I suppose he'll have to come up with a better name for it, now that his land is veiled no longer."

"'Well,' huh? Any chance you could be more specific?"

Vashodia let out a long, high-pitched sigh. "Yandumar has stabilized his domain, for the most part, with reforms all around to help equalize things for his citizens. Not everyone is happy with the changes. The great merchant families still push back, sometimes aggressively, but Paen, at my behest, is helping the emperor navigate their inner workings."

"Even after you left him behind?"

"Oh, ours was never a permanent arrangement, and he knew as much from the beginning. He's already grown too old for me."

"I thought he just turned sixteen?"

"Precisely."

Draevenus narrowed his eyes at her. "Fine. You've told me of his rule. Now, what of the man himself?"

She lifted her hands. "Who can say? Even I can't see into a person's soul."

"Please, sister. There must be something you can tell me."

"Plenty. But do you want to hear the truth? Or just some good news?"

"Can it not be both?"

She stepped close to him, reaching up to pat him gently on the cheek. Her red eyes burned like coals. "A father has lost his last child. No, it cannot."

Draevenus jerked his head away. Angry, though he knew he should not be. It wasn't her fault that things had turned out as they had. She might be able to manipulate events better than anyone who ever lived, but even her foresight had limits. That their revolution won didn't seem to matter much to the half million souls who died in the attempt, nor the countless families left to mourn the lost.

Mevon. Whatever it is you're looking for, I hope you find it. Soon.

Vashodia danced away from him, grinning. "But enough of this dour business. It's horrible for my complexion. What was the real reason you woke me up so early?"

Draevenus couldn't help but smile. "Ruul," he said. "I think I'm finally on his trail."

Vashodia's face gained all the expressiveness of a corpse. "How wonderful," she said.

Draevenus felt his smile wither. "Look, I don't expect you to be happy for me—"

"I'm not."

"—but the fact is, I *am* going to find him. And not just in some distant, theoretical future, but soon. Find him . . . and make him answer. Is there anything that I can say that will make you consider breaking your silence on the matter?"

Vashodia blinked. Slowly. "No."

"But I need to know what I'm heading into."

She scoffed. "Nothing of worth."

He shook his head, teeth clenched. "I don't believe that."

"Believe what you will. Most people shape their gods into whatever suits their purposes, good or ill. I thought you would be an exception." She sighed. "But I gave up hope long ago that you'd come to share my particular worldview. Looks like you're nothing more than a tool, after all. Useful, but unmindful. Most disappointing."

Draevenus felt a coldness growing within him at these words. A tired kind of anger. She seemed to be pushing him away, which only hardened his resolve to defy her. But he didn't know if he could trust the feeling. *Is even this a manipulation? I can no longer tell.*

"Will you at least tell me why you won't speak of your meeting with him?" Draevenus said. "What *was* it you found there?"

Vashodia's conjured form began fading, a crooked smile adorning her translucent lips. "Give my regards to Ruul, dear brother. You'll find out soon enough."

"You idiot!"

Jasside flinched, despite the fact that the words were not aimed at her. The daeloth guard standing before Vashodia dropped to his knees, clasping his hands in a beggar's pose. "Please, great mistress, forgive me."

The mierothi gestured sharply at the massive covered wagon, a veritable house on wheels, leaning precariously over an axle that was bent and jammed into a muddy rut. "Is the task of keeping us upright and on the road too much for your tiny intellect to handle?"

"No," he said. "My apologies. I won't let it happen again."

Vashodia giggled, a sound that drove a chill up Jasside's spine. "Oh, of course you won't."

She stepped within arm's reach of the prostrate man. A week's hard travel had seen their party to the edge of the swampy regions of southeastern Weskara, and Vashodia had abandoned her traditional full robe for a sleeveless blouse and skirt ensemble. They made her seem even more childlike than normal, an effect that was amplified by her proximity to the daeloth and the sharp lines of his bulky red-and-black armor. Only the dark scales decorating her bare arms and shoulders belied the image.

Vashodia raked her claws across the daeloth's face.

Blood sprayed as four red stripes blossomed on his cheek and scalp. Red dripped down, curling along his jaw to the tip of his chin. More pooled in his eye.

"A driver," Vashodia said, "needs to keep his eye on the road. Hard to do when yours is filled with blood."

Jasside kept careful watch. A tendril of energy probed his body, allowing her to read the man's physical responses like a book. Respiration, pulse, pupil dilation, the tension and contraction of each muscle—they all gave her insight into what he might do next. She was surprised to find little anger in him. Fear, of course. Pain. But no anger. A lifetime's worth of indoctrination had taught him the futility of resisting a mierothi, no doubt.

Vashodia had never even energized.

Her mistress now stalked away, ordering another of the daeloth into the driver's seat of the carriage. The man hopped up without hesitation, and without the barest glance—sympathetic or otherwise—towards his bleeding peer. Vashodia lifted one foot through the open door of the wagon, glancing over her shoulder at Jasside. "Fix this," she ordered.

Jasside nodded as Vashodia slammed the door.

She immediately went to the daeloth. *No time like the present to start putting the past behind me.* She reached down to him with a helping hand.

To her surprise, he took it. Though he had nearly half again her mass beneath all that armor, one year of war and another of endless marching had put more than enough strength into her limbs to pull him up—

right. He rose to full height, his chin level with the top of her head, then released her hand.

"Here," Jasside said. "Let me have a look at your wounds."

"No," he said, jerking his head away. "You'd best be getting on with the great mistress's wishes. I won't have you getting in trouble on my account."

With a sigh that was more angry than anything, Jasside energized, pulling darkness into her body from its resting place in the spaces between all things. She gathered the very limit of her capacity. She saw his eyes spring open in wonder. "Do you feel me?" she said, raising an eyebrow. "Do you understand the depth of my power?"

Carefully, he nodded.

"Do you trust that I know how to take care of my own affairs?"

"Yes, but—"

"Then please, shut your mouth and stay still, so I can heal you."

She brought her hands to both edges of his jaw before he could protest further. Delving into his flesh, she wove threads of power into the very cells of his body, finding the broken pieces and coaxing them into new life, into wholeness. It took all of two beats. She stepped back and looked up into a pair of green eyes set deep in a face as pure and healthy as sunlight. The touch of a smile crept into the corner of his lips.

"Thank you, mistress," he said.

"It's Jasside," she said, consciously omitting her last name. "And you are?"

"Feralt. Feralt K—"

"Just Feralt is fine," she interrupted. "It would be better if you forgot anything else. Better if all your kind did."

He furrowed his brow at this. Over the course of half a dozen beats, the expression reversed. "Oh," Feralt said. "I see."

"New beginnings," Jasside said, tearing her gaze away from eyes that seemed all too familiar. "That's what this is all about, after all. No use dredging up old memories. Old, painful memories."

Feralt nodded. "I understand. I will let the others know." He turned, clearing his throat. "But there's still the issue of the wagon . . . ?"

Jasside smirked. "Oh, that." She raised an arm, directing the power she still held. The wagon lifted on a cushion of air, and the wheel came up from the muck with a sucking sound. She reshaped the cursed thing, hardening every layer and joint to prevent another such occurrence. She whipped the hindquarters of all eight horses with a minute strand of energy, and they jostled forward, pulling the wagon free of the rut. "Better?"

"Much." Feralt smiled fully now, brushing strands of black hair away from his face. "It is good to know you, Jasside. Perhaps, in the days to come, we can get to know each other better?"

A tremor rattled up from the base of her spine. She pinched her lips together. "Perhaps."

The sound of approaching hoofbeats from the front of the column drew his attention, and he turned his head away.

Jasside exhaled as she closed her eyes, thankful for the reprieve. She had not been ready for that. For his gaze and his smile. For the reminder of all that she had lost. Of *whom* she had lost. *If only I'd gotten there sooner, Mevon might still be alive.* She had grieved, in her own way, and moved on, throwing herself wholly into her apprenticeship under Vashodia and soaking up oceans of knowledge. Drowning in it. She had been too busy to notice any other man.

I don't know if I'm ready. She took another breath, but it didn't quite help.

I don't know if I'll ever be ready.

The horse drew to a halt. The rider was no daeloth but one of the Weskaran border soldiers sent as their escort. The man lifted the visor on his cage-like metal helmet and eyed Jasside. "The captain wants to know what the holdup is and if you need any assistance?"

"It's nothing," Jasside said. "It's taken care of."

"Very well," the soldier said. "The captain would like me to also remind you that we'll be traveling in tighter formation from here on out."

"And why might that be?"

The man gestured to the fetid swamps that began less than a pace from the road's edge. Gnarled trees drooping with wet leaves and vines rose out of the mist like ghosts. A sour film covered the knee-high water, which writhed with the motion of countless creatures unseen. "Because," the soldier said, "this is where the reports say the attacks begin."

Jasside nodded once, then raised her chin and her voice. "Full wards in all directions, a third of you at a time. Switch every toll so no one grows tired." Each of the twenty-three daeloth who made up their personal guard shouted out their acknowledgment of the order.

Satisfied, the Weskaran soldier turned his mount and rode back up the narrow road. Jasside stalked towards the wagon. From the corner of her eye, she caught a glimpse of Feralt and turned her head to see him staring at her. He turned away sheepishly under her scrutiny but brought his sly gaze back just as quickly. Jasside didn't know, yet, if she welcomed such attention, and not knowing fanned the coals of anger within her.

As such, she burst into the interior, perhaps a tad too violently.

"My, my," Vashodia said, lounging on her bed compartment. She swirled a glass of blood-red wine and took a sip. "Feeling testy this morning, are we?"

"That," Jasside said, daring to glare, "was entirely uncalled for."

"Was it?"

The mierothi said no more, hiding behind another intake of wine. Humor sparkled in her gaze. Humor . . . and contempt.

Jasside gritted her teeth, stumbling slightly as the

wagon jerked into motion beneath her. "There is no reason to treat your subordinates the way you do."

"On the contrary, my dear apprentice. There is no reason *not* to."

"How can you even say that?"

"It is no less than they have come to expect. The weak must never forget how easily the strong can crush them, like ants underfoot. And if they ever do? Oh, a-stomping we will go!" Vashodia giggled. "Reminders like this keep them safe from the dangers of their own fickle pride." She gave Jasside a long look, one that said without words, "It might not hurt to remember *you're* my subordinate, too."

Jasside shook her head as images filled her mind of all those she had seen receive such reminders. Rarely had it turned out well. Her mistress's unsubtle prods only ever succeeded in filling their recipients with poison, a plague that spread to everyone around them, to everything they touched. Perhaps it achieved Vashodia's desired outcome, in its own way, but the side effects—all that pain and fear and hate rippling outwards like waves on the surface of a pond—did far more harm than good.

"There *has* to be a better way," Jasside said.

"And I'm sure there is," Vashodia said. "But I'd thought you'd learned by now that my greater concern is with efficiency. With . . . causality. Fear is a far more predictable motivator than love."

"Predictable, maybe. But not kind."

"Your point being?"

Jasside slumped onto a cushioned bench fixed to the inside of the wagon and rolled her head back. *I don't know why I even bother trying to argue with you anymore. . .*

She closed her eyes, letting the rhythm of their passage lull her into senselessness. Memories floated up of better times, before she ever met Vashodia. Memories of war, of companionship, of the death of her insecurity.

Memories of Mevon.

She clung to this last, rolling it over and over again until she saw clearly what it was they had shared. It seemed a pitiful thing from the outside, but still she cherished it. Something had awoken in her, back then. Something that refused to die. She could no more ignore it than she could channel it in another direction. The best thing for it—perhaps the only thing— was distraction.

But even that seemed to have its limits.

"Would you like to know what it is we're doing here?"

Jasside's eyes popped open. She sat up quickly, heart pounding in sudden excitement. "You mean you'll actually tell me?"

Vashodia had never been liberal about sharing information if she suspected even the slightest advantage in keeping it hidden, and so the reason behind this trip—the *real* reason, not the story about placating the Weskarans, which Jasside knew to be false—remained as tight-lipped a secret as any the mierothi had. Jasside had given up begging for information days ago.

"I suppose it's time you knew what we were dealing

with," Vashodia said. "After all, it will be you and you alone who will take care of this nasty business."

"Me alone? I don't understand."

"You didn't think we came all the way out here just to appease those weaklings to our west, now did you?"

"Of course not."

"Then tell me, clever girl that you are, why else would we bother?"

Jasside gazed at the ceiling, concentrating. *I and I alone . . .*

"This is a test," she said.

"And you've passed the first question, so it seems." Vashodia raised her glass as if in a toast. "Ready for the next?"

Despite everything, Jasside couldn't help but feel excited. *Finally, some action.* Vashodia's tests were always a challenge, but she looked forward to them all the same. Only by pushing herself, by struggling through these gruesome trials, could she expect herself to grow. All the power in the world was useless if one did not have the experience required to utilize it. "Always," she said.

"Then answer me this. What do the Weskarans fear?"

Jasside shrugged. "Sorcery."

"And why is that?"

"Because it puts some men and women above others, by no virtue other than the luck of their birth."

"Wrong. Children are born into privilege all the time. Princes and princesses, heirs to fortunes, scions of the famous and powerful—they all start out life at the top, a horde of the weak and powerless forming the mountain on which they stand. You don't see the Weskarans levying laws against *them*, do you? Try again."

Jasside took a deep breath. "They fear sorcery because they don't understand it."

"Wrong. They understand it perfectly."

"Do they? Yes, they must." She paused, thinking about it, scratching beneath her surface knowledge to the heart of things. "Then it can only be *because* of that very knowledge. They know that magic is chaos incarnate. That its lure, its inescapable pull, will drive the weak-minded to depths of depravity that border on inhumanity. To view those without it as . . . ants."

Vashodia sat up, gulping down the last swallow of wine and setting the glass aside. "At last. I was beginning to think you might fail."

Jasside shook her head. "Failure only comes to those who cease trying. Now, tell me, what is it we're after?"

"We're after the truest realization of the Weskarans' greatest fear. We're after the consequence of when fools gain access to power such as ours. When they decide to make themselves into gods. When they lose control." Vashodia smiled.

"We are—rather, *you* are—going to hunt us some monsters."

Arivana sat stiffly on her throne, trying desperately to keep her eyes open.

The council meeting had been dragging on for the

last three tolls. She knew because the great clocks of the city chimed eleven times just as she came in and were now ringing fourteen. She usually enjoyed the sound, a symphony of rising melodies plucked from the chaos of a thousand bells, but now they only reminded her of how long she'd been sitting there, in silence, being ignored by everyone else in the room.

Why do adults have to be so boring?

It would have been fine if she had something to do, a distraction or something to munch on or anything. She'd had Flumere bring a bag of candies, thinking she might share them, but one look at all the ministers and their aides told her how bad an idea it was. They all wore stiff, formal robes, made of spidersilk, bedecked with hundreds of gems woven into patterns matching the sigil of each house. Dour faces, painted to mask their age, sat beneath elaborate headdresses. No—no one seemed in the mood for candies, so Arivana kept the bag hidden.

She'd seen the way most of them looked at her. All smiles and politeness and deference to her position. But when they thought she wasn't looking, the number of eye rolls and sneers and wrists flipped in casual dismissal ate away at her confidence like the tide hitting a castle built of sand. She couldn't afford to lose any more respect.

She felt a pinch on her back and shot her eyes open. She hadn't even realized they'd been dangerously near to closing. Fighting off a yawn, she turned her head slowly. Flumere's worried face came into view, along with her retreating hand. Arivana gave her another nod of thanks. It hadn't been the first time she'd needed help staying alert.

She bit the inside of her cheek. The rush of pain drove some of the haze from her vision. For what seemed the hundredth time that day, she made an inspection of the chamber.

Six pillars decorated the corners of the hexagonal room, each a sculptured depiction of two split figures, male and female, spiraling around one another in twin hues of red and gold. White marble made up the walls and floor, enchanted to emit a glow halfway between starlight and sunlight. With no visible lightglobes, it made the whole room seem lit as if from everywhere at once. The ministers sat between each pillar in circular compartments, with a trio of younger family members behind them. The Faer family pod floated in the center of the chamber, having left its berth along the wall when Jorun Faer, Minister of Forms, began his oration.

He'd been speaking for nearly half a toll. Something about taxing the lesser houses to increase manufacturing on trinkets and vanity sculptures. Not for money but for labor. From what she had gathered, the great houses mainly concerned themselves with design and export, leaving the bulk of production and materials acquisitions, and a dozen other things she had no notion of, to their subordinate families.

So . . . very . . . dull.

She busied herself by running her fingers over the

lacy seams of her dress, a House Merune original. She had whole closets full of the like, each a masterpiece of high fashion. Supposedly. Arivana thought it was dreadfully uncomfortable.

At long last, silence descended on the chamber. Minister Faer had finished his speech. She turned to her left, blinking herself awake as Tior sat forward and cleared his throat.

"A reasonable proposal, Minister Faer," Tior Pashams said. "We all must give a little extra in times of war. I move that we vote."

"And I second," said Yuna Vandulisar, Minister of Art.

With no more ceremony than that—*thank goodness!*—the ministers all activated their private voting spheres. Less than ten beats later, they began sending them forward, each coppery ball floating on a small cushion of sorcery, which appeared to Arivana's eyes as nothing more than a blur, a thickening of the air. With a metallic clink, the spheres all touched and began spinning. They picked up speed, going faster and faster until she could not tell one from another. Then, with no warning, they stopped instantly and burst into a glow. Four were green, indicating an affirmative vote. The last was red.

Tior sighed. "Would the dissenter like to make himself or herself known and present the arguments against this proposal?"

For whatever reason, the chamber remained silent. Though all of this was new to her, Arivana thought she knew why. The dissenter wasn't likely to sway enough of the others to change the vote, so there was no point in identifying oneself. Even adults—even *these* adults—didn't like being the odd one out.

"Very well," Tior said. "The vote stands."

Jorun Faer bowed as the voting spheres all returned to their owners. "I thank you, fellow ministers, for your clarity and unity on this matter. Copies of the document I just described will be delivered to each of you by tomorrow." He activated some mechanism in his pod, and it floated up towards the empty space along the wall.

"Now," Tior said, "since there are no other proposals scheduled for today, we shall move on to routine matters. Minister Trelent?"

Across the room, Parvon Trelent, the greying Minister of Song coughed, straightening with some effort. Arivana could see his younger sisters, Mariun and Leruna, behind him.

She still couldn't tell them apart.

"Ah, yes," the man began in a halting, raspy voice, "there is some small matter that concerns us all." He paused, seeming to eye Arivana with a confused cast to his gaze before continuing. She swallowed the lump that formed in her throat beneath his odd scrutiny. "Yes, anyway, the last of the daughters of light have, erm, fulfilled the terms of their service. The valynkar consulate is in need of new . . . pledges."

"Chattel, you mean."

Every set of eyes in the room turned towards the speaker. Arivana nearly dropped her jaw as she angled her head to the right and saw Claris sneering at them all.

"Something to say, Minister Baudone?" Tior said.

Claris glared at him. "Nothing that I haven't already said a thousand times." She turned to Parvon. "Get on with it, then."

The old man shrank back from her, smoothing his white whiskers nervously. "Yes, well then. As I was saying, it has come time to poll your houses for fresh and willing participants though I'm sure you all have selections prepared already. I need not remind you what an honor and opportunity this is for the young women of your families."

Arivana scrunched her face in thought. *Daughters of light . . . where have I heard that before?* It had something to do with the consulate, as Parvon had said, but she couldn't remember what. *Did they go there to study?*

"You have our thanks for bringing this to our attention, Minister Trelent," Tior said. Parvon nodded, and Tior shifted his gaze once more to Claris. "Minister Baudone, would you care to give us all an update on the coalition's efforts in Sceptre?"

"You mean the punishment we are delivering?" Claris sniffed sharply. "If we're trying to even out the body count, we've outdone ourselves a thousandfold."

Minister Pashams stood, gritting his teeth. "Need I remind you, that as Minister of Dance, matters of armed conflict fall under your purview. It is your duty—"

"Don't talk to me of duty!"

Arivana sucked in a breath, holding it. She knew she wasn't alone in the reflex. No one else in the chamber but her adopted aunt kept breathing.

Tior was the first to let his out. He sat, exhaling slowly. Everyone else in the room, after a short pause, took that as permission to follow suit. Arivana did the same.

Through all of this, she never took her eyes off Claris. And now she was able to catch the woman's glance at her, with a look in her eyes that Arivana could only describe as sorrowful rage. She fought back a wave of tears that seemed eager to push their way out of her skull.

Arivana felt a hand on her shoulder and jerked around. Tior stood behind her, having left his house's pod and silently padded over to her. He leaned down, whispering in her ear, "Be still, your majesty. And be patient. The woman you call 'aunt' is having a difficult time of late. Take no heed of what she might do or say."

Arivana nodded, finding the strength to beat the tears into submission.

"The *war*," Claris said, finally, "goes well. Sceptrine forces fall back at every encounter, beaten and bloody. We've established a front line encompassing nearly a third of their considerable landmass. The captured are put into labor camps, working fields and mines to provide a source of local upkeep for the coalition's outposts and garrisons. Their children starve and break their backs so our officers can continue their extravagant lifestyles amidst bloodshed and squalor." Her gaze shifted to Arivana, not a glance, this time, but a glare, boring holes with its intensity. "Tell me, o' queen, has your family been avenged yet?"

Arivana's sorrow came flooding back, and, despite Tior's words, she could do nothing to hold them in check this time. Tears gushed forth amidst heaving sobs and sniffles. She buried her face in her hands.

What happened next, she wasn't sure, but she felt her feet shuffling beneath her as twin masses pushed gently on her shoulders. She continued crying, she knew not how long. Eventually, her emotions played themselves out, giving way to exhaustion, and she wiped the salty fluid from her nose and cheeks and chin. She looked up.

Tior and Flumere stood over her, concern writ plain on their faces. They were in the hall outside the council chamber.

Arivana took a deep breath. "Sorry," she said.

"No need to apologize, my queen," Tior said. "It was my fault to begin with. I thought that sitting in on a council meeting would do you some good. Help you to see how things were run in your kingdom. But, I must confess, I had an ulterior motive."

"Oh?" Arivana said, barely able to summon up a false show of curiosity.

"I'm afraid so. I had hoped your presence would temper Claris somehow. Keep her from making a scene."

"You knew she would?"

"Suspected. I've known for a while that she is opposed to our actions in Sceptre but not how vehemently until now. It is I who must apologize, for putting you in the middle of such . . . nasty business."

Arivana shrugged, as if that could dismiss all she felt. But a tremor in her lips threatened to prove the lie of that assertion. And a thought nagged her, a terrible thought, that could only find resolution in its release. "Why does Claris blame me?"

Tior slowly raised an eyebrow. "You don't know?"

"Know what?"

He stepped close, grimacing, and lowered his voice. "As queen," he began, "you have the power to put an end to the war. I did tell you, but that was nearly a year ago. I suppose the grief must have overwhelmed you. You truly do not remember?"

Arivana shook her head.

"It is your right, of course. It was, after all, *your* family who died in that tent. Either by burning or by suffocating as the air around them was lost to feed the flames, I do not know."

Arivana closed her eyes, conjuring memories of her family. Their mannerisms floated into her conscious mind. Tomil's mischief and Lisabet's temper and Beckara's strict adherence to etiquette. Father's roaring laughter. Mother's sad smile.

But for some reason, their faces refused to surface. All she could see when she tried to draw them out was fire, vague figures writhing amidst the flames, screaming and melting in the heat. This fanned not sorrow in her but rage.

"No," she said, firmly. "We make them pay."

Tior pressed his lips together. "Very well. I will make your wishes known." He pivoted and walked away down the hall.

Arivana turned to Flumere. "Let's go."

Her handmaiden stared at her, a strange mix of calculation and confusion painted on her gaze. The woman shook herself, smiling to banish the image so thoroughly that Arivana doubted it had ever been. "Yes, my queen? What did you say?"

"Take me to my chambers. I need to rest."

"Of course," Flumere said, gently guiding a hand across Arivana's shoulders. "This way."

Tassariel had always loved commune. It was like being on an impossibly high mountaintop at midnight on a perfectly clear night. Stars surrounded her, varying in intensity, each representing a living valynkar soul. She wondered what it was actually like, out there in the void where the real stars rested. Nothing like this, of course. Eluhar's studies in astronomy indicated that stars were, in fact, very large and very distant and so far apart from each other that every other one still seemed just a pinprick of light. She was almost intrigued enough to consider the practice for a future Calling.

But the world would soon be hers to play with, which would provide more than enough adventure. For a few lifetimes at least.

She could see a few others present here in commune, in conversations across domiciles or across continents. She paid them no heed, racing her disembodied soul out of the bright cluster of the valynkar city into the great gap of darkness without. A few dim lights dotted the landscape, here and there—half-blooded or less—but she aimed for a grouping so luminous by numbers alone that it rivaled her homeland.

Panisahldron.

She made her way towards a small grouping of stars far brighter than most of the rest and set apart. There was someone at the valynkar consulate that she needed to thank. She sought out his soul and brushed against it. Then she withdrew.

As she waited, she looked around. Much like the seat of the valynkar, the dark spaces dominated the area around this city. Though individual specks of light could be seen in most any direction, the area to the north and west seemed the most devoid. Spectre had almost no casters to speak of, and Weskara, of course, had none. Almost involuntarily, she found her gaze drifting instead to the northeast. Her vision seemed to shift along the countless leagues to a spot she knew well. In the waking world, it would be an island, tucked inside an inland sea in the middle of Yusan, another island, massive and horseshoe-shaped, just off the mainland in the Endless Sea. A place she'd never dared to go. A single bright star rested amidst a scattering of lesser ones.

Her father, and the spawn of his lusts.

She shook herself as the light before her dimmed and winked out. A moment later, the man she had come to see formed his corporeal body in front of her.

"Tassariel!" he said. "It is good to see you."

She smiled, admiring the strong lines of his jaw, the thick green hair and beard that made it appear as if spring grasses were sprouting from his head, the deep sparkle in his matching eyes. "It is good to see you too, Lerathus."

"To what do I owe the pleasure?"

"Just wanted to give you my thanks in . . . well . . . as close to 'in person' as I can, at the moment."

"You received the book?"

"Yes, and it's marvelous. How did you even get ahold of a copy? I've heard it's quite rare."

Lerathus waved a hand. "Oh, we have quite a few connections here, being nosed up against the Panisian council as we are. I'm only sorry it took so long to fulfill your request."

"Please. As you've done me a favor, it is ludicrous to expect an apology for delays. Besides, I'm simply thrilled to have it."

"Put the lessons to good use already, have you?"

Tassariel shrugged, grinning wryly. "Just in practice. So far."

Lerathus grunted. "As it is with most initial Callings. All study and theory and repetitive training, at least until your wings are no longer clipped. How foul this great sin called youth!"

She chuckled, warmed by his bright demeanor. A response that Lerathus never failed to draw from her. "Soon enough, I'll be able to fly free of this place," she said. "See the world. Find a new Calling. And maybe even put this one to use somewhere." A thought came to her, then. "Is there any demand for martial instructors in Panisahldron?"

"They call it 'dancing' here, which, at your level of competency seems as apt a description as any. Unfortunately, House Baudone has prime control of that particular commodity. And they don't tolerate outsiders encroaching on their territory. Their matriarch is a fierce one."

"It sounds like I would probably like her."

"No doubt. But if you're looking to take up teaching, I'm afraid you'll have to look elsewhere." He paused, his face twisting as if he were tasting something sour. "There are plenty of people up north in need of lessons in self-defense."

Tassariel bowed her head. "War. It's a terrible thing . . . I've heard."

Lerathus only nodded.

She had read her history thoroughly and knew that he'd seen a few conflicts in his five and a half centuries. Mere border skirmishes compared to what was taking place now in Sceptre, but he'd been far nearer to the action then. Far more involved. She hadn't pried, since she was pretty sure their friendship hadn't yet progressed to the point where he would likely feel comfortable sharing such experiences with her. But when the time came, she would gladly allow him to open up as fully as he wished.

The thought drove a spike of embarrassment through her, and she turned her head to hide whatever telling looks might cross her face. Hoping to cover herself, she asked, "Is there hope for a resolution to the conflict anytime soon?"

Lerathus shook his head. "I have it on good authority that the young queen does not wish it to end. And besides her, there are other factors at play, other interests, with far more of a stake in matters than the petty vengeance of a child."

"What do you mean?"

Lerathus blinked, as if waking up. Then, he shrugged. "Don't worry yourself over such things. I've said too much already."

"But—"

"Peace, Tassariel. Keep your mind clear. You'll have need of all your faculties for your birthday ceremony."

She sighed, letting go of her inquiry. *For now.* "Very well, then. Care to give me any intimations for my meeting with Elos?"

"Now *that*," he said with a smile, "would be cheating. You would dare come before our god with such behavior on your conscience?"

Tassariel's face went grim. "No. Of course not. Please forgive me for asking."

Lerathus laughed. "Oh, come now. It was merely a jest. I'm sure Elos would—"

"I'm sure he would like to speak for himself," Tassariel said, nearly shouting. She hung her head in shame. "It is written in his very precepts that people are not to share what they experience in his presence, in order to preserve the sanctity of the ritual. It was foolish of me to ask."

He sighed, chuckling softly. "You'll get over it."

She furrowed her brow. "Get over what?"

"Piety."

A squeak of indignity erupted from her throat, far beyond her hope of containing it. "Why would I ever want to?"

"Because," he said, "it has little place in a world dominated by . . . practical matters."

To this, Tassariel did not know what to say.

CHAPTER 4

"Would you take a look at that . . ."

They were the first words Draevenus had spoken all day, and they carried naked traces of wonder. Mevon, lifting his gaze from the trail, could easily see why.

The incline they'd been ascending all morning finally crested, revealing a wide swath of land gently sloping from the foothills in a series of stepped terraces. Each showed obvious signs of agriculture, a rare enough occurrence in these parts. Rarer still was the lake, a placid blue coin formed from the runoff of the farms, and the collection of dwellings clustered thickly around it. It was the closest thing to a town they'd yet encountered this side of the mountains.

Mevon inhaled in satisfaction, allowing himself a slight smile at the sight. With figures dotting the fields, collecting the final harvest before winter no doubt, and a breeze carrying scents of hearth fires, the picture conjured into his mind a single word.

Peace.

Which was shattered a moment later by a woman's scream.

Mevon dropped his pack and surged forward, kicking up dirt and stones as his boots tore ruts in the ground.

Draevenus was quicker.

Mevon felt a tingle, sharp due to their proximity, as the mierothi energized. Draevenus shadow-dashed once, twice, leaving an inky residue in his wake like thin, midnight smoke. On the third such dash, he disappeared behind an outcropping of rocks on Mevon's left. The scream sounded again.

Mevon vaulted forward, skipping across the tops of the man-height boulders in his path. Around the corner, a yurt came into view, round with a conical roof and a pillar of smoke drifting out of the hole in the center. Covered in animal hides and painted in colorful tones—dyes no doubt crafted from the vibrant mountain flowers nearby—the dwelling seemed to contrast sharply with the dull, squarish, wooden homes of the town below. It was no wonder it was set so far apart.

Mevon took in all of this in the two beats it took him to cover the distance. He pounced through the leather flap hanging over the entrance, legs coiled beneath him, hands raised in a fighting stance. As his eyes adjusted to the dim interior of the yurt, he realized what he'd just done.

Preparing for violence, without a second thought. He lowered his hands and stood upright, reversing the anger he felt until it was directed solely at himself. *Is this the test you thought I needed, Draevenus?*

Have I already failed?

The scene materialized before him. Thankfully, it appeared that the need for violence had already passed. Two men, wrapped in thick furs, lay sprawled to either side of the abode, unmoving except for the rise and fall of their chests. A third was suspended in midair by Draevenus's outstretched hand. Mevon could practically feel the sorcery that lent unnatural strength to the mierothi's limbs, allowing him to hold up a man nearly twice his bulk with ease. A man whose eyes bulged from a hairy face made red by a lack of air. Or embarrassment.

Or both.

Mevon almost failed to notice the last figure in the now-cramped space. The woman who, presumably, called this place home . . . and whose screams almost certainly had called Draevenus and him to her now. Her braided black hair hung past her waist, with bones and colored stones knotted up and down its length. Her face was smooth, young, and the vivid patterns on her shawl seemed to speak stories of ancient days. A quick glance around the room revealed shelves full of bottles containing colored liquids and powders, and pouches brimming with dried herbs and roots. Half a dozen black cauldrons of different sizes completed the picture, and Mevon knew exactly what she did for a living.

"You're the town shaman, my lady?" he asked.

The words broke the stillness holding them all like ice. The woman sniffed, blinking, and jerked her head towards him. Draevenus sighed, lowering the man until his feet were just able to press against the ground.

"Yes," she said. "I am."

Mevon gestured around him. "And these gentlemen were . . . customers?"

Her lips pressed thin. "Hardly."

"They were beats away from leaving her bloody and bruised," Draevenus said. "This one looked like he was about to enjoy it."

"Perhaps," Mevon said, "he had better explain."

Draevenus released him. The man crumpled to his knees, coughing and wheezing, one hand rubbing his throat. After a full score beats, he glared up at the mierothi with murder in his gaze.

"It's not me," the man barked, "who needs to explain himself. You two outsiders have no business interfering in the affairs of our town."

"I'd say we have whatever right we feel like taking," Draevenus spat. "Especially when thugs like you threaten a defenseless woman."

"The witch ain't defenseless. Just likes to attack in ways no one can defend against."

Draevenus bunched his hands into fists and took a step.

Mevon bounced forward and placed a hand on his friend's shoulder. He understood the anger, the sense of a hanging injustice and the power to right it. But if he were to truly turn a new leaf, he couldn't let emotions drive his actions. Not always. Perhaps not ever. And letting someone else perform the violence he so desired in his stead was not an answer. It was nothing but cowardice.

Somehow, he managed to convey all this to Draevenus in a single look. The mierothi nodded, exhaling, and stepped back.

Mevon peered down at the hairy man. "What's your name?"

"They call me Hakel." The man spat near Mevon's feet. "And you?"

"Mevon. And my companion there is Draevenus."

The woman flinched.

Mevon tucked that strange reaction away for later, trudging forward with his interrogation. "Would you like to tell me why you felt the need to attack this shaman?"

"She's been poisoning people, them that cross her. Killed the town chief just last night."

"And you've proof of this?"

Hakel grunted. "Don't need it. Ask anybody, they'll tell ya' it was her all right."

Mevon gritted his teeth. "If that's the case, then I suggest you leave. Now."

"Why's that?"

"Because I have no patience for those who think their strength over others gives them leave to enact justice as they see fit."

Hakel laughed, a roaring cackle that set his whole body to shaking. He took a breath, wiping the back of his hand across his lips. "Hypocrite."

Mevon's anger vanished. In its place rose despair. He lowered his head, eyes becoming blurry with shame.

Hakel resumed his derisive laughter as he pushed past Mevon towards the yurt's entrance. He grasped the collars of both his unconscious companions, hefting them one in each hand. "You want the witch? She's all yours. But don't expect that we'll be forgetting this anytime soon."

"And don't think my friend's reluctance to have you choked to death in any way makes you the stronger man," Draevenus said.

With a startled look, Hakel backed out through the flaps, dragging the other two men behind him.

A hand fell on Mevon's shoulder from behind. Draevenus, he knew without looking, reaching up to give him comfort. Mevon angled his gaze down as the mierothi edged around to his side. Just as he'd passed wordless meaning to his companion earlier, so, too, did Draevenus now return the gesture. The look in his red eyes bore all the compassion in the world, as well as a twinkle of flippancy. *Take no heed of the words some ignorant village tough spits in anger,* they seemed to say. Mevon expelled a deep breath, centering himself, and nodded in thanks.

Then they both turned to the shaman.

She stared out the opening of her home, face set

in grim resignation. "You've saved me from a beating, and for that I thank you," she said, "but I'm afraid you've only made matters worse."

"How is that?" Draevenus asked.

"Hakel would have settled for hidden bruises, but you've delayed his . . . satisfaction. I've no doubt he won't stop now until blood is shed, and far more than I'm willing to part with."

"Our apologies, then," Mevon said. "When men like us hear a woman screaming in terror, well, it's nearly compulsory that we run to her aid."

A ghost of a smile brushed her lips as she stared into his eyes. "Men like you. I see. It is good to know that there exists such a kind in this world."

Mevon smiled back, allowing his gaze to fall deeply into her eyes, brown wells so dark they seemed nearly black. Imagining, for the briefest of moments, that she was someone else.

Then he shook, breaking the reverie. Partly because too much of this wasn't true—she wasn't Jasside, and he and Draevenus weren't exactly paragons of justice and chivalry. At least, they hadn't always been. He was still trying to find out if he would be going forward.

But there was also his recollection of the reaction she had when he introduced Draevenus. First things first, then. "You've heard our names, shaman. Perhaps we've earned enough of your trust to hear yours?"

"I am Zorvanya," she said, dipping her head. "It is interesting that you call me 'shaman,' when the people around here simply call me 'witch.' I happen to know it is a title used more widely up north. Did you come from there?"

"More or less," Draevenus said.

"Less, I should think." She grinned deviously.

"And why would you think that?"

"Because," Zorvanya said, staring at Draevenus, "you can do magic." Her gazed flicked towards Mevon. "And you are immune to it."

Mevon glanced at his companion, but Draevenus could only shrug. He turned back to her. "So you've found us out. What now? Turn us over to Hakel and company?"

"No. I'm going to pack."

"Pack?" said Mevon and Draevenus at once.

"Yes. Did you not hear what Hakel said?" She began rifling through her stores, stuffing clothes and bottles and other provisions into a small travel sack. "I suppose it would never cross the minds of such *fine* men as yourselves to even question me about it."

Mevon closed his eyes and shook his head, unable to hide his amusement. "The chief. You really did kill him, didn't you?"

"Indeed."

Draevenus raised an eyebrow. "Something tells me he had it coming."

"He's been luring girls into his bed for years. Young ones, not even come to their first blooding. When he grew tired of them, he tied stones to their feet and released them from his boat in the center of the lake. I only found out recently, or I'd have done something sooner."

Mevon frowned, conflicted. What she had done appealed to his sense of justice, but he no longer trusted it. Such feelings had driven him to acts he'd rather not relive. To death untold. To innocent and guilty alike, falling prey to his blind loyalty as surely as they fell to his blades. Hakel's accusation of hypocrisy raked at his guilt like talons.

For every soul that lies quietly in my shadow, a thousand more cry out for my blood.

"Where will you go?" Draevenus said.

"With you, of course," Zorvanya replied. "And we'd better get a move on soon. There's another town a few days south of here, and I have a friend there who will provide us shelter."

"I'm not so sure," Draevenus said. "We're on pretty important business, and—"

"It's only for a few days. I promise I won't slow you down."

"But we hardly know each other."

She shrugged. "I may have only met you a few marks ago, but you've already displayed more character than any men I know. And I've already told you the worst there is to know of me."

"I . . . suppose that's true," Draevenus said although his tone didn't exactly match his words. "We're running low on supplies, and I think we'd best do our shopping elsewhere. What say you, Mevon? Up for an extra body in our little troupe?"

Mevon grimaced at the use of the word *body*, images flashing before his eyes of all the ones he'd caused. "One question, first."

Zorvanya cinched her pack shut and slung it over her shoulders. "What?"

He tilted his head towards Draevenus. "Why did you flinch when I said his name?"

She froze, eyes making a study of the floor. Mevon could hear not a breath in the room, not even his own, as he waited for her reply.

"Because," she said at last, "it's a name I've heard before."

Jasside sniffed, inhaling the swamp's fetid air. There was no movement in the thick mists around her, no sound. Neither the croak of frogs nor the buzz of insects nor the low bellow of alligators. Even the snakes and birds seemed chilled by unnatural fear.

Looks like I've finally found the right place.

She'd left the others behind three days ago, with her only instructions being to find and destroy all traces of the shadow beast that plagued the region. Her thoughts returned to her conversations with Yandumar during the revolution, when he told her of the tunnel he used to escape the empire, and later, with Gilshamed in tow, to return. He'd spun tales of his grand adventures beyond the Shroud with a perpetual smile and words always leading towards laughter. But of the tunnel itself, he spoke little. The horrors there must have been too unimaginable to recount.

And that's what she was making her way towards now.

She'd seen the corpses of the twisted monstrosities outside Mecrithos. What was left of them, at least, after Angla had finished with them. Most people had thought that all of the beasts had been consumed on those plains.

But some, it seemed, had escaped.

Jasside closed her eyes and energized. At Vashodia's behest, she'd been masking her signal for nearly a week. It had been a complex skill to learn at first, but now she could maintain the effect even in her sleep. No one, man or beast, could detect her through sorcerous means, neither in commune nor the waking world. Her mistress, before she'd fallen out of the emperor's favor, had done much of the initial research that laid the groundwork for these creatures' creation and had taught Jasside most of what she knew. The shadow beasts were able to sense magic, like a hound sniffing after a fox, and their raw, physical power gave them some resistance to it, making them ideal candidates for tracking and hunting casters. A producible army, nearly as effective as natural voids, but far more controllable. It was a good thing most had already been destroyed.

But not all.

She sent a wave of energy outwards in all directions. It searched, seeking out the heartbeat of any creature it might sweep through and returning the results to her. She waited a dozen beats. Nothing.

There was no balance between predator and prey here. No natural order. No life at all. This was a place of death, pure and simple.

They must be close. Perfect.

She drove deeper into the swamp, keeping to the dry areas when she could find them, and forming temporary bridges with her sorcery when she could not. The mist grew thicker, more foul, curling around crooked trees like smoke and coating her skin in grime. Besides the sound of her own boots pressing through the muck, the silence was absolute, a heavy blanket pressing down on her thoughts.

After ten marks, she came to a place where the land rose into mounds on three sides of her. Here, finally, something managed to overwhelm the normal stench of the rotting swamp: rotting *flesh.*

Jasside knelt, running her hands through the moist vegetation at her feet. Only beats passed before she found what she sought. She lifted her prize, inspecting it as she dangled it before her eyes: a human rib, chewed clean of meat by sharp, powerful jaws.

The barest hint of a growl was all the warning she got.

A monster sprang out of a hole in the mound to her front. It bore down on her, closing half the gap before she could blink.

Plenty of time . . .

Jasside thrust her hand forward. Razor-thin discs of pure darkness shot forward, aimed towards the beast's front knees. They connected, embedding deep into flesh, and exploded in a ripple of shadow with a sound like tearing fabric. Black blood burst from both forelimbs as they split in half.

The creature toppled forward. Its horned head thrashed in murky waters, and its hind legs clawed at the mud, pressing it forward in pitiful increments. The whites of its eyes shone wide as it stared at her with rabid fury and an intelligence far too human for her liking.

Jasside stepped back, steadied her breathing, and replenished her dwindling reserves of dark energy. She shot quick glances around because Vashodia had told her one more thing about the beasts.

They hunted in packs.

She felt, more than saw, seven more converge on her position, fanned out in a semicircle behind her. More than she had expected—a *lot* more.

She no longer had plenty of time.

Jasside eyed the top of the mound beyond the beast in front of her and shadow-dashed forward. She turned. A great, crushing paw swiped through the space she had occupied a moment before.

Her foes advanced, huge and dark, and snarling with something more sinister than mere animal hunger. Two of them snapped at their injured companion as they passed it, tearing out chunks of bitter flesh with knifelike teeth. Keening cries erupted from their throats. It almost sounded like laughter.

Jasside raised her hands before her, manipulating her energy into seven individual formations. Her mistress had been trying, repeatedly, to teach her how to cast without the use of her hands, but it was the one thing she was reluctant master. *I'm not even sure I want to.* The mind was a fickle thing, and keeping her sorcery tied to the motions of her body—to something requiring conscious effort—ensured that stray thoughts did not inadvertently turn into stray spells.

The seven formations solidified into spikes that were as thick as tree trunks, harder than steel, and longer than her body was tall. She guided their points towards their targets . . .

. . . and pushed.

The seven shadow beasts were dead before their bodies hit the ground.

Jasside admired her handiwork. "Another test passed. What else have you got for me, Vashodia?"

Her gaze drew towards the first shadow beast. It had rolled over onto its side, bellowing in pain as its blood stained the waters around it even darker. The head lolled, turning towards her and . . .

. . . savage lips curved into a smile.

She only had time to raise a curious eyebrow before talons gripped her from behind.

Her stomach lurched as she was lifted skyward by a feathered limb. A guttural howl raked her ears from less than a pace away. Hot breath blew her hair into her face. The talons bit into her torso, drawing waves of agony with every pulsing clench. Her skin split apart, spurting blood.

She screamed.

Energy lanced out from her fingertips, formless, destructive, searing the very air around her. The creature's shriek of victory turned into one of pain, echoing her own. Its flesh began to roast, emitting a sick, savory scent that churned her gut but was almost a welcome relief to the pain of the talons piercing her body.

It released her. She slammed into the ground. Crumpled. The wet grasses turned black around her as energy continued to writhe chaotically. She sucked in a breath. Then another. She twisted her head.

The shadow beast staggered, its outstretched limb curling inwards and shedding muscle, skin, and bone in flakes of ash as her power slowly ate it away. The sounds coming from its beak-like mouth chilled her to the core.

Time for silence.

Jasside formed a ball of power in her fist and punched forward. The energy crammed its way down the creature's open throat, gathering in its stomach. She opened her palm. The power . . . expanded.

Chunks of the shadow beast splattered in all directions. A shower of dark blood and flesh and feathers cascaded over her, coating Jasside from head to toe.

She wiped her face clean, gulping huge lungfuls

of air to still her frantic heart, and took one last look around. No more threats. No more sounds. Except, of course, for the wheezing laugh of the monster dying behind her.

Arivana waved to the crowds from atop her float, gaudy thing that it was. She hadn't minded it, in years past, when she'd ridden with her family, feeling Father's soft but firm hand on her shoulder, kicking Tomil's shin and having him kick back while trying to keep Mother from noticing, pulling Lisabet's hair, trading weird faces with Beckara.

The golden railing seemed empty now, with only Flumere for company.

The float drifted down the long curve of the avenue, with dozens more before and behind her, as crowds gathered, reveling in bright green clothes for the festival of . . . she couldn't remember what.

I'm not even sure what there is to celebrate anymore.

It was strange being down at street level. Her own chambers were hundreds of stories up, and she traveled from there by skyship anytime she had appearances to makes. This road was at least clean, being the main divide between the inner cluster of towers and the city beyond. Lightglobes lit the way every few paces, suspended by thin wires, and constables armed with shock-spears and wrath-bows stood straight and proud, holding back crowds that cheered for each passing float. She couldn't recall the last time she'd ventured any deeper into her own capital. There were so many people. So many . . . strangers.

Her smile wavered as her ceremonial crown tilted, forcing her to steady it with her nonwaving hand. She felt Flumere's deft fingers reach from behind, quickly right the bulky ornament without messing a single strand of her hair. Arivana gave the woman a smile—a real one—before once more presenting her queenly face to the masses.

The parade continued almost an entire toll, making a full circuit of the avenue and ending where they started. One by one, the floats turned in towards the central tower and began rising into the air. They made another revolution, fully airborne this time, until they were all lined up equidistant around her home and palace about thirty stories high. She had almost forgotten. The festivities were only just beginning.

"Ugh," she said. "This is guaranteed to be a dull affair."

"Oh, it can't be as bad as all that, your majesty," Flumere said.

"This is your first time, so I'll forgive you for not knowing. These parties are nothing more than an excuse for people to make themselves feel important."

"Well, as queen, I'm sure you have the right to tell them all what prancing fools they are."

Arivana gasped, opening wide eyes on her handmaiden. "Why, Flumere, I do believe that would be quite wicked of me." She smiled. "I'll have to keep it in mind."

They both giggled.

The float finally reached its destination, docking itself through some sorcerous means of control. Arivana stepped off, clearing her throat and fighting down a private smile. She walked straight onto a platform that held the throne she would sit in for the majority of the night while she waited on all the guests to pay—at their leisure of course—their supposed respects. She'd seen how her parents approached evenings like this. She'd paid careful attention and learned how to deliver an insult without breaking the pretense of propriety, but tonight would be her first chance to do so herself. *Maybe it won't be so bad after all?*

She sat down and graciously accepted a glass from a servant, whose eyes remained downcast behind a full-faced mask. Loose grey cloth covered him—or maybe her?—allowing him to blend in with the carved stone walls and pillars dotted around the pavilion. She took a sip from the glass, which contained wine watered to account for her age and weight, and mixed with a variety of frozen berries. She took one, a blackberry, in her mouth and squeezed it between her molars, savoring the cold, crunchy burst of flavor.

She leaned back, examining the crowd. Picking out targets ahead of time so she could plan how best to rattle them. A woman with her hair done up in a spire and laced with thin golden chains looked far too much like she carried a beehive atop her head. *The whole city will be abuzz with talk of your fashion.* A man grabbing double handfuls of pastries from every passing tray. *The breadth of your sweetness knows no bounds.* Way too much perfume. *I've heard it said that you teach men how to cherish the very air in their lungs.*

Arivana snickered through her nose, taking another mouthful of her drink.

A chair slammed down beside her and she jumped, nearly spilling the contents of her glass. Two grey-clad servants pushed the seat—nearly a throne itself—right up next to hers. The Minister of Gardens plopped down in it.

"Tior," she said, giving him a crooked smile. "I wasn't expecting . . . um . . . whatever this is."

He cast a wary glance over the crowd, then presented her with a tight smile of his own. "It is the royal *family* that is supposed to host the Festival of Blooming. Such duties are too much burden for one person, even one as radiant as yourself."

Arivana blushed under the praise.

"Plus," Tior continued, "you appeared lonely, to my aging eyes. I thought you might appreciate some company."

"And I welcome it," she said.

The statement was more than just social politeness. She *had* been lonely. So very lonely. Especially since that day at the waterfall. Claris had always been there for her, before and after the death of her family. Mother's best childhood friend, ever present in her life, was more a member of the family than any of the distant blood relatives who, by political necessity, never stepped foot anywhere near Panisahldron. Claris's shunning of her felt the worst sort of betrayal.

Arivana wiped a bead of moisture that had collected in her lower eyelids. *Sad, how I don't call her "aunt" anymore, not even in my thoughts.*

As she lowered her hand, it fell into Tior's palm, waiting on the arm of her seat. Though delicate, it held none of the soggy tenderness she'd come to associate with the elderly. He gave her hand a firm but gentle squeeze. She exhaled, feeling the twisting tension inside her if not dissipate, then at least dwindle to a tolerable level.

He must have observed the change in her, for he immediately sat back into his seat. "Now, my queen, I'm afraid I have confession to make."

"Oh?"

He returned his gaze to the celebrants, his expression strained but cordial. "What I'm about to say will be . . . upsetting. Can you promise to keep yourself calm?"

She took deep breath, smoothing out her gown over her thighs. "I can."

"Someone is plotting to kill you."

Arivana felt her heart take to thumping, as if threatening to tear free of her chest. She sucked in a harsh breath, unable to release it. What little preamble Tior had given to the message had not been nearly enough to prepare her.

Remembering his warning, and her promise, she worked to bring herself under control. "Why," she finally managed, "would anyone want me dead? And how did you find this out? And who is behind the plot? And—?"

"One question at a time, your majesty, please." Tior pressed his lips together as a servant drew near. He took a glass from the proffered tray and shooed the woman away with a backward wave of his hand. He swirled the wine around, brought the glass to his face, closed his eyes, and inhaled, all before taking the daintiest of sips. He tilted his head back, the barest smile decorating the corner of his lips.

His drink, she noticed, hadn't been watered down at all. She took a full gulp of her own and chewed on the half dozen berries that invaded her mouth.

Tior's eyes finally popped back open. He glanced down at her, as if he'd forgotten she was even there. "Where were we? Ah, yes, your questions." He cleared his throat. "The 'why' of it could be any number of reasons. We Panisians have always drawn the enmity of other nations. Or, perhaps, it would be more accurate to call it envy. We are a beacon, beautiful and pristine, shining among the filth and the darkness of the world. Those without will only ever despise that which they lack."

Arivana nodded, supposing that made some sort of sense. But somehow, it didn't feel quite right to agree. *After all, I've never lacked for anything.*

"As to how we found out," continued Tior, "we apprehended a man in the city yesterday. A foreigner. I'll spare you the details, but suffice it to say he found good reason to tell all he knew and revealed intimations of a plot against your person."

She shivered, trying—and failing—not to think of the measures taken to "persuade" the man to speak. Lisabet had always threatened to send her to the royal carnifex if she wouldn't stop bothering her. Arivana had never found such jests very funny. She'd never seen behind the man's mask but heard from numerous sources that he took far too much pleasure in his work.

"Who is behind all this?" Tior shrugged. "Any attempt that hopes to have even the barest measure of success would require help from within these very halls. That, you see, is the true reason I am here. I've seen assassins aim their blades and spells at six generations of Celandaris kings and queens. And I've had a hand in stopping four of them myself."

Realization slowly dawned on Arivana. "You're to be my protector? But why? Couldn't we just increase the guard?"

"And draw attention to the fact that we know something is afoot?" Tior shook his head. "Better to let our enemies, whoever they might be, continue thinking we are ignorant of their intentions. With your family gone, having your most trusted advisor close at hand will appear natural to outside observers. I'm afraid you'll have to get used to my presence. I'll try to be as unobtrusive as possible, but believe me when I say that this is absolutely necessary for your protection."

Arivana nodded. Something stirred in her belly, a sick feeling, drowning out all the pettiness of her life.

The mischief she'd been plotting earlier now seemed such a stupid thing. *Abyss, what a child I've been.*

It appeared she would have to start growing up, and quickly, if she wanted to survive.

"Do you understand everything I've told you?" Tior asked.

"Yes," Arivana said. "Unfortunately."

He patted her knee. "Try not to worry too much. It's not good for your complexion. Besides, our information suggests we won't have to wait long until our assailants strike. This will all be over before you know it."

"I see." She gulped, standing suddenly. "Please excuse me. I need to . . . freshen up."

Tior stood.

"You don't have to come with me," she blurted. "I mean, I'm sure I'm safe enough within these walls. With so many witnesses."

He smiled, grunting softly. "Merely giving my queen her due respects." He bowed.

Arivana gathered her skirts and, with a calmness she didn't feel, strolled off. She waited until she was out of sight of Tior and the other guests before breaking into a run.

She crashed against a balcony railing. The tears that she'd been holding in check now burst forth in a flood amidst chest-heaving sobs. Her sorrow was formless, directed at nothing and everything. *This is all too much for me.*

Flumere came up behind her, gently placing her long arms across Arivana's shoulders. She knew enough to say nothing. Her presence was comforting, though, and Arivana soon found exhaustion bleeding into the space occupied by her sadness. She straightened from the railing and turned. She stood impassively, drained of all emotion, while her handmaiden wiped her cheeks dry and reapplied a quick veneer of powder to her face.

"Thank you," Arivana said once the woman had finished. "Given how close you always stand to me, I take it you heard what Minister Pashams said?"

"Yes, your majesty."

She grasped the woman's hand. "I'm sorry."

"Whatever for?"

"You'll be in danger now because of me. I'm sure that wasn't what you had in mind when you became my handmaiden."

"Oh, don't you be worrying about me, my queen. I know how to take care of myself."

Arivana couldn't help but smile at Flumere's casual assurance. "I suppose we should return to the party now."

"It's probably for the best."

They started back the way they had come. As they crossed a hallway, movement drew Arivana's attention.

Three figures stood in a doorway. Two of them were foreigners, Fasheshish if their oiled beards were any indication. The third, a woman, had her back to them. One of the men handed something—she couldn't see what—to the woman, then stepped back and closed the door.

The woman turned. Arivana saw a brief flash of her face before she disappeared back into the main chamber of the pavilion. She recognized her, of course.

Claris? What are you up to?

Tassariel touched down upon the edge of Elos's Gaze, leaving her wings out for the moment. Evervines twirled around the borders of the path before her, and her own lavender glow mixed with their silver light to bathe the flagstones and lilies and hedgerows in a surreal cast that left her spellbound. Even the willows, dangling branches like threads high overhead, were caught in the interplay of color and light.

With a contented sigh, Tassariel furled her wings at last and stepped her sandaled feet up the trail. This was no domicile. The only structures present were the grand temple of the high council and the tombs of all the valynkar heroes. Elos's Gaze was the highest point in their city. Made that way, supposedly, so that the honored dead could rest closest to their god, and so the penitent living could worship without interference or distraction.

She passed throngs of her kin, usually sitting in small groups on the scattered stone benches, or en masse in one of the amphitheatres, paying their respects to Elos in whatever way they saw fit. There was no wrong way, according to the precepts, which was just as well; getting everyone to agree would have been impossible. She'd read stories of the days, eons past, when all of her kind had been united in purpose, one voice and one mind in all things. But to see such tales placed next to the people of the present made her think they were nothing but myth and legends, self-satisfying nostalgia on the part of the few left who might have lived through such times.

Tassariel shook her head, berating herself for the thought. *Remember why you are here. It is not to pass judgment, but to absolve yourself before Elos.* She inhaled deeply, renewed by the scents of flowers and grass around her and soothed by the murmur of the wind through the trees. Her purpose restored, she continued her uphill trek to her destination.

She passed groups large and small basking by ponds or lounging in gazebos. Around one curve, she spotted the sweep of Eluhar's blond hair over the side of his face as he sat with four others in quiet conversation. He turned as she approached and smiled.

She returned the smile but continued to march, shaking her head slightly as Eluhar motioned for her to join them. She did well one-on-one or as an observer in a large group, but the size in between made her feel nervous for some reason. *Too difficult to be myself, I suppose, when more than a single set of expectations are thrust upon me.*

Her friend did not seem upset, at least. He must have grown used to her predilections by now. Still, he never failed to extend the invitation, possibly hoping she might one day change. Not likely, but the gesture was sweet all the same. And besides, her observance today was in a place it was best to be alone.

Another mark later saw her to the gates of the necropolis. Stepping inside, she was greeted by a view of the newest structure, its entrance carved into the shape of a giant seashell, midnight blue like the aura of the man interred within. She'd heard he had always liked the sea.

Folding her hands respectfully, Tassariel shuffled into Voren's tomb.

The narrow stairs spiraled down, following the shape of the shell. A single evervine reached in, twisting along the roof as it released its soft, sad luminescence. Carved into the walls were images depicting Voren's life and deeds. It began during the War of Rising Night, when the valynkar had united to stand against the mierothi . . . and lost. A war, it seemed, they had never truly recovered from.

Tassariel reached the bottom step and peered down the length of the burial chamber. With a start, she realized she was not alone.

A figure knelt at the opposite end of the narrow space, head bowed, one hand resting on Voren's sarcophagus. Golden hair tumbled down, obscuring his face. But she knew who it was anyway.

"Gilshamed," she said. "I'm surprised to see you here."

He shifted his head, glancing once at her before turning forward again. "Why should that surprise you, niece?"

"I rarely see you out since you've returned. Not without . . ." She gulped. "Not without Lashriel anyway."

He moved not a finger's width, but Tassariel sensed a sort of deflation all the same. "Her turn with the healers today. The fools think there might still be something that can be done."

Tassariel stifled a sob. Swallowed. "Isn't there?"

"Not by them. Elos alone can restore her now. If he's even able." His hand clenched into a fist. "If he even cares."

"How can you say that? Of course he cares!"

"Such belief. Such . . . conviction." He slowly straightened, pivoting to face her. "As was I, in my youth. Enjoy your unflinching devotion while it lasts, Tassariel. The sentiment will pass."

She shook, struggling to contain the fury, and sorrow, that writhed within her. Finding fewer reasons to fight it by the beat. First Lerathus, and now her uncle. *I am sick of my age being used as a weapon against me.* "When," she spat, "did you become such a cynic?"

"When I came back from the Veiled Empire and realized how impotent our god truly is."

"But you returned with my aunt, with the others, too, after everyone had thought them all long dead. All those centuries, and Elos kept them safe—"

Gilshamed slapped the lid of the sarcophagus. "*He* kept them safe! Not Elos. Not anyone else. Voren. The man we had written off as a traitor. He did more for them than our god ever tried to. Even after that very same god abandoned him to his fate."

"But the Shroud. That was Ruul's domain. Elos couldn't help what went on there."

He raised an eyebrow. "Couldn't? Or *wouldn't?*"

Tassariel frowned, pondering the question, chilled by the implications if Gilshamed was even partially right. *What does that say about Elos if he didn't have the power to intervene? And if he did have it, why not do something?*

She folded her arms, tapping her foot nervously. "I don't know," she said at last. "But you can't argue that some good managed to come of it anyway. Some light, some hope, even when all seemed darkness."

He turned away from her, leaning over the interred body of Voren once more. "Perhaps. But, if so, it had nothing to do with our god. If he can even be called that anymore."

Tassariel gasped. "You . . . you can't mean that." She lowered her voice. "That's *heresy!*"

Gilshamed shrugged. "If that's what you want to call truth, then so be it. Too long have we played his games without proof that what we do has any meaning. I, for one, have had enough of it."

"Faith does not require proof."

He shook his head. "So all gods say."

She cried out in frustration. "Fine then. I can see debating with you will get me nowhere." She turned, placing a foot on the bottom step in desperate need to get away from him. She froze before lifting her back foot. In a week, she would turn one hundred and attend a ritual conducted by the Valynkar High Council. A council her uncle was a part of.

"Will you be there?" she asked. "At my centennial?"

"I don't know," Gilshamed said. "I and the rest of the council haven't seen eye to eye in a long time. A *very* long time. Why do you ask?"

"Let's just say, I wouldn't be upset if you weren't there."

"As you wish."

She stomped up the stairs, fleeing a darkness that had nothing to do with the crypt's lack of light.

CHAPTER 5

Mevon thrust his hands forward. Twin blades flew forth, spinning through the air. They whistled for a beat before crashing into their target with a dull crack.

He lifted his blindfold to check the accuracy of the throw. The ivory-handled daggers, which he'd carried for over a decade, were not meant for throwing, but he'd learned to use them in that capacity anyway. The blades stuck neatly into the tree trunk, one of many in loose formation at the base of a cliff. One blade cut halfway through the fist-sized circle Zorvanya had painted on the bark, and the other was just skirting the opposite edge. He smiled at his aim. Then he looked at the other tree. The smile vanished.

Two black daggers, nearly the size of shortswords, quivered in the wood. Completely inside their circle. And even from a distance of twenty paces, he could tell that they were nearly touching each other.

Mevon sighed, glancing down at Zorvanya. "You sure he didn't peek?"

The woman quirked a smile. "Quite sure."

Draevenus lifted his own blindfold, inspecting his handiwork. "A good effort, Mevon, but I'm afraid you're outmatched."

"I can see that. No need to rub it in."

"Not that," Draevenus said, marching to retrieve his blades. "But in matters of darkness, I've had quite a bit more experience."

Mevon grunted.

Zorvanya laughed, a throaty rumbling that sounded odd coming from a figure so small and so . . . feminine. "What is it with men?" she said. "Anytime a woman is present, you always feel the need to try to impress."

Draevenus yanked one dagger free. "Did it work?"

"Indeed it did. Perhaps I should leave the flap of my tent open for you tonight?"

The mierothi froze with his hand on the handle of the other blade. "I don't . . . I'm not . . . ."

"Yes?"

He gritted his teeth, then pulled the other dagger and slammed it into its sheath. "That won't be necessary."

Zorvanya darted her gaze back and forth between the two men. "Oh. I see. Then you two are . . . ?"

Mevon locked eyes with Draevenus. They both burst out laughing.

She placed her hands on her hips, taking on a playful, mocking look as she waited for them to stop.

"Well, if that's the case, then why do you reject me? Am I so hideous to look at?"

"On the contrary," Draevenus said. "You're a splash of paint on an otherwise-dull canvas. A fair treat for our deadened eyes."

She frowned. "Do I smell?"

"Near two days on the trail, and we've yet to come across running water. None of us are as fresh as we'd like to be."

Her eyes narrowed, cutting into the mierothi like thorns. "There's something holding you back. If I could only . . ." Her gaze shot open. "You haven't been with a woman in ages, have you?"

Draevenus flinched, then went still as a statue.

Mevon pondered the reaction. He'd thought he'd known the reason for his friend's standoffishness— that he wanted to keep his mierothi nature hidden from her—but now he wasn't sure. He'd never heard the assassin talk about any kind of love life, past or present. Mevon contained a smile. *She must speak too close to the truth for his comfort.*

Draevenus turned his head away, gazing out over the ocean beyond the Shelf and the sun now setting where even the waters faded away. "It will be dark soon," he said. "I'll go gather some firewood."

Mevon stepped forward. "I'll go with you."

The mierothi held up a hand. "No. Thank you. I'll be fine. You're not the only one who needs the exercise, Mevon."

He swung away and began marching through the trees.

"Exercise?" Zorvanya called after him. "You're just trying to escape me. Admit it!"

"I admit nothing!" he called back.

She laughed at the dark, retreating form, and Mevon allowed himself to join in. He gestured at a log he'd drawn up to their hasty encampment, and the two of them sat down. Mevon leaned forward and began preparing the ground for a fire.

"I've been meaning to ask," he said. "How exactly did you know what we were—regarding magic, I mean?"

"Finally worked up the nerve to ask, huh?" She sighed. "I'm afraid there's no big mystery. Draevenus flashed into my yurt faster than a blink, then held up a man twice his size without appearing to strain. He was the easy part."

"And me?"

"You were more difficult, but I figured you out all the same." She tapped her ear. Mevon could see a bead-like earring tucked just inside. "This tells me when someone is in or near my home. It is linked to other beads, enchanted as this one, that are woven into the skin of my entrance flap. It emits a low, ringing sound, alerting me whenever I have company, as it was when Hakel and his friends were visiting.

"The ringing stopped when you came in."

"Trinkets? Where did you get those?"

"The friend of mine, the one we are on our way to

see, she gave them to me. Though how she obtained them I've never been told."

Mevon nodded. He'd have to remember to ask the other shaman when they reached her. They'd encountered no casters of any kind since crossing the mountains, so the story behind how such devices came to be here would be an interesting one to hear. "Still, I am impressed that you noticed with all the commotion."

"I make it my business to notice things most others would miss. I like having insight into people's lives."

"Is that so? What have you discovered about the two of us, then?"

Zorvanya folded her hands in her lap and cleared her throat. "You've been traveling together for a while. There's an easy camaraderie about you, a cohesion of your movements that only comes to those who've shed blood side by side. You're both killers. Draevenus is stoic about it. He seems to have accepted that death is sometimes necessary, even inevitable, but he takes no pleasure in it. You, on the other hand, grow excited at the prospect of violence though you are trying to suppress that part of you."

Mevon realized he had grown still and forced himself back into motion, placing more stones around the edge of the growing fire pit.

"That," Zorvanya continued, "is why I tease your friend so. He looks like he could use a good jabbing now and then. But my flirtations with him are just that, a tease." She leaned forward, daring to caress his arm. "I prefer men who exude a certain . . . passion."

He felt a flush rising within him at her touch, and her words. There was no denying he welcomed both. Yet a twinge of guilt invaded his thoughts all the same. It wasn't that he didn't have the freedom to be with whom he wanted. But that freedom, he knew, only existed because he yet lived, while Jasside was dead. And while there had been no vows taken, no promises to her made . . .

He ground his teeth, willing the feeling away, so he could revel in the delightful possibilities of this encounter.

Mevon turned his head, gazing into her eyes with the full force of his attention. Her lips parted with an almost imperceptible gasp, which transformed her natural beauty into something far greater. He thought it might be called desire.

He smiled.

She edged closer.

They both jumped as a pile of logs dropped to the ground just beside them. Draevenus brushed his hands together, clearing off dirt and flakes of bark. "That should be enough to get us through the night," he said.

"Yes, thank you," Zorvanya said. She withdrew her hand from Mevon's arm with a sigh. But her gaze lingered a moment longer, a moment filled with promise.

Mevon grabbed a log and cluster of twigs and began arranging them in the fire pit. His mind wandered, pleasantly. He didn't know how much longer Zorvanya would travel with them, but he couldn't help but entertain thoughts on how best to use the time.

He felt Draevenus arrive at his side. The mierothi slapped something into Mevon's chest. "You forgot these."

Mevon reached for the two daggers, which he had left embedded in the tree. "Thanks."

He pulled back his cloak and inserted one into its sheath on his left side. As he repeated the movement on his right, something on the blade caught his eye. He brought it up to his face to inspect it.

A single sniff told him what it was. *Nothing but tree sap.* He pinched the dagger, sliding his fingers up the edge to clean it off. But something stopped him. In the day's dying light, it did not look like sap at all.

It looked like blood.

He closed his eyes as memories sprang forth, unbidden.

The Shelf on one side, a cliff on the other, and the day on the edge of darkness and light. Blood stained the end of a blade. This blade.

An encounter with a beautiful woman.

Mevon shook.

It was not excitement that set him to trembling, nor—as the memory recalled—fear, but something else new in his life.

Longing.

Longing for a dead woman.

But, more than that, longing for the effect she'd had on him. For awakening the realization that he could be something else. Something other than a killer. Something . . . good.

Her influence, more than any other, had set him upon the path he now trod. He had promised himself to do right by her, to see this path through, to make of his remaining days a worthy tale to tell. A worthy life.

He knew he had yet to succeed. Perhaps there would be time for his own happiness later, for . . . pleasant distractions. But not yet.

Mevon wiped the blade clean and slammed it home in its sheath. He dared the barest glance at Zorvanya's lounging form before shifting his eyes away.

Not yet.

Vashodia peeked over the edge of the boulder as she scanned the valley. She'd left the caravan soon after Jasside, but while her apprentice drove eastward into the swamp, Vashodia had gone south, ascending a section of the Nether Mountains that curled through the lower part of Weskara. A gust of wind fluttered her robe as it passed. It was cold, this high up, but the garment protected her from the worst of the chill. She was more than glad to be free of the hot, dank marshes.

Thoughts of the swamp turned to thoughts of Jasside. She was slow in coming back. *The girl must have gone and injured herself. My, what a foolish thing to do.* Vashodia smiled. A little pain, now and then, was good for keeping one humble. She knew she had at least a day before Jasside made it back to their little troupe.

Time to end the hunt. On the real quarry, that is.

She didn't feel bad for the deception. Those shadow

beasts were, after all, a nuisance that needed to be dealt with eventually. A test for the girl and a peace offering to the Weskarans were merely pleasant bonuses. She herself had a bigger mountain to crumble.

Vashodia energized. Her eyes swept over the whole of the valley below her. Thin droplets of her power spread out over the expanse, a million strong. None was large enough to warrant attention by itself, even from the most sensitive of wards. Her prey was vastly more intelligent than most others she had hunted. She would have to play it terribly careful to avoid falling into any unwanted traps, which was simply no fun at all.

The droplets reached the limits of her vision having found nothing. She had expected as much. The initial gathering of such power would have notified other casters in the area, so she'd started her search where she was sure none would be. She eyed a ledge a league distant, closer to where she thought her target might be found, and shadow-dashed to it. Once there, she simply pulled the existing droplets to her.

This valley proved empty as well. A second and third jump to new areas revealed identical results. On the fourth, however, one of the droplets, then another—then dozens, performed an action unattributable to her direct control: They bounced *away* from their path. The fact was, their function was not to find anything. Rather, it was to avoid. A much less obtrusive method of seeking out places soaked in manipulated energy. This trick was one she'd kept for herself.

Vashodia watched another mark, but the lone anomaly had been the only place to disturb her little pets. She chuckled. Eying the spot carefully, she shadow-dashed down towards it, landing in a clearing three hundred paces from a thick stand of evergreens, where she now knew her prey dwelled. She gathered her robe about her and skipped forward over a thin layer of pine needles and twigs. It wasn't long before she pranced past the trees, stopping just outside the wardnet.

She peered closely, examining the casting. A simple enough design, used to alert the maker whenever an unwelcome guest came traipsing in. She had ways of disarming it, but it would take a rather long time to do so. And besides: This close, she actually *wanted* her prey to know she was coming.

Vashodia gave one last command to her droplets of power and stepped forward. The ward quivered, releasing a strand of energy. She watch it snake along the ground, disappearing around the corner of a low mound. She followed. No doubt it would lead her right where she wanted to go. She was delighted to find an entrance cut into the side of the mound, hidden by folds of earth so that only someone who knew where to look would find it. She descended into the hole without hesitation. Into darkness. She couldn't help but smile.

A tunnel opened up before her, not damp or musty as one might expect. Vashodia scraped her claws across smooth, hardened walls, ravaging the passage with the shrill sound it made. The ground she walked was as level as a palace floor. She sniffed, inhaling what could easily be described as sterility. Her prey always was a bit obsessive about cleanliness. *I'm so very glad that some things never change.*

She strolled, following in the wake of the snaking strand, letting it guide her through several branches of the tunnel. She had no intention of beating the thing to its maker. Let the poor creature twist in the trap. Let him sweat. It would not change his fate. She sensed a snap of expelled energy as the strand reached its destination and delivered its fell message.

Reckoning has come.

Vashodia began to run, unable to refrain a moment longer from seeing the look on the man's face. Two more turns, and she broke into an open chamber, lit only by lightglobes that pulsed with a purple glow. Charts scribbled with complex formulae adorned the perimeter, and the floor space was cramped by half a dozen tables littered with alchemical tools—flasks and vials, clamps and droppers, clear amphorae holding a hundred body parts from as many different species, humans included. In the center rested a high-backed chair, facing away from her.

"Hello, Lekrigar," she said. "So sorry I couldn't visit sooner."

The chair swiveled, revealing the pinched face of the high regnosist, the last festering pustule of the regime she had destroyed. He sat, one foot propped on the opposite knee, fingertips of each hand resting together in a contemplative pose. He peered at her, fully lacking in the anticipated fear.

"Vashodia," he said. "I've been expecting you."

"And how might that be?" she asked, surprised yet unconcerned with his show of confidence. "I've been masking my signal for a week."

"Yet I still knew you were coming. I bet you're just *dying* to find out how."

"Seeking to impress me with your knowledge?" She giggled. "How pitiful. There are as many mysteries to solve as there are stars in the sky. I don't waste time on trifles."

"So besting you is merely a trifle now?"

She sighed. "I suppose you're right. The student has clearly surpassed the master. I'm sure it didn't even take a century for you to develop this one lamentable skill you think would grant you an advantage over me."

She watched, in exquisite satisfaction, as his right eye began to twitch.

Lekrigar cleared his throat, gripping the arms of his chair. "Why should I need an advantage? Surely you just came here to talk. I can't imagine you'd saunter in here, alone and deenergized, if you had something else in mind."

"Talk. Of course. How is your life these days, my oldest and dearest friend? Having fun unleashing my creations on the countryside?"

"They are *my* creations. Mine! You inflate your own involvement in their development, as you do in anything else you touch. Your idea was simple, childish. I took it and turned it into something beautiful."

"Beautiful? Even you can't believe that about such monstrosities."

Lekrigar cackled. "To some, power is the only true beauty."

"Oh, stop it. I'm blushing! You can't possibly think me the prettiest girl in the world."

His face scrunched in confusion for a moment. When it passed, a snarl took its place. He rose to his feet, pushing the chair back in his haste to stand. "I'm done with your games, Vashodia. Tell me why you're here."

She shrugged. "But we were having such a lovely chat . . ."

Lekrigar's fists bunched up as a growl rumbled from his throat.

"Fine. If you're going to get all pouty on me, I'll cut right to the point. I came to ask you one question. Depending on your answer, I will kill you."

He waited in silence four whole beats. "Or what?"

"Hmm? Oh, right. That statement requires another possible resolution, doesn't it? To be honest, I hadn't bothered to think of the alternative. I already know what you're going to say."

He sneered. "Out with it then."

Vashodia narrowed her gaze on him. "Are you willing to be civilized?"

He laughed, shoulders shaking like a slow shiver. "Are you talking about that pathetic colony of yours?

You are, aren't you? Ruul's light, girl, you must be desperate indeed if you've come to beg my help. What's wrong? Is it too taxing playing nice with the inferior life-forms of this world? Negotiating? Treating them like equals?" His laughter continued, becoming more unhinged by the beat.

She exhaled, shaking her head. "I thought as much."

"Just what is it you hope to accomplish with this show of civility anyway? Our people are *conquerors*, Vashodia. Or have you forgotten? You seem in the business of toppling rulers of late."

"What else do you think I'd be doing? I'm saving the world."

"From what?"

"Things they can't see." She smiled. "Things like you."

Lekrigar stilled, the sudden silence like a hammer strike. "You won't kill me, Vashodia. You can't. I figured out your weakness, you see. I know exactly why you didn't fight Rekaj yourself. His advantage over you in combat meant that you would always be too cowardly to face him." He stepped forward, pushing his hands to each side. "That advantage is one he and I shared."

Vashodia rolled her eyes, adopting the most bored-looking stance she could think of. She yawned.

Lekrigar's forward momentum wavered, then stopped.

Slowly, so he'd be sure to hear every word, she said, "I've devoted myself to the observance of things most people aren't even aware of. Almost two thousand years of it. Did you really think, in all that time, I would never once turn that gaze upon myself? I know all about my own weaknesses, Lekrigar. More importantly, I know how to counteract them."

"I . . . don't—"

"You feel it now, don't you?" she said. "And perhaps you finally remember the most important thing there is to know about me."

He grew rigid, unmoving, unblinking, as shadows slowly crept up his legs like a black mass of ants. The sweat she had expected at the start, and the fear in his face, finally deigned to show themselves.

She crossed her arms. "I plan for *everything*."

The shadows swelled, converging on his torso, sweeping up his neck, clawing across his face to darken bulging, frantic eyes. They continued to the top of his scaled head as a formality. Finally, with a single constriction, like the twisting of a wet towel, the shadows consumed him.

Vashodia energized at last, but only for half a beat. She gave the order, and the shadows dispelled once more into the million droplets of power she'd conjured nearly a toll ago. At her command, they'd been seeping in through the cracks and pores in the earth, surrounding this very chamber. Only her staying hand would have saved him, but she'd known the outcome of this encounter before she'd even left the colony. Not that there was much left to save. Neither bone, nor scrap of cloth, nor a single drop of blood remained.

She turned to leave but heard a sound behind her. A whimper. She sighed. "Of course he'd have one."

She tramped to the back of the laboratory and pushed through a door into a bedchamber. It was empty, but the sound came again, drawing her towards another door farther in. This one was made of metal and had a sturdy lock. She marched up to it, shattering the lock with a single wave of energy, and pulled it open.

A woman huddled inside. Chained up. Bruised. But, unsurprisingly, lacking in dirt or grime. Vashodia laughed. "He always did like to keep his things clean."

The woman jerked at the voice. She lifted her head and stared in obvious awe at Vashodia. "Who are you?"

"Today? An executioner."

A glimmer of hope splashed across the woman's features. "You mean he's . . . dead?"

"He's less dead than he is, how shall I put it, *unmade.*"

"Gone is gone." She spat into the corner of the closet. "You'll hear no cry of mourning from me."

The woman stumbled to her feet, rattling chains and pained groans competing to be the loudest sound in the room. She lifted her arms forward in supplication. "Are you here to save me?"

Vashodia tilted her head. "What an odd thing to say."

"**O**uch!" cried Arivana. She pulled her throbbing hand back from the stem. "Stupid thorns."

She brought the pricked tip of her finger to hover a hand's width from her face and studied the wound. A single drop of blood bloomed, like the cap of a tiny crimson mushroom. So small, yet it still hurt like the abyss. "Gardening. Pah! I've had enough of this."

"So it seems," said Tior from behind her.

As promised, he'd been her constant companion this last week. She'd performed a cursory inspection of the barracks, presided over an art contest for children of the great houses, watched skylights in celebration of another pointless festival, and, of course, continued with all facets of her education. It seemed as if he'd not left her side even once. He set others to watch her as she slept—people, he'd told her, whom he trusted implicitly—but since he was present from when she woke in the morning until she drifted off once more to sleep, he might as well have tied a cord between their wrists.

She stood, brushing soil from her dress. It was a sturdy ensemble, long and thick and layered in shades of brown and grey. Made for work in a garden but still pretty in its own way. She'd always thought beauty could be found in the usefulness of a thing. As it was not a popular opinion to have, though, she mostly kept it to herself.

Tior reached towards her. "Here, let me heal that."

"No," Arivana said, jerking her hand away. "It's the fool who grabs a rose without heed of its thorns. Pain is a lesson. And this fool, it seems, needs all the instruction she can garner."

Tior stepped back, quirking a smile. "Wise words, for one so young."

Arivana shrugged. "It's just something my father used to say." She lifted her finger again, hissing a breath though the sharp ache. "Never thought I would experience it quite so literally."

"Well, then, since you've decided to endure a penance of self-imposed torment for your folly, I don't think it would be fair to test your horticultural skills any further today."

"You mean we can be done?" She peeked over her shoulder at the hundred towers rising to the south, hope rising with the thought that she might soon be in her bath, so Flumere could wipe the grime from the day's lessons away. Such hope had nothing to do with the fact that it was the one place Tior would not accompany her.

Of course it doesn't.

"I'm afraid not," Tior said, smashing her hope on the ground like a porcelain vase. "Demonstrating your botanical knowledge requires no use of your hands, does it not?"

She slumped over, sighing, not even trying to hide her opinion on the matter. "I suppose not."

The minister began up the path, and Arivana followed without the need for him to beckon. She already felt enough of a child in his presence. She couldn't stand the thought of another scolding.

They left the training area behind, sashaying along one of the private pathways. Arivana saw numerous guardsmen tucked into every corner, watching all angles of approach. Tior said he hadn't increased the number of them, in keeping with his plan to avoid attention, but she swore there were a lot more than usual lately. Maybe it was the armor, which, through some sorcerous means, blended in with their backgrounds, or perhaps it was just her own wariness driven into hyperactivity by the looming threat of assassination, but she couldn't recall ever noticing their presence so acutely before. Her heightened state of alertness was beginning to drain her, and part of her wished that her unknown enemy would just try it already, so she could relax.

They turned and entered a grand veranda overlooking the gardens proper. Arivana caught the eye of one particular guard through the slit of his visor. Even from that narrowed view, she could tell he was young, bare years separating them. She thought she saw a faint crinkle around his eyes. It took her a moment to translate the motion to the hidden parts of his face and realize he was smiling. She blushed, returning the gesture, after which they both looked hastily away.

She let herself be led to the veranda's edge. Below them, plants of nearly every variety in the world blossomed in curving rows between sections of the meandering, stone walkway. All the ones considered pleasant to the senses, at least. Tior pointed to one grouping of bushes. He didn't need to say any more. Arivana knew what was expected of her.

"Azalea," she said. "Flowering shrubs that typically come in pinks and reds, native to Phelupar. They prefer the shade of trees and bloom annually."

Tior nodded, then pointed to a pond.

"Lotus. An aquatic perennial flower with a variety of uses across horticultural, culinary, and artistic disciplines, native to Yusan."

He pointed again.

"Orchid. Another perennial with almost as many different types as there are grains of sand on the shore. They can be found just about everywhere but exist in greatest concentration in the jungles on our southern border."

He pointed again, and again, and again, and each time she gave the right answer. He'd been quizzing her hard the last week. It seemed like his wealth of knowledge had finally decided to stay put in her mind.

At last, he lowered his hand. He patted her on the shoulder, giving the barest nod of approval. "Very good, my queen. Very good indeed. Now, can you tell me why it is so important for you to know all this?"

Arivana twisted her lips in thought. This wasn't one of the things he'd taught her. Never explicitly anyway. He must want her to draw her own conclusions. No—he wanted her to draw *his* conclusions in her own way.

She took a deep breath. "I think it's for political purposes?" She stared at him, questioningly. When he did not interrupt, she went on. "Yes, if I receive a gift of flowers from a visiting dignitary, or wear petals or their fragrance at a gathering of important people, or something like that, it would be highly embarrassing if I, the Queen of Panisahldron, the supposed embodiment of all things beautiful, could not correctly identify them."

Tior sighed. "A good answer. Only, there is no 'supposed' about it. You *must* be what your ancestors have been for the last five millennia, what the world expects of you, and, most importantly, what our people need from you. A symbol of beauty for all to look upon, the standard against which all must measure themselves." He smiled. "It has already begun. The latest trend among teenaged girls in the city is to dye their hair in shades of the sunset." He gestured towards a loose strand of her hair. "Some grown women are even adopting the style."

Blushing, she looked away. But that only brought her gaze in line with the young guardsman she'd noticed earlier. And he was staring straight at her. He quickly looked away but brought his eyes right back a beat later. Arivana failed to stifle a giggle.

"What is it?" Tior asked.

"Nothing. It's just . . ." She paused, for she did not want to get the young man in trouble. She glanced past him to the sun setting over the protective wall on the south side of the gardens, looking for some excuse.

Now, to her horror, she found one.

Figures began appearing at the top of the wall. Five, ten, a score of them, dressed in dark, hooded cloaks with veils concealing their faces. They leapt down from a height of twenty paces, touching lightly upon the garden soil as if sinking into a pool, then shot forward, directly towards her, at incredible speed. Bare steel filled every hand.

Tior must have seen the fright on her face, for he swung around. She heard a growl sound from his throat. "Up arms!" he called. "Protect the queen!"

Guardsmen flocked out of their hidden places, more than she remembered counting on the way in. The numbers looked equal, but Arivana shook in fear. The men advancing moved faster than humanly possible. She didn't need to be told that they were under the influence of heavy sorcerous enhancement.

Her protectors had no time to form ranks. Crossbows twanged from the intruders. Most bolts deflected off armor, but one guard crumpled, choking and gurgling, as one caught him in the throat. Another crashed backwards at the impact from four simultaneous hits.

Arivana rushed to Tior's side, her breathing ragged, clutching him like a toddler. She'd never seen bloodshed before. Her earlier wish to get this attack over with came back to haunt her, and she cried tears of bitter fear.

"Stay behind me," Tior barked, shoving her. She continued gripping him, burying her face in his back, but as the cacophony rose, and men screamed in pain, she slowly edged her head around so she could see the fight. But her mind could not comprehend all the chaos at once, instead processing each frame of violence individually.

A guard released an arrow from his wrath-bow.

The glowing red missile streaked over a flower bed and erupted into a gout of virulent flame, immolating two attackers who, somehow, trudged onwards a few steps more.

Another guard thrust his shock-lance forward, activating it. Sparking tendrils reached out and caught three men in its cone. The one in the center froze, twitching. The two on the edges spun free. They converged on the guard from each side, scything curved sword towards him. A sickening amount of blood sprayed across a row of white lilies.

A man swung a two-handed axe, knocking two guards to the ground. He lunged atop them, stomping a boot down to crush one skull like a melon and chopping through the neck of the other.

The young guardsman who'd been looking at her parried a sword thrust from one attacker, then spun to bash another with his shield. A third man pounced, daggers aimed for his throat, but the guard dodged at the last moment and skewered his assailant's groin with an outthrust blade.

A beast of a man, hands slick with blood, lost hold of his spiked mace. He kicked it as it fell, sending it smashing into the knee of an advancing guard, staggering him. The man gripped the guard by his pauldrons and heaved him a dozen paces. He crashed into a tree trunk, bones and armor crunching like twigs.

Arivana blinked as the scene seemed to pause before her. Three guardsmen were left standing, along with ten of the assassins. All of them panting, drenched in blood. One of the cloaked men slumped over, and now there were only nine.

"Back to me," Tior commanded. The three guards backpedaled until abreast of her and the minister. The attackers advanced.

Tior took one step forward, then lifted his hands. Light began filling them. A shock of worry went through the assailants and, with a cry, they dashed forward. But whatever sorcerous augmentation they'd been blessed with must have waned, for their charge seemed pitifully slow compared to their earlier movements.

Tior's conjured light flared, filling the whole of the garden around them. Arivana turned away and covered her face to protect herself from the blinding brilliance. She felt pulses of energy thump through the air. Heard bodies crash to the ground.

The light diminished, and Arivana hazarded a peek. The nine would-be assassins lay on their backs, knocked over like sunflower stalks, each with a gaping, smoking hole in the center of his chest. Her nose and lungs filled with the distinct scent of burning human flesh. She struggled to calm her racing heart and quivering. She spun away, breathing through her mouth to try to settle her roiling stomach.

"It's done, then," Tior said, weariness evident in his voice.

Arivana couldn't respond. Facing away from the others, she was the only to notice someone step out from behind a hedgerow thirty paces away. Tight, dark clothes, with hood and mask as the others, but a figure most decidedly female. The woman stalked towards them, slim rapier in one hand. The other glowed with magical light.

"Behind us!" Arivana screamed.

Two of the guardsmen jumped in front of her at once, and Tior lunged to their side a beat later. Too late, though. A barrage of light, sharp and fast like arrows, careened towards the minister.

He lifted a hand, conjuring a wall of light, but it was hastily made and unable to do more than deflect the attack. The sorcerous projectiles veered sideways— straight into the two guardsmen. Dozens of fresh holes ripped through each of their bodies.

The woman swiped a hand, slashing a ray of energy across Tior's defenses and popping his shield with a sizzling crack. Arivana toppled backwards, and the minister plopped down at her side.

This is it. We're done. I'm so sorry I failed you, Mother . . .

She heard stomping feet and managed to lift her head. An armored figure lunged for the woman. The last guardsman. His helmet had come off at some point, and she saw the full face of the eye-wandering youth at last. Her only thought, as tears rolled down her cheeks, was that he was far too young to die. *Especially for me.*

He jabbed his sword, and the woman met it with her rapier, turning it expertly. She spun, smashing her elbow into his jaw. He staggered and reached out with a wild swing, but she cartwheeled away. The woman sheathed her blade and thrust both hands forward, filled with light. The guard rose into the air. She turned her hands outwards and clawed them apart.

The guard split in half.

The legs and waist flew off the veranda, bloody intestines flapping madly behind. The rest tumbled across the ground, coming straight towards Arivana. She clenched, rolling away, as he crashed into her.

Tior, however, had regained his feet. With fist held high, he formed what she thought looked like a hammer of light, massive and raging. He brought it down on the woman.

She put hands over head, raising a shield of her own. The hammer bounced off it, and she winced. Tior pounded her again, and she cried out, falling to a knee. A third time, and her shield shattered. The woman crashed down, her head smacking the ground, and lay still.

Arivana rolled back over and sat up. The young guard's head and shoulder were between her legs. He wheezed. His eyes met hers, and her heart broke.

Tior had staggered over to the unconscious woman. He bent over, pulling off the mask.

"Well," he said, "I suppose this explains her odd behavior lately."

Arivana glanced only briefly, confirming what she'd already known in the deepest part of her soul.

Claris. How could you?

She bent her head, rivers flowing freely from her eyes. The young man's lips started to move, but she heard only mumbling.

"Wh-what's that?" she managed to say between sobs.

He ground his teeth, sucking in a rasping breath. "So . . . beautiful."

She cradled his head, forcing herself to watch, to honor him, as the life left his eyes. The finger she'd pricked on the rose stem, a lifetime ago now, peeked out from behind his neck, still sporting a single dried spot of blood.

CHAPTER 6

"Put your arm in mine, Draevenus. No, not like that. Hold it bent and up around your chest. There, doesn't that feel nice? Now, keep your eyes forward and greet anyone you walk past with a nod, or a handshake if you simply must converse. If they're dressed nicer than us, address them as sir. That will probably be most everybody. Don't speak to the women—no, I'll do that if the need arises—and definitely do not *touch* any of them. Got all that? Good. Off we go, then."

Mevon watched in amusement as Zorvanya schooled Draevenus on the intricacies of being a respectable citizen in these parts. He'd thought they'd done well picking up most behaviors along the way, but with things changing as often as from village to village, she'd taught them a great deal they hadn't already known. An education they were both grateful for.

"Come along, servant boy," Zorvanya said, grinning over her shoulder.

Mevon smiled, hefting the pack as they stepped into motion. He kept his eyes averted. Down, but still alert. They'd yet to enter a town this large, and they didn't know what to expect. If things went bad, they'd have far more than a single tavern full of men to contend with.

They rounded the last bend in the road, and the town walls came into sight. Striking, for the fact that it had walls at all. The town by the lake, where they'd met Zorvanya, had been one of the largest they'd seen since the farthest northern reaches. This place was bigger, almost a city.

"How much farther until your friend's place again?" Draevenus asked.

"If we stay here tonight, we'll be there before the next morning is gone," Zorvanya said. "It's a bit steep, but I'm sure the two of you aren't adverse to a little climb."

"Not at all," Draevenus said. "But does that mean there's an inn? An *actual* inn?"

She laughed. "Of course."

"With real beds?"

"Yes."

"And maybe even a bathing room?"

She nodded.

"Sounds wonderful!"

"Keep your voice down. Look, we're almost here."

They passed through the outer gate, manned by a spearman on each side. The two gave their party scrupulous looks but said nothing and did not bar the way. Inside the walls, Mevon saw slate-roofed houses sitting in neat rows. Mothers chatted while balancing baskets on their heads. Fathers skinned the day's hunt, or chopped wood, or smoked. Children ran between the legs of adults, chasing each other and squealing in boisterous delight.

"This seems a peaceful place," Draevenus said. "A real community. Where people look out for each other, care for each other, and—"

"Keep especially wary of strangers," Mevon said.

Zorvanya hushed him with a look he knew well. "Yes, that may be," she said. "Just be courteous and say as little as possible. We'll be fine."

"Right," Draevenus said.

Mevon nodded in agreement but kept feeling eyes on them as they strolled through the town. He hesitated to catch someone in a stare. He was supposed to be playing the servant, and it would not do to be seen as too curious for his own good. *It's my size, that's all. I doubt these people have seen anyone as large as me in their lifetimes.*

The thought seemed logical. But it did not reassure him at all.

Eventually, they reached the inn and stepped inside. Draevenus negotiated, briefly, for a room, and they soon marched up a narrow flight of stairs and into a room with three beds.

Mevon dropped the pack with a thump, staring at the mattresses. "Not sure if I'll fit in any of these."

"Oh, you can pull two together and sleep sideways," Zorvanya said. "Draevenus doesn't mind sharing one with me, do you, husband of mine?"

The mierothi rolled his eyes. "I'll sleep on the floor if it comes to that."

"Nonsense," Mevon said. "Wasn't it you who was slavering at the mouth just *thinking* about a bed? I'd not want to rob you of your fantasy."

Zorvanya put her hands on her hips. "But you both seem to have no problem robbing me of mine!" Mevon glanced over at Draevenus, and was unsurprised by his friend's look—a mix of shock, horror, and embarrassment.

Zorvanya laughed as her campaign of teasing—or terror, as Draevenus likely thought—the mierothi resumed once more.

"Very well," she said. "I'm off to take a bath. Try not to stir any trouble while I'm gone."

She plucked her small pouch of essentials and danced towards the door with swaying hips. Mevon moved aside to let her pass. As she neared, she whispered in his ear, "The bathing rooms here are private, isolated. You're welcome to join me. If you'd like."

He sighed. He hadn't given in to her advances, tempting as they were, but neither had he yet told her off. Unsure if doing so was cruel or kind, he merely shook his head.

She pursed her lips but said nothing, nodding once to herself before pushing out the door.

Draevenus flopped, spread-limbed, onto a bed. A soft groan escaped his lips. "Thanks, Mevon. I owe you for this."

Mevon chuckled. He hung up his travel cloak, then sat on the edge of a mattress, unlacing and tugging off his boots. He pushed backwards off the floor, squeezing the remaining two beds together.

Draevenus sat up, a horrified look on his face. "But I thought you said . . . ?"

"That's for tonight. Doesn't mean I can't take advantage while our lady friend is otherwise occupied."

The mierothi exhaled. "Ah. Well, in that case I'll leave you to your rest. I think I might partake of the baths as well. In a separate room from Zorvanya, of course."

Mevon smirked. "Of course."

"I mean it. I have no interest in her. You know . . . in that way. I can't."

"Still afraid to let her see your scales?"

"Well . . ."

"Or is her assessment of your experience to blame for your hesitation?"

Draevenus ripped off his gloves. "Do these look made for tender caresses? These"—he spread his lips—"for playful nibbles?"

"Point taken."

The assassin sighed. "I tried, you know. A few times. Relationships, and all that. But without the possibility for children, no human women could stand to stick around for long. And mierothi women? Pah! Don't get me started."

"Too temperamental?"

"Among our kind, everything is a constant power struggle. Sometimes, that gets literal."

"I can see how that might put a strain on intimacy."

Draevenus hopped off the bed and began pulling fresh clothes from the pack. "Besides all that, we both know it's not me she's really interested in."

Mevon lay back across the double mattresses. "You see that, huh? Good. I was beginning to think you'd lost your edge."

"Worry not about that, my friend. The closer we get to Ruul, the sharper I'll become."

Mevon closed his eyes as the door closed shut. The silence welcomed him, the stillness called. It wasn't long before he drifted off to sleep.

His dreams, as always, were filled with blood.

He knew not how long he slept. Sometime later, the door creaked opened. He awakened at the faint sound and sat up immediately, one hand going to the hilt of a dagger.

Draevenus stood on the threshold.

"What is it?" Mevon said.

"The inn is too quiet, and I haven't seen Zorvanya in three tolls. Has she been here?"

"No."

"Not in the bathhouse either. Or the dining hall."

Mevon stood, dragged on his boots and armaments. He was out the door in a beat.

Draevenus leading, they descended the stairs in a rush. The mierothi stopped dead in his tracks a pace after reaching the landing. Mevon looked past him and saw why.

The dining hall was quiet. Dark. Devoid of even the barest scent of food or drink. With no fire roaring in the hearth, a chill crept across Mevon's skin.

A single figure stood shadowed before them.

Mevon saw clearly, though, as he knew his companion also could. He recognized the man. A blotchy bruise still clung to his temple from where Draevenus had struck him.

One of Hakel's two friends.

The man lifted a hand, spinning a bone dagger around a thumb before catching it in his grip and waving. Mevon wasn't sure if the gesture was meant as an invitation or as a taunt. The man turned and strolled out the tavern's front door.

"Do we follow?" Draevenus asked.

"What kind of question is that?" Mevon pushed past him, bounding for the exit. He crashed through the door.

Outside, darkness greeted him. A darkness of two kinds.

Night had fallen, and a flickering ring of torchlight bathed the street in an orange glow. People crowded around the inn's entrance. Their eyes burned, reflected as much from without as within. A weapon was in each hand he could see.

Hakel stood at the center of them. The fingers of

one hand gripped Zorvanya's hair tight, while his other hand held a knife to her throat.

Mevon shook. He felt something building inside him.

Draevenus stepped out on his left. "Let her go, Hakel."

"No," Hakel said.

"No? You obviously mean to use her as a bargaining tool. What use is she if you won't negotiate?"

Hakel sneered. "She is not a bargaining tool. She is merely bait."

More men pushed in behind the two of them, closing off any hope of escape.

Not that Mevon had been thinking of escape at all.

The storm . . .

"I see," Draevenus said. "I'd rather not have to kill a whole town full of men tonight. Why don't you tell me what it is you want?"

Hakel jerked Zorvanya's head back. She cried out in pain, terror. "I want this murderer to pay for her crimes. And I want her accomplices to share in that punishment."

The storm is coming . . .

Draevenus shook his head, sighing. He cast his gaze around the crowd. "Is this how justice is done in these parts? Do you all swallow the words of a bloodthirsty lunatic without question? Do you kill a woman whose life is devoted to making yours easier without proof? Do you waylay strangers in the night because you don't like the look of them?"

"These people trust me," Hakel said. "They know I

am a man who speaks truth. This woman has revealed herself to be full of treachery and lies, and anyone she touches becomes plagued by her filth. The only way to keep ourselves safe is to cut away the infection."

The storm is . . . here.

Mevon inhaled.

The world slowed to a worm's crawl. He felt every breath in the crowd around him, smelled every drop of sweat. Every twitching muscle became as loud as beating drums, and a single batting eyelash seemed to fall and rise for tolls.

Abyss take me, not now . . .

Mevon leaned forward, placing a foot to catch himself. Then another. And another. Before anyone could so much as widen their eyes in surprise, he'd reached Hakel. He drew up, towering over the other man. His raised hand quivered, screaming to be released, to crush flesh into pulp, to let the flow of blood begin.

It took every last ounce of his will to stay it and say three simple words.

"Let.

"Her.

"Go."

Hakel growled.

Mevon saw the man's bicep clench, the wrist curl inwards, the shoulder start to pull. A sharp edge touched trembling skin.

Mevon reached out, casually, and pinched the blade between two fingers. He yanked, sending it spinning through the air. It bit deep into the inn's roof with a crack. A single tear of blood wept from the woman's neck.

Hakel shoved her aside. "Get him!"

Mevon stilled himself, counting the moments in a breath as half a dozen daggers lunged towards him. He remained a statue as each pierced his flesh. He didn't move. Didn't cry out in pain. He barely even grimaced. The men who'd attacked him stepped back, hands falling from the blades wedged inside his body. Horror filled their gazes.

Mevon made the mistake of looking down.

So much blood, and for once, all of it my own. Is this the price I must pay for the peace I seek?

He did not know the answer. And now, the comment Draevenus made at the foot of the stairs came back to him in a new light. His friend wasn't asking if they should try to rescue Zorvanya. He was asking if Mevon wished to keep blood off his hands. Even in this, the man was willing to protect him from his own nature, to safeguard his pursuit of peace. But that quest was a lie. He was merely attempting to escape the violence that had wholly defined his life.

It seemed he hadn't fled fast or far enough.

Mevon lifted his eyes, drilling Hakel with his gaze. One by one, he grasped each protruding handle and pulled it from his flesh, tossing the bloody blades to the ground. When the last had fallen, he stepped once more to within a hand's width of the antagonizer. There was so much he wished to say, but he knew letting loose the dam of words would allow other things to flood through. Other things, as it stood, he could barely keep contained.

"Let her go," he said, finally. "Please."

Hakel could only stare.

Zorvanya shrugged from the grip of the men who'd caught her. She straightened her clothes, then, chin held high, marched freely into the open space behind Mevon. No one moved to stop her.

Mevon spun and followed her, meeting up with his traveling companions. He gave them a nod. "I'm sorry, Draevenus. It looks like you won't be enjoying that bed after all."

Jasside was the first to see it.

She stood on the bench as the wagon rumbled beneath her on the coarse dirt road. Feralt held the reins at her side. She saw it again, there, through the trees, unmistakable this time.

A banner fluttering in the breeze.

"What's that for I wonder?" she said.

"Something amiss?" Feralt asked.

She glanced down at him, smiling. Her near death at the hands—talons—of the shadow beast had given her a new appreciation for life. Perhaps she would never be ready to truly let Mevon go, but she could no longer imagine wasting what little youth she had left pining over a corpse. Feralt had proven pleasant company.

"A flag of some sort," she said. "Flying up ahead. I wasn't expecting company."

"Neither was I. Feel up to a scrap if it comes to it?"

Jasside probed her ribs, searching for any remaining tender spots. "It seems so. I'll have to repay you for the healing somehow."

"No reparations are necessary. I was glad to put you back together."

When she'd stumbled back to the caravan, she'd been too embarrassed to ask Vashodia for healing even though she'd seen the mierothi pull people back from the brink of death without blinking. And since manipulating energy inside her own body with such precision was tricky, she'd asked Feralt to heal her instead. He'd done a splendid job of it.

The trees broke out into open ground of red clay and bristly patches of flora. Just ahead, a tent had been set up, and two hundred soldiers encircled it. Their armor and swords shone silver in the sunlight, their formations indicating they were ready for trouble at a moment's notice. A sharp contrast to the rough-looking border guards who were playing escort. Professional soldiers, then. Whoever was in the tent must have been important.

A horseman broke out from the glittering ranks, trotting towards them. A scout or messenger, she presumed. The man reached the foremost border guard a hundred paces to her front and conferred with the captain. After a mark, the leader of their escort spurred his mount around and rode back towards her, drawing on the reins just beside the wagon.

"Your gracious presence is requested," the captain said in tones that made it clear he was glad to be rid of her. "You and that . . . that great mistress of yours."

"Who, me?"

The captain's horse reared, neighing in a frantic voice that was mirrored by its rider. Jasside spied the black smear in the air, behind Vashodia, marking the path of her shadow-dash. "You can't resist a chance to make an entrance, can you?"

"There are so many pleasures to be had in this life," Vashodia said. "Why fight against them when you can instead indulge?"

The captain, at last, had brought his mount under control though he was a considerable distance away now. "As I was saying—"

"I heard you quite clearly, thank you." Vashodia peered at Jasside. "Shall we?"

"Yes."

Jasside energized, narrowing her gaze on a spot between the encircling soldiers and the tent. It was a good distance, but she knew she could make it in one go. She gestured forward and dashed.

Reality itself seemed to bend around her. She landed three paces from the tent's flap, which was pulled back and held by tasseled golden ropes. Vashodia appeared at her side a beat later.

No less than thirty swords pulled free of their scabbards, bared tips pointed in at them.

Vashodia, shoulders squared on the tent, twisted

her head around and gave the soldiers a sharp-toothed smile. "Would one of you be a dear and announce us to your king?"

Every blade dipped slightly.

A woman burst out from the tent. "What's all this?" she said, then jerked to a halt and studied them. "Are you them? Of course you're them. How many other little girls with scales and red eyes do I know of?"

Jasside's eyes widened. The woman stood as tall as most men, youthful and regal in posture and possessing a kind of indescribable beauty that drove a flush of envy through her. The woman's auburn hair, twisted behind in an elegant bun, seemed to shine brighter than even the most polished soldiers' armor. Jewels of every color glittered about her hands and neck.

Jasside almost missed seeing the crown on her head.

She leaned down and whispered to Vashodia, "What is the protocol for addressing a queen?"

Vashodia grinned deviously. "Just follow my lead."

The queen raised an eyebrow. "Well, don't stand there all day. My husband dragged me halfway across the country for this, and I'd really rather get it over with."

"As would I," Vashodia said. She strolled in past the waiting queen, and Jasside followed right behind.

The tent interior, lit only by muffled sunlight through the thin canvas roof, displayed an odd mix of rustic and luxurious appointments. Across from the entrance sat an old man on a simple wooden chair. A crown nested in his grey hair. Two men flanked the king, one on each side. One she did not recognize, but by his stance and the casual but confident way he carried the narrow sword at his hip, she took him to be a protector of sorts. The other was the emissary who had first greeted them two months ago. He did not appear happy.

The queen drew up to Jasside's side and waved an arm in front of her. "May I present King Daryn Reimos of Weskara, the illustrious and magnificent and what have you. Here they are, o' husband of mine, as requested. Do remember to be kind to them. They just did you a substantial favor, after all."

The king straightened in his chair. He coughed, squinting. "That remains to be seen, Halice."

The queen sighed. Loudly. "Oh have it your way, you distrustful old codger. Don't blame me if they decide to fry the meat from your bones, as our dear emissary seems to think they will."

"That one," the emissary said, pointing at Vashodia, "outright threatened as much. And worse!"

"Yes," the queen said, smiling slyly. "And I'm sure it had nothing to do with your humble-yet-charming personality."

"None of that matters now," the king said. "I have to see. With my own eyes." He began to rise from his seat.

The emissary stepped in front of him, putting a hand on the king's chest. "I don't think—"

The other man grabbed the emissary's wrist and jerked it away. He pulled their faces so close together their noses touched. The silent man shook his head.

The emissary lowered his eyes.

"Enough of the theatrics," the king said. He pushed between the two men, prying them apart with force not born of touch or muscle. Hunched over, leaning on a cane, he brought his eyes up to Vashodia. "May I see your hands?"

The mierothi stepped forward softly. Jasside could only wonder at her compliance. No doubt Vashodia had something to gain from this exchange, but she could not figure out what. She watched as the king took the clawed hands in his palms, gently rubbing the dark scales.

"*Mierothi*," the king said. "The word has almost become synonymous with ghosts and nightmares in my country. With fables of the darkest kind. Yet, here you stand, solid and real as the rest of us."

"Strange how some tales grow in the telling, becoming entirely separate beasts from the source of their inspiration."

Jasside hid a smile. *Sometimes, the tales get it right.*

The king released the small hands and leaned once more on his cane. "Thank you, my child."

"Satisfied?" Vashodia said.

The king nodded. "I do have to wonder, though."

"About what?"

"Why it is, exactly, that you left the Veiled Empire."

"Oh, it's simple enough, really. We were no longer welcome."

Something sparkled in the king's eyes. "Lost the war, did you?"

Vashodia laughed. "Me? I *never* lose."

The king frowned. "Then . . . ?"

"Oh, let them be, Daryn," the queen said, having laid herself out upon a lounging couch. "They've done enough for us already. They don't deserve to have their entire life stories dragged out upon the ground for you to inspect. Besides"—she grabbed a pitcher and cup from a low table next to the couch—"we haven't even offered them refreshments yet."

Vashodia smiled, strolling over to the queen. "How gracious of you, Halice. But there is no need—I've brought my own." Never one to miss an opportunity to impress, Vashodia energized and formed her own crystal goblet from thin air.

"That's a neat trick," the queen said, although her tone indicated "neat" was even more effusive than she planned. She poured. Vashodia sat opposite her on the couch, and they clinked glasses together. "A shame we don't have more of that around here."

The king sighed. "Knew I never should have married a northerner."

"Would you rather have your last wife back from the grave? A stoic who likely died from her own revulsion to any form of pleasure?"

"No. Abyss above, anything but that."

"Then stop complaining and get on with the rest of your business."

"What business is that?"

"Nothing much," Vashodia interrupted. "But I do

believe you owe my apprentice here your most heart-felt thanks."

The king turned, glancing at Jasside. "Why?"

"Because it was she alone who . . . took care of the matter."

His eyes flared, and he saw her as if for the first time. "You?"

Jasside had grown accustomed to reactions like this. Being in Vashodia's shadow, she either had to embrace her role or reject it. It was far easier to just go along with things.

"Yes," Jasside said. "Me."

"I don't understand."

"There were nine shadow beasts in that swamp, creatures of nightmare and war. Most had been wiped out, but a few must have slipped away. I destroyed them."

The king's eyes still bored into her with confused scrutiny.

Jasside sighed as she energized. *Some people have no imagination.* Like her mistress did before her, she formed a goblet in her hand, then waved a finger at the wine bottle, forming a funnel in the space between them. Red liquid floated up, spiraling through the air to slosh gently into her cup.

She took a sip. "Any more questions?"

Jasside had expected the move to amuse the man, or at least placate him. She wasn't ready for the storm of rage that took over his visage.

"Just one." He held up a finger, quivering.

"When are you people going to get off my land?"

Jasside felt her heartbeat quicken. Her breath became a thing of effort. *After all we've done . . .*

The queen jumped up and began shouting at the king. The emissary moved to his lord's side, throwing arguments back in her face. The king simply stared at Jasside.

She glanced at Vashodia, but the mierothi remained on the couch. She drained her cup, laughing, with her gaze locked on the trio, and poured another. Jasside knew, then, that she was on her own.

Another test.

But not one I'm sure I know how to pass.

She studied the king and the emissary, recognizing them as the obstacles to be overcome. Their stubbornness infuriated her. Their hatred of all things sorcerous was irrational in the face of the practicality of the situation. It was a belief set in stone, unmovable by any words she might say—so that tactic seemed pointless to try.

Think, damn it . . .

In the deepest part of her, Jasside clutched at a solution. She dismissed it at first, for she couldn't fathom following through with it, but it came back stronger, more logical, each time it ran through her mind.

She lifted a finger, drawing in more power, until she felt bursting at the seams with darkness. She traced lines around the two men with her eyes.

It would be so easy. The obstacles could be removed just . . . like . . .

Her hand was raised, fingers poised to snap: a gesture she'd trained herself to use when releasing a prepared conjuration of energy.

She'd been less than a heartbeat away from letting it all go.

Instead, Jasside stepped back, pulling both arms in close. She shook. It was bad enough, even entertaining the idea, but she hated herself all the more for letting such stray thoughts overwhelm her conscious actions.

Power ever begs to dominate. It was something she'd learned from Vashodia, not as a lesson itself but rather a tenet that weaved through and around all other lessons. She thought she had shielded herself against it but now knew that no defense ever holds for long without a strong arm propping it up. She'd grown complacent, and her victory over the shadow beasts had made her arrogant. The combination proved a potent concoction that had nearly drowned her in its poison.

Jasside took a breath. She glanced over at Vashodia. *So this is what you've been dealing with your whole existence. A few thousand years of it, and no one to tell you what the limits are, what should or should not be done. No one to teach you the value of every single life.*

Her heart, for the first time, went out to Vashodia. She'd made a vow, once, while overlooking a barrow of countless dead, that she would help heal the darkness that held sway in her mistress's soul. She hadn't been doing a very good job of it lately. *There is a light in all of us. I just have to find it in her and, somehow, fan the flames until it burns bright again.*

But first I have to make sure the light in me is never dimmed as it almost was today.

Jasside smiled to herself, set in purpose once more. A difficult road lay ahead of her, but she now knew what to keep watch for in herself and her mistress as well.

As her introspection faded, reality set in. The debate was still in full swing. If anything, it had become more heated. Vashodia remained disengaged. Jasside realized she still had to handle this herself . . . and that perhaps there were words that might actually make a difference.

She thought about all the people she knew who excelled at settling arguments, at diplomacy. One face popped into her mind almost immediately. "What would Yandumar do?"

The king stepped towards her, silencing the others. "What did you say?"

Jasside tried to hide her surprise. "I said, 'What would Yandumar do?'"

"Yandumar, eh?"

"He's a friend of ours, you see, and I couldn't help but think he'd be useful in resolving this situation."

The king looked up and to the left, smiling faintly. "Did he ever find his daughter?"

Jasside furrowed her brow. "It was his son. And yes." She shivered. "He found him."

"Had to check," the king said, eyes glimmering with vigor. "You should have told me you were friends with Yandumar in the first place. Of course I'll let you stay!"

Oh . . . of course.

No matter how hard she tried, Arivana could not stop the trembling. It had taken all of her effort just to limit it to her hands. They fumbled around in her lap as she sat once more on her throne in the council chamber, waiting for the unimaginable.

"You know what you must do," Tior said, leaning close to her ear.

She nodded even though she knew it was no question. Her role in all this had been driven into her like a nail into wood, and Minister Pashams was the hammer.

Arivana lifted a shaking finger to her eye, wiping away another of the tears that never seemed to stop coming. Flumere had been forced to reapply powders to her face three times as they were getting ready. Eventually, the woman had given up and wiped it all away.

If only this mess could be cleaned up so easily. She probably appeared like a sickly commoner, but she didn't care.

Sometimes, being a queen seemed the worst job in the world.

Tior straightened, then announced, "I call to order this special judiciary meeting. Bring in the accused."

The circle in the very center of the floor shifted away, and a platform rose in its place with a clear, flat board, standing at a slight angle. Strapped to it was Claris Baudone.

The trembling in Arivana's hands intensified.

Tior cleared his throat. "Now then, to the evidence . . ."

He spoke at length, but Arivana could barely stand to listen. Agents of the crown had somehow seized documents with Claris's personal seal, linking her with surety to the other attackers, who had all been identified as expatriates from Fashesh. War dodgers.

Filth.

He also produced a lesser groundskeeper and two other people who happened to be in the gardens at the time of the attack. Arivana remembered them all, but only as one remembers a dream. They each told how they came upon the scene and ran for help, picked up a weapon and stood guard, or comforted their queen, who had clearly been in shock. As they spoke, the dream sharpened, becoming reality. Arivana wished, now, that she had plugged her ears.

After they had gone, Tior recounted his own experience. He seemed to notice many details that she had missed at the time and told the tale with a grim adherence to fact. He didn't mention how it made him feel. Such an approach would undoubtedly have caused a resurgence of all the horror she'd gone through at the time, and with far more potency than had the words of the others. For that, Arivana was almost thankful.

But all too soon, his words dwindled. He turned to her with eyes both hard and soft at once. "And now, your majesty, it is time for your testimony."

Arivana stood. She felt a sudden calmness take over, which both surprised and gladdened her. This was nothing but a performance, and she knew all her lines by heart. Her voice firm, she said, "My own account of events coincides with that of the Minister of Gardens. All he has said, as far as I am aware, is the truth. Claris Baudone, in concert with the twenty deceased Fasheshish men, attacked me with obvious intent to kill, and it was only by the brave actions of Tior Pashams and the ten guardsmen that I am still alive."

"Have you anything else to add?" Tior asked.

"No."

Arivana sat back down. She hadn't missed a single word of the script. One performance down. One to go.

The shaking in her hands resumed.

Tior, at last, turned towards the center of the room. Frowning grimly, he said, "Does the accused have any-thing to say in her defense?"

Silence engulfed the chamber. Arivana fixed her eyes on the floor.

But the silence stretched for ten beats, twenty, a mark. Arivana heard a murmur among those gath-ered. She felt her gaze forcing its way upwards, until at last she peered into the face of a woman she had once loved as family.

It did not look as she expected.

There was no hate, no rage, not a whisper of defi-ance. If anything, Claris's skin seemed slack. Her eyes returned the stare, but lazily, almost as if she were bored with the whole process. *Almost.* The tears streaming down the woman's cheeks, strong as rivers, belied the otherwise-complete image of apathy. Arivana had no idea what to make of it at all.

After what seemed an eternity, Claris gently shook her head.

"Then the testimonies are complete," Tior said. "It is now time for judgment."

The ministers all activated their voting spheres, as they had the last time Arivana had been here. But this time, they weren't after some stupid law. They were after justice. After blood.

Five of the six rolled into the center within ten beats of the announcement. Two glowed red. The other three were green. Rather than a simple yes or no, however, this time they stood for guilty or not guilty. Arivana's heart jumped as she remembered that four greens would see the woman go free.

She looked up. The last sphere was held in the hands of a man she didn't recognize. She knew, however, that he belonged to House Baudone. He must have been the one to step up into Claris's position after her . . . demise.

Surely he'll vote to save his kin. Then my second performance won't be needed at all.

The thought gave her a strange sort of hope. Strange, because she didn't know she actually *wanted* Claris to live. Until now. Despite everything, the woman was still the closest thing to family she had left, and losing her would make Arivana lonelier than she could imagine.

She watched as the man from House Baudone sent his voting sphere forward. It touched the others.

It glowed red.

Arivana's hope died from one breath to the next. She knew what had to happen now.

Tior turned to her once more. "In the case of a tie, the ruler of our great nation must cast the deciding vote."

She closed her eyes and nodded. Somehow, it seemed, he had known it would come to this. He'd preached of the dangers of letting assassins run free. The respect her family would lose in the sight of every citizen. The unrest it would cause. The bloodshed.

Gasping in a breath, she said, as quickly as she could, "I vote guilty."

Tior gave her a sad smile before facing the room. "The vote is settled. The accused is found guilty. As is our way, punishment is left in the hands of the betrayed."

Her final performance for the night. This, more than anything else, had been drilled into her mind beforehand. There could only be one penalty for traitors. *Death.*

"I sentence Claris Baudone . . ." she took a breath. Then two. The trembling came back. Her performance was forgotten. "I sentence her to deepest prison for the rest of her days."

Tior's eyes flared for a beat. His hands gripped the edge of his family pod, turning white with rage although his face showed no other signs of emotion.

Arivana left her seat and strode promptly from the room as the platform holding Claris descended to the bowels of the tower. A descent from which she would never rise. She pushed through the doors, out into the hall, dragging Flumere behind her.

As soon as the chamber disappeared around the first corner, Arivana hiked up her skirts and ran. She made it to the lift, up to the top of her tower, and into her bedchamber before she broke down crying.

Her handmaiden sat on the bed beside her as she bawled into a pillow. The woman patted her gently on the shoulder. It didn't help. She needed more than that just now. Arivana flung herself into Flumere, wrapping her arms around her like a constrictor and burying her face in the woman's chest.

For one beat, Flumere sat like a frozen log. The moment stretched. Her handmaiden still did not move.

Arivana lifted her soggy face, staring into the older woman's eyes. "Please," she said. "Please, can't you just hold me?"

With a trembling lip, Flumere gave the briefest of nods, then brought her arms around Arivana and squeezed.

Tassariel stepped in among the pedestals. One hundred years, and she would finally be allowed to meet her god. Her stomach fluttered, and she fought to control her breathing. As intended—as had everyone before her—she was walking into the encounter blind, with little knowledge of what to expect. Her imagination ran wild with the possibilities.

The flowing folds of her simple ritual robe swished awkwardly around her ankles. She wasn't used to attire so loose. She made sure to keep her steps measured, solemn, resisting the urge to skip or prance along. At last, she came to the center of the circle, firmed up her spine, and waited.

All twelve members of the Valynkar High Council were present. Even Gilshamed. She hadn't known he'd resumed his duties. After their spat in Voren's tomb, she wasn't sure she'd ever see him again. His unexpected appearance disturbed her for some reason though she could not say why. Too many things pulled at her attention, threatening to shatter the frail solemnity of the occasion. Figuring out her uncle would have to wait.

Inarius, an ancient-looking man and leader of the council, stood on his pedestal directly in front of her. All the others followed suit. He lifted his arms, casting a warm gaze down upon her. "And so," he began, "we have gathered here to witness and espouse the first holy visitation of this obedient servant, our friend and kin, Tassariel of the martial calling."

As one, the others chanted, "Welcome, daughter of Elos."

Her heart skipped a beat as everything suddenly became real, became *now*. Somehow, she managed to smile.

"As we have with all our children before," Inarius continued, "we send you now to commune with our god, to bask in his light and his glory, to absorb his wisdom and his power. Enter into his presence with an open mind and a humble heart, and your time with him will be a cherished thing indeed."

Tassariel dipped her head in supplication. "My soul is ready to receive this most holy gift."

"Then let our shepherd take your hand and guide you through to our god's embrace."

She squinted, feeling someone land beside her. Golden light glowed in a ring around them. She turned, staring into Gilshamed's eyes as his wings stood erect behind him. He put out his hand.

"Are you ready, niece?"

She hesitated, blurting out in a harsh whisper before she could stop herself, "What are you even *doing* here?"

If he was surprised by the question, he did a good job of hiding it. "I've resumed my duties as a member of the council."

"After all this time? Why now?"

"In a way, I have you to thank. Our conversation in the crypt forced me to begin thinking about things outside myself. About the greater good, and how little I've been doing to further it since I've been back. It may not amount to much in the end, but working within this system—to change it if I can—will be better than the nothing I'd accomplish elsewise."

"Yes, but are you sure you're the most qualified person to be doing this? I mean, you and Elos . . . ?"

"He and I have to come to an . . . understanding.

Believe me, when it comes to being your guide, I have all that it takes." Gilshamed smiled wryly, grunting. "And more."

Tassariel took a deep breath and nodded. She placed her hand at last into his waiting palm.

She felt Gilshamed energize, just the barest amount, and the others around the room did the same. She waited patiently as the disparate pulses of energy slowly came into sync and finally snapped together as one. Gilshamed gasped softly and shuddered.

"Now," he said. "We fly."

She unfurled her wings. The lavender light competed with his golden aura for dominance. The resulting interplay of color shimmered like the sun off the sea, hypnotizing her.

They both angled their faces up towards the starlit void and launched into the air.

Hand in hand, they lifted skyward, the air caressing them as they ascended. The pedestals below fell away into murky shadow, and the tops of the great pillars came level with them. Gilshamed led her to land on a small glass platform, suspended by ropes of ancient magic to the twelve edifices around them. He dismissed his wings, and Tassariel mimicked him. Without their glow, she couldn't see the glass at their feet and felt as if she were standing on nothing at all. She swallowed the lump in her throat.

"Nervous?" Gilshamed said.

"Yes," she said.

"Good."

"Is it really going to be that bad?"

He wagged a finger at her. "No prying. Blind faith, remember?"

She grimaced. "And so my own words come back to haunt me. Thanks, uncle. You're really putting me at ease."

"Is that what you wish me to do? Very well, then. This will be an experience you never forget."

"That didn't help."

Gilshamed laughed, turning his back to her and peering at the sky. She followed his gaze. Among the stars smeared across the night now flared a single brilliant light. The Eye of Elos, peering down. Gilshamed began to frown.

"Something the matter?" she asked.

"We'll find out shortly."

Gilshamed, still harmonized with the others despite the distance—a testament to his will and power—pulled in energy in amounts Tassariel had never even dreamed of. The air thrummed, and her skin tingled. And still he gathered more.

She winced, shielding her eyes as the pooled energy seemed to start leaking from his very body as rays of light. So close, she felt pain from their passing and wondered how a single person could hold so much and not be consumed.

With a jolt, the rays coalesced into a single beam, arcing through the night towards the resting place of their god. All but one, that is. This last ray, tiny but virulent, touched her chest, seeming to connect with her very soul. Heat surged through her.

Pain, like a flame's caress, wracked every fiber of her being.

She gritted her teeth. "Is it . . . supposed . . . to hurt this much?"

Gilshamed did not answer. He seemed enwreathed in a swirling whorl of energy, light that blinds, power overwhelming. She staggered to his side and peered at his face.

His jaw hung open in terror.

Something is very wrong.

Tassariel grasped his shoulder, shaking him. "Stop this, Gilshamed! It isn't supposed to be this way!"

His eyes swung to her. Only for a beat, but she saw in them . . . helplessness.

Fear drove Tassariel to her knees.

Gilshamed cried out, a shout of anger and frustration and raw force of will. The power around them seemed to ebb, to wane. And with a shock of silence, it vanished.

He, too, slumped to one knee, panting desperately, a look of weariness in his visage she'd not seen since he'd first returned with Lashriel and the others. Whatever had happened, it had drained him, body and soul.

Tassariel reached out to him. "Are you all right?"

"I . . ." He shook his head. "I don't know."

"What happened?"

"I'm sorry," he said. "I never meant for this to—"

Power exploded outward.

Tassariel rocked backwards, and her vision blackened.

She came to a moment later, falling.

The floor far below grew closer by the beat. The figures on the ground, heads craned to the sky, became larger and more distinct, and she could soon make out the horrified look on their faces. She shook loose the lightness in her head, then flexed her back to unfurl her wings.

Nothing happened.

She tried again, with the same result.

Panic set in. A chill filled her, taking up residence in the space once occupied by the ever-present warmth of her ethereal wings. A voice spoke. She knew, somehow, that it came from within her.

But the voice was not her own.

"So," it said, "this is what a body feels like. It seems I had forgotten."

The ground came up to meet her, and she knew no more.

PART II

PART II

CHAPTER 7

Draevenus peered down the trail behind him as he waited for his companions. Zorvanya hadn't been joking about the climb. The ascent had lasted all morning, carved switchbacks up a rocky mountainside bringing them to where the air chilled to the bone, borne on winds that snapped his cloak about him like a banner. The town they'd left peeked out from behind a hill, and the hollow where they'd spent a bitter, silent night rested just this side of it. He smiled, remembering when the shaman went to tend to Mevon's wounds, only to find nothing but faint scars and smears of drying blood.

It was the only amusement the previous night had brought.

Movement below caught his eye. Zorvanya, panting as she struggled to keep up with Draevenus. A quaint effort, especially considering how much both he and Mevon were holding back. If he were willing to divulge his true being to her, he could move like lightning. Mevon had often kept up a jog all day during their journey, a pace that equaled most men's sprint, but he remained in the rear to guard her back. Still, the urgency in her steps was appreciated, for while no one from the town had given chase, that they could tell, they all thought it best not to take any chances.

Draevenus turned from them, eyeing something farther up the trail. The reason he had stopped in the first place. Set in a recess beneath an overhang of yellow stone sat a yurt not unlike the one they'd found Zorvanya in. The differences were small but telling. Once-bright colors faded into browns and greys, and many parts of the outer hide layer sagged or flapped freely in the wind. A small garden lay beside it, wilted and overgrown with weeds.

Can the answers I seek truly be found here?

He shook his head, despair holding strong because of what he saw before him but hope still scratching away at his mind, unable to stay buried for long. Ruul was closer than ever. He could feel it. A dark presence lingered just beyond a horizon that never seemed to grow any nearer, but now he sensed what lay beyond with something close to clarity. He quivered faintly with excitement.

He waited impatiently a few marks until his companions hiked to his position. He let Zorvanya catch her breath and take a single swig of water before insistently asking her, "Is this the place?"

"Yes," she said, wiping moisture from her lips. She bent down, groaning as she stretched, then straightened with a smile. "Come," she said. "I'll introduce you to Mother Poya."

Draevenus gestured to the narrow dirt path, and Zorvanya took the lead. Mevon followed close behind her.

As the former Hardohl passed him, he noticed the forlorn look on his face and realized the man had not said a word since the incident the evening before. Draevenus, too relieved that the night had not ended in bloodshed—well, not *massive* bloodshed, as he had feared it would—had not bothered to wonder how the event had affected his companion. He now saw what a tribulation it had been. An ordeal in which he'd helped little. He'd been too busy assessing targets and preparing himself for the mass slaughter he thought would ensue, never sparing a thought for Mevon's efforts to end the night peacefully.

He'd made a promise to Mevon, to be there to guide him through such trials. Last night, he had broken it.

Agony clutched his chest, a pain born of regret and hatred towards himself. *I've done it again. I've let someone down in the worst way. When will I learn how to get it right?*

He reached out to Mevon, opening his mouth to begin an apology that he already knew words could not fully express. He was interrupted by Zorvanya's wordless call, though, and realized they had arrived at the yurt. His atonement would have to wait.

No answer came, so the woman called again, adding, "Mother Poya? Are you there?"

Draevenus strained his senses, woken to alertness by Zorvanya's pinched brow. He held his breath. After three beats, he finally heard the faintest of coughs.

"Go," he said. "She's inside, but weak. I doubt she can hear us."

Zorvanya's worry morphed into alarm as she pushed through the thick hides covering the entrance. He and Mevon followed.

His first breath inside told him most of the sordid story.

The stench of rot hung thick in the air, enveloped in threads of mold and sweat. The combination suffocated. He looked past a room covered in dust to where a thick bundle lay wrapped in at least a dozen blankets. The cough sounded again, and the bundle shook.

Zorvanya dashed to the bedside and knelt, running her hands through the blankets until they met flesh. "She's burning up," she cried, voice full of tremors. She leaned in close, querying softly and bending her ear to hear murmured replies. She reached into her bag and began pulling vials of oil and small pouches of dried herbs, lining them up on the bedside.

Draevenus stepped close. He laid a hand of Zorvanya's shoulder, causing her to tense. Her face lifted to his, revealing red eyes and wet cheeks.

"It's bad, isn't it?" he said.

Zorvanya nodded. "She may be too far gone already. I don't know how long she's been ill."

"Perhaps I can take a look?"

She scoffed. "You're no shaman, Draevenus." Her eyes cleared, then widened. "Wait, do you mean . . . magic?"

He nodded. "I may not be an expert healer, but my skill and your herbs together might just be enough to save her."

"Let's do it, then."

They worked to peel back layer after layer of woolen blankets, until the woman beneath was revealed at last. Knotted grey hair, matted with sweat, spread out under a face sunken by age and infirmity. Her eyes fluttered. Lips mumbled incoherently. Even he could tell she had not long to live.

He laid a hand on her forehead and energized. "It's a good thing we got here when we did."

He quested inside her body with his power. Unnatural heat drew his focus into her lungs, where he found an infection raging. *Come on, Draevenus. Concentrate. You can do this.* The reknitting of wounds had all but eluded him during his infrequent attempts to harness sorcery for anything but death. Infection, however, was something he knew how to handle. Darkness always seemed a natural antithesis to such alien fire.

He guided his power, seeking out the strongholds of the infection and smothering them with icy dark. Sweat beaded down his scalp as he worked. His breath became heavy.

At last, he could find no more traces and withdrew. He sagged, worn from his efforts. "How is she?" he asked.

"Breathing has evened out, pulse is steady"—Zorvanya paused, smiling—"and some color is even returning to her face. I think you did it."

"I've done what I can, but she will still be weak. It may take some time for her to—"

A hand reached out, grasping his wrist with surprising strength.

"'Weak' am I?"

He looked down and saw a hint of a smile around the old woman's mouth. "Mother Poya, I presume?"

"Yes. And you are?"

"This is Draevenus," Zorvanya said. "And he healed you . . . with magic."

Poya arched an eyebrow at him. "Now why would you go and do a thing like that?"

"I had some questions," Draevenus said, "that Zorvanya here thinks you might be able to answer."

"Questions, eh? How 'bout you help me sit up first. And get us a drink, will ya'? Can't be blabberin' on with my throat turned into a sandbed, now can I."

Draevenus pulled. Poya retained her grip on his wrist and came upright, wobbling only slightly. Her eyes peeked over his shoulder. "Not that one," she said. "The big one, with the white rim up top."

Draevenus turned to see Mevon setting down a small brown jar and picking up another, this one twice as tall. He brought it over and held it out to the old woman.

Poya reached for it. Her fingers brushed Mevon's hand, and she squeaked. Mevon gazed at her curiously.

"You are one strange fella," she said.

"And you," he replied, "are the first person we've met this side of the mountains to have even a drop of sorcerous blood in your veins."

"A drop it is, all right. Can't do much of anything with it. Takes months just to make a simple charm." She eyed Draevenus. "And I sure as snow can't do what you just did. Who the abyss are you two?"

Draevenus sighed. He needed answers from her. Honest answers. He couldn't afford to give less in return. He cast a glance at Zorvanya. *Are you ready to see me for who I truly am?*

Finger by finger, he tugged off his gloves. He swept his hood back, pulling his wig along with it. A small wave of energy dismissed the enchantment that made his eyes appear brown. He took a cloth from his belt and wiped away the skin-darkening paste on his face.

"I am a mierothi," he said. "A child of the dark god Ruul. I need to find him, so I can make him answer for his crimes. Will you help me?"

Both women's eyes were wide as moons. Draevenus prepared himself for their judgment.

"Well," Poya said, "looks like my great-grandmother wasn't crazy after all."

Draevenus tingled with excitement. "She saw one of my kin, didn't she?"

Poya took a swallow from the jug she held, then passed it to him. "She was a little sprout at the time, almost two hundred years ago now, but she told me a story of the day a scale-skinned creature with claws came through these parts. Body of a girl, but those red eyes of hers were just like yours. They were ancient. Claimed to be after some dark god as well. I can't remember what she called herself . . ."

"Vashodia," Draevenus said. "My sister."

He took a gulp from the jug, surprised but delighted that it was full of kefir. It had been a while since he'd last had a drink. He could see the wheels inside Poya's head turning, putting the pieces together, and a sly smile spread across her lips.

"Do you happen to know what came of her travels?" he asked.

She shook her head. "She never came back this way, far as I know. Kept on south, across the plateau."

He rose, filled with energy. "Then that's where we'll go as well."

"Now hold on a mark, there, young man. Winter approaches. That plateau will be an empty, frozen wasteland in a week, if not sooner. If you were smart, you'd wait until the spring thaw."

Draevenus waved a hand in dismissal. "We're used to hard terrain."

"Not like this. The land is cracked, filled with crevasses so deep you can't see the bottom, and wider than twenty men are tall. There's no game to hunt, no forage, no wood to build a fire, and the wind howls like a thousand wolves, day and night. You may be hardy men, but you'd be fools to try to cross it now."

Mevon stepped next to Draevenus. "Perhaps she's right," he said. "We aren't in a rush, are we?"

Draevenus grimaced, fueled by the desire to see this task through, to confront Ruul once and for all. He couldn't fathom even the slightest delay. He peered sharply at Poya. "Do you know what lies beyond the plateau?"

The woman quivered. "Every few years, a haggard traveler comes from out of that waste, often days from death's door. None of them wish to speak of that what goes on there, however. It is a place of darkness."

"Ruul's corrupting influence." Draevenus felt a growl building in his throat. "I've seen the like before." He turned to Mevon. "We go now."

Mevon shrugged.

"That's it?" Zorvanya said, rising from Poya's side. "You'll leave just like that? Without even a proper send-off?"

"What did you have in mind?" Mevon asked.

"More games, I'll bet," Draevenus said, resisting the urge to spit. "To be honest, they're getting rather tiresome."

Zorvanya clenched her fists but turned her head away and took a long breath before responding. "No more games then. Ever. But please, won't you at least stay a few days, to rest and restock? This quest you're on—whose importance so *obviously* outweighs all other considerations—promises to bring far more hardship and suffering before it's done. Something tells me you'll be glad of these last few moments of peace."

Impatience warred with civility, and Draevenus

found it was he who could now not meet *her* gaze. He twirled a knife through his fingers, unsure how to respond.

"We'll stay," Mevon said, rescuing him. "Thank you."

Zorvanya grinned. "It's settled then. I promise you won't come to regret it."

"No one knows what the future holds," Draevenus said, gritting his teeth. "Not even the gods."

"So as it turned out," Jasside said, "Yandumar had made a name for himself as a mercenary while waiting around for Gilshamed to show up. Caught the attention of King Reimos and worked out a deal to put down a revolt of miners in the Weskaran Wastes. He ended the whole ordeal in only a few months with a surprisingly small amount of bloodshed and became fast friends with our ruler to the west."

Angla smirked as she popped grapes into her mouth. The woman lounged beside her on a picnic blanket spread out on a flat patch of grass just south of the main mierothi settlement. "He was quite a formidable man, as I remember. Only met him once, but that encounter was enough to tell me he's far better to have as ally than adversary."

Jasside reached to the basket between them, plucking a plump strawberry. "Isn't it better to have no foes at all?" She plopped the whole thing into her mouth and bit down. Tart, sweet juices gushed down her throat, eliciting a moan from her. She hadn't eaten fresh fruit the whole time she'd been away.

"Pah!" Angla said. "We're measured as much by our friends as by our foes. Pay attention to those who hate you the most, what they believe, how they treat those in their power. If cruelty runs through all they do, you're better off having them as enemies."

Jasside bowed her head, grateful for the sharing of wisdom. Still, such words seemed strange coming from a mierothi, knowing all that her grandmother's people had done over the centuries.

Some of her musing must have shown on her face, for Angla said, "I'm not a hypocrite, you know."

Jasside blanched. "I didn't . . . I never said . . ."

"No, but you're thinking it."

"Yes. I'm sorry. It's hard not to . . . given your history."

"And who wrote that history? Certainly not me, nor the others locked up alongside me. If we had, it would have read much differently. There was a reason, after all, that we ended up as we did."

Jasside didn't have to ponder long before figuring it out. "You didn't agree with Rekaj's methods."

"His *methods*? I didn't even agree with his *face*!"

Jasside broke down laughing, warmth soon replacing the tension inside her. Angla joined in. The sound of their merriment lasted until it was interrupted by clashing steel behind them. They both turned.

"Oh, bother those men," Angla said. "At it again, and still using sharpened blades no doubt. It's only a matter of time before one of them loses a limb."

Jasside peered over the grassy hill behind them. The heads of Harridan Chant and Feralt came into view, swords swinging into sight every few beats. Chant backed up, parrying a slash, then ducked under a wild swing that left the daeloth off-balance. The old Elite followed with a punch to Feralt's side that made him cringe and crouch back into a defensive stance. The daeloth gasped for breath, smiling all the while.

Without armor, Feralt seemed younger, happier. Almost as if the weight of it bore all the gruesome necessities the job had once entailed. Things Jasside hoped would never be required again.

"So tell me," Angla said, cutting herself a slice of cheese, "how has it been putting your own advice into practice?"

"It's been an . . . interesting experience."

"Rough times bedding the boy?"

Jasside blushed, hugging her knees to her chest. "We haven't done that. And besides, isn't it usually the men who do the bedding?"

"Usually. But this is my granddaughter we're talking about. I know you well enough by now to see that, whether you're willing or not, no man will ever be able to dominate you."

Jasside glanced at Feralt, who was attacking Harridan once more. She thought about what they shared. Laughter and company, pleasant smiles, an occasional touch on the arm. It wasn't much, really, but it seemed to be exactly what she needed at the moment. She hadn't given much thought to what *he* wanted. And though he'd made known his desire for things to progress physically between them, she didn't wish it, so it didn't happen.

Right as always, Grandmother. I am dominating him. And I've done it without even thinking. Is this a symptom of the power I wield? Or is this just who I've become after suffering from one too many broken hearts?

She turned away, realizing in that moment that nothing serious could ever come of her relationship with Feralt. She knew she would never feel safe being vulnerable around him, letting him take control. Even the thought drove spikes of ice up her spine.

There was only one man who made her feel at peace with simply being herself. One man around whom she wouldn't mind letting go of control.

Jasside jerked as a hand touched her knee. Angla, reaching out and patting her gently. "It's okay, Jasside," the mierothi said. "There are worse things to be than a woman who knows what she wants."

Jasside let out a peal of laughter, and even she could hear the bitterness strung throughout that solitary note.

It seems all I want is death. Fitting, then, that I should be so good at delivering it.

Such musings only served to spark her own outrage, an emotion directed at no one but herself. Vashodia had been distant all the way back from Weskara. Her own efforts to get closer to her mistress, perhaps even to begin prying open that arctic heart, had proven futile. There was no danger driving them at the time.

No *need*. In such instances, Vashodia seemed to separate herself entirely from reality. Jasside knew that idleness didn't suit either of them.

We need something to do.

Jasside leaned back on one elbow. She reached for more fruit, grabbing a pear this time, and peered down over the fields being harvested by daeloth half a league below them. It was good work she'd done there. The settlement had a wide variety of crops to choose from and a short enough cycle that no one was ever in danger of going hungry. With trade slow in starting, and the hunting parties forced to range farther and farther each day—and still not finding enough meat to fill every stomach—what they now grew more than made up the difference.

Still, she sighed. The work was mostly complete. She didn't fancy waiting around for some small problem to arise that would keep her occupied for a time. That Vashodia had stuck around as long as she had surprised her. She couldn't imagine the two of them playing administrators the rest of their days.

Her gaze wandered as she bit into the pear, absently wiping away a stream of juice that dribbled down her chin. The vast plains of Weskara dominated the view westward, and to the east, the deserts of Fashesh. North, past their fields, grew a forest thick with evergreens sloping upwards to a mountain range that covered the horizon as far as she could see. Sceptre lay beyond. A nation, she'd heard, as enigmatic as the mierothi themselves.

Movement at the edge of the forest caught her eye. She squinted at the tiny figures in the distance. Unable to discern their identity, she energized and formed a tunnel of darkness between them, narrowing the space so that they appeared to her eyes no more than a hundred paces away.

"Who is that?" Angla asked.

"One of our hunting parties," Jasside replied, having taken stock of their woodland cloaks and longbows. Then, she noticed something else. "I think they may be in trouble."

"Why is th—"

Jasside never heard the rest. She'd stood and shadow-dashed across the league between them in a heartbeat.

The six daeloth stopped as she appeared in front of them. Four stood, carrying a pair of unconscious forms on makeshift litters. They set their burdens down with no effort to hide their exhaustion.

"What happened?" she asked.

For five beats, no one answered. Finally, one of them, a female daeloth well past the days of youth, managed to get her panting under control. "Ran into some trouble," she said.

"What kind?"

"We don't rightly know. Had to go all the way up to the passes of these here mountains so as not to over-hunt this area. Some folks up there must have had the same idea. Only, we're pretty sure they came from the other side."

"You fought them?"

"It wasn't so much a fight as it was a mad scramble under a hail of hissing arrows. These two"—the daeloth gestured to the pair on the litters—"got hit pretty bad. We healed 'em, but they were too weak to march on their own. Our rations fell low. We were counting on the meat we found to hold us up on the way back."

"I'm sorry. It must have been difficult. But why didn't you commune to get aid?"

One of the men on the ground lifted his head at this. "Didn't . . . want to be . . . seen as . . . weak."

A new voice spoke from behind Jasside, startling her. "A little too late for that, I'm afraid."

Jasside turned, unsurprised to find Vashodia standing not three paces away. "We need to get them help."

"Hmm? Oh, of course, of course, it's already on the way. You and I have more important matters to attend to."

"What do you mean?"

"Why, someone has made an aggressive incursion on our most sovereign border. Is that not worth investigating?"

Jasside smiled, shaking her head. "I'll round up the crew."

There was no doubt in her mind that, somehow, Vashodia had been expecting this all along.

Arivana's reflection wavered in and out of focus in the mirror as Flumere ran the brush through her hair. The strokes came in a measured, languid rhythm, tugging at her scalp, causing a pleasant sensation when few others filled her life. The sun rose over the sliver of ocean just visible between the towers of House Baudone and House Pashams, cutting through her balcony to light the bedchamber on fire. Pinks and reds and sparkly things adorned every surface, brightening under the assault. This was the room she'd grown up in. She had never before considered moving into the chamber where her mother and father used to sleep.

Perhaps it's time I stopped acting like such a little girl and instead started acting like a queen.

She sighed, unable to envision what that was even supposed to look like. Putting aside childish things would be easy, at least. The child inside her had been dying a little each day. It wouldn't take much to put it down for good. But as for what she would put it its place, she came up empty. It seemed she had finally run out of role models.

Flumere finished and set the jeweled brush down on the surface before the vanity. "There, my queen," the handmaiden said. "All ready for any occasion. Do you think you'll be going out today?"

"If I should find sufficient reason? Perhaps."

"Very good, then. I'll call for your breakfast."

Arivana smiled a bit as Flumere stepped to the wall and raked her hand across the chimes. She was glad of the woman's demeanor. Never questioning, never shaming with word or gesture, her handmaiden always did her duty with businesslike efficiency. Like a soldier. She could almost imagine the woman on a battlefield somewhere, shouting commands to her troops with prim precision, fully expecting them to be obeyed simply because she had given them.

Then again, Arivana had never seen a real battle. She'd only heard about them in stories. Most of the times she'd been around soldiers had been on her rare visits to the barracks, where they'd dress their finest and parade around. None of that was real, she knew. Just the shiny surface of things. Just dazzle and distraction. Her brief brush with bloodshed in the gardens made her realize that all she'd been told of war was a lie.

And I am sick of being lied to.

Arivana's nose filled with scents that made her stomach rumble in anticipation a moment before Flumere pried open the dumbwaiter door. The woman spun around with the tray in her hands, then set it gently on a table. Arivana stood and stepped over to one of the two high-backed chairs around it.

Without a word, they both dove into the food. Boiled duck eggs half-shelled in tiny silver bowls, fried alligator tail wrapped in bacon and stuffed inside pastries, sliced mangoes drizzled with honey and mint, a carafe of guava juice—they devoured it all in less than five marks, not caring about the grease and crumbs that got everywhere.

Arivana sat back, patting her belly. It felt good to be full though her dance instructor would likely berate her for putting on so much weight in the past month. If she ever went back to the lessons, that is. She wasn't yet sure if she could look any member of Claris's house in the eye.

"Why did she do it?" she said, then covered her mouth. She hadn't meant to say it out loud.

Flumere cocked her head as she wiped her hands clean with a towel. "Well," she said, "there's the official answer—"

"Yes, yes. She was opposed to the war. It makes a sort of sense, I suppose. But why wouldn't she come to me and plead her case? We were so close to each other. She *had* to know I would have listened."

"Did she, your majesty?"

"I . . . I thought so." *What a strange question to ask.*

"Something obviously made her think she could no longer confide in you. What happened to change her mind?"

Arivana moaned. "I don't know!"

"I see," Flumere said, crossing her legs. "Why don't you start with what you *do* know?"

Arivana leaned back, rubbing her temples. "That's just the problem, though. It feels like I'm being kept in the dark. Tior probably thinks he's doing me a favor, what with my being his delicate little flower and all, but I can't stand staying ignorant any longer. I need some answers."

"What's stopping you from finding them?"

She rolled her eyes. "Please, as if I didn't already appear as pathetic as can be. Coming to beg for scraps of information will only make it worse."

"Who said anything about begging?"

"What?"

"I don't see why you have to go through your advisors at all. Better to just find out what you want to know yourself."

Arivana threw up her hands. "I wouldn't even know where to begin looking."

Flumere stayed silent a long moment, staring out the balcony. The sun's rays fell low enough now to dance across her handsome face, forcing her to squint. She drummed her fingers across her knee for an entire mark.

At last, she nodded to herself, saying, "If you'd like, my queen, I might have an idea where to start."

Arivana felt her heart stammer at the words. "Truly?"

"Yes, your majesty. Being your handmaiden, I have a surprising amount of access in this tower, among the affairs of both the high *and* low. I can ask the questions you can't."

"What questions?"

Flumere lowered her eyes. "Oh, I'm not so clever as that. You'll have to come up with what to ask. I can only make sure it reaches the right ears."

"Hmm." She leaned forward, resting her chin in her palm. "So you'd be, like, my own personal spy?"

Flumere jerked slightly at the last word. Taking a breath, she said, "Yes, my queen. Something like that."

Arivana had to wonder at the reaction. She had no idea of the woman's past and didn't want to pry. Perhaps she'd done similar work before she became her handmaiden? If so, she'd let the woman tell her in her own time.

I think I finally have a friend. I don't want to ruin it with intrusive questions.

She reached out and grasped Flumere's hand, squeezing gently. The woman returned the gesture. They shared a smile.

"I think," Arivana said, "that I would like that very much."

"I am pleased to serve, your majesty."

"Good. Are you ready for your first task?"

"Of course."

"Good. Then the first order of business: As long as we are in private, I insist that you begin calling me Arivana."

Sensation returned to Tassariel with agonizing slowness, as the void of her dreams faded to mist. Disturbing impressions of things unseen, amorphous shapes stalking shadows, had been haunting her for what seemed time unending. She was glad for the respite.

But that cold spike in her back was still there.

She snapped her eyes open and jolted upright, flexing the muscles that would unfurl her wings on demand. But nothing happened. Just a stirring of the ice in her spine. A pale dread filled her as she began breathing faster and faster, wishing, praying for this one truth to be undone. The nightmares seemed preferable to this reality.

A hand came down on her shoulder. "Are you all right, Tass?" Eluhar said.

She twisted, peering up into his eyes. Eyes full of concern and compassion, sympathy and relief. She shivered, wrapping her arms around herself. "I don't think so," she said.

He stepped away. "I'll go get the caretaker."

"No!" She grabbed his hand, pulling him back towards her. "Just stay with me. Can you do that, please?"

"Of course." He sat next to her on the bed. "Why don't you lie back down?"

She let him guide her head to the pillow. He pulled the blankets up to her neck. "How long has it been?" she asked.

"Four days."

"Does anyone know what happened yet?"

"I haven't been told anything really. No one has. The only information the council let out was that something went wrong during the ritual and you . . . fell."

Her memory flashed back to the experience, to the ground rushing up, to her sudden fear of the wind.

Tassariel rolled onto her side. She pressed her eyes shut, clenching the sheets to her chest.

Eluhar was silent for a time but remained a warm, welcome presence at her back. His breaths evened out. She felt his rigid form begin to sag. She rolled over and caught his head bouncing up from his chest. "Do you need anything?" he said quickly, slurring his words slightly.

"Oh, El," she said. "You haven't left my side this whole time, have you?"

He shook his head. "I just wanted to make sure you were all right."

She reached out from under the blanket and grasped his hand. "You're a good friend, El. The best I could ever hope for."

A slim smile broke through the exhaustion on his face.

"But I think I'm going to be fine," she said, nearly choking on the words. "There's no point killing yourself over nothing."

"The healers don't think it's 'nothing,' Tass."

Her eyes widened. "Wh-what do you mean?"

He sighed, running his free hand through his hair. "They found some . . . peculiarities with your injuries. Something they've never seen before. Do you . . ." he looked away, ". . . do you know anything about that?"

"Get rid of him."

Tassariel tensed, going stiff as a statue.

The voice. It was back.

She'd been holding on to the hope that it had been a hallucination. A trick of her mind as a result of the trauma. Perhaps, even, an unexpected side effect of the botched ritual, an echo of Elos as he attempted to communicate with her. But the words then, and the fact that the voice still spoke inside her mind, put any such notions to rest.

She had become . . . inhabited.

"What *are* you?" she whispered.

Eluhar leaned in close. "Sorry, I didn't hear that?"

"You cannot let on about me, my child. Do please put an end to this line of inquiry before it becomes uncomfortable for us both."

Her heartbeat raced. Cold sweat trickled down her temples. She shivered violently.

Eluhar stood, releasing her hand. "I'm sorry, Tass. Forgive me. You've just woken up, and here I am battering you with questions. You look freezing. Is there anything I can get you? Something warm to drink? I know how you love hot cider."

"Yes, thank you. That would be lovely."

He marched towards the archway of the room.

"Oh, and Eluhar?"

He stopped and turned.

"Of course I forgive you."

His shoulders lifted, back straightening at the words. He departed the room with a smile on his face.

"Finally. Some privacy at last."

Goose bumps sprouted on every surface of Tassariel's skin. That cold knot in her back seemed to be pulsing with waves of dread. Being alone with the voice was the last thing she wanted right now.

But I need to find out what the abyss is going on.

She clenched her fists. Opening her lips, she started to speak, but couldn't form more than half a word at once. She realized she had no idea where to even begin.

"Strain yourself not, young one. All will be revealed in time. We can speak freely now that the pest is gone."

"Pest!" she spat. "Eluhar is my friend. How dare you speak of him that way?"

"A friend, is he? Good luck convincing *him* of that."

"What's that supposed to mean?"

"Nothing. Now, where were we? Ah, yes. You were going to ask some very pointed questions that, no doubt, seem of utmost importance in your mind."

"H-how did you know that? Can you hear my thoughts?"

"If only! That would make all of this so much less difficult. Well, in some ways. Have you any idea what a jumbled mess the subconscious is? Thoughts and ideas and dreams and fears all crashing into each other like waves breaking in a storm. I'd get pulled under just from dipping in a toe!"

"Please stop. Just stop. I can't make sense of any of this."

"I'd be worried if you could. But enough musing. Can you do me a favor?"

"I don't know."

"Nothing vile, I assure you. I just need you to stand up."

"Why?"

"This would all be pretty pointless if you couldn't. And seeing as how it took a tremendous amount of effort to get this far, I'd know sooner rather than later what state my chosen vessel is in."

"Chosen . . . vessel?"

"In a moment. Now stand."

Sighing, she moved to obey. To be honest, she was curious what shape she was in as well. She swung her legs off the bed and pressed her feet into the tiles. Pushing off the bed, she rose. The grey walls spun slightly, and her head seemed to drain of all blood at once, but otherwise she felt fine. A bit stiff, but that was to be expected after four days in a bed.

She took a few steps and stretched out all her muscles, groaning in delight as she began to feel herself again. "Nothing damaged beyond repair," she said. "I'm actually a little exuberant, to tell the truth. I feel ready for anything."

"Excellent. Now, before we go any further, I need you to make me a promise."

"What's that?"

"You must tell no one about me unless I give you explicit leave."

"Right. Like I was about to go shouting in the streets about the voice inside my head."

"That's the spirit!"

Tassariel took a deep breath. "Okay, I've done as you've asked. Are you ready to tell me who you are and what you want with me?"

The voice laughed, like a grandfather amused by the antics of babes. "Oh, Tassariel. My dear, sweet, devoted child. Have you not figured it out yet?"

A word bubbled up from its hiding place beneath the surface of her mind. A name she'd hoped and feared to hear herself speak. Somehow, she had known from the very beginning.

"Elos."

"The one and only."

"B-but you're a—"

"A god? I suppose I am. As far as the colloquial use of the term is concerned, at least."

"My lord, I am honored." She bit the inside of her cheek, afraid to say more. *To think I've been swapping words with my own deity. And with such irreverence!* She couldn't help but cringe.

"No need to fret, my dear. I'm no stickler for formalities, despite what your high council may think. You've done nothing to upset me . . . yet."

Yet. The word echoed in her mind. She knew it was only a matter of time before she disappointed him. This was not at all what she had in mind when she'd been craving the chance to bring her questions before him. But everything she'd been planning to ask had escaped her mind like smoke through her fingers. None of it seemed to matter anymore.

"What," she said at last, "do you wish of me?"

"Nothing you haven't been doing your whole life already. And doing splendidly, I might add."

"Which is?"

"Obedience."

Tassariel nodded. "If you truly are Elos, then that is something I can do. But, if you don't mind me asking, to what purpose will my obedience lead?"

"Well, to be perfectly frank—and please believe me when I say I am not placating you—I'm not exactly sure. I may excel at examining available information and extrapolating the most likely outcomes, but even I can't foresee the future."

"What does all that mean?"

"It means I will send you where I think you may be needed. Where you can do the most good."

"I see." She closed her eyes, struggling to absorb all that she had learned. "But I still don't understand one thing."

"And that is?"

Tassariel swallowed. "Why me?"

Elos laughed, a warm sound that offset the lingering web of frost. "**Because, my dear, you alone may have what it takes to save us all.**"

She smiled, feeling a ball of joy surge up within her. Reward, at last, for the years of faithful devotion, dedication to her Calling, and adherence to the precepts. It had all been worth it.

Then why am I still crying?

She wiped a tear from her cheek, knowing exactly why it was there.

"What happened to my wings?" she asked, shaking.

There was silence for a time. Elos seemed to sink away from her, as if he had simply gone to sleep. But she knew that wasn't the case. After several marks, his presence returned.

"I needed room, and there is nowhere else for me to go. I'm . . . I'm sorry."

Her eyes stayed blurry with moisture until the smell of hot cider approached from down the hall.

CHAPTER 8

Mevon watched as Draevenus reopened his pack, checked the contents, and cinched it closed for the eighth time already that morning. The mierothi resumed wearing a rut in the yurt's floor with his pacing, the naked agitation in his manner making him seem as young as his age-frozen features suggested.

Seated on a wooden bench, Mevon sighed and resumed honing his blades.

Mother Poya shuffled up behind him. She'd been able to maintain her feet longer, and steadier, with each of the last few days. He took that as a sign she'd recover fully, or at least as far as her years would allow.

"You'd think," she said, low enough that Draevenus could not overhear, "that one so old as he would have learned a thing or two about patience over the centuries."

Mevon grunted. "You'd think."

"What's got him so riled up, then?"

"Ruul. While I agree that he has much to answer for, Draevenus has taken it upon his shoulders alone to make the god atone. Or die trying, it seems."

"The latter looks more likely."

"Aye."

"And yet you still accompany him. Blindly. Tell me, what reason could a strong, smart man such as yourself have to participate in such foolishness?"

"*Someone's* got to keep him out of trouble. As much of it as possible anyway. Besides"—Mevon shrugged—"I made a vow."

"One that will see you *both* in pointless graves."

"Neither of us could have done otherwise and still lived with ourselves." Mevon slid the blade into its sheath on his hip and shoved the honing strap into a pocket of his travel pack. "Ruul isn't the only one in need of atonement."

Before she could respond, Draevenus let out a loud huff from across the room. "Where *is* she?" he said.

"Zorvanya will return in due time," Mother Poya said. "Bearing gifts, if you recall her promise. I only wonder if you remember yours?"

Draevenus glared at her. "We promised to stay until she gets back. But if this is another one of her games designed to make us dance to her tune, don't expect me to—"

"To what?" Zorvanya said, pushing through the yurt's hide flap. "Wait forever until I return?"

The mierothi sprang his gaze upon her, his scowl deepening. "I wouldn't put it past you."

"I told you the time for games had ended, and I meant it. You may not have known me for very long, but you should at least be able to tell when I'm being sincere."

"Should I? I seem to recall nothing but jests from your mouth these many days. What part of that is supposed to instill confidence in your supposed honesty?"

She took a deep breath. Mevon couldn't help but marvel at her ability not to rise to his bait, not to escalate the conflict further even though she had ample cause. An admirable trait, and one he'd not seen in her before. Though, perhaps, he hadn't been looking hard enough.

Perhaps I didn't want to.

"I promised you gifts for your journey," Zorvanya said after a lengthy pause. "To you, Draevenus, I give this."

She handed over a bundle of reddish herbs wrapped in a thin leather pouch. Draevenus narrowed his eyes as he accepted it. "What is it?" he asked.

"Winterweal," she said. "A rugged flower that grows in the mountains around here, blooming even during the harshest freeze. Chewing on a few leaves will stave off frostbite and other cold-related maladies. For a time, at least. Where you're going, I'm more than certain you'll have need of it."

Visibly taken aback, likely by the thoughtfulness of

the gift, Draevenus at last managed to muster enough grace to bow his head in thanks.

Then, Zorvanya turned her soul-searching eyes towards Mevon.

"I have something for you as well," she said. "But it's . . . best given in private."

Mother Poya was at Draevenus's shoulder in a blink, pushing him towards the exit. "Get you on now, young man," she said.

Draevenus raised his hands in protest. "I'm not—"

"I know very well what you are. And isn't a quick exit what you wanted anyway?"

"Yes, but . . ."

Mevon heard no more as their voices faded away outside. He slowly turned back to Zorvanya, suddenly nervous to hear what she had to say.

One glance at her, however, revealed that she was far more nervous than he.

Shaking fingers pulled a vine from her dress pocket. A twisted thing, it let off a pungent fragrance that, even from across the room, made him feel invigorated. He'd never seen or smelled the like.

"Vir vine," she said in response to his unasked question. "A common cure to the ailment of many a young wife. I've administered it many times, but never to myself. No such reason until now."

"What does it do?"

"It acts as a . . . fertility aid."

Mevon inhaled sharply. "You mean . . . ?"

"Yes," Zorvanya said. "I wish to have a child.

"And I wish it to be yours."

He sprang to his feet and turned away from her, unable to make sense of the request. Fatherhood had always been the furthest thing from his mind. He was a warrior, built for war, knowing he had nothing else to offer a woman but a cold, lonely bed as he sought one battlefield after the next. It was simply out of the question.

"I can't," he said at last. "That's not who I am."

"It could be. You can be anything you want, Mevon. All you have to do is make a choice and stick to it."

Mevon shook his head but knew that she wasn't far from the truth.

After all, I made the choice to love someone once before. To try to make myself something more. Why shouldn't I choose to do it again?

He had to know something first. "Why me?" he asked.

"You're strong," she said, "and far more intelligent than your brutal exterior would suggest."

"So I'm . . . what? Good breeding stock?"

"That's part of it, I'll admit. But there's more. I can't afford to let any man in these parts become the father of my child. It would give him a claim over me that I'd have no power to subvert. What little autonomy I have would disappear."

"You ask too much. I'd have to abandon my friend in his greatest time of need."

"Only for a toll at most."

"What? I thought you wanted me to be . . . ?" He swallowed hard, unable to finish the statement.

"If it's that upsetting, you don't have to think of it like that at all. I merely need a . . . donation. After that, you can continue on your merry way. If, in time, you feel the desire to return, and fulfill . . . other roles . . . well, I'd consider that well beyond what any woman could reasonably hope for."

He turned to face her and knew immediately that it was a mistake. Her eyes met his, sparkling with beauty and desire enough to melt away his objections. He felt his mouth go dry, and his heart began to race in his chest.

She stepped closer, hips swaying, lips parting ever so slightly.

He held up a hand, and she stopped, for which he was grateful. Another pace, and his already wavering resolve would have likely shattered.

"I must finish this," he said through gritted teeth, wishing it didn't have to be so. "Until then, I won't be able to think straight, much less trust myself with a decision as big as this. Please."

He almost expected tears, or perhaps a furious outburst, but he underestimated her once again.

She merely took a halted breath and snapped the vine in two.

"Take this," she said, tossing one half to him. "The potency will fade by day's end, but it will still serve as a reminder. Should you find the steps of your path ever winding my way again, know that I'll be waiting."

Turning away, she stuffed the half she'd kept between her breasts and left the yurt without a sound.

Mevon could only stare after the memory of her retreating body, wondering if he hadn't just made a huge, huge mistake.

The peaks rose up to either side of the narrow game trail, lost in low clouds that rolled through the pass. Jasside marched, boots squishing through soil moistened by the mists. She rarely rode on the wagon anymore. The trail was so steep, she felt as if she might roll right off it, and Feralt would insist that she ride at his side. She didn't have the heart to tell him it was over between them.

As she had done the last few days, Vashodia strolled beside her. The mierothi had surprising stamina for one with such short legs. Though summer approached, the rising elevation, and the fact that they marched farther north every day, dictated continued wearing of their cloaks. Gusts of wind spattered them with hints of frost and pine.

A chill surged up from Jasside's toes, rolling through her body and making her shudder. It reminded her of the frozen heart of the small figure at her side and the private task she'd taken on to thaw it.

It would not be easy.

How do you change the soul of someone almost two thousand years old?

Just thinking of the vast stretch of centuries made her head spin. She must seem a fly to her mistress. Here one day, gone the next. She wondered what the mierothi even saw in her, and—perhaps more vitally—what she ultimately *wanted* from an apprentice. To unfreeze Vashodia's heart, Jasside had to be able to grasp it without turning to ice herself.

But first, she needed to understand it.

Of course, such things could not be done directly. Most people didn't tolerate overt probings of their souls. Jasside knew she would have to be subtle, but she wasn't worried. *I'm learning from the best, after all.*

"So," Jasside said, "what are we about on this little trip?"

"Nothing much," Vashodia replied. "Just bringing a nation to heel."

"Another one?"

"Worry not. I promise I'll actually help you this time."

"I'm not worried. This place, at least, doesn't have a crippling fear of the metaphysical to complicate things."

"What makes you think that?"

Jasside shrugged. "The Weskarans kept harping on about how they're a haven against the 'foul misuse of sorcery.' And they didn't exactly have anything nice to say about their neighbors to the north. It stands to reason that the Sceptrines do not share the same aversions."

"Oh, that sounds quite reasonable. Quite reasonable indeed."

"But?"

"But things are never as simple as they seem."

"Meaning?"

"Meaning the relationship Sceptre has with magic

has always been strained, and recently, it has become more so. Much more."

"How would you . . . ?" Jasside's eyes widened with realization. "You've been here before."

"An excellent deduction, my apprentice. And it's even correct this time, too."

How? When? Why? These questions nearly burst forth of their own accord. Jasside clamped her lips shut, though. Vashodia had a familiar look in her eye that told Jasside that her mistress would say no more on the subject. Still, she couldn't help but speculate, and the places her logic led drove cold spikes of dread into her bones.

You're planning something big, aren't you? Big enough to make what we accomplished with the revolution seem a mere footnote in the annals of history. A history you'll write no matter the cost.

Even if the price is countless souls.

Jasside twisted her lips. She needed time to sort her thoughts and feelings and decided to walk in silence. It wasn't long, however, before she noticed how quiet the woods around them had become.

Too quiet.

She energized and sent a pulse outwards, checking for signs of life. She found none. Not even a squirrel or a sparrow. *That shouldn't be possible.*

Furrowing her brow, she altered the shape of her energy and detected something faint, neatly hidden on the edges of perception. Another spell, masking the heartbeats of everything in the vicinity. She followed the trail back to the caster and discovered him two hundred paces away to their front.

With a few flicks of her fingers, she dissolved the energy strands, feeling the other caster stagger. Then she counted the heartbeats that did not belong to her party.

She froze in her steps.

"Halt!" she called.

The daeloth guards obeyed, pulling swords from their scabbards.

"Something the matter?" Vashodia said.

Jasside shook her head. "I just want to avoid any . . . misunderstandings."

"Ah. In that case, why don't you introduce us?"

"Gladly."

Pulling in more energy, Jasside formed a cone of excited air in front of her to amplify her voice. "Soldiers of Sceptre," she began, "we are representatives of the sovereign nation of the mierothi. We come in peace."

She modified the casting, forming a dome of silence encompassing her party. "Sheathe your weapons," she ordered to the twenty-three daeloth. "But keep your shields ready."

As they obliged, she removed the dome, resuming her announcement. "Take this as a gesture of good faith. I ask that you show yourselves so we may converse in a civilized manner."

For a mark, nothing happened. Then, slowly, figures began emerging from the mist between the trees. Three hundred, all told, dressed in camouflage patterns that blended seamlessly with the surrounding foliage. A longbow was in each hand, arrows fitted to strings. Thankfully, they were not drawn, but the men holding them looked as if they could release before she could blink. What little she could see of their faces revealed rough, muddy skin, wide cheekbones, and narrow brown eyes. Black hair peeked out from every hood.

Still, no one came forward to speak. She reversed her spell so she could receive sounds, and began roving it around. After a few beats, she heard voices whispering. One, breathless and near to panic, she knew to be the Sceptrine sorcerer by his position.

"—you cannot!" he was saying. "Every one of those soldiers is a caster ten times as strong as I. And the two in the middle?" She heard him shudder. "Those two can tear down mountains."

A sigh sounded, close to the first man. "I fear no caster," said a second man, whose voice betrayed weariness yet still maintained a resolute quality she could admire.

"They aren't even normal casters, though. Their power is strange, born of darkness. I've never seen the like."

"Well, we're not exactly allies with the light right now, are we?"

"But we don't know what they intend."

"That is why I must speak with them. Stay behind me. If it goes to the abyss, run and tell my brother—"

"My lord, I beg you!"

"Enough!"

Jasside withdrew her eavesdropping spell as a lone figure emerged onto the path ahead of her. She glanced down at her mistress. "Ready to meet their leader?"

"Of course." Vashodia smirked. "But is he ready to meet us?"

They sauntered forward together, emerging outside the encircled daeloth and marching another score paces to meet with the man in a spot of relative privacy. She studied him as they approached. He stood taller than any of his soldiers, the bulk of his armor protruding from beneath his woodland cloak. A greatsword rested in a half scabbard on his back, the hilt peeking up over his right shoulder. His helmet was a steel mask in the shape of a scowling skull, with horns sweeping forward past the jaw. He stopped five paces away and reached to remove the headpiece.

"I am Daye Harkun, Prince of Sceptre," he said. "Or, at least, the closest thing to a prince we can manage these days."

A shock of chestnut hair tumbled out as he pulled off the helmet. The skin beneath was travel-worn but otherwise fair. Blue eyes gleamed as they studied her. He didn't appear anything like his fellows. In fact, he looked . . .

"You're Weskaran," Jasside blurted.

He smiled. "Aye, by birth I am. But I've long called Sceptre my home."

Jasside felt a spot of heat rising to her cheeks. "Apologies for my rudeness. It was surprising, is all."

"You're not the first to think that."

She cleared her throat. "Yes, well then. I am Jasside Anglasco. I'm human, as you may tell," *well, mostly,* "but I'm here on behalf of the mierothi nation, newly settled in the mountains south of here." She turned. "This is my mistress—"

"Mistress! But she's just a little girl. What kind of sick people are you?"

Jasside stifled a laugh, however, with little success. "Ah, sorry. I'm using the word as a feminine version of *master.* Not . . . that other way."

He jerked his head back. "Now you have me even more confused."

Vashodia, at last, stepped forward, exhaling with a high, keening noise somewhere between a sigh and a patronizing laugh. "What she means is that I let her make the introductions. It helps smooth over any . . . unfortunate reactions."

She flipped her hood down, revealing her face.

To his credit, the prince did not flinch or reach for his weapon. His eyes, however, made a thorough study of Vashodia, taking in all the differences—or malformations, as he more likely thought—in only a few beats.

"She called it the *mierothi* nation," Daye said, "I take it that's what you are?"

"I am."

"You're not as young as you look."

Vashodia laughed again. "My, aren't you a sharp one."

His hand cut the air. "My brother got all the brains in the family, not me. Tell me why you're here."

"Straight to business, then? I like it," Vashodia said. She waved a palm towards Jasside.

Jasside stared hard into the prince's eyes. "Some of our people were hunting to the south of here a week ago and came under attack. It is our understanding that this land is unclaimed by any nation. *Was* unclaimed, I should say. The mierothi sovereignty has chosen to call it theirs."

"Your point being?"

"You owe us an apology."

He shrugged. "How were we supposed to know? I don't see any of your flags planted in the soil."

"Is that what you want? Eight hundred of my mistress's kin, and nearly ten thousand daeloth stand ready to erect fortresses and stand watch along the border we now claim."

"Daeloth?"

"Sorry." Jasside gestured towards the darkwatch behind her. "Half-breeds."

Daye's eyes widened. "Ten thousand you said?"

"Yes."

He sighed, sagging, a simple deflation that made him instantly seem a lesser man. The weariness she'd first heard in him as she stole in on his conversation with the sorcerer now suffused his entire body. A wild, desperate look entered his eyes.

"If it's an apology you want, then you'll have it." He drew up with obvious effort. "On behalf of the people of Sceptre, I, Prince Daye Harkun, express my sincer-est remorse for any injury our ignorance may have caused you. I am . . . sorry."

Jasside could tell how much the statement had wounded his pride, yet still he barely hesitated. Here was a man burdened with duty and wracked by sor-rows she could not even name. She felt sick with her-self for forcing an apology from him.

She cast a dome of silence around her and Vashodia, then turned to her mistress. "Why are you doing this? Can't you see that it's destroying him?"

Vashodia's face remained neutral. "A man must be broken down to nothing before he can be rebuilt. As the man, so too the nation."

"Rebuilt into what?"

"What else?" Vashodia said, shrugging. "A weapon."

"Why do we need a—?"

Jasside spasmed as her spell vanished, the energy lancing back into her like lightning. She pivoted to see the prince step through the place it had been, dread knowledge filling her.

You're a void!

On instinct, she began weaving the spell that crip-pled Hardohl, threading it towards him a beat later. Her second surprise came when it vanished as well. She shook her head, shivering. *Of course it doesn't work. He doesn't have any blessings to act as a buffer. We're com-pletely helpless.*

He stepped closer, an arm's reach away now. She felt her heart begin to race.

The prince stopped, shaking his head as if saddened by her attempts to subdue him with magic. "Please," he said. "I must know if you accept our apology."

Jasside backed up, dropping her hands to her sides. She felt for the small knife sheathed at her hip.

Vashodia, seemingly unperturbed, smiled up at the man. "No."

His fists clenched at his sides. "Why not?"

"Because I only accept apologies from those who are *actually* in power."

His brow scrunched up. "I don't understand. I am a prince—"

"A prince in charge of only three hundred men? A prince relegated to the farthest corner of his country? A prince scrounging outside his borders for scraps?" Vashodia shook her head. "That doesn't sound like someone who has any *real* authority to me."

Jasside steeled herself for the violent outburst she was sure would come, but it never did. Her mistress's words only deflated him further than before. She even thought she saw a hint of fluid start to brim in the prince's eyes.

"We are at war," he said, each word falling like a hammer. "Not all is as it once was. Not all is *right* anymore." He shifted his eyes back and forth between them for several silent beats.

War changes everything and everyone it touches. Just not always in the same way. She'd managed to come out of it stronger than ever but could tell his story would read far differently than hers. And what was worse, it was still being written.

"Fine, then," Daye said at last, as if pronouncing a death sentence. "I will take you to my brother."

Steam rose from the fountain as Arivana tiptoed along its edge. Her bare arms remained clasped behind her back as she darted glances at the figures standing in ankle-deep water. Twelve in all, boys about her age, wearing nothing but tight swimming breeches. They came tall or short, muscular or lean, with skin, hair, and eyes every possible combination of hues. One thing they had in common, though, was that they were all breathtakingly gorgeous.

She twisted her head towards Tior as he pushed aside a palm branch hanging down over the path. "I don't understand, Minister. What are they here for?"

Tior pulled his gaze from a family of cockatiels singing in a nearby tree. He smiled down at her. "They are here for you, my queen."

"Yes, but what *for*?"

"For your entertainment, of course."

She arched an eyebrow. "What? Do they sing or something?"

"Why not? They will do whatever you wish. You can make them dance or wrestle, leap from the boulders above the waterfall, paint you a picture, feed you sliced fruit, or shower you with praise and affection.

Whatever your imagination can conjure. Their only desire will be to fulfill all of yours."

Heat that had little to do with the sorcerous constructs spewing steam around the expansive, jungle-like room rose into her cheeks. The plunging neckline and soaring hem of her swimming gown suddenly didn't seem so innocent.

She swept her eyes across the boys again, noticing, this time, many peeking her way with smiling faces. A few even stared openly. "That seems like it might be . . . awkward. I don't even know the first thing about them."

"Oh, you'll have plenty of time to learn. They will be here, day and night, whenever you have need of them."

"They'll be living here?"

Tior nodded. "As is tradition. You have many floors of your tower devoted to leisurely pursuits, one typically for each member of the royal family above courting age. It's about time they were put to use again."

Courting. The very mention of the word stirred up bile in the bottom of her throat.

"Surely this isn't necessary, Tior. I appreciate your efforts, truly, but I don't need to be kept in a constant state of distraction."

"Is that what you think this is about?"

She stopped, peering up into his face. "Isn't it?"

Tior sighed. "You are a woman, yes? Physically, I mean."

Arivana squirmed inside at the thought of talking about her monthly cycle with him. "Yes," she said curtly.

"And you are the last surviving member of the royal line, correct?"

The blood drained from her face as she realized where the conversation was headed. "Yes."

"Then it's high time we changed that."

She twisted her lips. "You seek to make one of them my king."

"Yes, your majesty. The attempt on your life made it very clear, to all the nation, that such things cannot be postponed until they are . . . convenient."

"Until I'm in love, you mean."

"Oh, my queen. You are so young. Please do not let the ignorance of youth obstruct the way of your duty."

"Funny. Claris said something similar not long before she tried to kill me."

Tior's body went rigid. He lowered his chin, and said through gritted teeth, "Do not speak to me of Claris. By letting her live, you failed in your responsibility, Arivana. You made us all look like fools."

She hung her head, making herself as still and small as she could. An instinct she'd been obeying her whole life. Today, though, something made her lift her eyes once more. Some part of her, deep inside, that was tired of being knocked down and trampled on every beat of her life.

"I did what I thought was right," she said. "Is that not what a queen should do? What she should *always* do?"

"Yes," Tior said. "So long as it falls within the law."

"And did the law say I *had* to put her to death?"

"Not . . . specifically," Tior said through gritted teeth. "It seems you've been doing some reading."

It had actually been a wild stab in the abyss, but Arivana couldn't let him know that. *Though if I can discover interesting bits like that, reading might be an excellent hobby to pursue.* She masked her giddy surprise by turning to face the twelve boys, still lined up patiently. "I am trying, Tior. Really I am. But how can I take responsibility for anything if you won't trust me to learn from my mistakes?"

For a long moment, he was silent. She feared her small burst of defiance might have been a step too far. At last, however, he let loose a low chuckle, one ringing with genuine amusement, not scorn. He stepped past her, smiling. "You may have some of your mother in you after all."

The corners of her lips curved as she met his gaze.

He began marching in the direction of the exit, threading between palm trees and beds of ferns. "Enjoy yourself, my queen," he called.

"I will."

Once Tior was fully out of sight, she turned to the boys. "Go play," she ordered. They obliged, whooping and hollering and splashing around.

She watched them, feeling amused and confused and a hundred other emotions, sure they were all the things young women were supposed to feel when surrounded by beautiful young men.

And it was at that moment Arivana resolved never to enter that level of her tower again.

The caretaker laid a wreath over Tassariel's head. Strands of woven silk, white as pearls, signified the purity of a patient's well-being. She had been healed as far as the temple's skills could manage. She accepted the symbolic ornament with what little grace she could muster, nodding in unfelt gratitude. It felt like a betrayal.

"There now, love," the caretaker said. "You're fit as can be. Lovely as your face is, I hope it doesn't end up back in here anytime soon, yeah?"

Tassariel did her best to smile. "Yes. Thank you for all you've done."

The caretaker patted her shoulder once, then strode from the room. Tassariel was glad the woman hadn't lingered. Her body had recovered from the fall, but nothing could be done for the loss of her wings. She had shed every tear she had for it. Now, keeping the sorrow at bay paled before the difficulty of holding back the rage.

Elos remained . . . distant. It was as if, having divulged his bidding, he had nothing else to say until she could fulfill it. He seemed to be waiting. For what, though, still wasn't clear. Tassariel trudged out of the room, glad to see the last of those four bland walls. The temple exit lay less than a hundred paces away, down the corridor to the right.

She turned in the opposite direction.

If Elos will not answer my questions, perhaps someone else will.

She extended her fingertips, brushing them against the smooth stone walls on her left. She turned one corner, then another, passing rooms occupied by the sick and the dying. Aging valynkar filled only a small fraction of them. The rest held humans from all corners of the world who had traveled here to receive the best care possible. It had not always been this way. Once, she'd read, valynkar ran healing centers scattered around the planet, so that few died who could be saved by sorcerous arts. Now, only those who could afford the price of the considerable journey enjoyed such a boon.

My people look ever inwards. How long until we stop bothering altogether and even turn away those in need?

Eventually, she came to a cut in the stone wall like a curved, inverted "V" and peered into the room beyond, finding whom she sought. Gilshamed, sitting stoically at Lashriel's bedside.

The ice stirred as she gazed at the back of his golden head.

For the hundredth time, she wondered why the god of light had to be so cold.

She tensed to step inside but was stopped short by the urgent rush of Elos to the forefront of her mind.

"What are you doing?" he said.

Tassariel paused, gripping both edges of the archway and pushing herself backwards out of the room. "I must speak to him, my lord," she whispered.

"Why?"

"He owes me an explanation." She sighed. "And I suppose I owe him one as well."

The chill churned, driving slivers of frost to every extremity. Elos faded. "**Do not betray me,**" he said, as if from far away.

"I will try." *If I can help it, that is.* Gilshamed was shrewd, she knew, and skilled at drawing truth from the most uncooperative of subjects. Vulnerable as she felt at the moment, it was the best promise she could give.

She stepped into the chamber.

Gilshamed's head snapped round after she made an effort to add force to her stride. He jerked upright and bowed. "Tassariel. Niece. I am honored by your presence."

She returned the bow. "Uncle. I trust you are well?"

"Fine." He glanced at the wreath on her head. "I see you've healed nicely. That is quite a relief."

"I'm not *all* better," she said. "Only . . . mostly."

"Mostly?"

She lowered her eyes. "There was one thing the healers could not fix."

Gilshamed glanced down at Lashriel as she slept. "There seems to be a lot of that going around these days."

"Yes, well, I was hoping you might be able to tell me something about that. You were the one channeling the ritual, after all."

"So I was."

"Did you notice anything . . . unusual?"

His eyes widened, boring holes into her with his gaze. "The very fact that I was present—and the seemingly endless series of coincidences that led me there—was unusual enough."

"Prod and pull," said Elos. "A thousand times a thousand times. Each, by themselves, no more noticeable than a mote of dust, but together, they're almost able to make up a man's mind. It's all I can do, nowadays. And only to those with even a speck of faith left in their bones."

"Do you still have faith?" Tassariel asked.

"Faith?" Gilshamed grunted. "I had thought it all but dead. He was great, once. Powerful. Present in the lives of all our kin. But in my four millennia on this world, I've witnessed the influence of Elos dwindle to almost nothing."

"And now?"

"Now, I'm . . . not sure. Something happened, up on that platform. Some power took over, far beyond any hope I had to control it. I might have nudged the connection open a bit wider than usual, but I never expected . . ." he shook his head, " . . . whatever it was that happened."

"Is that an apology?"

"Would you like it to be?"

"To be honest, I don't know yet."

"You don't know? How can you say that? From my perspective, nothing good came of the experience, whatsoever."

Tassariel bit her lip.

Gilshamed stepped closer. She felt him energize. "What are you—?"

"Just hold still."

Hands glowing with power reached to cup her jaw.

"Keep him away!"

Tassariel lashed out a palm, striking Gilshamed in the chest. He sprawled backwards, crashing off the edge of Lashriel's bed and tumbling across the floor.

She gasped, horrified by her own reaction. The physical response seemed almost involuntary, her training and her faith combining for a sordid outcome. "Uncle! I'm so sorry. Are you all right?" She took a timid step forward, not knowing if he would welcome her aid.

He held up a hand, stopping her advance. Gasping for breath, it took him half a mark before he could respond. "You've done enough," he said at last.

"Please forgive me for reacting like that. I was just surprised. And the last time you used sorcery on me . . ." She shrugged, as if that would explain everything.

Gilshamed coughed and laughed simultaneously. "It's funny what happens when the gods get involved. Isn't that right, Elos?"

Ice contracted into her spine. "Now you see why I wanted you to be careful."

"It wasn't my fault," she said.

"I never said it was," Gilshamed said.

"I wasn't talking to you."

His eyebrows rose. "Oh? Interesting. Can he hear me? Can he see my face?"

Tassariel turned her head to the side. "Well, can you?"

"I can."

She glanced back towards Gilshamed and nodded.

He shook, hands clenching into fists. "I must apologize in advance then, niece. None of this is meant for you."

Gulping, she said, "I understand."

She closed her eyes as Gilshamed began a rampage of words. Spittle flew from lips on a face turned red as her uncle broke the dam on his long-held rage. She'd never seen him like this before. Words poured forth, so vitriolic she was surprised her skin wasn't melting. More surprising still, the fact that she could find no fault in the accusations, all of which came down to pretty much a single question:

What kind of god would allow such atrocities to befall his faithful?

Through it all, Elos never even stirred.

CHAPTER 9

The bear thrashed about in the bushes two hundred paces away, foraging, no doubt, in preparation for the long winter to come. Mevon peeked around the thick trunk, downhill and downwind of the creature. They'd been tracking it for three days as they scoured the countryside for food, furs, and other things they would need to aid them through the trek to come. The pickings had been slim. They were lucky to have found a bear this close to the plateau.

Mevon pulled his head back. He turned, inhaling the sweet, almost cinnamon scent of the tree as his fingers stuck to the dripping sap. Draevenus leaned against the other side of the trunk, caressing the hilts of his daggers.

"Plan?" Mevon whispered.

"Get you a new winter coat," Draevenus replied,

grinning. "And enough meat to last a month, if he's as big as the tracks suggest."

"I meant what's the plan of attack?"

The smile vanished. "Sorry. Just give me a moment, will you?" The mierothi turned away to study the terrain for the fifth time that morning.

Mevon frowned. Draevenus had been doing that a lot lately. Starting with a playful attitude, then dropping it as soon as he realized what he was doing. Almost as if he felt guilty about it. But for the life of him, Mevon couldn't think what could have caused such a shift in his demeanor.

Though the assassin had been driven, almost obsessive since they'd left Mother Poya's, Mevon hadn't objected too harshly to the haste. If anything, he had become infected by it himself. Despite the dangers, he now found he was longing for a conclusion to this quest almost as much as his companion was. Holing up for the winter—with or without Zorvanya—seemed less appealing by the day.

"How do you cook bear meat anyway?" Mevon asked, trying to keep his tone light.

Draevenus shrugged. "Same as any other wild game. Steaks, stews, and sausages mostly. You've never had it before?"

"No. My rangers would go hunting on some of the longer missions, but they mostly brought back venison or fowl. Rogue casters avoided bear country. No way to defend themselves without giving away their position."

"Well, you're in for a treat, then. Bear's good eating. And that coat of his ought to be big enough to keep even *you* warm."

"You're sure it's alone?"

"No cubs. No mate. It's probably only got a few years left anyway. Poor thing." Draevenus scratched his nose. "Want to hear my plan for killing it?"

"Go ahead."

The mierothi pointed to their left. "See that boulder? The one covered in moss? I'll dash over there and wait behind it. When I'm set, you'll charge towards the bear, making as much noise as you can. The terrain is pretty constricted here, so I'm betting it will run right past me." He jabbed out a hand, mimicking a knifing action. "Straight to the heart. Easy. Clean. Quick."

"What if he doesn't run?"

"In that case, he'll likely come after you."

"This is sounding like a good plan less and less."

Draevenus dismissed that with a wave. "Just fall straight back, into that clear spot fifty paces behind us, then circle around and come towards me again. I'll dash in and catch it the same way."

Mevon frowned, rubbing his chin. "I don't know."

"What is it?"

"There's no denying you're fast, but one lucky swipe, and you're done for. I should be the one that faces it."

"Is that going to be . . . safe for you?"

"Safe?"

Draevenus sighed. "Violence, Mevon. It's like any

addiction. Most people, when trying to kick a habit, either need to abstain from the barest hint of their chosen vice or find some alternative that's similar, but less destructive, and wean themselves off it. I'd always thought you fell into the former category."

Mevon's eyes lost focus as he contemplated the words. He thought back over the last few weeks and realized Draevenus had not let him so much as skin a rabbit. He felt gratefulness as an ache deep inside him that the assassin would go to such lengths just to keep him safe from his own sin.

He felt something else, too, and peered now into the other man's eyes, finally seeing the guilt writ there, plain as ink on parchment. Guilt the mierothi had been carrying around since that night. Since Mevon had almost lost control. He'd been too tangled in his own thornbush of melancholy to realize it until now.

"Draevenus," Mevon said, "this journey of mine is a personal one. While I appreciate any advice you can give me, you have never been, nor will you ever be, responsible for my actions. Some ghosts a man has to face alone."

Draevenus leaned his head back against the tree. "I know. I just . . . I promised I would be there for you, and back in that town, I failed to keep that promise."

"You owe me nothing, you understand? Nothing." He fixed Draevenus with a grateful expression. But not for too long. The moment of shared vulnerability—of *feelings*—was already dragging on too long. *It will only grow more awkward if I let it linger.*

Mevon smiled. "And besides, it's only a beast."

"No prohibitions against animals then, eh? Good for letting off a little steam?"

Mevon pulled both of his daggers, examining the curved steel in the sunlight. "Something like that."

"Well then," Draevenus said, twiddling his fingers as if in mockery of some circus magician, "I'll do my best to keep him distracted. Ready?"

Mevon nodded. As one, they sprang out from opposite sides of the tree.

Jasside stared at the woman standing beside the road ahead of them, who was rocking a tiny infant in her arms.

Tattered rags hung about the woman's body. Hollow cheeks, smeared with dirt or something worse, puffed in and out as she sang a wordless lullaby. The child bounced upon limbs more bone than flesh, itself little more than a bundle of wrapped cloth. The mother cradled its head against her withered breast.

Jasside wiped away a tear that had found its way down her cheek. She glanced down to Prince Daye Harkun, who rode his black stallion at the side of her wagon. He must have sensed her regard, for he turned his face to her. A face that mirrored her own lament.

"What's going on here?" she asked.

"Didn't I tell you?" he said. "War. And our people are losing. Badly. Few of our casualties come from actual combat. The rest . . . well . . . you'll see in a moment."

"I don't—"

"Look."

The road straightened ahead, and through a break in the trees, she viewed a vast valley sprawling below them. Every acre was infested with humanity.

"That's no city," she said.

"No. It's not."

Not a building could be seen. Ramshackle tents and lean-tos filled a massive maze of swarming men, women, and children, a hive of languid activity that spoke of life hanging by a thread, lost to hope, waiting for a salvation it knew to be a dream.

It made Jasside very, very angry.

"Who are all these people? Why are they here?"

Daye sighed, shaking his head. "Refugees, my lady. A million strong, the last time we attempted to make a count. They've nowhere else to go. My brother tasked me with doing what I can to keep them safe and fed." He looked about in despair. "I haven't been able to do much."

"Why not?"

"Have you seen war before?"

"I have."

"Then you must know that it makes monsters out of men. Wives become widows. Children become burdens. Everyone becomes desperate as the things they took for granted are stripped away all at once, leaving them destitute in their flight away from chaos and bloodshed. Tell me you haven't seen these things before, with your own eyes, and I'll say you haven't seen war in its most honest form."

Jasside swallowed hard, her anger evaporating in an instant. "You're right, I suppose. I guess I haven't seen war. Not really. I was too caught up in the fighting to pay attention to the . . . peripheral effects."

The prince lowered his head. "My apologies if I seemed harsh. Despite my best intentions, I am made a failure every day. People pay for that failure with suffering I cannot even fathom."

She shuddered at the pronouncement, wracked with guilt for her judgment of the man yet still furious at the dismal situation. There had to be *something* that could be done.

"What are your greatest needs?" she said.

"We have plenty of water, thanks to the summer melt running off the mountains," Daye said, "but food is scarce. Ten thousand new mouths arrive every day, bringing with them stomachs we can't fill and a host of diseases that our few casters are sore pressed to keep contained. Women and children are dragged away in the night, used for abyss knows what end, while most of our fighting force is out throwing their lives away to stall the inevitable.

"What do we need?" he asked, steel in his voice. "We need a miracle, my lady. Have you got one lying around somewhere?"

"I might."

Jasside stood on the wagon seat and called a halt.

The daeloth obeyed within a beat, and the Sceptrine soldiers, marching in columns along the edges of the road, drew up short after seeing their prince stop alongside her.

She hopped down and marched past the front of the formation, throwing a smile to the mother who still hummed while rocking her baby. Daye followed close by her side. Unobstructed, she was able to gain a clearer view of the valley. She pointed to a spot in the distance—just visible in the horizon's haze—that seemed clear of milling souls.

"What's that out there?" she asked.

The prince squinted, shading his face with a hand against the early-morning light. "That? Just some local fields. Wheat, mostly, but a few other crops as well."

"Are they growing?"

"Aye. But the harvest won't be ready for months. I have to keep half of my soldiers stationed around them to prevent theft of seeds and half-grown crops. People still risk it almost every night."

Jasside nodded. *One.* "Have you anyplace to collect the sick and wounded?"

"So they can catch something else and die all the quicker? No, my lady. We've not enough healers to even bother."

Two. "What about the men, those without families to look after? What are you doing to keep them . . . occupied?"

"What's there to do?"

Three. "My prince, with your leave, I think I might be able to—"

"What are you *doing?*"

Jasside flinched at the sound of Vashodia's voice but immediately berated herself for the reaction. *I can't keep playing the wide-eyed apprentice anymore. If I'm to reach her, I need to show her what's right.*

"It's called 'helping,' Vashodia. Have you ever heard of it?"

The mierothi glowered. "Don't get snippy with me, Jasside. We're in a hurry if you didn't notice."

"No, actually, I didn't. These people are in desperate need of assistance we are uniquely suited to provide. Pray tell, what manner of haste could outweigh that?"

Vashodia ran her gaze over the throbbing masses below, her disdain so palpable it seemed to thicken the air. "These people are useless. Saving them means nothing."

"No person is *useless.* Look around—it will mean *everything* to them!"

The mierothi's eyes widened.

Jasside held her breath.

After what seemed an eternity, Vashodia shrugged. "Very well. I can see that you're set on this. Just know that our little caravan will continue to march. It should take no more than four days to move beyond all this riffraff. You *will* be with us when we exit the far end of the valley."

Jasside exhaled. She'd pushed her luck already by making a stand. *No use poking a viper after it has decided to let you pass.* She bowed her head in obeisance. "Of course, my mistress. I wouldn't dream of missing my ride."

Vashodia threw her one last, exasperated glance before twirling away and disappearing back inside the wagon. Jasside turned towards Daye.

"You really think you can help?" he asked.

"I do."

"Then I may just ask for your hand in marriage before this is all over."

Jasside pressed her lips together but couldn't stop the laughter from bursting forth. Even the prince cracked a smile.

"Let's make sure there's actually food before we start planning a wedding feast," she said after composing herself. She pivoted around and ambled softly over to the woman on the side of the road, stopping before her and smiling broadly.

The mother gave no indication that she acknowledged Jasside's presence.

"Hello? Are you well? I just wanted you to know that I'm here to help. I'm going to make everything all better."

The woman continued her wordless humming, oblivious.

Jasside narrowed her eyes, peering from the mother's face down to the child in her arms. Her breath caught in her throat.

The baby's face was white as milk, the lips blue. No breath had stirred from the tiny lungs in days.

Jasside brought a hand to her lips, quivering. Tears fell down her cheeks, not a trickle this time but a torrent. With shaking hands, she reached to pry the infant corpse from the woman's grasp. Between the weight of the child and the strength of the mother's protest, it hardly took any effort at all.

She passed the body off to the prince, who had come up behind her, then turned and wrapped the woman in an embrace, letting sobs loose with aching abandon.

Through it all, the lullaby never stopped.

"**W**hat have you found?" Arivana asked.

Flumere cast her gaze about as they sauntered through the colonnades on the floors of knowledge. "Not here, my qu—Arivana, I mean. Maybe when we have some privacy."

"Is your information that scathing?"

"Perhaps."

Arivana nodded as they marched through the entranceway of the royal library. Pillars of marble dotted the chamber, encompassed by gilded shelves filled with all manner of books and scrolls. Silk ribbons twirled around the top of the posts, coded by color to indicate the category of the works held below. Sunlight streamed through stained-glass windows on every side, warming her skin, augmented by rings of light-globes placed to illuminate every nook and cranny.

Arivana inhaled, expecting the must-dust aroma of old books. She smelled nothing of the sort. The place seemed almost too clean for its own good.

"Your majesty!"

Arivana nearly jumped out of her skin. A woman stood at her side, and she hadn't even heard her approach. The thick, golden carpet must have absorbed all the noise. Other than the sound of her own, newly frantic breathing, the place seemed as quiet as a tomb.

"Yes, what is it?" Arivana said at last.

"I'm just surprised—and delighted, of course—to have you in my library," the woman said, tucking stray strands of brown hair behind her ears. "It's been so long since a member of the royal family came to visit."

"You are the head librarian, then?"

"Well, being the only one, I suppose I *am* the head librarian after all. Imagine that."

Arivana studied the woman's features but couldn't quite place her family. "Which house are you from?"

"House? No house for me, I'm afraid. I only got this job because my father owed someone important a favor. But enough of me prattling on, your majesty. I can't imagine you'd be interested in hearing about my dull little life. I suppose you'll be wanting a tour?"

Arivana shook her head. "No, thank you. Just point us to a quiet spot to lounge, please."

"Oh! You came to read."

"Yes."

The librarian listed the various locations with couches and chairs and explained the color coding.

Arivana walked away from the woman, perplexed by her own thoughts.

"Something the matter?" Flumere asked, as they maneuvered between the bookcases.

"I'm not sure. She said I wouldn't be interested in her life, and . . . I'm afraid she's right."

"How so?"

"She's only a normal person. No one of any particular importance. No one with *influence*. Just like those boys that Tior keeps dangling in front of me. I've never taken an interest in the lives of the people I supposedly rule. I don't really know the first thing about them."

"Perhaps we ought to change that, then."

"How?"

"I don't know. Maybe we could take a trip through the city?"

Arivana rolled her eyes. "Right."

Flumere only stared at her.

"Wait, you're serious?"

"Why not? We could wear disguises to hide who we are and wander wherever our fancy takes us. Might be a good way to better understand the day-to-day affairs of your nation's citizens."

"But how would we even make it clear of the tower without being noticed?"

"Oh, leave that to me. I've gotten to know a few people here. Shouldn't be too hard getting some of them to help a poor maid escape from the greedy clutches of her lady's lecherous husband."

Arivana furrowed her brow for a moment before perking back up. "You mean me!"

Flumere smiled deviously.

Arivana chuckled, rolling the idea around in her mind. "I don't know. It might be dangerous."

"But educational, I think."

Arivana shrugged.

They rounded another bookcase and found themselves between a pair of curving couches resting in a patch of sunlight.

"I'll check to make sure we're alone," Flumere said.

Arivana nodded as the handmaiden made a circuitous route around the pillars surrounding them, ostensibly searching for a book. Arivana stepped up to the nearest shelf of the right color and began perusing the titles in truth. It took her a mark before she found a likely candidate. She pulled the book and settled down on a couch about the same time Flumere returned from her scouting.

"All clear."

"Good. Now, please tell me what you've learned from the queries I asked you to put out."

"For the first, I'm afraid there's nothing much to tell. I spoke to at least a dozen tower servants, many of whom have been around long enough to remember wiping your mother's bottom as a babe."

"And?"

"Nothing. Your mother and Claris had plenty of spats over the years, as even the best of friends often do, but nothing so drastic as to cause a permanent rift between them. As far as anyone can say, the previous queen left this world on good terms with your adoptive aunt."

Arivana shuddered, fighting back the tears. "I feared as much. Then it truly was something *I* did that set her off."

"Now, Arivana, we don't know that for sure."

"What else could it be?"

Flumere turned down her eyes.

"None of that," Arivana said. "I need you to be completely truthful with me."

The handmaiden twisted her lips. "It's not that. Honest. It's just, like I told you before, I'm not that clever. I wish I had an answer for you, but I'm afraid you'll have to figure it out on your own."

Arivana sighed. "Very well. What about the second question?"

"As for that, I was able to get an answer, but don't think it's a good idea . . ."

"Just tell me. Please."

Flumere hesitated. "I know where Claris is being held."

Arivana felt a tingle of excitement sprout up and down her limbs. She almost shot to her feet. "Well, what are we waiting for? Let's go ask *her* what this is all about."

"It's impossible. Just learning the location of her cell cost me all the goodwill I'd built up with the wardens. They're staunchly loyal to protocol and won't let anyone in without proper authorization."

"Even me?"

"*Especially* you. Minister Pashams gave them strict orders to keep you out. For your own good, he told them."

"What about sneaking in?"

"Getting you out of the tower unseen is one thing. Getting down there?" Flumere shook her head. "Even if I could, I'm not sure I'd want to."

Arivana frowned at her. "It can't be as bad as all that."

"I could practically smell the despair in the air, and I didn't even come within a hundred paces of the outer door. That . . . pit . . . it is an evil place. You would not leave it the same person you were going in."

A chill drove up her limbs. She hadn't even considered that. She'd heard only the vaguest rumors about the deep dungeons, mostly stories by her siblings meant to scare her. She wasn't ready to face the horror of such a reality.

And yet I sent a woman there to spend the rest of her life, a fate that might very well be worse than death. What kind of monster am I?

"What's that you're reading?" Flumere asked.

Arivana shook herself, peering down at the book in her lap. "What, this? I suppose you could say it's the next phase of our little intelligence-gathering plan. Did you not wonder why I wanted us to meet in the library?"

"Very clever. But that still doesn't answer my question."

She held up the book so her handmaiden could read the title. *Statutes Regarding the Power and Limitations of*

House Celandaris, Vol. I. "We're doing some research. Grab a book that you think might divulge what the law says I can and cannot do. Let's see if we can find us a way to make my council do what *I* want for a change."

Flumere rose. "As you wish."

"Oh, and Flumere?"

"Yes?"

"Regarding your offer to take me on an unrestricted tour of my city: I accept."

The woman patted her shoulder as she passed on the way to the nearest bookcase. "It will be an experience to remember, Arivana. I guarantee it."

Tassariel slung her travel pack over her shoulders and pulled the straps tight. It rested comfortably over her plain grey cloak, which dangled nearly to her toes. It seemed sad, somehow, that everything she needed for the foreseeable future could be held in so small a satchel.

"Are you at least going to tell me where I'm—where *we're* headed?" she asked.

"Patience, my dear," Elos said. "Good things come to those who wait. Or some nonsense like that. You know what I mean?"

"No. I don't."

"Just as well. I'm not exactly clear on it either."

She took a deep breath, gritting her teeth. *This is your god, Tassariel, even if he's the furthest thing from what you expected. Keep a firm grasp on your temper.*

"Very well. I'm to go to the docks and book passage to the mainland, correct?"

"Correct. Have you brought everything I instructed?"

"Weren't you paying attention while I was getting ready?"

"Not a bit."

She sighed. "Yes, I have it all. Coin, a jewelry case, my best robes, and a bag full of cosmetics. Why is all this necessary again?"

"You obviously haven't spent much time among humans."

"No."

"Appearances are everything, Tassariel. Nowhere is this more true than among the people we're headed towards."

"Stringing me along with cryptic clues, are we now?"

"Maybe?"

"I've already agreed to obey your will, my lord. I don't know why you can't . . ." She shook her head. "Never mind."

She took one last look around her dwelling. Everything seemed in order. She briefly wondered if this would be the last time she saw the place but realized she didn't actually care. It had seemed a cage for most of the last century. She should be ecstatic to leave it behind.

Then why aren't I?

And yet she trudged out her front door without another moment's debate.

Walking down the path, Tassariel took in all the

sights of Halumyr Domicile, making a point to capture the images in frozen slices of memory. The dwellings, the gardens and parks, the library, the shops, the learning centers for each calling, a hundred other places she'd visited countless times over the span of her life. She knew not when she would return and wanted to be able to recall it all with clarity. Despite her long desire to leave it behind, this place would always be her home.

All too soon, she reached the edge of the floating island. She peeked down over the ornate silverstone railing. The Phelupar Islands lay in the shadows of both their own peaks and the greatvines that connected them each to the valynkar city. The seas between them shimmered like a sheet of scattered rubies under the setting sun.

Tassariel marched along the rim, destined for a place she'd never had reason to visit before. Five marks later, she reached it.

Eluhar waited there for her.

Though his face glowed at her approach, as it usually did, his body seemed unusually rigid. The smile he gave her was tight.

"Thought you could leave without saying goodbye?" he asked.

Though he meant it in jest, something seemed off. Perhaps it was the strained timbre of his voice as he said it. Perhaps it was how humorless they both knew the words to be.

"How did you know I'd be here?" she asked.

Eluhar looked away sheepishly. "I've been . . . keeping an eye on you. To make sure you were all right. Everyone was worried about you."

"Everyone? You and my cynical uncle are the only two people who even know I exist!"

"That's not—!"

"Don't lie to me, Eluhar. Name another person who actually voiced a concern to you on my behalf."

He hung his head, scuffing his sandaled foot across the ground for several beats. "Fine. It was just me. It's *always* been just me. Can't you see that?"

"See what?"

He filled his lungs, holding the air until his face turned red. Then, all at once, he spurted out, "Don't you know that I love you, and we're meant to be together forever?"

Tassariel stepped back, quivering in rage.

"Go easy on the boy," Elos said. "At least he means well."

"Shut! Up!"

Eluhar blinked rapidly, cowering beneath the force of her scream, and she realized that it was meant for both him and Elos.

"Did you not stop to think for one moment about what I wanted? About my desires and dreams? Or does none of that matter to you at all?"

"I—"

"No. You didn't. You wanted what you wanted, and abyss take all else."

A pair of tears streaked down either cheek. He

bounded forward, closing the distance between them in a heartbeat and grabbing her wrists. "It's not like that, Tass. Please. After all I've done for you, why won't you listen to me!"

Have to get away. Have to get away. Have to get away. . .

On instinct, she twisted her arms around, wrenching free of his grip, and shoved him with both palms. He staggered back, wincing.

Tassariel pivoted. Lunged away. Stepped off the edge. Flexed the hidden muscles in her back.

Nothing happened.

A strange sensation took over her body. It took her a moment to realize what it was.

Falling.

"Now you've gone and done it, girl."

A moment of panic set in. It stretched to eternity.

Something latched onto her pack and began to pull, halting her unobstructed descent. Slowly, painfully, the force wrenched her backwards onto solid ground.

Her frantic heart beat in time to ragged breathing that was not her own. She rolled over. Eluhar lay next to her, face red with exertion as his chest heaved up and down.

Tassariel jumped up. She methodically brushed the dirt from her cloak. "I thank you for saving me, Eluhar. But this changes nothing between us. I cannot stay here."

Before he could answer—she didn't have the heart to hear it—she spun away and stepped onto a platform attached to the lip of the domicile. A single lever sprouted from a pedestal at waist height. She moved it from UP to DOWN. The lift, meant for flightless humans, began its descent.

Like a feather, she fell away from the only life she had ever known, unfamiliar moisture drenching her cheeks and jaw.

CHAPTER 10

Mother Poya had lied about the wind. It didn't blow like a thousand wolves all howling at once.

It felt more like a million.

Which made Mevon conflicted about the giant crevasses.

"You doing all right down there?" Draevenus called.

Mevon craned his neck to see the assassin perched on the top of the ridge, holding his cloak closed against the cold, biting wind. Down where he climbed, Mevon didn't even feel a breeze. "Just fine, thanks," he said, pulling himself up another few arm lengths on the knotted rope. "Not all of us can cross thirty-pace gaps as if they were a single step."

He thought Draevenus might have laughed at that, but the sound was lost as an abrasive flurry swirled snow up into the mierothi's face.

Mevon chuckled, yanking himself higher as he

stepped up the vertical surface of the crevasse wall. This was the sixth time today. Though he'd had little trouble with the climbing itself, they'd been forced to stop every other one so he could get some food in his body. Their progress had ground to a crawl.

At last, he reached the top and tumbled over the edge onto flat, frozen ground. The wind returned with all the fury he'd been dreading. He sprang up and shivered inside his bearskin coat.

"Care for a bit of warmth before we continue?" Draevenus asked.

Mevon spied the blue flame hovering above the mierothi's palm. He crowded in without a word, reaching out to collect some of the heat with his hands.

"Not too—"

Mevon's fingertip dipped into the dancing flame . . . just before it winked out.

"—close." Draevenus sighed. "I suppose I can make another one?"

"Don't bother," Mevon said. He reached down and grasped the straps of the pack, flinging them over his shoulders. "Let's keep moving. That will warm me up just fine."

Draevenus pulled up the rope, wrapped it around his shoulders, and began marching.

The flat expanse stretched out before them, a seemingly endless white blanket whose edges disappeared in spirals of dancing snow. The Shelf lay somewhere on their right, and to the left, a series of jagged ice cliffs soared towards the very summits of the Andean Mountains, so frail-looking that a single shout would likely send them tumbling down to crush them. They stayed between the two extremes, where, unfortunately, the worst of the crevasses split the land open.

The cloud cover broke. Mevon looked skyward. The sun offered no warmth but far too much light. And it looked like it would last awhile this time. He felt a tingle as Draevenus waved a hand across his eyes. A spell of darkening, to protect from the insidious glare. Mevon, of course, could not be helped the same way.

He reached into a pouch on the side of his pack and withdrew a thin, white cloth. He wrapped it around his head, covering his eyes. The sunlight bouncing off every snowflake and patch of ice nearly blinded him already. Crude as it was, this was the only defense he had against it. He trod forward, guided by the tail of his companion's flapping cloak, just visible as a shadow ahead.

"So," Mevon said, "ready to turn back yet?"

"Just when we're beginning to have such a lovely time?" Draevenus replied.

"If this is your idea of lovely, I'd hate to see you on a dreary day."

"Of course it's lovely. Every step brings us closer to Ruul, after all. And I've got some words saved up for him that will bring all the warmth I need."

"Do you, now? What words might those be?"

"A most thorough scolding, I assure you." Draevenus chuckled. "But what's this nonsense about turning back? Surely the great Mevon Daere isn't thinking about quitting?"

"Quitting? Never. But right now, I think I'd prefer the company of Hakel and his cronies over this cold. And if that means I get to dish out a bit of justice at the same time, all the better!"

They both shared a good round of laughter at this. But the wind still whistled by, drowning out the sound and putting an end to the mirth. The effort of conversation warred with Mevon's dwindling energy reserves. Though they made better time than normal men, and the wind kept the snow from piling too high, the chill seemed a permanent occupant in his bones, making each step seem harder than the last.

At least out here there's no one to tempt my desire for blood. Indeed, they'd not even seen an insect in days, nor an animal in weeks. Of men, there was no sign. No one could call this place home. No one sane anyway.

They walked in silence for a time. A long time. Eventually, though, Mevon spoke.

"Draevenus?"

"Yes?"

"Back then, when I talked of meting out justice, I wanted you to know that I was only joking."

Draevenus paused, turning slowly. "As was I."

Mevon nodded. He could imagine the difficulty. He had no idea what he would say were he to meet a god he once had faith in and who he believed had betrayed him.

The assassin began trudging forward once more but stopped again almost immediately.

"What is it?" Mevon asked.

Draevenus gestured forward. Mevon lifted the cloth over his eyes.

Another crevasse cleaved through their path.

The mierothi lifted the rope from his shoulders and began tying it to the pack before Mevon had even finished dropping it. "Ready for another go?"

Mevon glanced down into the icy shadows. "At least I'll get a break from the wind."

Jasside yawned as the sun set over the fields. Four days, and she'd only slept once, and briefly at that. These people had needed her far too much to allow any further rest.

She shook her head to banish the exhaustion and focused once more on the task at hand. A clay jar sat on the table before her. She energized, cringing against the pain that came from excess use of sorcery before managing to ignore it. She arranged the elements of the fluid within the jar, forming another batch of her elixir.

A million refugees, and almost half were beset with ailments of some kind. Many were life-threatening. She didn't have enough days left in her life to heal them all individually, so she'd come up with this remedy, which could scour a body clean of most common illnesses.

Jasside slumped down into her chair, the transformation complete. A young girl in twin braids came and lifted the jug, grunting with the effort. "Thank you," Jasside said.

The girl flashed her a smile, then carried her burden over to a wagon filled with similar containers. She hefted the jar into the wagon then jumped up and sat on the back edge, feet dangling in the tall grasses. She slapped the sideboard. The wagon driver flipped his reins, kicking the mule team into motion.

Jasside watched through blurry eyes as the sixth such vehicle this day pulled away to deliver its goods to those in greatest need. She only hoped it would be enough.

It had better be. I have nothing left to give.

She glanced around at the cadre of volunteers who had come to her aid. Hundreds of men, women, and children, all bustling about with the tasks she'd given them. There was the old woman and her six grand-daughters, who had categorized the elixir distribution, the triplet boys, who'd taken to guarding her at all times, the young couple, who saw to the proper place-ment of the harvest constructs, the one-eyed matron, who'd organized round-the-clock patrols by enlisting idle hands, and many others, who aided in smaller but no less important ways.

She felt terrible that she hadn't had time to learn their names. The smiles on their faces, though, re-minded her why she was doing this. It felt right to be using her power for something wholly and undeniably good.

Jasside only regretted that her time was up—there was still so much work to be done here. So many ways in which she could help. But the fourth day was nearly over, and she had promised Vashodia that she would rejoin the caravan. Something told her that disobedience now would put a permanent end to her apprenticeship. And she doubted any of Vashodia's previous pupils ever got out of such a show of defiance alive.

She stood, stretching and yawning once more. A quick glance around told her that no eyes were focused on her at the moment. She used the opportunity to slip away quietly, knowing better than to make a show of her departure. The praise and veneration they'd heaped upon her as she began her "miracles" were already more than she could bear. If she let them give her the send-off they wanted, she wouldn't be able to leave before morning. If ever.

Jasside threaded her way between a pair of tents into a small copse of trees. From there, she came clear out the far side, peering at the road heading north out of the valley. A smudge on the otherwise-unbroken path indicated the presence of the caravan, nearly cresting the gap to the lands beyond. She took one last look over the fields filled with workers harvesting the newly sprouted crops.

I've done the best I can for these people. Now, let's see what we can do for the rest.

Smiling with a sudden surge of elation, Jasside energized, then shadow-dashed forward. Four quick leaps bridged the gap between her and the caravan. She landed, breathless, just outside the ring of daeloth. None was startled. They had been expecting her, it seemed.

She strode towards Vashodia's house on wheels. Curiously, she didn't see any Sceptrine soldiers about, and the prince was now astride a horse. She marched up to him.

"Are your men hiding in the woods again?" she asked.

He twitched at her voice, from surprise no doubt. Unlike the darkwatch, he'd not yet become used to people showing up out of nowhere. "No, my lady," he replied. "Every man of mine is still needed here. I venture forth in your company alone."

"Alone? Isn't that a little risky for a prince?"

He shook his head. "I've seen what your kind can do. The power you wield. If you meant ill, having more men around would only mean they died along with me. That, at least, is one risk I don't have to take."

"And that," she replied, "is a decision I can respect. Please know, however, that I intend you no harm."

"I believe you. But we both know, it's not *you* we need to worry about."

Jasside eyed the wagon. "Is she inside?"

He nodded.

"I'll do my best to discern her intentions. I'll let you know if I have any—"

"Luck? Yes. You'll definitely need that."

Jasside shot him a crooked smile, then pulled open the door.

By noon, Arivana's neck hurt from gazing upwards. The towers of her city seemed so different from street level, now that she was actually in a mood to study them. Each one held a personality all its own, a little piece of its owners making its way into the construction of the buildings that, from here, seemed to scrape the sky.

The one on her right was built from some greenish stone, with arched windows at regular intervals and over a dozen discrete peaks pointing into the clouds like emerald spears. The tower on her right was bulbous, topped by a brass dome, with vines hanging like teardrops from enormous, circular windows. Ahead, the building was square and made of grey stone, but it more than made up for this supposed plainness by draping itself in glittering strands of glass every shade of the rainbow that bathed the street below in a wash of dancing color.

"Stop gawking," Flumere said for at least the tenth time that morning. "You look out of place enough as it is."

Arivana pulled the cotton shawl tighter around her shoulders. It, and the dress beneath, were as plain as the tower before her but intensely comfortable. *High fashion could learn a thing or two from my maid's wardrobe.* The disguise proved useful in getting them out of the palace. No one had looked at her twice.

"I don't know what you're talking about," Arivana said. "I thought you said I fit right in?"

"Your clothes, maybe. But you still carry yourself like a queen."

With a sigh, Arivana slumped her shoulders and

brought her eyes to stare at the ground a few paces in front of her. "Why must commoners walk like this? It's as if they're afraid to let anyone know what they're interested in. What things their eyes are drawn to."

"Not everyone must do so, Arivana. Just those who are trying to remain unnoticed."

"I see your point. Dejected it is."

Flumere sighed. "Besides, it's not the architecture we're here to see, is it?"

"No." Arivana said, darting a glance at the people on the street around them. "But I'm not sure what I *am* supposed to be looking for."

"Nothing in particular. You need only to watch the people of your city. Get a feel for their lives. Just . . . observe."

"How can I do that with my chin in the ground?"

"Use your peripheral vision."

"Peripheral?"

"It's how the rest of us tend to view the world. The perspective might do you some good."

And so, for the next few tolls, they simply walked the streets. And Arivana was given the chance to observe her people, unfettered by the bonds of privilege or position, from the corner of her eye for the very first time. She couldn't help but smile at the purpose evident in every motion as they partook of their daily routines.

But when Flumere led her down a street leading away from the city center, away from even the most fringe of the hundred towers, the smile slowly vanished.

The change came gradually, but potently. The pristine cobbles faded to dirt. Pungent odors drifted from refuse piled in corners. The clothes on every back lost all color but dust. The tallest building didn't climb past four or five stories, and those that dared seemed brittle, ready to topple before a stiff wind. Faces once painted with joviality were now painted with desperation. And the city guard, patrolling down the center of the lane, commanded the same wide berth as before, but out of fear instead of respect.

"What have you brought me to, Flumere?"

"Truth, Arivana. Were you not ready to see it?"

"Not like this. I thought . . ."

"What? That everyone was happy?"

"I don't know. I . . . don't know."

They shuffled to the edge of the road as the patrol made its way past them. A surge of dread swept over Arivana. She had no protection here. No authority. Declaring herself the queen would likely garner laughter from people who had never seen her face before. If they got into any trouble, they'd be on their own.

"Let's get out of here," Arivana said. "I don't feel safe anymore."

"Are you sure?"

"Yes." She pulled on her handmaiden's sleeve. "Please."

"All right. Let's just—"

"Get him!"

They both jerked their heads towards the voice barking out angrily. A man darted through the crowd with frantic eyes. He didn't make it far. Three city guards grabbed hold of him and dragged him back to their commander, the man who had first yelled for his capture.

"Well, now," the commander said to the captive, "if it isn't old Jarrick Wanes. Fancy meeting you here. Word is, you've been late with your payments again. Isn't that right, corporal?"

"Right as rain, sir," another guard said.

"I'll get the money," Jarrick said. "Just give me more time."

The commander laughed.

A woman threw herself against the commander, dropping to her knees. "Please, our children are starving." She waved to three bedraggled youths behind her. "Can't you have mercy, at least for their sake?"

"Corporal?"

"Yes, sir?"

"In your most honest opinion—"

"I'm as honest as they come, sir."

"Of course you are. In your opinion, do these here people meet the requirements laid out in statute eighty-seven of the Citizens' Refinement Act?"

The corporal gave the man and woman a quick glance. "After careful review, I can say without a hint of uncertainty that they fail to meet those requirements, sir."

"And what is the punishment for that failure?"

"Immediate seizure of all assets, sir."

The commander grinned. "Best get to it, then."

The rest of the guardsmen snatched up the woman—obviously Jarrick's wife—and their children, placing them all roughly into metal bindings. They marched off amidst Jarrick's cries of vengeance and his wife's pleading wails. The children wept.

Everyone else on the street turned back to their business, emitting a collective sigh of relief. Arivana instinctively understood the gesture.

They aren't relieved justice has been done. No—they are all just glad it hadn't been them.

Tassariel moaned as the ship rocked upon another swell. She was sure this would be the one that capsized the rickety wooden vessel. She clutched the edge of the bucket with damp fingers, averting her eyes from the stomach ejections already sloshing around inside.

For some reason, Elos chose this, of all moments, to surge forward into her mind.

"Something the matter, my dear?"

Fighting the rumble in her esophagus, Tassariel muttered, "The sea was much nicer from *above* the clouds. There, at least, it didn't try to kill you."

"Kill you?" The icy presence surged out and back in, as if testing the waters of sensation. **"Nonsense. This is barely even a storm."**

"How comforting."

"Is that sarcasm I hear? How dare you! Such behavior is most unbecoming the holy vessel of Elos!"

She stiffened, her sickness forgotten as a wave of

shame swept over her, more violently than the very *real* waves crashing into the ship's deck. "Apologies, my lord. I didn't mean any disrespect."

"Oh, come on. You had to know that was a joke."

The shame turned to fury in an instant. She pressed her lips tightly together, then took a deep breath before answering. "Sorry. I'm not in a joking mood."

"It's a flaw of yours, I'm sure. Too much seriousness is bad for one's health, you know. Didn't anyone tell you?"

"No valynkar would, that's for sure."

"That flaw is systemic, I'm afraid, despite my most persistent efforts to prevent it. Alas. All children outgrow their parents. I suppose it was only inevitable you people would end up as aloof miscreants."

"Miscreants! I wouldn't—" Further words were forgotten as the ship lurched again. Tassariel lost her tenuous hold on the remainder of her stomach contents.

After a mark had passed, and no further expulsions seemed forthcoming, she rolled onto her back. The cot beneath her dug its fists into her spine, but she was too exhausted to care anymore. The bare walls of her cabin, lit only by a single wick lantern swinging wildly with every wave, closed around her, spinning. She shut her eyes, but it did little to stave off the dizziness.

Three days under sail. Halfway or better, the captain says. I'm not sure I could take much more of this.

The cramped confines only worsened her feelings of bondage and imprisonment. Ever since Elos had taken refuge inside her, it seemed she'd not made a single decision for herself. Try as she might to be obedient to her god, the constriction on choice would soon drive her mad.

"So," she said to the empty room, "you're not happy with the direction my people have taken."

"Hardly."

"There's something, at least, we can agree on."

"Why do you think I chose you?"

"Wait, you *chose* me? I thought it was only because Gilshamed tampered with the ritual that you were able to come to me the way you did."

"Well, I chose him, too, but his was a much smaller part to play. You know, despite your difference of opinion on most matters, the two of you actually have a lot in common."

"Is that so."

"That didn't sound like a question."

"It wasn't."

"I see. Good to know my inflection receptors are still in working order. But aren't you curious as to how you and your uncle are similar?"

"I don't see how you could think that. I can't imagine two valynkar more different than he and I."

"Oh, there you go again. Focusing on all the wrong things. Surface things. Deep down, where it matters, you both desperately want to make the world a better place."

Tassariel popped her eyes open. She pondered the statement and found that she could not disagree. "All right, then. Supposing that's true, wouldn't it be in your best interest to tell me all of your plan, so I can prepare well in advance of any obstacles that present themselves?"

The icy presence throbbed within her. The lantern above her swayed a full cycle every two beats. She counted forty-three swings before Elos answered.

"I see things . . . differently. You know how small the waves below you seemed from up in your domicile? Well, I'm as high above your city as your city is above the world's surface, and then higher still. I see farther, deeper, more thoroughly than you can even imagine. I say this not to boast but to inform. I observe, categorize, evaluate patterns, calculate odds, then extrapolate likely conclusions. I cannot see the future, as I have told you, but I *must* act as if I actually can. To do otherwise would be to give in to despair."

Tassariel swallowed the growing lump in her throat. "I understand, my lord."

"I don't think you do."

"Perhaps not fully, but I'm beginning to. All I ask, going forward, is that you don't blame me for my inquisitiveness. I only seek to extract some measure of control over my own fate, however slight it might be."

"Fair enough. But I must ask something of you in return."

"What's that?"

"Do not think me cruel for withholding information. If you couldn't already tell, there's more at stake here than you can be allowed to know. Please understand that all I do, I do with that in mind. Sometimes, the greater good leaves no room for small kindnesses."

Tassariel nodded. She took the words of her god and wrapped them around her soul, making of them a lifeline she could cling to when all else seemed bleak.

She had a feeling that she would be needing it often.

CHAPTER 11

The blizzard raged into its third day, with no end in sight. Draevenus struggled forward through the snow, which rose to his knees in the easy places. He had cast a spell about himself to ward off the worst of the cold and the wind, but he could feel the effects starting to wane. He hesitated to renew it. The chill in his bones warned him that the environment was worse than what he felt. Far worse. And any energy expended on sorcery was energy he didn't have to keep his feet moving forward.

I am not going to let a little weather defeat me.

Draevenus remembered Zorvanya's gift at last. He reached into a pocket for some of the winterweal, threw a handful into his mouth, and began chewing. The effect was immediate. It didn't eliminate any of the cold's bite, but it did at least take the edge off.

Forgiving her in his mind—a little bit anyway—he trudged onwards.

After another mark, or another toll—it was difficult to tell—he heard a sound behind him that made him stop and turn. His own tracks had already disappeared not two paces away, scoured clean by the icy tempest.

Also missing was his companion.

The noise sounded a bit like a voice, but he didn't quite trust it. With nothing but wind to fill his ears these last few days, he'd begun to have auditory hallucinations, phantom sounds so real they nearly drove him mad.

The noise came again, clearer this time. A deep voice, faint and stuttering, calling out. Draevenus dashed back along his erased trail.

A few moments later, he came upon Mevon, barely staggering forward. The man's bearskin coat seemed a single cloak of frost. Draevenus soured inside as he realized he hadn't been keeping close to his companion.

"H-have t-t-to stop," Mevon said.

If Draevenus's own weariness was any indication, Mevon had to be in terrible condition. He was pretty sure those Hardohl blessings would heal frostbite but would drain the man's stamina to do so. Mevon's sunken, frost-rimed cheeks spoke volumes about his state. The man barely hung on.

We need shelter.

He immediately energized and began crafting a sorcerous dome around them to block off the wind.

"Hold still," he said. "I've got to make sure nothing touches you."

Shaking, Mevon nodded.

Around them he pulled at the surrounding snow, piling it upon the dome, layer by layer, until it formed a solid barrier of ice a hand thick.

Mevon slumped to a knee.

Draevenus resisted the urge to rush forward. Contacting a void right now would sap all his energy, sorcerous and otherwise, making his efforts meaningless. "Lie down, Mevon. Take off your pack. Can you manage that on your own?"

Though he moved with all the dexterity of a man on his deathbed, his companion complied. Draevenus cut a few holes around the outside of the shelter, to ensure they didn't suffocate, and conjured a dozen flaming orbs, placing them carefully in an oval around Mevon's sprawling form. The effort taxed him. Darkness shimmered at the edges of his vision.

Shaking away his exhaustion, Draevenus circled Mevon and pulled two logs from the man's pack. They were frozen solid. He risked another spell to thaw them, tottering against a wave of dizziness as he did so. Next came the hatchet. Aching fingers made the work longer than necessary, but he eventually turned one log into kindling and the other into four arm-thick wedges of wood.

He knelt, clearing a patch of ground in the snow, and arranged the sticks into a cone. With a weak gesture, he pulled the flaming orbs on the near side of

Mevon's body and arrayed them beneath the kindling. Draevenus sighed in relief as they caught fire.

Once the flame crackled steadily, he pushed a larger piece into it, then slumped onto his back, chest heaving with labored breaths. He peered sideways. Mevon, rolled onto his side and shivering, fought to keep his eyes even halfway open as they gazed into the flames. Draevenus snagged a bear steak from his own, smaller pack, skewered it on a dagger, then propped it up over the fire. The dome, warming comfortably now, soon filled with the aroma of sizzling meat.

"Sorry," Mevon said after a time. "I never meant to be a burden to you."

"Nothing to be sorry about," Draevenus said. "If anything, it should be me apologizing to you. I nearly left you behind, after all."

"I *fell* behind. I should have been able to keep up."

"Nonsense. I've got an unfair advantage in that I can shield myself from the worst of the elements. You're pretty good at absorbing damage, but even those blessings of yours have their limits."

"So I am discovering."

Draevenus smiled, relieved that Mevon seemed to have at least a small measure of his humor left to him. It was a good sign. He flipped the steak over, juices spattering on the coals.

Later, after they'd both filled their bellies with warm food and arranged their bedrolls comfortably, they leaned back on their elbows across the dwindling fire from each other. Draevenus felt rejuvenated, and

Mevon appeared to have recovered from the effects of his exposure. As best as he could tell, it was still early afternoon. They had plenty of time to kill.

"So," Draevenus said, "what does the great Mevon Daere actually do in his spare time?"

Mevon rubbed his chin, eye glazed in thought. "That's a good question."

"What, no hobbies? No pastimes? Not *every* toll has to be about the mission, you know."

Mevon raised an eyebrow.

"It's true," Draevenus continued. Then, he realized something about his companion that had never occurred to him before. "That's why you came with me, wasn't it? You saw an end to your purpose, the life ahead full of uncertainty and doubtful meaning and far too much free time. You feared that more than death."

"Yes."

"Life isn't always about purpose, though. About achieving some goal."

"Then what *is* it about?"

"Mevon, if you can answer that, you'll be the wisest man who ever lived."

The former Hardohl managed a tight smile at that. "What about you? You've walked upon this world for twenty lifetimes or more. Surely you've picked up a useless skill or two along the way?"

"Hundreds, probably."

"Probably?"

Draevenus shrugged. "Only the most important events seem to keep inside my memory, in the place where I can recall them at will. The rest is just . . . mist." He chuckled. "I think I tried my hand at wood-carving once, though."

"How did that turn out?"

"I don't remember."

"Hmm. Must not have gone well at all."

"Probably."

"What *did* keep, then?"

"What do you think?" Draevenus sighed, sagging onto his bedroll. "Killing."

Mevon, thankfully, merely nodded.

Draevenus closed his eyes. *Who am I to think I can judge a god for all the things he has done? I, who have so much blood on my hands. More, possibly, than any other living soul.*

The wind howled around the outside of their shelter, but Draevenus found no answer in the cold, uncaring storm.

All it held was fury.

In that, he found something in common with it.

"This," Jasside said with an eyebrow raised, "is your capital?"

Prince Daye Harkun shrugged. "More or less."

Though more sizable than any of the towns they'd passed on the way, Taosin was barely large enough to be a city. Most of it would fit inside a single district of Mecrithos. Half the buildings were burnt-out, and the other half appeared to be built from the ashen bones of the first. The air, as they rolled down the muddy path that passed for a street, reeked of sweat and char. Refuse clogged the runoff channels. For every person going about on normal affairs, three or four faces were crammed into alleys and stairs.

"What happened here?" she asked. "I thought all the refugees were back in the valley?"

"All? No. Those were just the ones longest separated from their homes. These here are mostly fresh. It takes time to find a more permanent solution."

"What about the buildings? It looks like you were attacked."

"We were."

"Care to elaborate?"

He sighed, clearly not wishing to revisit the tale he was to tell. Jasside didn't rescind the query, though. She needed to know.

"For it to make sense," he said at last, "I think it best to start from the beginning."

Jasside nodded, gesturing for him to continue.

"Almost a year and half ago, the nations gathered in response to—" He furrowed his brow, then turned his head to glance back at Vashodia, who rode on the wagon, behind them. He grunted. "Can't believe I didn't see it before."

What happened a year and a half ago? Then, she remembered. *The Shroud. Of course. The whole world must have felt its collapse.*

Their eyes locked, and somehow, the awareness of each other's knowledge passed between them. The prince broke his gaze away first. She could almost swear he blushed. "Yes, anyway," he said finally. "Representatives had met to discuss the event when the Panisian royal family was assassinated. Witnesses claimed it was soldiers from our nation that did the deed."

"And was it?"

"We don't know. Our king and all of our princes barely escaped the summit with their lives, but no sooner had they returned to San Khet—that was our previous capital—when a southern assault force laid waste to the city."

"How did you escape?"

Daye shook his head. "I wasn't in that city."

"I thought you said all the princes were there?"

"Yes."

"Then . . . ?"

He ran a hand through his hair. "In Sceptre, we choose our leaders based on character, competency. On courage. Not because someone was lucky enough to be born to the right parents. My brother and I were being groomed for princedom. Once all the others died, we took it upon ourselves to step up into that role."

"I see. But that doesn't explain the devastation here in Taosin."

The prince looked away. "Some other time, perhaps. We're almost there."

Jasside peered forward. Straight ahead, the road split around the front structure made of wood and steel, larger and better kept than the rest. Spearmen stood guard at the entrance, and bowmen walked the parapets, lighting torches to ward against the coming of night. A banner above, adorned by a bear backed by brown-and-grey stripes, flapped in the breeze.

As they approached, the two guards flanking the gate stiffened, then bowed. Daye dipped his head towards them. They straightened, eyes narrowing on the prince.

"Is my brother in?"

"Yes," said the one on the right, in a gruff voice. "He's where he should be. My lord."

Jasside caught the subtle interplay, the slight hesitation before the honorific, the tightening of Daye's jaw. They perceived a man not doing his duty and challenged him without breaching courtesy. The prince did not dress them down for it. *Interesting people, these Sceptrines.*

"Foreign guests," the prince muttered, gesturing to Jasside. "*Powerful* guests. They needed personal attention."

The two guards eyed her for a moment, but their gazes soon drifted past, gaping for a beat, then narrowing. Angled downward. She didn't need to look to know that Vashodia approached from behind. Probably had her head exposed, too.

The soldiers waved them in without further protest.

As a trio, they marched through the gate into a shallow courtyard, tiered with spiked barricades manned by fierce and alert-looking soldiers, ready to repel anything short of a full-scale invasion. Daye returned bows with another pair of soldiers, but the exchange stayed brief, wordless, as the men pulled open the steel doors.

They stepped into a hallway lined by torches. The sudden narrowness caused Jasside to bump shoulders with the prince. She gasped as she felt her power momentarily sapped.

And, perhaps, for other reasons.

"Sorry!"

"Sorry!"

He smiled at her. "Best if we go single file, I think."

Jasside nodded, catching her breath. "Lead the way."

As she settled in step behind him, she wondered at her reaction. True, it was always surprising, and a little unpleasant, having her power taken away so casually, but she had felt little fear. She'd gotten to know the prince during their journey and had learned enough about him to know he wasn't the type to take advantage. She thought she might have actually begun to trust him.

It was good to know that trustworthy men still existed in the world.

After a few twists and turns and staircases—more defensive measures, no doubt—they emerged into a squarish room with arched support beams soaring towards the peaked ceiling. A single table rested at the far end, ringed by a dozen men on stools. Several were speaking at once—loud, but not exactly argumentative. A figure in the center of them rose, holding out his hands. All talking ceased immediately.

The man who had stood locked his eyes on Daye.

"Chase," Daye said. "Brother. I come on important business."

Chase looked to each man around him in turn. "We'll reconvene tomorrow, gentlemen." They left, not ungratefully, bowing and muttering, "Prince Chase," as they stood and walked out a side door. The looks they gave Daye were not nearly as respectful.

Chase came slowly across the room. It was a strange walk, soft and precise, like a cat's. A slim sword rested on the man's left hip, one hand weighed on the plain, sturdy hilt. The prince was much the same as the blade. His resemblance to Daye was obvious, but Chase was shorter, and his eyes glowed with intelligence, seeing and calculating everything in the brief glances he gave to the three of them.

With only a few paces left between them, Chase paused, narrowing his gaze on Daye.

The two brothers each pounced forward.

They embraced, laughing and slapping each other's backs. Tension visibly receded from them both as each sought to outdo the other with the strength of his squeeze.

"Oh, it's good to see you, Daye," Chase said. "It's been too long."

"We've been apart for longer," Daye said.

"Never by choice." Chase pulled back, grinning. "How are things going with the refugees?"

"Better, now that they're here."

Chase followed his brother's gaze to Jasside and

Vashodia. "Well met. I am Prince Chase Harkun of Sceptre."

"Jasside Anglasco," she said. "I have no official title, but I'm here on behalf of the newly founded nation of mierothi. This"—she gestured to her mistress—"is our de facto leader, Vashodia."

"Whether they like it or not, huh?" Chase said. "I'm sure there's a story behind why they let a child lead them."

"They're all too afraid to stand up to me," Vashodia said. "If anyone actually had the balls to do so, I'd gladly hand over the reins, so to speak. Oh, and I'm actually almost two thousand years old. But letting people perceive me as a little girl has led to so many wonderful occasions of underestimation. Care to join the club?"

Daye leaned in close to his brother. "They're from the Veiled Empire."

Chase glowered instantly. "It always comes back to that, doesn't it? I'd gladly let the abyss take me if I never hear that name again."

"Prince Daye told me of your troubles," Jasside said. "I wish we could claim innocence, but I'm afraid that's not possible."

"How do you mean?"

Vashodia smiled. "That little disturbance that drew all the rulers of the world together? My doing. The Shroud was an . . . inconvenience. I got rid of it."

Both princes' eyes flared at this.

"But enough gibbering." Vashodia glared at Daye.

"You promised to bring me to your leader. I expected a king."

"We've no king at the moment. Chase refuses to take the title though he holds more respect than the past ten monarchs combined."

Chase punched his brother in the shoulder. "They revere me because they're desperate. Not because I actually deserve it. Once this crisis is over, Sceptre will be able to think clearly again. They'll find a king worthy of the position."

"You say that like victory is certain."

"We will never give in. *Never.* That is victory enough to give the people reason to go on, to keep fighting. We may be outmatched in numbers, in quality of weapons, and in the sorcerous arts, but we will never be outdone in spirit."

"That's all very inspiring, I'm sure," Vashodia said. "I suppose you'll have to do, then. Tell me, Prince Chase, why is it that you are losing this war?"

"Did you not hear what I just—?"

"Oh, I heard you all right. I heard a pretty speech that might light a fire in the soul of the insipid masses. But I am not so easily swayed. Tell me why you're losing and how you plan to win. Make me believe if you can."

"Why should I?"

Vashodia only smiled. Jasside shivered at the sight of those pointed teeth.

Chase turned, showing them his back. He walked

away, his previous grace lost in the slump of his shoulders. He leaned over the table. Jasside thought she might have even heard a sob.

"Get them out of here," Chase said, voice quivering.

"Brother, pl—"

"Now!"

Daye sighed. He turned to the two women. "Come on. I'll find you some rooms."

The doors swung open before them, and they took a single step inside. They stopped before being able to

"**W**e know what we're looking for," Arivana said, as they marched through the halls of the now-familiar level of her tower. "We just need to find it. I *must* know why that family was arrested and where they were taken. This kind of arbitrary justice will not stand in my city."

"But what good will that do?" Flumere said. "It is the council that shapes the laws, not the crown."

Arivana froze midstep. "It is?"

"I . . . that is . . . at least I believe so."

Arivana huffed and began striding forward once more. Her handmaiden squeaked, racing to catch up.

"One more thing I know too little about," Arivana said. "I may just have to move my bedchamber down to this level. It will save countless tolls spent walking with all the trips I'll be making here."

They turned a corner. The doors of the library came into view.

"That may not be the best idea."

"Why not? I mean, I'm sure I could use the exercise—"

"No, not that. I don't think it wise to spend too much time here, is all."

They arrived at the doors, and each grabbed a handle. Together, they pulled.

"You pick the strangest things to object to sometimes, Flumere. Why could coming to the library be a bad thing?"

The doors swung open before them, and they took a single step inside. They stopped before being able to take a second.

Tior lounged in chair directly before the entrance.

"Ah, my queen," he said, smiling. He set aside a book, then rose to his feet. "I was hoping to catch you here."

Arivana felt her heart begin to race. "Tior! I didn't expect you."

"You should always expect me, your majesty. It is, after all, my solemn duty to see to your well-being. And it is a duty I take quite seriously."

She flashed him a smile in return at last, then bent her lips towards Flumere's ear. "Go," she said. "Find it. This may take a while."

Flumere nodded, then stalked off.

Minister Pashams watched the handmaiden disappear into the stacks with cool eyes, but turned them, warm once more, back to Arivana as soon as the woman was out of sight.

"Come, sit," he said. "This is as pleasant a place as any to discuss the business at hand."

Arivana cringed, nearly choking to keep the reaction from showing on her face. She had a feeling she knew what "business" he had in mind and dreaded the conversation that was about to happen. She stepped forward daintily, smiling to hide her sigh, and floated down into the seat opposite him.

He sat as well, groaning the way old people always seemed to do. "Now, your majesty, what have you been up to lately?"

The question caught her off guard. Casual and harmless on the surface, yet all too direct. She didn't have a response prepared and stuttered over her reply.

Tior held up a hand. "No need to dissemble, my queen. I know all about your little trip to the city the other day."

The blood turned to ice in her veins. "You . . . you know about that?"

"Indeed. I was only surprised it took this long for you to take it."

Her head spun with a hundred scenarios, each with a thousand questions of their own, and the room started to spin with it. "I don't know what you mean."

"Oh, most Celandaris heirs get it into their heads, at some point or another, to discover the supposed 'truth' about our people. It usually happens at a younger age. Your oldest sister, Beckara, took her own tour of the city at the age of eleven. Now that I think about it, it's no wonder that you waited until now to make the journey, considering you were never properly groomed to take the throne."

All the careful planning, the secrecy, the fear at being caught—all pointless. He'd known all along. She wouldn't be surprised to find that he'd sent guards to follow her while keeping out of sight. She shrank into her seat, feeling more like a child than ever.

"Fret not, my dear," Tior said. "I take this as a good sign."

"You do?"

"Of course. It shows me that you may finally be ready to learn what it means to rule."

I passed some test, did I? Didn't know I needed your approval to do what is mine by right.

The thought steeled her will just a bit. "I see," she said. "Are there secrets you're going to let me in on, now? Some hidden knowledge that will grant me the keys to unlocking the wisdom of my authority?"

Tior chuckled. "Oh, Arivana. Haven't you been paying attention? I've been giving you that information all along. By showing an interest in the fate of your people, you have shown me that you're finally ready to start fulfilling your role. In earnest."

"And what role would that be?"

"That of queen, of course. Of beauty and grace, of knowledge and inspiration, of . . . stability." He paused. "Arivana, you haven't been spending any time with your suitors, have you?"

She hung her head. *No use trying to lie my way out of this one.* "No."

"Hmm. If none are to your liking, we can arrange for a new batch to be sent." He chuckled. "There's no shortage of pretty young men dying to earn a favorable glance from you."

"No. I'm sure they're all very, um, nice. But I don't think—"

"There's your problem, if you don't mind my saying, your majesty. Such things do not require thinking. Only feeling."

"Is that really all the guidance you can give me for choosing the future king?"

"There must be peace within the royal household. Forcing two people to marry who can barely stand each other is counterproductive to the purpose of the throne. Without love, there can be no peace. And no citizen sleeps easy in a realm without an heir."

Arivana furrowed her brow. He offered her everything a girl could want. The luxuries of being a queen with the ability to marry for love. Just like the princesses in all the storybooks. His reasons even sounded logical.

Then why does it seem so wrong?

"Peace," she said, more to herself than him. "I suppose that's a worthy enough goal."

She tried to sound convincing, but the words rang hollow even in her own ears. There had to be more to ruling than that. What about wisdom? Judgment? Leadership? Courage? A hundred other traits that someone in charge is supposed to have? Did they mean nothing at all besides the power of stomach flutters after stolen glances? Was there no greater requirement to becoming a king?

Or a queen?

Arivana painted on a smile. "Thank you, Tior. This conversation has been most informative. I shall try to be more faithful about fulfilling my duties from now on."

"Good, good." He rose. "Enjoy your time among the books, my queen. But not too much time, I hope. There are, after all, more important things to be doing than reading."

He left without waiting for a response. As the doors closed behind his retreating form, Flumere emerged from behind a bookcase.

Arivana sighed. "Find anything?"

Flumere's eyes darted around, then she nodded. She pressed forward a slim book, titled *Citizens Refinement Act*, tapping a finger on the open page.

Arivana read the words:

Statute 87—all citizens of Panisahldron must maintain a respectable appearance at all times, as would befit a representative of our glorious nation.

That was it. No other stipulations. No guidelines as to what qualified for "respectable" or not. Just a note at the bottom indicating the penalty, which matched the patrol captain's words: immediate seizure of all assets.

She flipped back and forth through the book, skimming every other statute. Most consisted of pages and pages of rules, stipulations, exceptions, and enough legal jargon to make her head spin.

"What makes this one so special?"

"Don't you see, Arivana? It has no boundaries. It

can be exercised at will, without procedure getting in the way."

"But why?"

Flumere shrugged. "What better way to get rid of those considered a stain on your precious society?"

In answer, Arivana released a single tear from her left eye.

But only one.

Though frustrated by an impossible task and negligible resources—and the outright horror of the situation—she found the prospect of backing down and forgetting all this was happening too sickening to fathom. The only way out of this, she saw, was to keep going, straight through until the end.

She wiped the tear away and clenched her fist, at last finding a measure of resolve.

After her short but miserable time at sea, Tassariel had never been happier to have solid ground beneath her feet, despite the fact that she'd been walking for a week, with an unknown number of days yet to come. Anything was better than that perpetual rocking and the insatiable nausea it spawned. Step by step, she'd almost forgotten about all that had been taken from her.

Almost.

Tassariel fanned herself, a vain attempt to cool the sweat drenching every bit of her skin. "Is it always this hot on the surface?"

"This near the equator, yes," Elos said. "Didn't you study geography at all?"

"A little. Fifty years ago, or so. I can't remember much of it."

"I don't suppose you committed anything to long-term memory, then."

"No."

"Didn't think so. While it may be uncomfortable for you, life thrives in abundance in the warmer climes. Just look around you."

Tassariel did, marveling at the diversity and beauty in the natural world around her. A dozen different types of trees enfolded the road, every last one bustling with bright birds and inquisitive monkeys. Flowers and other plants, in more hues than even a rainbow could account for, dotted an underbrush indelibly marked by the passage of countless boars and snakes, elephants and crocodiles. The air smelled crisp. Even the faint miasma of mildew and scum floating atop nearby stagnant water did nothing to diminish the smell of *aliveness* permeating the air around her, a scent that seemed to be missing from the valynkar city. And the warmth, despite its penchant for making her sweat, felt more real than the sorcerous heaters back home.

"A shame I couldn't make this whole world as vibrant as it is here."

Tassariel nearly tripped. "Wait, what are you saying? Did you make the world, or not?"

"Make? No. I suppose I misspoke. I might have

given a nudge here or there, but raw creation is far beyond even me. What do you take me for?"

"Um . . . a god?"

"And what does that mean, precisely?"

"I . . ." She shook her head. "How should I know? You're the supposed deity, here."

"A word with as many meanings as there are minds to think it. More. I wouldn't touch that if I were you."

Tassariel froze with her hand about to push aside a branch hanging over the path. She peered at it and soon realized that it was moving ever so slightly. Not a branch at all, then. Her first thought was snake, but the motion was too chaotic and omnidirectional for that.

"Insects?"

"A particularly nasty variety, I assure you. Necessary, though. Like all forms of life, if you look hard enough. Just go under without contacting them if you want to avoid a few thousand tiny bites that will eventually leave you paralyzed, followed by a slow death as the swarm digests you over the course of the next several days."

"Ew. No touching. Got it."

She got down on all fours, then rolled under the fake branch, giving herself far more room than was strictly necessary. *Better safe than devoured by a million murderous bugs.*

On her feet again, she continued up the road. It had been climbing most of the last two days, but she thought she could see sky up ahead, indicating that it might start leveling out soon. Her legs and lungs, though grateful for the exercise, practically jumped for joy at the prospect of a break from the uphill march.

Not for the first time, she wondered what she might be walking towards.

Or why she had to walk at all.

Tassariel lowered her eyes, trying to fight off another bout of melancholia at the thought. She'd thought she had gotten over it already. Thought she'd resigned herself to her fate. But no one, it seemed, liked being held in a cage for too long. *Even when my god holds the key.*

She took a deep breath to dispel such blasphemy from her mind. It would do no good to dwell upon the impossible.

A burst of cool air made her lift her head again. She realized she'd come to the crest of the hill. The land opened up before her, spread out like a vast, rumpled blanket of green, sussurating in the breeze. Mountains marred an otherwise-flat horizon, strange and bright, with countless steep peaks.

A hundred paces ahead, an animal stood in the road. A great cat, striped black and orange. It was nothing she had ever seen before, and she therefore had no name for it.

She gasped, shaken by fear, as it hunched its shoulders and began stalking towards her. She began energizing before she'd even made the conscious decision to do so.

"Destroy the beast quickly, and from afar," Elos said.

Her arm lifted, energy gathering in her palm.

"Wait. No." She shook her head, a movement taking far too much effort than usual. "It's just an animal. Why should my errant trespass equate to its death?"

"To risky to let it live. Do you see those teeth? Now imagine them around your throat."

"I don't—"

"Kill it!"

The cat was nearly upon her now. It gathered powerful legs beneath it to pounce.

Tassariel pounced first.

She internalized the energy, blessing herself, and moved with speed even this great predator could scarcely comprehend.

Bared claws swiped through empty air where she'd been half a moment ago. She lashed out a fist. Connected with the creature's jaw as it flew past. It landed sideways, sprawling. But only for a beat. It shook its head, turned towards her, and lunged again.

She skated back, kicking the beast aside. It spun, roaring. The thing must not have been used to prey that walked upright. Not that knew how to fight back anyway.

"Stop this now! There is too much at stake to play such games!"

Tassariel didn't answer.

The cat reared, widening its forearms as if to give her a hug. She grasped it by the wrists and held. Teeth snapped out, hissing, hot breath blowing a few finger widths from her face. Its strength and mass weighed down on her, fighting on a level with her own magically enhanced physique, yet she did not give.

"You will not kill me, beast," she said. "But neither will I kill you."

She lunged upwards, driving her knee into its belly. She let go with her hands, and it faltered, skittering back. Before it could land, she gathered power in her hands, turning them bright with fire, and struck her palms forward. Twin handprints branded themselves into the beast's chest, and it crashed onto its back.

It was sluggish to regain its feet. A pained gaze tracked her though it drew no nearer.

"That's right," she said. "I'm not prey. I'm dangerous. Too dangerous for you. Go. Find an easier meal."

Though she knew it could not understand her words, she could swear it grasped her intent. The wide head lowered as it turned its flank to her. She surged more power into her hands, flaring flames that reflected off those feline eyes.

The beast darted off the road and became lost in the shadow of the jungle in beats. Tassariel relaxed, bleeding off her excess magic with a sigh.

"That," Elos said, "was a very stupid thing to do."

"Why? Because it wasn't according to your perfect plan?"

"You might have been killed, that's why."

"And what would that have mattered?"

"You're important. My chosen vessel. If the time ever comes for you to play hero, I'll let you know. Until then, let *me* calculate the risks. I *am* rather good at it."

"This risk never would have happened if you hadn't—" She clamped her teeth shut, screaming behind closed lips.

"What?"

She exhaled, letting her anger seep away on the winds of her breath. The calmness of her next words surprised her. "You took the sky from me. How *dare* you ask for anything else!"

The icy presence retreated, which was fine by her.

Still under the effects of her blessing, every sense tingled with acuity. She looked again to the horizon. Those mountains, she now realized, were not mountains at all.

They were towers. Dozens of them.

"No—not dozens," Elos intoned. "One hundred. Exactly."

Ah. Panisahldron. It was good to finally know her destination.

CHAPTER 12

Mevon crouched behind the boulder, smiling at the tufts of grass poking up through the snow. In the last few days, the plateau had begun to dip. There were places he and Draevenus had simply slid down for hundreds or even thousands of paces. Even so, signs of life remained rare.

Until now.

The crunch of hooves across the cold slush brought his attention forward. Mevon quivered in anticipation. He didn't know if that was a good thing or not. Despite all his efforts to abstain, he still grew excited at the prospect of violence, even that not directed at men. Maybe he'd been wrong about himself. Maybe letting off steam was the last thing he needed. Maybe he'd been the biggest fool in the world to think he could change.

Maybe he was just really, *really* hungry.

Another crunch, and now the ram's head edged into view from behind an oblong stone, nose scuffing around in the snow to get to the grass trapped below. Mevon caressed his dagger hilts, coiling to pounce.

A family of dark birds screeched into the air across the field. The ram turned towards it, startled. But only for a moment. It bleated once, then retreated in great, four-legged hops that took it away from his position with incredible speed.

Seeing his next meal escaping, Mevon charged after it.

He leapt forward, feet launching his body off boulder after boulder, staying high to keep an eye on his prey. His blades stayed sheathed, for now. The ram had not fled directly away from him, and he caught up to it in a dozen beats. He aimed for the creature's back and surged forward, ready to wrestle it to the ground.

The very instant before his hands were to meet the beast's neck, however, something crashed into him from the side. The breath was knocked from his lungs. He tumbled from the impact, rolling and kicking up gouts of snow.

He righted himself a moment later, fighting the storm that threatened to break within him.

Draevenus lay sprawled nearby. He held a hand to his head and groaned.

"Are you all right?" Mevon asked.

"Ruul's light, Mevon. I'd rather dive headfirst into a quarry than run into you again. What are you made of anyway? Steel?"

"A man of steel. Now *there's* a thought." He reached

down, clasping hands with the assassin, and pulled him to his feet. "Better?"

"I will be in a mark or so. Did you see where the abyss-taken beast got to?"

"No. And we'd be skinning and butchering it now if you hadn't interfered. What was that all about anyway?"

Draevenus shrugged. "Same as you, I guess. Our plan was ruined by those birds, so I just took off after it, quick as I could. It was just bad luck that we reached it at the same moment."

"True. But that doesn't make me any less hungry."

"It can't have gotten far." Draevenus squinted, peering into the distance. "How 'bout a little wager?"

Mevon arched an eyebrow. "Name the terms."

"Simple. First to catch it gets to divvy up the portions. Choicest cuts to the victor."

Mevon didn't ponder long. "You're on." He smiled, pulling his daggers. "No accidents this time?"

Draevenus performed a mocking bow. "I shall endeavor to abstain from such clumsy displays."

Mevon didn't see the mierothi rise from the ridiculous posture. He was too busy getting a head start.

Pouring his focus into speed, Mevon tore across the ground. The wind of his motion whistled past his ears, whipping his hair behind him. Instinct told him to stick to the flat ground, but he knew the ram would not keep to such restrictions, so instead he angled towards the steep edge of a hill. His choice was vindicated as he spied his prey on a level with him less than half a thousand paces away.

Blackness streaked across his vision, killing his elation. Draevenus emerged from his shadow-dash just ahead of the ram. He smiled towards Mevon. Waved. Pointed his daggers at the beast and made to dash again.

The stones beneath the mierothi came loose of the hillside. His attack seemingly forgotten, he spun his arms in an attempt to keep his balance.

The attempt was in vain.

The assassin tumbled down the slope, battered by a shower of pebbles. The ram spun, fleeing the disruption . . .

. . . right towards Mevon.

It sensed him coming but too late. Mevon, with a series of leaping bounds twice as far as the ram's, boxed the beast in. It turned in a circle. Once. Frantic bleats erupted from its throat.

Mevon pounced for the kill.

His weight crashed into the creature as he curled one arm around its neck. They rolled together, sliding across a patch of ice. Mevon came out on top, straddling the furry chest and avoiding the hooves lashing out at his face. He drove a dagger into the pounding heart.

It stilled in beats, all fight lost. Mevon smiled.

Draevenus slogged up the hillside, hand over hand, groaning with each twitch of motion. Mevon began skinning the beast.

"Today is just not my day," Draevenus called.

Mevon peered down at the mierothi, who was bleeding from a score of superficial lacerations. "So it seems." He paused to snatch a drink from his canteen. Blood dripped from his hands to his elbows as he raised them. "Are you going to be all right?"

"Nothing is hurt more than my pride, thankfully. A little fresh meat will cure the worst of my physical ailments."

Mevon grunted. The chase had invigorated him at the time, but now his stomach rumbled. He had half a mind not to wait for a cookfire but knew he'd pay for it later if he gave in to impatience now. Still, a cookfire would take too long. Sorcerous flame would sear the meat in beats.

A glance at his companion, however, revealed a figure clinging to handholds in the stones just below the ledge before the hill leveled out, as if surmounting that one last barrier took more effort than the mierothi had to give. If his own hunger-born weakness was any indication, Mevon's assessment might not have been far from the truth.

He rose from his kill and marched over to the ledge, reaching a hand down. With obvious gratefulness, Draevenus took it, too wearied to even flinch at the contact. "Thanks."

"Think nothing of it." Mevon finished hauling up his companion, then jerked a thumb over his shoulder. "She's almost ready. A few more cuts, a little fire from your fingertips, and we'll be feasting in no time."

"Feasting on what?"

Mevon spun to face his kill, pointing. "On th—"

The ram was gone.

A trail of speckled blood lay in a straight line away from where their meal had just lain, and a dark shape streaked into the woods a hundred paces away.

Mevon glanced at Draevenus. Information passed silently between them in that brief meeting of eyes. He knew they were both thinking the same thing.

Trouble.

"But we've no reason to provoke them," Jasside said. "Why do you insist on it?"

Vashodia eyed her coolly, sipping wine as she lounged in a feathered chair. "I must know the heart of a man before I can offer him my aid."

"Aid? You mean you actually intend to help them?"

"Perhaps. It all depends on their reaction to my little challenge."

Jasside sighed. It had been three days, and no official response had come from either prince. The rooms were cozy enough, and they had little restriction on their movements, free to come and go as they pleased, but Jasside felt as if her time was better spent doing something, anything, else. She only wished she had a better way to direct her energy.

Idleness, once again, proved ill-fitting to her temperament.

She slumped down onto a couch, burying her face in her hands. "Is there anything you need me to do?"

"Get some rest," Vashodia said. "One way or another, you'll be needing it. And soon."

"Vague and cryptic as always." Jasside rose, knowing a dismissal when she heard it. "Let me know if you're ever in the mood for a real conversation."

With that, she stomped out of the room.

The torch-lined halls, all steel and stone and wood, offered her no comfort. She'd walked them a hundred times, it seemed, and had come no closer to discerning her purpose here. To say it was frustrating would not even brush the heart of the matter. Jasside knew she could help—she had already, with the refugees—but now she didn't know enough of the political situation to even begin thinking of possible solutions.

Vashodia had brought them here for a reason, but her penchant for withholding information was getting old. Really quick.

She stalked to the next door down the hall and pushed inside. Her own room, graciously provided, was identical to her mistress's. Warm and soft and comfortable. And aggravating. She kicked the rear leg of a high-backed chair as she passed.

It did not give as she expected. Jasside cringed, pain radiating from her toe and lancing up her shin. She bent down, leaning on the arm of the chair to massage her injury.

Prince Daye Harkun's face turned, his nose half a hand's width away from hers as he sat.

Jasside jumped upright. "Oh!"

"My apologies," Daye said. "I didn't mean to startle you."

"Well, you did."

"Sorry."

"It's fine."

Her heart raced, half from the surprise, half from the man's very presence. She hadn't ever been truly alone with him. Not like this. Certainly not in her own bedroom. She stepped lightly across the room and settled in a chair opposite him. The space between them was now great enough to give her room to breathe.

"You know what you are, right? I mean, your . . . peculiar relationship with magic?"

"Yes. I am a void. A nullifier."

"Ever think about the effect of sneaking up on a caster unannounced?"

He smirked. "Often. You think it rude, I suppose. No one likes having all his advantages stripped away."

"No."

"After all, it must be how everyone else feels when near someone like you."

"Is that an accusation?"

"Just an observation."

"Then let me put your mind to rest. Power such as mine may grant an advantage, but no civilized person would exploit it."

"No *good* person, you mean."

"Isn't that what I just said?"

He shook his head. "The two aren't always synonymous. The Panisians and their allies are indisputably more 'civilized' than us northerners. But I'm hard-pressed to find anything decent about them."

"You think all progress immoral, then?"

"No. Just that not checked by ethical considerations. At every step."

Jasside nodded, troubled for some reason she couldn't explain. She drummed her fingers on the arm of her chair, studying the man across from her, finding—to her surprise—that she didn't mind his presence one bit.

"Why are you here?" she asked.

He looked up at her slowly, sadness brimming in his eyes. "I've come to beg for your help."

"Help with what?"

"Everything."

He stood, turning parallel to her, and began pacing back and forth. "My brother has not had an easy life. I was abducted as a child. Taken from Weskara because of my unique abilities, which are prized here. Chase spent the better part of his youth training furiously, and most of his early adult years searching. For me. For a brother who did not need rescuing.

"He could have been happy, you know. He was going to take over the family business, silversmithing. He was always good at it. Then again, he excelled at pretty much everything he set his mind to. Instead, he wasted his life because of me."

"You can't possibly blame yourself for that."

"Oh, but I can. I was treated well, respected, given

training and every honor. I fell in love with this land and its people. But never once did I think about home, about the life I'd left behind. About my family.

"Never once did I send word."

"It seemed to turn out all right for him, though. He's a prince now, after all."

"But he does not *love* it, don't you see? He is only here because of me. He only leads because he feels he must and because there's no one left alive who can do it better." Daye shook his head. "That is why he will not answer your mistress's challenge. He does not know how to win. He only knows how to hold on for another day against impossible odds. He feels that he is only delaying the inevitable."

"He can't be so hopeless as that. I heard rumors that he's already led the charge in some stunning victories."

Daye sighed. "When the coalition first invaded, they rolled hard and deep. Taosin was where we finally turned them back. Chase became a hero that day, and a prince. But he shouldn't have had to."

"Why not?"

"I . . . I was in charge of the city's defense. I failed, and half of it burned to the ground. Chase led the counterattack that retook the city, rescuing me from a cadre of enemy sorcerers, no less. The very kind I'm supposed to be most potent against. He almost died saving me from my own failure, my own weakness.

"For that, and for everything else, I will never be able to repay him."

He stopped his pacing and, before she could even

blink, fell to his knees in front of her, gripping her forearms. She tensed, as much from surprise as from the sudden loss of her power.

"Please, Jasside, you must do something to help him. I will convince him to hold another meeting with you and Vashodia, but I beg of you, please, find some way to change your mistress's terms. We are desperate—*I* am desperate—and we need all the help we can get."

She peered into his eyes, pleading and honest, brimming with tears. She couldn't find it in herself to tell him no.

Moreover, she wasn't sure she wanted to.

Arivana and Flumere had scoured the library for any other mention of statute eighty-seven but had come up empty. She spent the next several days in a perpetual state of anxiety. She kept up appearances, performing her duties and even visiting the boys on the entertainment levels once. They took turns reading her poetry, most of it vain ramblings of writers overstuffed with their own supposed brilliance. She thought it boring. The whole affair seemed sordid, but for some reason she couldn't quite place, she felt as if she had to start pleasing Tior.

Then, she *could* place it. She was going to confront him about the statute—she *had* to—and knew she must give him no reason to chastise her.

But every time he was near, she found some excuse

for not bringing it up. Her throat was dry, she needed a rest, she had some other appointment to keep. Today, though, she had worked up enough courage. She would finally do it.

Now, I just need to find the old man.

She and Flumere asked around, for tolls it seemed, yet found no one who could give them a definite location. She even dared send a summons, but the porter came back empty-handed. Her resolve faltered with each passing mark and was nearly spent when they stumbled into a servant who swore she'd seen him down at the tower reception hall not too long ago. Arivana thanked the woman, took a deep breath, then headed for the lift.

"Ground floor, please," she said to the elevator operator.

The man bowed. "As you wish, your majesty."

As the lift began its descent, she turned to Flumere. Her nervousness must have shown on her face, for the woman reached out, squeezing her hand affirmingly. "You'll be fine."

Arivana squeezed back. "I hope so."

They passed the rest of the way in silence, then emerged into the ground-level hall. Banners for every nation lined the walls, lit by crystal chandeliers that floated and bobbed. Sculptures and statues made a maze of the marble floor. All of this and more was designed to impress visitors. Beyond that, at the end of the hall near the entrance, sat another copy of the Jeweled Throne, barely used by her, where she could sit to receive ambassadors, foreign rulers, and other so-called important guests.

Tior stood next to the throne, turning at their approach. "My queen! That was quick. I only just sent the request for your presence a few moments ago."

Arivana stumbled over her next step. "You . . . asked for me?"

"Yes, of course. Is that not why you're here?"

"No. I mean . . . what is this about?"

"Visitor. Should be arriving shortly. Do you remember the proper addresses and such?"

"Yes."

"Best get seated then."

"Okay, but—"

"No time to waste, your majesty. Please." He gestured towards the throne.

Flumere gave a little pat on her shoulder. Arivana nodded. "No. I must speak with you first. It is important."

"Oh?"

"Yes." She swallowed. "I must gain a clear understanding about statute eighty-seven of the Citizens Refinement Act. What do you know about it?"

Minister Pashams lifted a brow, intertwining his fingers in a thoughtful pose. "Eighty-seven? Hmm. That sounds familiar . . ."

She gritted her teeth. "Do. Not. Lie to me. I will not believe that you are ignorant of its existence."

Tior's eyes widened. Both cheeks twitched, but not from mirth. "I see."

Arivana folded her arms and waited.

With a great sigh, Tior began. "Beauty is our nation's greatest export. People have come to expect nothing short of stunning when looking upon anything with our name stamped upon it. The purpose of the Citizen's Refinement Act is to ensure that everyone who deigns to call our city home adheres to standards of beauty in all aspects of their lives.

"Perception is reality, to most people anyway. Those that matter. Those in control. If the world were to perceive that we could not keep our own streets resplendent, what would they begin to think about our exports?"

Arivana shivered. "That doesn't explain the statute."

Tior shrugged. "Ugliness can manifest itself in many forms. You are too young to—"

"I am NOT too young! I—"

Just as she had cut him off, so too did the herald's trumpet interrupt her.

The doors began to open.

This isn't over.

Tassariel stared through the opening doors, the trumpet blast still ringing in her ears.

"This isn't the consulate," she said.

"No," Elos said. "Is that where you thought we were going?"

"I . . . don't know. I assumed—"

"A fiendish thing to do."

"Yes, but what am I to do here?"

"You're here to offer your services."

"To whom? For what?"

"That, I must leave up to you."

"You can't be serious."

"It's just one of those things. Foresight, remember? If I tell you too much, my predictions become, well, unpredictable. Just follow your instinct."

"Instinct. Right. Whatever that means."

She had half a mind to do the exact opposite of her instinct, just to spite him. But then again, that might be just what he was counting on. She had no way of knowing how precise his calculations could possibly be.

Just be true to yourself, Tassariel. Don't let him change who you are.

With a deep breath, she walked in through the bright opening.

Still blinking, a man appeared at her side. "How shall I announce you, madam?"

"Umm. As 'Tassariel.'"

"Just . . . Tassariel?"

"You can add 'of the valynkar,' I guess."

The herald smiled. He shouted out her title, eliciting another ache from her already throbbing skull.

She stepped forward, lifting her eyes past the dozen guardsmen lined up at the sides of the room, standing rigidly. A young girl sat on a gaudy throne, orange hair gleaming under the light of a crystal chandelier. Tassariel had never been overly concerned about her appearance, but the girl was so beautiful, it made her feel plain. Dowdy. She shook that feeling and glanced to the girl's side. An old man stood next to her in ornate robes.

Let's just get this over with.

"Greetings," the girl said. "On behalf of the people of Panisahldron, I, Queen Arivana Celandaris, welcome you to our city."

Tassariel froze, uncertain about the proper protocols, and feeling ever more awkward for facing a child queen. "Thank you," she said at last.

The old man stepped forward. "And I, Tior Pashams, Minister of Gardens and supreme advisor to the crown, welcome you as well. What is it that brings you to our fair city?"

"I have come," she began, clearing her throat to buy her a moment to think, "as . . . a representative of Elos."

"What?" Elos said.

She ignored him. "The power of his light is used in abundance in this city. He has sent me to . . . umm . . . oversee its proper administration."

"Really?" the minister said. "My dear, you must be mistaken. We already have the consulate, which performs this very task."

Abyss take me! Why did I say that? And why didn't I ever research what it was that Lerathus did here?

"Maybe," she said, desperate to cover her mistake. "But they only speak with the will of our council. I speak with the direct voice of our god."

"You just couldn't help it, could you?"

She muttered under her breath, "I'm not lying, am I?"

The god seemed to sigh. **"Technically? No."**

"Interesting," the minister said, folding his hands together. "You must know that this is all quite unprecedented."

"I understand."

The queen opened her mouth to speak but shut it again, twisting her lips and glancing at the minister. She almost appeared afraid to speak, anger and uncertainty plaguing her gaze.

At last, though, the girl took a breath and met Tassariel's eyes. "If that is the case, then know that you are most heartily welcome by me. If your god wishes to inspect his own power, then by all means, I shall make sure to aid you in any way possible."

The queen glanced again at the back of the minister's head, cringing as if afraid of reprisal. Just what was going on here? Whatever it was, Tassariel didn't like it. And the minister seemed to be the one towards whom her distrust naturally inclined.

Very well, Elos. Watch me follow my instinct.

Tassariel stepped forward and knelt before the throne. "Your majesty, that is very good to hear, for Elos has sent me specifically to offer *you* my services. As of this moment, I am pledged to you and you alone."

The minister sucked in a hissing breath.

The queen smiled. "It would be my honor." She stood, holding out her hands. "Please. Rise."

Tassariel obliged. She reached out to grasp the girl's hands. From the corner of her eye, she witnessed a woman's face poke out from behind the throne. A servant of some sort, by her plain clothes.

Under no control of her own, Tassariel felt herself begin energizing.

"Kill her. Kill her!" Elos screamed. "KILL HER!"

Her hands, not yet touching the queen's, glowed with power. They turned of their own accord towards the woman behind the throne. A spell formed at her fingertips.

Death was but a beat away from release.

No . . .

She snatched her hands back at what seemed the last possible moment, dispersing her energy harmlessly into the floor.

The queen tilted her head. "Is . . . everything all right?"

"No it's not," the minister said. He stepped up next to her, energizing himself. With a start, Tassariel realized he was her equal in sorcerous power.

Stamping boots drew up behind her. She felt a faint breeze as half a dozen swords swung towards her, stopping so close she felt sure she would bleed if she so much as sneezed.

As far as first impressions went, this was, by far, the worst one of her life.

PART III

CHAPTER 13

Draevenus wasn't sure if he or Mevon stopped first. The air held something. A menace. A promise borne on breezes across the steppes that blood lay in wait for those who trespassed. He felt it in the squishy release of oils between his hard-packed scales. He saw it in the stillness of the stones and the trees. He heard it in the silence.

They'd been tracking the thing that stole their last meal for days now, barely scraping by on roots and berries. They'd seen no other game. Hunger had driven them, but where to find their next meal would be the least of their worries if they didn't survive the next few marks.

Without a word, they both ducked behind trees on opposite sides of the narrow game trail. Arrows zipped through the air, punching holes in the bark and the space they'd just vacated. A shout went up, harsh cries of beastly rage, all the more twisted for ringing from human throats. Countless animal growls joined them, guttural and rabid, deep as boulders, filling the shallow bowl of the hillside with their fury.

Draevenus pulled his daggers, energizing, and glanced across at the Mevon. "I'll leave the beasts to you?"

And without waiting for an answer, he shadow-dashed away.

Mevon sighed.

"Yes, I'll take the beasts," he said to the trail of black that was already starting to fade.

More arrows spat towards him. One got lucky, embedding in his shoulder. He pulled it out with a grunt and ran to the next tree thick enough to hide his bulk. The growls sounded again. Closer. He felt rhythmic vibrations through the rocky soil as heavy limbs struck the ground, again and again.

Men only lashed out without warning from fear or from the blackness staining their souls. He didn't know which these men were. Right now, he couldn't afford to care. Death came calling. Violence. Blood. One way or another, he had to give answer.

And today was not the day that he would choose to die.

He leapt sideways, onto a flat stone outcropping. Twin blurs of darkness scythed around the tree, just missing their intended target. Mevon finally got a good look at them.

Draevenus alighted upon the shallow ridge and immediately enshrouded himself in shadow. With the sun high overhead, darkness would not be the best concealment, but it might just buy him a beat or two of confusion from his assailants. More than enough time to assess his targets. To execute.

He peered down but did not see anyone. Strange smears, dark and low, darted across the battlefield, somehow able to avoid the thick bramble. Not men. He would leave them for Mevon. He turned his gaze up the hill towards where the beasts had emerged. A tangle of trees and shrubs and rocks provided plenty of places to hide. Even as he watched, more arrows streaked from hidden nooks.

I've got you now.

The foliage would be a problem. Drawing all the dark energy he could hold, he thrust his hands forward, emitting a jet of blue flame. It lanced down, igniting the undergrowth in a swath as he swept it from left to right.

An arrow whizzed by, grazing his thigh. Draevenus released the spell and dashed behind the smoking conflagration.

One of the creatures lunged for Mevon. He reached out and wrapped a hand around its throat. Forepaws gouged at his arm, tearing strips of fur from his coat as they sought the flesh beneath. The rear legs raked towards his belly.

Mevon studied it.

Black fur, black eyes, black drool dripping from black teeth. He thought at first it was a wolf—the size was about right—but the snout was too long, sporting thick whiskers, and the body too bulbous.

He held in his hand the biggest rat he'd ever seen.

Movement in his peripheral. Three more of the vile things.

Mevon spun, wielding the beast in his grip like a club and smashing it into another. He let the two collapse in a heap, then stepped back. The other pair crashed together, heads cracking in the space he'd just occupied. He jumped. Boots stamped down, crushing twin skulls. Dark blood burst onto the boulder and hissed like boiling tar.

The first two rats pounced on him again. One landed on his shoulder, scraping his cheek with an errant swipe. The wound stung like acid. Mevon wrenched his blades free and buried one in the heart of each beast.

He lifted his head as two more creatures came into view, yipping wildly. Not rats this time.

Black jackals, big as horses.

Draevenus waded through the smoke. The sorcerous shadows enveloping him now found a purpose, a home, concealing him within the chaos. He much preferred to be the one laying an ambush, but still, there was something brutally sweet about turning the tables, like finding hot peppers in a pastry.

Two enormous men staggered towards him, coughing. He froze, curious to see if they would even notice him. They didn't. He watched them approach, clutching bows in one hand. Some sort of dark, fuzzy suit surrounded each of them, almost like they were sprouting their own fur. Draevenus waited until they drew abreast of him.

In a single motion, he struck. The two men took one step more, then fell to the ground, dead before they hit.

More movement. Draevenus shadow-dashed towards it without thinking. He landed amidst five men as they slid into place behind a hollow of large stones, a place relatively free of flames.

One managed a surprised shout before Draevenus whirled, blades gleaming as firelight reflected off blood-soaked steel. He cut two throats in a heartbeat. The men fell to their knees, spitting red and obscenities.

The other three swung at him. Draevenus parried two stone hatchets, then ducked under a wild blow by a heavy cudgel. He kicked at the knee of this third man. The sound of crunching bone reached his ears. The man toppled into one of his fellows.

A hatchet chopped down again, and Draevenus twisted out of its way, using his motion to empower an upward slice. Wrist tendons snapped apart, and a hand went flying, weapon still in its grip, spraying black blood across the survivors.

Not survivors for much longer.

He stepped towards them. The one still standing swiped his hatchet. Draevenus batted it aside, then lunged, driving a dagger up through the soft part of the man's chin and into the brain.

The downed man cracked his cudgel into Draevenus's shin, but he barely felt it in the rush of adrenaline. He flipped his left blade into a reverse grip, then drove it down. It sank into the back of the man's head, to the hilt.

Draevenus straightened. He closed his eyes, sniffing and straining his ears. Distant, bestial growls sounded, but he didn't worry about those. Mevon could take care of himself. The crackling flames he'd spawned grew nearer by the beat, drowning out any hope of sensing human presence nearby. He sauntered out into the clear air.

Once away from the smoke, his eyes were all he needed to find his next targets. Two men crouched behind trees, facing away from him.

Still wrapped in shadow, Draevenus advanced.

The massive jackals trotted towards Mevon, tongues lolling from creepy, happy-looking faces. They seemed unconcerned by him or the dead rat-things at his feet, circling almost lazily. They paused, just out of lunging distance. Black eyes sparkled with twisted delight.

Behind me . . .

A weight slammed into his neck. And with it, pain.

He spun, reaching behind him. His hand grasped . . . something. Teeth tore free as he pulled, slicing across his spine. A jolt of pain ran through him, and he fell to a knee.

He crushed the ball of fur in his hand. He didn't have time to examine it. A dozen more, at least, leapt atop him before he could so much as breathe.

Mevon rolled, bouncing off the boulder. Long fangs punctured his legs and arms, another in his side. His movement prevented penetration as deep as the first attack, throwing some clear, crushing others. He pressed against the ground, coming to a standing position, and swiped to dislodge the few still clinging to him. Creatures the size of hounds. Long ears, compact bodies.

He blinked, trying to reconcile the image before him.

"Rabbits?"

The jackals, laughing still, decided that this was a good time to pounce.

Mevon jumped back, avoiding their first assault. But the second came too quickly, and he found himself on his back, barely holding back a jaw as wide as his shoulders as it snapped and slavered, dripping drool onto his face.

He raised a foot, planting it in the beast's belly, and kicked up. The jackal flipped over his head. Mevon surged upwards. He'd lost one dagger somewhere but held the other firmly as the second jackal leapt at him. He danced to the side, swiping along the creature's flank. Black blood poured from the gash. The beast twisted its head towards him and laughed.

Mevon drove his blade through the thing's eye.

The other jackal, cackling madly, crashed into his side. Teeth clamped down, tearing a bite out of the flesh around his ribs. Pain reached nauseating levels. Mevon punched the feeding head once, twice, thrice, but it kept on chewing.

It ate him as he watched.

Mevon screamed. He thrust his hands into the jackal's mouth, gripping each half of the jaw, interrupting the meal. He began pulling them apart. Yipping turned to yowling, turned to whimpering, turned to . . .

The jaw cracked wide open.

. . . silence.

Draevenus stepped up behind the first man, who hadn't even twitched at his approach. One hand wrapped around the forehead, pulling back. The other ran a blade across the exposed throat.

He pushed the thrashing, dying man to the ground and turned to the next.

The man wailed and fled.

Draevenus dashed forward, ahead of him, cutting off his line of retreat. The man changed direction. Draevenus did the same thing again.

Three more times.

Eventually, the man collapsed, shaking with fear and fury. Draevenus drew near.

"You made a grave error," he said, "crossing the likes of us."

The man growled, staring back with wide eyes.

Eyes whose irises were as red as blood.

Draevenus froze in midstride.

Mevon pushed off the massive corpse and staggered to his feet. His whole body burned like coals as his blessings worked to heal the damage he'd sustained. It had been awhile since he'd been this badly hurt. He remembered feeling much the same the day his army had run into the Imperial force next to the Shenog Ravine, and the daeloth had somehow managed to lay a trap for him.

The day Jasside had fallen off the cliff.

He shook his head to clear the memory, breathing deep. He couldn't afford to dwell on the past no matter how much he wanted to. No matter how much he was filled with regret. With longing.

With despair.

Lurching with each step, he waded through the trees, searching for more enemies or for a sign of his companion.

He found both soon enough.

Draevenus stepped towards a man on his knees. The grim flash of his blades thrust forth.

Mevon sucked in a breath to tell his friend to stop, to

show a little mercy or at least question the man before his end. But the call never came. Weakness from blood loss and hunger finally caught up to him, and he collapsed to hands and knees, struggling for mere breath.

He heard the knife go in. The gurgled cries. The body slump to the ground.

Another growl. But this one from a voice he knew well.

Mevon lifted his head enough to see Draevenus, drenched in dark blood, shaking as he stood over a pair of corpses. Fear, sorrow, and anger brewed in the assassin's distant gaze.

"What wrong?" Mevon asked.

"It's happening again," Draevenus said, face twisting into a snarl. "Ruul must have felt he failed with us, so he simply started over."

"What do you mean?"

"The fur gave it away. Not a garment. They're growing it right off their skin. And the eyes . . ." Draevenus shook his head. "Malformations, Mevon. Darkness making monsters of men and beast alike. Sound familiar?"

Mevon couldn't hold down the word that floated up into his mind.

Mierothi.

"Yes," Mevon managed before a darkness of his own took hold and he fell face-first into the dirt.

Jasside shuffled into the same chamber as before, led by Daye, with Vashodia following. The first thing she noticed was Prince Chase's lips, pressed together into a thin, pale line. It seemed Daye had gone to great lengths to secure this meeting. They were sure to have their work cut out for them.

She stopped a respectful distance away, folding her hands before her. Vashodia came abreast of her, planting hands on her hips and spearing a grin across at Chase. It was a casually amused look that Jasside knew well, which said the mierothi was perfectly in control of the situation, the world bowing to her whim and will, mostly without even realizing it. As it should be.

As she thinks *it should be anyway.*

"Brother," Daye said. "Thank you for agreeing to this meeting."

Chase shook his head. "It pained me to see my own brother reduced to begging. It is for that alone that I relented."

"Still. Thank you."

Chase waved away the sentiment, eying both women in turn. "Say what you will, so we can be done with this."

Jasside cleared her throat. She had been preparing for this moment since Daye visited her chamber a few nights ago. A whole speech, well rehearsed, sat waiting in her head. If it couldn't convince Vashodia to see reason, nothing would.

She parted her lips to speak.

Vashodia beat her to it. "My dear prince, please know that I am deeply sorry for my actions during our first meeting."

Jasside turned to her mistress, jaw hanging wide open.

It was the first time she'd ever heard Vashodia apologize. For anything.

Chase, too, seemed taken aback. His face softened, the tension and anger vanishing like smoke in the wind.

Jasside leaned in close to Vashodia. "Are you feeling ill?"

"Strategic calculation," her mistress whispered back. "Watch and learn."

Jasside nodded and straightened.

"That is very kind of you to say," Chase said. He furrowed his brow. "That still doesn't answer why you're here."

Vashodia broadened her grin. "We're here to offer an alliance."

"An alliance?" Jasside and both princes said at once.

Jasside glanced at the brothers, who, understandably, seemed equally as surprised as her.

Vashodia giggled. "Of course. Why else do you think I dragged myself out here?"

"I thought you wanted an apology," Daye said, "for that incident between my scouts and your hunters?"

"Oh, don't be silly. We're new to the area and still figuring out the lay of the land. Petty squabbles with neighbors is hardly worth getting worked up about."

Daye looked betrayed. "Then all that guilt you laid on me was just . . . what? Pretense?"

"I'm afraid so."

He hung his head. "Then maybe I was wrong to

bring you." He turned to Chase. "I'm sorry, brother. I am a fool. It seems I've brought nothing but liars into our midst."

Jasside quivered at the accusation. "No," she said. "Enough of this."

"You deny your own falsehood?" Daye said.

She took a deep breath. "I've been denying far too much for far too long. The lies have to end." She turned her glare on Vashodia. "Now."

It was Vashodia's turn to be surprised. The slight widening of her eyes was more victory than Jasside had ever hoped to accomplish.

"No more manipulation," Jasside said. "What is the real reason for this alliance?"

"You want the truth, do you?" Vashodia smirked once more, falling back into her self-assurance as if her momentary falter had never taken place. "Very well."

Jasside held her breath. She was sure both princes did the same.

"This war," Vashodia began, "is unfounded. I know that not a single soul from Sceptre had anything to do with the murder of the Panisian royal family. This invasion of theirs—this 'coalition'—is being manipulated by forces most foul. It is an injustice I intend to correct." She narrowed her gaze on Jasside. "And I'm very good at that, in case you have forgotten."

Jasside shivered. "I haven't forgotten."

"Good. Then the only thing that remains, is the *king's* answer." Vashodia turned her eyes to Chase, and Jasside followed.

Tears streamed down the man's cheeks.

Daye stepped up to him, grasping his brother by the forearm and bringing the other around his shoulders, hugging him close. They touched foreheads, breathing heavily. Chase nodded. Daye stepped back, allowing his brother the room he needed.

"You mean to help us in this war? Truly?" Chase said.

"We do," Vashodia replied.

"What do you want in exchange?"

"Peace along our shared border. Open trade and travel."

"That's it?"

"And one other thing. A trifle, really."

Chase grunted. "That nonsense about calling me 'king'?"

She nodded. "Nothing nonsensical about it. A nation needs a strong leader, especially in a time such as this. Refusing the title only denies your people the assurance they need. It is childish of you."

"So, we're back to petty insults again, are we?"

Vashodia shrugged. "I thought you wanted the truth."

Chase sighed, the corners of his lips tugging upwards. "Very well. I'll make the announcement today."

"That's good to hear," Jasside said. "Thank you again for agreeing to see us. We look forward to continuing cooperation." She smiled at Daye, receiving like in return, then spun on her heels to leave.

"Wait," Chase said. "Before you go, can you at least let us know when we can expect reinforcements?"

"Didn't you know?" Vashodia said. "Our expeditionary army is already here."

Daye raised an eyebrow. "I'd hardly call twenty-five men an army."

"What, the daeloth?" Vashodia giggled. "No, no. Not them. They are merely the escort." She held up both hands, one towards Jasside, the other towards herself.

"*We* are the army."

"Is it bad," Tassariel asked, "that no one has come to see us yet?"

"See *you*, you mean. I'm certain my presence is still safely masked, despite your antics in the receiving chamber."

"*My* antics? That was all *your* doing, you miserable ass."

"Hey, now, what happened to all your piety? I could use a good dose of it about now."

"Good luck with that. Next time you plan on murdering someone using my body, give a girl a little warning first. I almost couldn't stop you."

"The fact that you did, however, is most worrisome. Believe it or not, I've never done this before. I was expecting to be more . . ."

"Arrogant? Selfish? Insufferable?"

"Effective."

Tassariel shrugged, not knowing—or caring—if Elos could discern the gesture. "Well, I guess that's just what a god gets when he messes with lesser life-forms. Did you forget that we have this little thing called 'free will'?"

"No. I didn't forget. I just . . ." Ice stirred within her.

"What *is* that?"

It took him a moment to respond. "**Pardon?**"

"That coldness, like a whirlwind of liquid frost. It only happens when you stop speaking. Sometimes I hate it."

"**It's . . . I'm . . .**" The god paused again, and the ice swirled once more.

Tassariel nearly screamed.

"Calculation," Elos replied at last. "It requires a certain cold detachment. It is an unfortunate side effect that it causes you such discomfort."

She scoffed. "That's putting it mildly. I want to roll around on burning coals every time you do it, just to balance the temperature out."

"Sorry."

"Whatever." He clearly wasn't going to stop. "So, what is it you're calculating anyway? The odds of my jumping off the nearest cliff if I have to listen to one more abyss-taken word from you?"

"Something like that, yes."

"Don't tempt me."

"I'll try to steer us clear of any high ledges in the future."

Tassariel sighed. "Of course, falling wouldn't even be an issue it you hadn't taken my wings away."

"How many times must I say it—there was no other choice."

"There's always a choice. Anyone who says otherwise is either a fool or a tyrant."

To that, Elos had no reply. The ice didn't even stir this time.

Tassariel sighed, leaning back in her chair. It wasn't very comfortable. Opulent, yes, but far too stiff for curling up and relaxing. It seemed much the same with the rest of the room she'd been given. The bed was too soft, and the embroidered sheets itched. The carved table legs, made to look like the branches of some exotic tree, kept knocking into her knees. The horn-shaped goblets spilled water down her chin. It was an interior chamber and thus had no balcony—no natural source of light—but the lightglobes placed in every corner left no room for even a sliver of shadow, bathing the whole space in an eerie, perfect glow.

Tassariel hadn't left the room once. Not since she'd been brought here after meeting the queen and told, in very polite terms, that she wasn't to step foot outside without explicit permission. A day and a half later, and she was still too scared to crack open the door.

"Just what the abyss are we even *doing* here?"

In answer, a knock sounded at the entrance to her chamber. Tassariel jumped to her feet with a squeak.

"Come in?" she said.

The door swung inwards. One, two, four guards piled in. A pair posted by the door. The other two approached.

"Sit," one ordered.

Tassariel obliged.

They took their places at either side of her, facing in. She noted, with equal parts amusement and disgust, that their waists were both eye level with her and less than half a pace away, and that their ridiculously festooned armor formed comical bulges around their groins. She felt manic laughter rise into the back of her throat.

The next figure to enter stifled it.

The minister shuffled in, still wearing those same ornate robes. Tassariel cringed internally at the sight of him. He put her on edge, for some reason, though she could not explain why. She'd only just met the man.

She found herself breathing a sigh of relief, however, when the queen came in behind him. Tassariel had a feeling the ensuing conversation would be much different if the minister had come alone.

The relief was short-lived. On the heels of the queen came one more figure.

The woman.

If her reaction to the minister had been hidden, she could do little to keep from broadcasting her feelings at the sight of her. And Elos did far more. He awakened within her, not as a cold, calculating blizzard, but as a red-hot flow of lava.

Tassariel recovered quickly, making sure to keep every limb, every finger, every single strand of hair, firmly in check. Elos writhed against the bonds she placed over him, but they seemed to be holding.

For the moment anyway.

The three figures lined up before her, just inside the

doorway, fifteen paces away. The minister was fully energized. *It seems like they're taking no chances with me. Best not give them a reason to act.*

"Your majesty," Tassariel said, bowing her head. She couldn't do much else from her seat. "Minister. I'm honored that you've come to see me."

"Our apologies for making you wait so long," the minister said. "But I sense that you do not blame us for that. The situation is quite . . . unusual, wouldn't you say?"

"Unusual. Yes. That word sums it up well."

"And if it weren't for the queen's good graces, you'd have been locked up in the dungeons rather than housed in her own guest chambers."

Tassariel locked eyes with Arivana. "You have my deepest gratitude, your majesty."

"Think nothing of it," the queen said. "I'm afraid my dear friend Tior here is a little overprotective, especially since the recent attempt on my life."

"Someone tried to assassinate you?"

Arivana nodded. She lowered her eyes and, almost imperceptibly, shook. "Yes, well, I'm sure the incident when we first met was simply a misunderstanding. I thought you would appreciate the opportunity to explain yourself."

Tassariel took a deep breath. Elos had helped her prepare the story. And, like all the most convincing lies, it held a measure of truth. Far too much of one, in fact.

"My mother died in childbirth," Tassariel began,

"and the only memory I have of my father is when he left me. I was barely twenty years old, a child, still, by valynkar standards.

"When he left, he was with a woman. And that woman"—Tassariel glanced briefly at the queen's handmaiden—"looked just like her."

The minister let out a sound somewhere between a cough and a grunt. "Not a happy parting then."

"No."

"I suppose I can forgive such a reaction as you had the other night, in light of this information. Do I have your assurance that the incident will not repeat itself?"

Tassariel gazed once more at the handmaiden. She smiled. The hot rage of her god rested just behind the warmth she was attempting to convey.

She graciously bowed her head.

The minister cleared his throat. "Well. Now that that's settled, there's still the issue of your supposed 'service' to the crown."

"Tior," Arivana said, "please—"

"My queen, I must insist. I have no problem giving Tassariel status as a guest, with full privileges, including freedom to wander as she chooses throughout your tower. But granting her an advisor position—above even me, no less—is something the council cannot in good conscience allow."

Tassariel stood at last. The guards at her side flinched, reaching for their swords, but Tior halted them with an upraised hand. He raised an inquisitive brow towards her.

"It need not be so formal as that, your majesty," Tassariel said. "I simply wish to help. Any way I can. My faith demands it."

"Faith?" Tior huffed. "I've seen men do despicable things for faith. Far worse, even, than for any other cause."

"And I've seen wonders, Minister. Miracles. Compassion to make even the most cynical person shed tears in awe. All only possible by the power of faith. What's your point?"

She averted her eyes from Tior and missed whatever reaction might have shown on his face. She didn't care what he thought. The speech hadn't been directed at him anyway.

Elos, however, began to squirm, ice and lava mixing together in a chaotic stew. Tassariel wasn't sure if she should smile or sob. *Let him chew on* that *for a while.*

Soft feet approached, and Tassariel looked up. The queen stood less than a pace away. The guards quivered, looking ready to pounce at the slightest questionable gesture.

"I already said I would be honored by your service," Arivana said. "And I'd be remiss to take back my own word."

Tassariel gasped, looking down to realize that the queen had taken hold of her hands.

"Please," Arivana continued, "coordinate your efforts through Minister Pashams. I look forward to seeing what your help may bring."

Tassariel bowed her head, squeezing the queen's fingers gently. "As do I, your majesty."

The party left her room without another word. Tassariel smiled, sat down, then unfolded the note the queen had passed to her.

> Tassariel,
>
> If you are serious about helping me, you must do so in secret. Meet me tomorrow at noon in the royal gardens, between the fourth and fifth hedgerows on the north side, just past the tulips. I will explain everything I can, and, hopefully, you can do the same.
>
> With utmost secrecy,
> Arivana

"Well, now," she said. "Perhaps we're in the right place after all."

CHAPTER 14

Draevenus stumbled through the woods, losing his grip on a bundle of sickly-looking berries. He stopped, wheezing as he bent to retrieve them. They weren't much, but it was the best he'd found in a day and half of searching. Mevon needed something to eat. Desperately. Still, it took all of his willpower not to gobble them down himself.

He reached a familiar place on the path and knew he was close. Cutting through another thicket, Draevenus came in sight of a low overhang, leafy branches leaning over the entrance. He contemplated calling out, but thought better of it. Though he'd seen no other threats in the area—neither beast nor beast-like man—he'd occasionally heard cries that sounded all too close for comfort.

Instead, he paused outside the concealing brush, and whispered, "Mevon? You awake? It's me."

All he got in reply was a feeble groan.

Draevenus carefully lifted and set aside a few branches with his free hand, revealing a shadowed alcove behind. Sagging to his knees, then his side, he slithered into the cramped, redolent space.

"Find anything?" Mevon asked, barely above a whisper though not by choice.

Draevenus rolled onto his back, panting, and reached his hand out. "Here."

Mevon grabbed the berries. Draevenus didn't even notice when their fingers touched, having no more energy to siphon, it seemed.

He tried not to be jealous as his companion inhaled the meager meal.

It seemed less than a beat before Mevon sighed. "Not enough. Thank you, my friend, but it's not nearly enough."

"I know. I'm . . . sorry."

For a time, they lay at each other's sides, in silence except for their labored breathing and the all-too-audible rumble of their stomachs.

"Funny, isn't it?" Draevenus said.

"What is?"

"My sister once called us the two most dangerous men on the planet. Can you help but laugh that we're going to be done in by nothing more than hunger?"

"Indeed I *would* laugh," Mevon said, "if only I had the strength."

"Me too."

Another passage of time. Another long silence.

Draevenus wasn't sure, but he might have lost consciousness once or twice. His head throbbed, and his limbs quivered. His belly begged for bread. The pain was a good thing, though. If it stopped, he knew then he'd be in *real* trouble.

Taking a deep breath—which sounded more like a whimper—Draevenus rolled onto his hands and knees and began shuffling out of their shelter.

"Where are you going?" Mevon asked.

"To find more food, of course. There must be *something* around here we can eat."

"There is. And close by, too."

"Wait, what? Where? How long have you known about this!"

"Since before our little skirmish had even ended."

"You can't mean . . . ?"

"Yes. I do. But I didn't want to bring it up except as a last resort."

Draevenus swallowed hard. "You think it might kill us."

"Aye. But we don't have much choice now, I think. It's take a chance or die."

"I know." Draevenus sighed. "Abyss take me, I know."

"Then you know it has to be me that tries it first. Just in case it turns . . . sour."

Draevenus didn't have the strength to argue against his companion's brutal, practical logic. He crawled back out into the open without another word.

He staggered down the shallow hillside, falling only once, before entering the site of their ambush.

Dark bodies lay about in various deathly poses, yet he was surprised to find only the faintest odors of rotting flesh. Whether that was a good sign or not, he took it as one anyway; they couldn't afford another setback.

He sank his claws into the smallest one he could find, unable to trust that his grip could hold, and dragged it back the way he had come. Stopping just outside the alcove again, he cut a few thin slices from what had once been a rabbit and cradled them in a palm before entering.

Mevon propped up a dagger. "Here," he said.

Draevenus selected the top morsel and impaled it on the blade's tip. Calling upon what dredges of dark energy he could find, Draevenus conjured the barest spark of flame and held it up to the meat.

The sizzle set his mouth to watering.

Mevon pulled the now-cooked bite towards his lips. "Here goes."

Draevenus heard the grinding of teeth, slow at first, but quickly picking up speed. The swallow a moment later seemed as loud as thunder.

They waited.

"Feel anything?" Draevenus dared at last.

"Yes," Mevon said, lips twitching into a barely perceptible smile. "I feel like . . . seconds."

Draevenus cooked the next piece right off the end of his claw. Reluctantly, he pushed it towards his friend.

"No," Mevon said. "If you're to keep up with those flames, you'll need your strength as well. This one is yours."

Smoke still curled around the charred meat as Draevenus stuffed it down his throat. It was chewy, and a little bitter, but he didn't mind at all.

He'd attended royal feasts less satisfying than this.

Chase rolled the map out onto the table inside the command tent. *King* Chase, now, Jasside reminded herself. She pulled her attention away from the noises outside the tent. Men shuffling about, metal clanking on metal or sliding across leather, fires crackling, the constant mutter of a thousand voices, each indistinct, yet adding up to a whole that could not be misplaced.

An army on the march.

It brought back memories of her time with the revolution. With Yandumar and Mevon and Gilshamed and the rest. She'd had a purpose then, clear and definite. Personal. She wondered if this current endeavor would be able to match that. If anything ever could.

Chase pulled a slim dagger from his belt and pointed at the map. "This is us now," he said.

Jasside leaned over the table, crowded on one side by Vashodia and the other by Prince Daye. The metal point rested just outside a crooked red line. Scrawled next it were the words *Enemy-held territory*. The area beyond it encompassed more than half of Sceptre.

"And this"—Chase moved the dagger tip over the red line, east and a little north—"is where they're holding the bulk of our people."

"What people?" Jasside asked.

"Sceptrine citizens. Innocents. Why?"

"Are they soldiers?" Vashodia asked.

Daye grunted. "Sceptrine soldiers are not taken prisoner. We win or die fighting. *Surrender* isn't in our vocabulary."

Vashodia gestured dismissively. "They're useless then."

"Useless?" Chase said. "Our people are made to slave away in mines and fields, which were stolen from us by the Panisians. They suffer daily under foreign whips, aiding our enemy directly by their pain. I don't care if you think they're useless. They *must* be freed."

Vashodia sighed, shaking her head. "Do you want to win this war or not?"

"Of course I do."

"Then listen to your elders. I do have a few centuries on you, or have you forgotten?"

"But our people—!"

"Will still be there tomorrow. We may very well end up rescuing them as a matter of course, but not as our first move. That must be here."

Jasside followed Vashodia's finger, which rested at the very edge of Sceptre's southern border, on the symbol of a castle. Deep inside the red line.

"Impossible," Daye said. "We've brought fifty thousand men on this expedition. We'd lose half just making it there, and the other half taking it. I don't see—"

Chase held up a hand, silencing his brother. His eyes stayed locked on Vashodia. "We've a fortress there that controls the pass into Fasheshe. It was the first place taken over when the Panisians invaded. But you knew that already, didn't you?"

Vashodia giggled. "Catching on at last? It's about time."

"We control that, we control their supply of troops and resources," Chase continued. "But my brother is right. We won't be able to march our army in there unscathed."

Jasside smiled, realizing the only possible option. "Then I guess *our* army will have to do."

"That's too dangerous," Chase said. "You haven't seen what their war machines can do. Enormous catapults that lob magic-wrought projectiles, each one capable of obliterating a hundred men in an eyeblink. Bows held by a single man whose arrows explode in a burst of fire. Lances that spit lightning. The two of you going in alone is suicide."

Jasside shrugged. "It sounds like a reasonable risk. I'd almost say sending both of us is a waste of resources."

"Truly?" Chase said.

"My apprentice never exaggerates," Vashodia said. "It's one of her better qualities. Still, I don't think it's a good idea for us to go alone. We don't know the terrain, after all. And we'll need someone capable of guarding our backs."

"I'll go," Daye said. Chase opened his mouth, but Daye trudged forward. "Hear me out, brother. They need me. And you'll need someone across enemy lines whom you can trust. I'll take a caster with me and send messages regularly, so you can be kept abreast of the situation. I know what these two are capable of. Just seeing how they helped the refugees left me in awe. Imagine that level of power translated to combat. Panisahldron doesn't have a dozen casters combined on the war front who can match either one of them. This is an opportunity we can't afford to pass up."

Chase chuckled. "You had me at 'I'll go.'"

The brothers clasped forearms over the table, each grinning ear to ear.

Jasside smiled along with them. It would be good to have the prince along. Spending too much time alone with Vashodia could be hazardous to her health. And besides, Daye was . . . nice.

She peered down at the map again, as much to clear her head of distraction as anything else. "So much red to erase," she said, snatching a peek at her mistress. "We've got our work cut out for us."

"Six months," Vashodia said.

"Until what?" Chase asked.

"Until the coalition forces are in full retreat. Provided, of course, that you follow my instructions to the letter."

Chase grunted. "If it drives those bastards back to their own lands, I'm willing to try almost anything."

"Good. Now, split your army and send them northeast and southwest of our current position. Probe the enemy positions, raiding when you can, but do not let yourself be drawn into a pitched battle. You're here as distraction, for now."

Chase nodded. "Understood. We keep their attention while you drive a spike into their back. It will unbalance the whole line. We can pick them apart, little by little, and they'll have no reinforcements to come to their aid."

Vashodia nodded. "Very good. Once the fortress falls, you'll be able to collapse their western front with ease. Sweep in and occupy the pass. In the meantime, Mierothi territory is not far away. I'll call in some daeloth to reinforce the position and guard against sorcerous counterattacks."

"Where will you be after that?"

Vashodia dragged a claw across the map, scratching the red line along its length. "Knocking down every stronghold they have."

Jasside could not help but feel a surge of elation at the announcement, a feeling she knew both brothers shared in by their exuberant faces. If they could actually pull this off, it would go down in the chronicles as the greatest military upset in history. And she and Vashodia would be solely responsible. Her whole body shook in excitement as she pondered the possibilities.

The whole world will know our greatness.

But her eye was drawn to a lonely spot on the map, a slight depression still visible from where the king had laid his dagger.

The place the prisoners were being kept.

Compassion, as ever, played second fiddle to practicality. The people would have to suffer a while longer.

Why is it that greatness so often precludes the possibility of goodness?

Jasside wished she had an answer. She only hoped that, sometime during this campaign, she would have the opportunity to find one.

Arivana stared at the bloodstained stones, completely forgetting how to breathe.

"Are you all right?" Flumere asked.

Arivana barely heard her. Heartbeats thumped inside her skull, drowning out sound and thought. Her mouth went dry. Every inch of her skin tingled and shook. She hadn't been back to the gardens since the . . . incident. She'd tried not to think about it at all.

"It was a mistake coming here," she said. "I'm not ready to face this. Not yet."

She spun, but Flumere grabbed her by the shoulders, turning her back around again. "Easy there," the woman said. "You called this meeting, didn't you?"

"Yes, but—"

"And wouldn't it be rude to miss an appointment you arranged yourself?"

Arivana sighed. "I suppose."

"Good. Now relax. You'll scare the poor woman off if you approach her so rigidly."

"If she even shows."

"She will." Flumere began kneading her hands into Arivana's shoulders. "I'm sure of it."

The queen groaned as the woman's strong hands seemed to leach the very tension from her muscles. After a mark of this, her whole body began going slack. She jerked upright, blinking away her exhaustion and sucking in a puddle of saliva that had found its way to her outer lip.

"Come on," Arivana said. "The meeting place is just ahead."

She made sure to keep her eyes averted from the ambush site as they strolled past and into the hedgerows. The towering shrubs blocked off the world beyond, helping her focus her thoughts and prepare for the meeting ahead. This was no time for distractions.

They came, at last, to the agreed-upon location, a secluded spot well away from prying eyes and ears. Though they had arrived early, the valynkar woman was already there. She pivoted to face them, looking just as surprised as Arivana felt.

"Greetings, your majesty," Tassariel said. Her eyes flicked to Flumere but snapped back without lingering. "I'm sorry for getting here early. I wasn't sure if you would actually come."

Arivana let out a burst of laughter. Then immediately covered her mouth in embarrassment. *So much for a good impression.*

Tassariel smiled. "You were thinking the same thing, weren't you?"

"Yes." Arivana sighed, and it seemed the tension that had been gripping her since she had slipped the note into Tassariel's hand evaporated like dew before the morning sun. She gestured at a nearby bench. "Come, sit. I'm dying to hear what brought you all the way out here."

After arranging themselves, Arivana allowed herself a good study of the woman's face. This close, she seemed younger than her previous estimate. Perhaps only a few years beyond herself. But the eyes seemed positively ancient, glittering with the weight of ages. The disparity seemed . . . strange.

"So," Arivana, "you said you had come to help me. What, exactly, did you have in mind?"

"To be honest? I was hoping *you* could tell *me*."

"I don't understand."

Tassariel lowered her chin and stared at a spot a few paces ahead of her. "I came at the behest of my god. I've got a sort of direct channel to him, you might say."

"Really? What's that like?"

The valynkar twisted her lips before saying, "Eventful."

Arivana laughed again. Tassariel even cracked a smile this time.

"Excuse me," the queen said. "Do go on, please."

"Yes, well, he sent me here with instructions to aid the person most in need of outside help, and to trust my intuition as to whom and what that might involve. Which led me to you.

"So, your majesty, I must ask: What is it that you need assistance with?"

"I'm . . . not sure. I mean, if I ever needed help from a valynkar, I could always go to your consulate—"

"Those are your minister's words, not yours. If I may be so bold, you should spend less time worrying about how not to upset him. No relationship should be based on fear."

Arivana cringed, folding in on herself, making her body small on the bench. Emptiness rumbled in her stomach. She nearly flinched when Flumere put an arm around her shoulder.

She turned to her handmaiden, fighting back tears. "Is it so obvious?"

"Yes," Flumere said. "I've been meaning to say something, but I had not the courage. Forgive me, my queen."

"Oh, stop it. If anyone is to blame, it's I. I can't expect you to shoulder my burdens. And don't you dare start with that 'my queen' and 'your majesty' talk again."

Flumere managed a thin smile. "As you wish . . . Arivana."

She rotated to face Tassariel once more. "You want to know how to help me? It seems you already have."

"Perhaps as a start," the valynkar said. "I could tell from the very beginning that Minister Pashams had his claws in you. I didn't realize they were so deep that you couldn't even see them."

"Is it really so bad as all that? He's been so kind to me. After my parents and siblings died, I only had my aunt to look after me. But he's been taking care of everything since she tried to kill me."

"She *what*?"

Arivana nodded, suppressing a tremble. "In these

very gardens, not two hundred paces from where we now sit. It's why I wasn't sure I'd be able to make it here today."

"Smart thinking then, deciding to meet here. If *you* didn't even expect to come here, I doubt anyone else would either."

"I hadn't thought of that, to be honest."

"My feeling is some part of your mind knew it would be a good idea, nonetheless. Some small voice, lurking in the depths of your consciousness. I'd start listening to it more often if I were you."

"I think I will."

"And what does it tell you now about this minister of yours?"

Arivana closed her eyes, trying to quiet her thoughts. She took a deep breath. "That even if he means well, he thinks he has the right to control me, as one would a pet or an infant. I am neither. I may be young, but I'm still a queen. I think it's time we both learned that."

Tassariel smiled. "Maybe I can be a help after all."

"You have already. Truly. I cannot begin to express my gratitude. How ever can I repay you?"

"Just tell me one thing."

"Name it."

"What else is troubling you?"

Arivana sat back on the bench. She thought of all she'd been through these past few years. The loss of her family. The assassination attempt by Claris. The subtle molding by Tior. The family taken as slaves over nothing. A young guard, cut in half, whose dying thought was only of beauty.

"There's something wrong with Panisahldron," Arivana said. "A sickness lurks at the very heart of our society. It *must* be excised. Will you help me do that? Can you?"

Tassariel's eyes grew wide. "That's a rather hefty task. I don't—" She stopped and looked away, furrowing her brow.

Arivana tilted her head, gazing at the woman curiously. "What is it?"

The valynkar shook, clutching her elbows as if cold. "I'll do it," she said. "I came here for a reason, and it appears this is it."

Arivana wouldn't let herself be bothered by the woman's peculiar behavior. This was an opportunity she couldn't afford to miss.

She smiled. "Where should we begin?"

CHAPTER 15

Mevon ran.

It felt good to be in motion again. Blood flowed through limbs returned nearly to full strength after too many days spent in lethargic recovery. His chest heaved as he sucked in cold-yet-humid breaths. Balanced sweetly upon that edge between exertion and strain, Mevon was once again glad to be alive.

The pack of dark creatures nipping at his heels made him smile.

He darted through the trees, sticking to the easy footing of the path as their growls and barks and ragged caws crowded him in. Birds took flight in droves, squawking in fright, as bulky black forms disturbed the underbrush below and the branches above. The gap closed by hairs every few paces—as he intended. For their plan to work, he'd have to get the timing just right.

Draevenus had been seeking out packs for the better part of three days. It had taken that long to find one that fit the criteria: few in number, all of a similar size, and none of them men. Despite their primal nature, the feral humans had displayed far too much intelligence to let their pack fall prey to such a simple trap.

And Mevon still wasn't sure if he was willing to kill them or not.

The proscribed place came into view, and Mevon slowed. An ambush site of their own, to make up for the one they had foolishly fallen into. The one that had nearly done them in. Mevon narrowed his stride, keeping his feet even more strictly to the path. The beasts howled, thinking victory—and their next meal—to be close at hand.

From six different directions, they pounced.

Mevon sprang forward, pushing all of his considerable if slightly diminished strength into clearing the area in time.

Surprised yelps sounded behind him.

He skidded to a halt, spinning with blades bared in case any had managed to evade capture. The precaution proved unnecessary. All six creatures twisted in suspended nets, thrashing like nightmares.

Mevon straightened, sheathing his weapons. "Perfectly placed," he said. "Not that I expected anything less."

"And perfectly executed." Draevenus sauntered out of the shadows on Mevon's left, dancing daggers across his knuckles. "Like leading mice to cheese. You have a talent for animal wrangling it seems. If you ever find yourself in need of employment, you now have something other than slaughter to turn to."

Mevon grunted. "I'll keep that in mind."

Draevenus drifted closer to their captives, narrowing his eyes at each in turn.

"Not too close," Mevon advised. As if to emphasize the point, one beast swung a long talon towards Draevenus, missing by only a hand span.

The mierothi chuckled at the creature's effort. "Not to worry, my friend. I think we've found our candidate."

Mevon nodded and stepped close. The foul creature barked at his approach, swiping ever more wildly. He watched, studying the movement of dark limbs, then thrust his hand forward at just the right moment. The talon caught in his grip.

Screeching with renewed fury, the dark animal clenched, seeking to pull Mevon close to its slavering beak. He didn't give it the chance.

His free hand unsheathed his dagger, and in a single motion, chopped off the taloned foot.

The beast's cries of fury morphed into cries of pain.

Mevon stepped back, tossing the severed limb to the side. The yelps from the other creatures intensified, becoming nearly unbearable. He tried to ignore it as he wiped the black blood from his hand.

"One wing, too," Draevenus said. "This would all be pretty pointless if it could simply fly back to the source."

"You're still sure that's where it will go?"

The assassin shrugged. "It's the best lead we've got. Something, somewhere, caused all these beasts to transform. I'm betting that's exactly where they'll return upon receiving a grievous injury. If that doesn't lead us to Ruul, nothing will."

"I suppose if anyone would know, it'd be you." Mevon approached the net again and stabbed surgically, snipping through tendons in the wing opposite the severed limb. He stepped back and nodded. "Ready to go."

Draevenus went behind a tree and released the rope holding up the woven lattice of rope.

Beast and net alike crashed to the ground, and the occupant flapped madly to free itself. It almost looked like it would make one more try for a kill, but a gust of conjured wind from Draevenus sent it screeching and hobbling away.

Mevon watched it disappear down the path, dark smears of its blood indelibly marking its trail. It would be next to effortless to track.

"Are we done here?" Mevon asked.

"Almost."

He felt a tingle as the mierothi energized again. Clawed hands lifted towards the remaining beasts, letting fly blue flame. The growls soared in volume and pitch until their sudden absence gave way to the crackle of cooking meat. A savory aroma filled Mevon's nose.

"Dinner," Draevenus said with a smile. He withdrew a dagger. "And even enough left over for the road."

"That's it," Daye said, pointing through the trees. Jasside saw the stone walls of the fortress, glowing orange before the rising sun. "Are you sure you don't want me coming with you?"

"Quite sure," Vashodia said. "We wouldn't want to be disabling their wards, now would we?"

"Why not?"

"Because that would ruin the surprise."

"Ah. You're electing the stealthy approach. I should have guessed."

"No, no, my dear prince. The surprise is for *you*."

"I don't understand."

"You will." Vashodia pivoted away.

Jasside moved to follow but stopped short when a hand gripped her arm gently. And her power fled.

"Be careful," Daye said.

She turned and peered into his eyes. The sun framed his face, and she stood in his shadow, surprised to find herself completely content. *Being under the power of a void isn't so scary when a good man lives under the nullifying skin.*

"I will," she said, smiling up at him. "I promise."

"Come, apprentice," Vashodia called. "Battle awaits."

Jasside gave the prince a helpless shrug, then followed her mistress. They traversed a forest floor smothered in pine needles and doused in mist, climbing uphill towards the fortress. Jasside prided herself that she wasn't winded when they reached the crest and came within sight of where the outer walls met the ground. A few years ago, she'd have been huffing halfway up and likely would have had to stop for a rest. The constant travel had been good for her physical health.

But the killing wasn't good for her soul.

The first time she took a life, it had been her own father. Justice, she thought. At the battle of Thorull, when she'd killed her first mierothi, she'd thought much the same even though she hadn't even known the man personally. He was guilty simply by virtue of his race. It had all seemed so simple back then.

Now she walked at a mierothi's side on their way to kill some humans. She let out a snort of laughter.

"Something funny?" Vashodia asked.

Jasside shook her head. "Just life. It never turns out the way you expect, does it?"

"For most people, no."

"I suppose you don't include yourself in that 'most' category, do you?"

Vashodia flicked her wrist. "Please."

They strolled a few more paces, then came to a halt. They stood now at the edge of a field filled with tree stumps and coarse grasses, all blackened by flame. A kill zone, three hundred paces deep. Jasside felt a thrumming sheet of energy so close she could touch it, and beyond that several more, layered inside each other in hemispheres around the fortress. The perimeter walls were simple enough, but two great constructs poked up behind them. Hollow tubes charged with sorcerous energy that, according to Sceptrine reports, could launch projectiles a hundred paces or a thousand, with the accuracy of a dart and the devastation of a tornado. Artillery, Daye had called them.

The Panisians knew their business it seemed. At least when it came to war.

"Attack or defend?" Vashodia asked.

"Attack," Jasside replied without hesitation.

"Feeling eager, are we? Gone too long without a corpse to your name?"

Jasside resented the accusation. "Nothing of the sort. I thought you knew me better than that?"

Vashodia smiled. "Just stoking the flames, my dear. You'll need the heat for what's to come."

"I think the cold will do just fine, thanks. Wouldn't want things to get out of control."

"Is that why you chose attack? Think I'll cause too much collateral damage?"

"With you, that always a valid concern. People near you always seem to get burned."

"Only those I intend, my dear. You'll do well to remember that."

Jasside scoffed. "I can hardly forget it."

Vashodia sighed, then lowered her hood to her shoulders. "Let's begin, shall we?"

Stepping forward through the first layer of wards, they both began energizing.

A shrill noise blared throughout the fortress immediately—the alarm sounding. Other responses took a moment to take effect. They obviously weren't expecting any sort of attack.

And certainly not one like this.

Figures stirred on the battlements as they sauntered across the killing field. Dozens of them. Now, hundreds. One man stood above the rest, waving and shouting something made incoherent by the distance. Probably telling them to stop and state their business, coupled with thinly veiled threats for failure to comply. Jasside paid him no mind. They weren't here to negotiate.

Energy pulsed out from Vashodia, forming into a bubble that moved as they did. A complex shield that would stop just about anything that came their way. Jasside had reached her own capacity a few beats ago but didn't want to strike before Vashodia's defenses were up.

There was nothing to stop her now.

She raised her arms, one each towards the two artillery pieces.

"Still with the silly hand waving?" Vashodia said.

"Always," Jasside replied. "I don't trust my own mind just yet, and I don't think I ever will. Not in one mere lifetime anyway."

"You're limiting yourself, you know."

"That's exactly the point."

Energy spun into the form she desired. Something

flashy to get their attention. Her hands came down. Twin bolts, like lightning formed of darkness, lanced out of a cloudless sky.

The two artillery pieces exploded into a million sizzling shards.

Jasside had time for a single breath before the arrows began streaking down.

They struck Vashodia's shield and burst into flames. Fire blanketed Jasside's vision, thumping in her ears with each concussive blast. The smell of fresh char filled her nose as the heat scorched nearby tree stumps and clumps of grass.

"I can't see a thing," Jasside said, waving an arm forward. "Would you mind?"

"Making demands of me now?" Vashodia said in mock exasperation. "I thought I'd beaten that out of you long ago."

Jasside shrugged. "I've regressed. More beating will be required. Some clarity, please?"

"Oh, very well."

The shield morphed at Vashodia's gentle urging. It widened and softened, becoming an almost gel-like layer between them and their adversaries. The arrows kept whizzing towards them, but instead of exploding, they merely slowed, then stopped altogether, caught in the shield like fish in a net.

Without the flaming obstruction, Jasside had a clear view of the gate. She lifted her hands again, slicing upwards with pointed fingers. A sharp line along the outside edges of the gate glowed white-hot from top to bottom. The massive iron doors squealed like stuck pigs as twisted metal crumpled to the ground.

"Oh, come on!" Vashodia said. "We're trying to make an *entrance*. How can we dazzle and delight our foes when we're stumbling across debris?"

"Have a little faith," Jasside said. She chopped down, striking the collapsed gate with a strand of energy like a whip. The whole mess split down the middle, and Jasside pushed the two halves aside. She gestured at the clear path ahead. "You're not the only woman with a plan."

Vashodia twisted her lips into a smile. "It seems you're learning something after all. Glad to know my patience isn't being tested for nothing."

Together, they strolled to the very center of the fortress courtyard. Arrows continued converging, forming a floating, wood-pricked sphere. Some soldiers tried rushing them but staggered back after getting mired in the shield. It was then that Jasside felt a new presence: a dozen enemy casters, fueled by light, began assaulting their position with direct spells. Vashodia grunted.

"Trouble keeping up?" Jasside asked.

"Impertinent little tart."

Jasside counted that a victory. Her best one yet.

"Do get on with it, please," Vashodia said. "I'd rather not be here all day."

"Gladly."

Jasside took a single glance around her at the soldiers swarming like ants, their cacophony an unwelcome distraction, and she knew what she needed to do. Something to quiet them. Something to make them listen. She rubbed her hands together.

I think I've got just the thing.

She thrust her hands outwards. The very air slammed against itself, breaking like waves, and from the center of it she yelled, "Silence!"

The spell crashed throughout the fortress, toppling those caught unbalanced and staggering the rest. Not a soul moved. The wind seemed to howl, but Jasside knew that was only by comparison. She heard few other sounds that could compete.

She had their attention, it seemed.

With space now to breathe, she looked around at the soldiers arrayed within the fortress. Not all were the same, their differences marked as much by their attire as their disposition. Slender, narrow-eyed soldiers in studded armor, similar in style to the Sceptrines, manned the walls with their bows. Another group with bodies wrapped in layered cloth, with oiled beards and wide-curved swords, were centered around the wreckage of the two catapults. Small, dark men with spears and feathered vests guarded every doorway. A few others who didn't seem to fit any other group were scattered among the rest. And it all created a problem.

Jasside wasn't sure who was in charge.

She angled her head and lips towards her mistress. "Which ones are the Panisians?"

"How should I know?"

"This is no time for games. I know you've traveled the world before. There's no use denying it."

Vashodia looked at her sternly, but Jasside soon realized the mierothi was suppressing a smile. It was a strange look on her mistress. She almost thought it might be pride.

At last, the mierothi waved a hand before her. "The fairest ones in all the lands. Or so I've been told."

Jasside sighed. She'd have to do this the hard way. She cleared her throat, lifting her chin and her voice. "Who is in charge here? I demand to speak with the commander of this fortress."

Every eye turned towards the group of casters standing on the ledge of an interior bunker. A heartbeat later, a woman stepped forward, dressed in jeweled armor more artistic than functional. Though fair, as Vashodia had promised, the woman's stony gaze made Jasside suspect the woman knew her business.

"You're in command here?" Jasside asked.

"I am," the woman replied.

"Then, on behalf of the mierothi sovereignty, and the nation of Sceptre, I—"

The commander's body exploded.

She could only stare, dumbfounded, as blood and bits of flesh splashed across the other casters. Everybody in the fortress flinched, coiling to make an escape should the destruction continue.

Jasside hadn't cast the spell that destroyed the Panisian woman, but its flavor was similar.

She glanced down, horrified, at Vashodia. "What the abyss was that about?"

Vashodia giggled. "I said it before, didn't I? We are not here to negotiate. It sounded like you were coming dangerously close to such pointless discourse."

"I was trying to get them to surrender peacefully."

"And it worked. Look."

Jasside spun in a circle, noting that every last person was throwing down his weapons and raising his hands. No one looked in the mood to challenge them further.

She turned again to Vashodia. "Your methods are effective, I'll admit. But shortsighted."

Her mistress giggled again. "I don't think I've ever been accused of *that* before. Bravo, Jasside, you continue to surprise me. Care to explain your unorthodox position?"

"It's simple, really: Dead people make horrible hostages."

"Ah, so you do have a practical bone in your body. I was beginning to think you'd gone soft on me."

Jasside shook her head. "If our enemy expects no mercy, they'll fight all the harder."

"Mercy only makes us look weak."

"If mercy makes you weak, then I don't want to be strong."

"Yes you do. Else I'd never have considered you for my apprentice. And I surely wouldn't have kept you around for as long as I have."

"There is strength in restraint. Taking prisoners

alive is far more difficult than mass slaughter. Even *you* can't debate that."

Vashodia sighed. "If you insist. It really isn't worth getting worked up over." She smiled. "Let's go deliver our surprise to Prince Daye, shall we?"

"Finally," Jasside said, "something we can agree on."

Tassariel looked up as soft footsteps approached. She smiled at the newcomer. "Glad you could make it, Arivana," she said. "Any trouble slipping your minister?"

"Not at all," the queen said. "Flumere here is quite adept helping me escape notice."

The handmaiden blushed. Tassariel felt fire erupt inside her as she looked at the woman. The rage of Elos never failed to respond to Flumere's presence though he still had not told her why. She'd given up asking.

Tassariel drew her eyes away from the handmaiden, and the fire subsided. She shivered. The cold was still there, always lurking in her bones. Elos rarely spoke anymore, but he was always calculating, churning his ice inside her. She'd almost grown used to it, again, but the sudden arrival—and equally sudden departure—of the fire drove her awareness of the chill towards agony.

"Is that him?" Arivana said, inclining her head towards a man seated across the courtyard.

Tassariel set her jaw to banish her acute focus on her inward turmoil, and nodded.

"Best go say hello, then," the queen added.

"I've a better idea."

Tassariel tiptoed behind the man, drawing within a hand's width without his realizing she was there. She sidestepped right, then tapped his left shoulder. She smiled gleefully as he dropped his book and jumped up, spinning almost in a complete circle before finding her.

"Tassariel!"

"Lerathus!"

He threw out his arms wide, and she fell into his smothering embrace. Though they'd never met in person, the correspondence they'd had over the years made him feel closer to her than almost any person alive. The hug was exactly what she expected and not a bit awkward.

At last he pulled away, laughing merrily and shaking the grasslike hair sprouting from his head and face. "I'd no idea you were in town, lass. When did they let you out of that prison called home?"

"A few months ago."

He eyed her up and down. "Adulthood looks to be agreeing with you."

Heat rose to her cheeks. "Thank you."

Lerathus glanced past her shoulder, and his eyes widened briefly. He stepped clear of Tassariel and bowed. "Your majesty," he said. "Your presence is an unexpected pleasure. Please be welcome to the consulate."

Arivana inclined her head. "Thank you, Lerathus. Tassariel has told me so much about you."

"Has she now? In that case, I must apologize. Tass

here has a flair for the dramatic. Likes to tell lies and such. I'm not half so bad as I'm sure she's made me out to be."

Arivana hid her mouth behind a hand. "It's been nothing but good things, I assure you."

"Nothing but good things? She's a worse liar than I feared."

Tassariel punched him in the chest. Lightly, for her, but he still staggered back half a step. "Oh, stop it, Lerathus. You're making me look bad."

"Using me to make a good impression was your first mistake."

"I'm beginning to realize that now."

Lerathus chuckled, squeezing Tassariel around the shoulder. "So what brings you here?"

"I'll give you one guess."

His eyebrows rose along with the corners of his lips. "Books! Of course. What else would it be with you? By Elos, I swear, you've read half our archives already. Looking to get started on the other half, eh?"

Tassariel shrugged. "Something like that. It appears the queen here is as avid a reader as I am."

"Quite so," Arivana piped in. "But I'm afraid I've read everything in my own library. All the books worth reading anyway. Tassariel has been telling about all the amazing things she's learned from your archives, and I thought it would be wonderful to sit down amidst a fresh group of tomes."

Lerathus frowned, then leaned in close to Tassariel. "You do know it's for valynkar only, right?"

"Yes," Tassariel replied. "But surely an exception can be made. She is the queen, after all. And . . ." she lowered her voice to a whisper, " . . . only a child."

He whispered back, "Some say it's children who are the most susceptible to the influence of dangerous literature."

"Is that what you'd call our archives? Dangerous?"

"Not for me to say."

He withdrew a step, then eyed Arivana. "If it were up to me, your majesty, I'd give you the grand tour, even let you take a peek at the restricted section. Alas, I'll have to confer with the consul before I can do that. They'd take my wings if I even tried!"

Tassariel flinched.

"Please do," Arivana said. "I wouldn't want you getting in trouble on my account."

He bowed, then turned and strode away. Tassariel stepped around the corner and watched his progress through the vine-wrapped pillars of the consulate. He didn't have far to go. Less than a hundred paces away, he approached another valynkar male. This new man was ancient, older-looking than most members of the council even. She assumed someone so elderly and holding a prestigious position would be well-known, but the man was a complete stranger to her.

"Think they'll let us in?" Arivana asked.

Tassariel nodded. "If they'll bend the rules for anyone, it will be you."

"I hope so. My own library seems to be deliberately lacking anything that could tell me what is *actually* going on in my own kingdom. These archives sound like they'll be a different story."

"We valynkar have a tendency to write everything down. If there's something to be found, it will be here."

Lerathus and the other valynkar conversed for a while, complete with several curious glances towards her and the queen. After a few marks of this, the ancient valynkar stepped behind a pillar. Lerathus crossed his arms, as if expecting a long wait. Tassariel felt a faint flash of energy.

"What is he doing?" Arivana said.

"No clue. If I had to guess, I'd say he's . . ." No. It couldn't be.

"What?"

Tassariel furrow her brow. "Give me a beat, please?"

"Of course."

Tassariel placed one hand against the nearest pillar to steady herself, then energized. Inhaling deeply, she stepped into communion.

She made out the star of Lerathus directly in front of her, but there were no others close to him. The ancient valynkar should have been practically merged with Lerathus, as close as they were physically. There was only one explanation.

He was in communion, too.

Panisahldron was a busy city. Dozens of people were there at the moment, sending messages or conversing with other casters. Tassariel ignored them all. The consul would be seeing someone important. If he was anywhere, it would be at the very heart of the city.

She turned towards it, an unmistakable pillar of light, thick with powerful casters. She moved swiftly towards it. Closing in, she observed a hollow area in the center of the cylinder, devoid of all stars, and realized what she was seeing. The towers of the six great houses were filled with magic users, but the royal tower was empty of them.

No, not entirely empty. She spied two figures, huddled close together. One wore a hooded robe, concealing the face beneath, but the other she recognized as the consul.

Almost as soon as she spotted them, however, they both vanished, returning to their corporeal bodies. She glanced over her shoulder. Another star now rested next to Lerathus. But who was the other man?

With no time to contemplate, she released her hold on communion. Blinking, she stepped into the sun shining into her eyes, her mind and body once more combined. Lerathus approached. His smile seemed forced.

"I've good news," he said.

"We'll be allowed in?" Arivana asked.

"Yes. But . . . you'll have to come back tomorrow."

"Why?" Tassariel said.

"It's quite old, and is undergoing a bit of a restoration at the moment. But it should be cleaned up come the morning."

"He's lying," Elos said, the first words he'd spoken in days.

"I know," Tassariel said. Then, realizing what she'd done, added, " . . . that you've done us a huge favor, Lerathus. You have my thanks."

"And mine as well," Arivana said.

Lerathus bowed to the queen once more, then winked at Tassariel. A toll ago, it would have sent her heart to fluttering. Now, she only felt cold. At least this time, the cold was of her own making and not that of the god inside her.

"See you tomorrow, then," she said.

She turned away, and the queen followed her. They walked in silence until outside the walls of the consulate.

Tassariel sighed. "You do realize what the delay is all about, right?"

Arivana nodded. "They need time to remove any . . . controversial books. The only question is why? What do they keep there that could be so damaging? Why would they need to specifically keep it from *me*?"

"I don't know. But I peeked into communion, and caught the consul in conference with someone inside your tower. If I had to guess, I'd say he was asking permission."

"From Tior? That doesn't make any sense."

"Little of this does."

The queen practically growled, frustration plain on her face. "I guess we'll have to come tomorrow regardless. It will raise more questions if we go to all this trouble and don't even show up."

"Agreed," Tassariel said. "We may be lucky, though. They don't know what we're looking for."

"And we do?"

"Good point."

CHAPTER 16

As expected, tracking their quarry had been easy. *So* easy, in fact, that Draevenus had started to grow bored.

He almost would have welcomed it if the crippled bird-thing had joined up with another pack along the way. Such an encounter would have at least led to a little fun. But the beast stayed arrow straight on its path, veering only to *avoid* other creatures. And they, in turn, steered clear of it. The dark animal hobbled along despite its injuries like a creature coerced, as if some force outside itself drove it to keep moving, keep striving for something it could not explain or deny.

It was a feeling all mierothi knew well.

Ruul's power had changed them, all those centuries ago. And not just in the more obvious ways. Indecipherable at first, they only become more apparent as those so inclined among their tribe began testing the limits of their newfound abilities, putting them to use against those who once oppressed them. It had seemed a good idea at the time.

History had proven otherwise.

In all that time, Draevenus had come to learn that adversity was such an easy thing to overcome; next to the burden of power, it weighed little more than a feather.

"Might be trouble," Mevon said.

Shaking to clear his reverie, Draevenus returned focus to his senses. "What is it?"

"Listen."

He closed his eyes and held his breath. A moment later, a faint conglomeration of noises reached his ears, coalescing into an unmistakable image that chilled his bones: the roar of a bestial crowd.

"Trouble indeed," Draevenus said.

"Should we check it out?" Mevon asked.

Draevenus glanced up the path. The dark blood of their quarry, though diminished in quantity, still left fresh stains on tree trunks and leaves hanging across the trail. They'd have no difficulty resuming their hunt.

"Very well," he said. "But let's make it quick."

"Do we know any other way?"

Draevenus shared a smile with his companion before crouching and turning off the path.

Stalking forward, he angled towards the haunting sounds. He pushed aside branches with care, avoiding tangled patches of brush when he could and stepping lightly over them when he couldn't. Mevon, for all his bulk, did a fair job of following his lead. They arrived at a shallow ledge overlooking a glade, crawling the last dozen paces to avoid being seen by whatever was making the grotesque sounds just below them.

Poking his head over the crest, Draevenus was not prepared for what he saw.

A score of stick-and-grass huts formed a tangled web in a tree cluster at the glade's edge. Below it foamed a pack of dark men and beasts larger by far than any they'd yet seen. At least fifty black-furred bodies crowded around the base of the elevated village, circling and roaring in displays clearly meant to threaten. An occasional arrow zipped upwards to little effect except to make their presence felt.

Movement, at last, began showing among the huts.

"What are they doing?" Draevenus asked. "Can you see anything?"

"Aye. I can."

"And?"

Mevon shook his head. "You'll see soon enough."

His companion's words became prophetic a mark later when the villagers began lowering something by rope from the center of the huts: a bundle wrapped in darkly stained cloth.

"Some kind of tribute, maybe?" Draevenus said. "Or . . . ?"

The bundle twitched.

"Oh."

"Oh?" Mevon said. "*Oh?* That's all you can say?"

Draevenus shrugged. "What do you expect of me?"

"They're sacrificing people over there, Draevenus. *Living* people. Shouldn't that matter to us?"

"It does. But we didn't come here to involve ourselves in local affairs; we came to find Ruul. We can't let ourselves get distracted when we're so close to achieving our goals."

Mevon didn't respond. Draevenus peeled his eyes from the scene below, finally glancing at his companion.

The man quivered with rage.

"What?" Draevenus demanded, feeling his own anger spike. *Must I deal with your reticence yet again?* "Do you want us to march down there now and try to put a stop to this, just the two of us?"

Mevon remained silent yet tilted his head slightly. Draevenus could almost see the words *why not?* written across his friend's mind.

"No," Draevenus said. "Even if we could prevail—which isn't guaranteed—there are other packs besides this one. Not to mention the fact that it's half made of men. Are you willing to put aside your vows for what may amount to a pointless gesture?"

Mevon shuddered, lowering his eyes.

"I didn't think so."

"But we must do *something*!"

"We will. But not here. Not now. Once we find Ruul, we'll make him answer for everything he's done, this included. If we stopped to help everyone he's hurt, we'd just be applying bandages to a bleeding wound, and we'd never have time to actually repair the ruptured vein."

Mevon furrowed his brow, returning his gaze towards the sickening scene below. He sighed. "I suppose that makes a kind of sense. Still, I can't help but feel guilty—"

"Yes," Draevenus interrupted. "You can. Guilt lies with those who caused the injury. No one can be held at fault for another man's sins."

Unhesitant, Mevon nodded.

Finally, a point we can agree on.

They crawled backwards away from the ledge, readying to leave and resume following the injured beast. Draevenus forced himself not to look back as the bundle finally crashed into the ground, and the pack's howls reached a fever pitch, a chorus of savagery accentuated by a single, human scream.

"The main force is in position," Daye said. "They're only awaiting your signal."

"Make sure they do," Jasside said. "If Chase assaults too early, the coalition artillery will tear his army to shreds. Too late, and we'll be caught inside a very angry city, with fifty thousand enemy soldiers chasing us down."

"Sceptrine will do its part. I have absolute faith that you'll do yours."

She and the prince exchanged smiles.

"Done with the chatter?" Vashodia asked. "Or can we go ahead and capture this highly strategic location?"

"A city full of helpless people, you mean," Jasside said.

The mierothi waved the sentiment away. "This is a choke point. All enemy supplies and reinforcements come through here for distribution. Cut this limb off, and the whole beast writhes."

"And almost half a million civilians languish under Panisian martial law."

"If they actually cared about their freedom, they'd have won it long ago. Are we going to have this same old argument every day?"

Jasside took a deep breath. "I suppose not."

"Good." Vashodia peered up at Daye. "Be a dear and guard our backs through this?"

He furrowed his brow. "You want me to come along? I thought you said I would stand out, or worse, be recognized?"

"Oh, none of us can hope to avoid that. But my apprentice and I don't know this city half as well as we should. If we run into any trouble, we'd have a hard time finding our way back to our targets. Plus, having a void in tow has certain . . . tactical advantages. You don't seem to know quite how to use your skills to their fullest advantage. But believe me—*I* do."

"I see," Daye said. Jasside could tell he struggled to say even that, much less anything else. Compliments from Vashodia were rare enough to have that effect.

"Ongshaith awaits liberation," Jasside said. "I'd say the city has waited long enough, wouldn't you?"

No further deliberation seemed imminent. Together, the three of them descended a hillside strewn

with thick brush towards the southern wall of Ongshaith.

Jasside marveled at their success so far. She and
Vashodia had stormed three other forts in the last
month, and King Chase's army had dealt critical de-
feats to the coalition's westernmost position, which
had been relying on aid from the very places she and
her mistress had struck.

As much as it pained her to admit, Ongshaith
was every bit as important, strategically, as Vashodia
claimed. The whole war could tilt in Sceptre's favor if
they were successful today. And Jasside *knew* they would
be. It was, perhaps, that very confidence that ensured it.

She reached the wall ahead of the others and energized. Gesturing forward, she rearranged the particles
in front of them, spreading them apart just enough to
allow them passage through. They couldn't risk the
gates, and this small use of energy would go unnoticed
this far away from the military-controlled zones. They
slipped through the gap and continued on. Vashodia
gave Daye the lead.

They slunk through the winding streets of the city,
turning to avoid dead ends and paths too choked with
civilians or coalition soldiers. The prince instinctively
avoided crowds, a decision Jasside could find no fault
in. Though they'd likely be able to blend in better,
any confrontation would mean increased collateral
damage. And more dead Sceptrines would defeat the
purpose of their coming here.

Several times, they were forced to duck behind market stalls or into doorways as enemy patrols passed by. Jasside watched, horrified yet enthralled, every time they did. The coalition soldiers marched in a close knot, surrounded by Sceptrine citizens who were chained hand, foot, and neck. A wall of humanity between them and the rest of the populace. It would make any dissidents think twice about assaulting them, for they'd have to carve down their own people first.

The brutal practicality of it sickened her. Though, not quite as literally as it did Prince Daye, who vomited after seeing it for the first time.

By all reports, the enemy held positions in a cluster at the very center of the city. As they drew nearer to the heart, signs of the occupation grew in frequency. And intensity.

Houses, and sometimes even entire blocks, lay in burnt-out ruins. Screams erupted with regularity as whips fell over those pressed into forced labor. Raucous male laughter and soft female whimpers leaked out of second-story windows. Fewer people who weren't also in chains roamed the streets.

Avoiding patrols became nearly impossible on the main streets, so they stuck to the alleys, carefully sneaking from shadow to shadow. After what seemed an eternity, they at last drew near to the place occupied by the Panisian military. Daye paused at a corner, peeking around.

"Five men," he whispered back to her and Vashodia.

"One of them is a caster. An entrance to the main compound is just behind them. What should we do?"

"We can't do any casting," Jasside said. "Not this close. That will alert them to our presence too early. We need to know the layout before we make any overt strikes."

Daye turned to Vashodia. "Please tell me you have an idea?"

"Perhaps. But I doubt you'll like it."

"I'm all ears."

Vashodia flipped up her hood, gesturing for Jasside to do the same. Once both of their faces were properly concealed, the mierothi did the last thing she expected.

She reached out and grabbed Jasside's hand.

"Come, 'mother,'" Vashodia said. "Let's go on a little trip to the market, shall we?"

Too stunned to disagree, Jasside and her "daughter" waltzed past an equally surprised Daye out in the open space of the alley.

The coalition squad noticed them immediately.

"What have we here?" one of them said.

"A couple of lost souls, I'd wager," said another.

"Best show them the way home, then," said the first.

Jasside spied two of them rushing their way and began dragging Vashodia as fast as she could. They reached the opposite corner with only ten paces separating them from the approaching men.

Vashodia dropped her hand and spun, eying Daye behind them and pointing down the adjacent alley. He nodded.

"Ready your dagger," the mierothi said.

Jasside flattened herself against the wall, pulling the small blade from her waist. "A little warning next time?"

Vashodia shrugged, lifting her claws. "That would only give you time to start thinking. You're no good at killing when you think too much."

Jasside opened her mouth to retort but lost the opportunity. The guards came around the corner with vicious smiles on their lips.

She pounced.

Vashodia had been right. It was easier with no time to think.

Jasside pulled her dagger free from the man's neck, then stepped back as he fell to the ground, gurgling. She looked over to see her mistress wiping her claws clean. A spatter of blood painted the wall next to her victim. She heard a noise from the alley.

Daye!

She spun towards him, but he was already gone from his spot opposite them. Jasside dashed around the corner.

She found him, chest heaving, as he stood over three corpses. Enemy blood dripped from his blade. His eyes seemed far away.

"Did their caster get off a spell?" she asked.

He peered down at the sword in his hand. "I did it," he said, ignoring her question. "I found my courage again."

Jasside froze. She hadn't realized this had even

been an issue for him. Looking back, however, she didn't know how she could have missed it. She had been too wrapped up in herself, in the mission, to notice even the simplest truths and needs about the people around her.

"You did well," she said, slowly edging closer. "But keep your blade ready, prince. There are more enemies ahead."

He nodded.

"Done with the emotion session?" Vashodia snapped, coming round the corner. "Or can we get on with our business?"

"Yes," the prince said. "Finally."

Jasside drew near to him and gently laid a hand on his arm. She gave him a smile. "Lead on, prince."

He marched forward without another word, and Jasside noticed something in his stride that hadn't been there before. Confidence. A sense of purpose. Pride. It almost seemed a new man was there before her. Or, perhaps, it was the old one rising once more. Either way, she was glad of the change.

The prince pushed open the door mounted on the recently erected wall ahead of them, which served as a barricade for the coalition forces at the center of Ongshaith. He bounded through alone. Jasside heard a short struggle ensue and came inside to find two more fresh bodies at his feet.

The warrior in him had indeed returned. And not a moment too soon, by the looks of it. Four more enemy soldiers converged, and they were still out of sight of the main yard. She still couldn't risk a casting.

Daye charged in among them, slashing high. One man ducked the swing, but another caught steel in his throat and spun to the ground, dead.

The one who'd dodged staggered towards her, then turned towards Daye. Jasside lunged at him and sank her dagger in the back of his head. The body fell, bringing her with it. By the time she managed to untangle herself, one of the remaining enemy soldiers was on his back, clutching a bleeding leg, and the other was skewered on Daye's sword.

Vashodia strolled in behind her and stepped on the downed man's leg. He screamed. She leaned down, putting the tips of two claws a scant breath away from his eyeballs.

That shut him up quick enough.

"Numbers and disposition," Vashodia said. "Answer true and fast, and I'll make sure—"

"You live to see another day," Jasside interrupted. "You have my word." Vashodia rolled her eyes at her apprentice, but Jasside ignored it. "Fail to satisfy, however, and I'll leave you to *her*."

The man made a choking sound and began shaking. Jasside took that for consent.

"A little space for our guest?" she said.

Vashodia sighed but withdrew her claws.

The man swallowed hard. "Please, I'll tell you anything. Just spare my countrymen."

Jasside inspected the beaded armor dangling from his chest and guessed him to be among those soldiers hailing from Phelupar, some island nation beyond even Panisahldron itself.

"Why so afraid?" Vashodia asked. "What harm can we two little girls do?"

"I know who you are," the man said. "Word's gotten round about some witches knocking over every fortress in their path. If you aren't part of that group, I'm a blind man."

"What other words have been going around about us?"

"That you kill without mercy. That you take no prisoners except those you keep around to eat later. That you made deals with devils from beyond the abyss, and that's where you got your powers from."

" 'Devils from beyond the abyss?' " Vashodia giggled, that trill familiar sound Jasside had come to know so well. Jasside almost couldn't help snickering herself. "My, my, that *is* a new one. Yet, ironically, dangerously close to the truth."

Jasside felt her jaw drop. "What?"

"Why should we spare your countrymen?" Vashodia asked, ignoring her.

"We're all conscripts, my lady. None of us wants to be here, but the coalition treaties demanded troop tributes. Nearly all the men of age from every village back home are taken. We've no stake in the war. No purpose. We don't want to die for nothing."

"What about the other nations?" Jasside asked. "Are they all as innocent as you?"

The man shrugged. "Fasheshe has been skirmishing with Sceptre for centuries. I'm sure they've no qualms about this invasion. Can't speak for the others."

"So," Vashodia said, "we're to spare your people, kill the Panisians and the Fasheshish, and ignore all the rest, hoping they'll do the same to us. Is that all?"

"Shouldn't be too hard if the rumors about you are true. Besides, they're all laid out neatly for you." He gestured deeper into the compound. "Bad ones to the left. Everyone else to the right."

Jasside nodded, turning to Daye. "Mind guarding him?"

"For how long?" Daye asked.

"Until stealth is no longer a factor."

"How will I—?"

"You'll know soon enough."

He nodded. "Be careful in there."

"I will. And thank you."

"For what?"

"For being concerned. It's been awhile since anyone has cared what happened to me. It's comforting." She swallowed. "Especially coming from you."

Jasside brushed past him, chin held high, without waiting for his response. She wasn't sure she was ready to hear it yet. Vashodia was right on her heels.

They came free of the alley into an open space that looked to have once been a park of some kind. It had since been repurposed and was now the staging ground for the main enemy force occupying Ongshaith. At least three dozen of the massive, magically charged artillery pieces rested in two long rows, pointing tubes in all directions so that they could rain down destruction within or without the city walls.

They would have to be destroyed first.

Jasside began energizing, then stepped to the right.

Vashodia grabbed her elbow. "This is war, girl. No time for playing nice. I won't lose my most promising apprentice in ages because she died from a fit of conscience. Understand?"

"I'll be careful," Jasside said. "But I only kill those who deserve it. You'll do well to remember that."

"Throwing my own words back at me?" Vashodia laughed, not her normal high-pitched giggle but something throaty and unnervingly adult. "So be it. Your fate is your own. Don't come crying to me when your own foolishness comes back to bite you in the ass."

Vashodia released her and stomped off to the left, energizing. Jasside finished filling up her own reserves, then began eying her targets. The double row of artillery pieces gave her a perfect opportunity for surgical obliteration.

Head down, she strode quickly between the two nearest tubes. It wouldn't be long, anyway, until the enemy casters felt their presence. Might as well make the best use of the surprise she could.

Thrusting her hands to each side, Jasside released some of her dark energy. The four nearest artillery pieces erupted into molten flames.

She ran forward, not bothering with a shield. The massive weapons themselves provided a barricade between her and whatever lay beyond. The enemy would have to get extremely lucky to hit her with either arrow or spell. At her tenth stride, she reached outwards again, setting another group of artillery pieces alight with blue fire.

A crewman stumbled into her path. Without thinking, Jasside elbowed him in the gut, then shadow-dashed past. She landed in perfect position to destroy a third group of the huge weapons. Running, she now realized, made her an easier, more predictable target. Dashing worked better, and faster. And she had plenty of energy to spare.

Inhale.

She shadow-dashed forward again. Pulsed destruction outwards at the malign weapons placements. Dashed again.

Exhale.

It took less than a mark to vanquish the last of the artillery pieces on her half of the compound. The signal had gone up with the very first, the flames themselves a beacon to her allies outside city. King Chase and his army should begin their assault any moment, and the coalition would find itself lacking the most potent tool in its arsenal.

A job well done, Jasside, she told herself. *You should be proud.*

The moment she emerged past the last flaming ruin, arrows and spells began streaking towards her.

Jasside threw up a shield, barely warding off the first blows. Soldiers converged on her position. She sent a pulse outwards, flinging them all to the ground. It bought her a moment. She closed her eyes, sensing for the enemy casters. Two, four, ten, a score. Now, a lot more. It didn't matter. Vashodia had been right about one thing. This was war. Jasside wasn't sure the morality of killing mattered when people were doing their best to tear you to shreds. Never mind that she was the one who had initiated things here—Panisahldron had started it *all* when they chose to cast blame in the face of Sceptre's denial. Undoing that great wrong was the whole reason she was here.

She would do her best to kill as few as possible, but with the casters, she had no choice. Power such as this could not be easily contained. And, she guessed, no one with sorcerous blood in his or her veins who strode within a war zone could ever be entirely innocent.

That she herself fell into that category bothered her. But only a little.

She had work to do.

Jasside reenergized, then prepared her spells. One by one, she funneled her energy towards each of the enemy casters. One by one, they fell. Some, probably sensing the scope of her power, formed their own shields in defense, but they provided little protection. Her spells ripped right through them like a sword through cloth.

More soldiers raced towards her now, hundreds of them. She recognized many of them to be their captive's brethren, fellow Phelupari. Had she given her word to spare them? Right now, she couldn't remember. But, based on his testimony, she wasn't sure they were deserving of the same fate as the casters.

She peered back over her shoulder. The artillery pieces lay in smoking ruins behind her. Farther back, the other half of the encampment writhed in furious swaths of chaos and death. Vashodia, apparently, hadn't been nearly so restrained in her use of sorcery. Jasside heard what seemed like a thousand screams from as many paces away, a discordant sound that chilled her to the bone.

Disengage.

Wherever the thought came from, Jasside had no problem obeying. They'd done their part, and now the Sceptrine army would do the rest. She couldn't let the fact that these men might very well still die in the coming battle affect her decision. War was an ugly thing. Until they got to the root of it, this was the best they could do.

Jasside turned around and shadow-dashed back the way she had come. Other than the occasional crewman futilely trying to salvage an artillery piece from her flames, she ran into no resistance.

Sighing, she walked back towards the alley just as Daye came out, pushing their captive ahead of them. Before she could say even a word, Vashodia strolled towards them, explosions and cries of agony still erupting behind her.

"Is it finished?" Daye asked.

"More or less," Vashodia said.

"Let's get to the rendezvous point," Jasside added. "Your brother can handle the rest from here."

"What about him?" Daye said, giving the Phelupari man a gentle shake.

Jasside met the man's eyes. "Release him," she said. "The Sceptrines will win the day, with or without his kinsman's involvement. Perhaps he can convince them that surrender is the best option."

"Without question," the man said.

Daye sheathed his sword. The limped man ran off without another word.

"Let's go," Vashodia said, casting cold glances towards both Jasside and the prince. "I've had enough of your sentiment for one day."

"**T**his. Is. Pointless!"

Arivana threw down the book she'd been reading.

Tassariel lowered her own book to her lap as Flumere dutifully picked up the queen's discarded pages. She sighed, wishing she could find some reason to disagree. The bookcases held too many empty spaces, bereft of even a hint of dust. Anything useful had been hastily removed.

"You're probably right," Tassariel said. "I'm sorry this turned out to be a waste of time."

"We suspected as much coming in. I guess I just hoped those fears would be proven false."

"I was a fool to trust the consular personnel simply

because they were my kin. I should have known better. All the worst people I know are valynkar."

"You just haven't met enough humans, then. Give it time."

Tassariel chortled at the joke.

Flumere looked aghast, darting her eyes back and forth between Tassariel and the queen. "You—" she began then paused, shaking her head. "We aren't all that bad. Many are choked by greed and lies, only thinking of themselves, but there are still good people out there. Selfless people who think only of the welfare of others. Who are . . . compassionate."

Arivana leaned back in her seat, folding her arms. "Name one."

"Arivana Celandaris," Flumere said without even a breath of hesitation.

The queen squeaked, then fidgeted in her seat. "You really mean that?"

"Absolutely. I'd not be going this far beyond my duties for just any old queen, now would I?"

Moisture glistened under Arivana's eyes. The girl reached out to Flumere and clasped her hand. "Thank you, Flumere. It means so much to me to hear you say that."

Tassariel wondered at the exchange, marveling that these two people had managed to look beyond their respective stations and, somehow, become friends. They were both exceptional people, in their own way. No wonder Elos had brought her to the two women.

Even if he *had* tried to kill one of them.

"Shipping logs."

Tassariel flinched at the sound of her god's voice. She hadn't heard it in a while. Hiding her mouth behind a fake cough, she whispered, "What?"

"Sorry. Couldn't see the covers from here. Had to wait for the right angle of sunlight to bounce off . . . oh, abyss, you don't care. Look, up there on that shelf past the queen's right shoulder."

Tassariel glanced up. A pile of ragged parchment, ancient by the looks of it, sat atop a bookcase she hadn't even seen before. They'd been in here long enough that the shifting sun had finally deigned to drench the spot in light. In shadow, it had been all but invisible. She supposed he wanted her to fetch them.

She stood.

Arivana's eyes whipped towards her. "Ready to leave? I'm about done with this charade as well."

Tassariel made a show of stretching, touching her fingertips above, then behind, her. "Not quite. I'd like to do one more sweep. See if they missed anything that could be useful to us."

"Good luck," Flumere said. "I've searched about every bookcase in this section already. If there's anything to be learned, I doubt it will be here."

"I don't know," Tassariel said, edging closer to the place Elos had indicated. "Maybe we just need to redefine our parameters. Look in pages we haven't previously thought would hold the information we seek."

"That implies we actually know what we're looking for." Arivana sighed. "Which means our systematic approach has been worthless. Anyplace really *is* as good as another."

"Exactly," Tassariel said. She reached out for what Elos had called shipping logs, moth-chewed parchment wrapped in frayed leather, and blew dust free from their top. "Abyss, even these old rags might hold the hint we need."

The queen shrugged. "Might as well. Bring them over, and we'll have a look."

Tassariel returned and plopped the crinkled mess down on the table between them, kicking up a cloud of dust and setting them all to coughing. What she'd blown off the top had only been a fraction of the whole.

"Trying to kill us?" Arivana said as she waved the air clear in front of her.

"Slowly, maybe," Flumere said. "These pages are as likely to give our lungs the rot as they are a clue."

"Sorry!" Tassariel said.

"Get going," Elos said. "There's something in here. I know it. Read!"

She passed out the first three of the six bundles. All three of them set to the sacred task of poring over pages packed with tedious accounts of goods shipped, including buyer, seller, shipper, price, package, procurement, origin, destination, all planned stops along the way, and some categories she didn't even recognize. After half a toll of silent skimming, replete with many yawns and sighs and droopy eyes, they all seemed to reach the last page about the same time.

They'd found nothing.

Tassariel handed out the other three.

Within a mark, Flumere sat up straight. "Hold on a minute."

"A what?" Arivana said.

"Nothing. Look at this."

Tassariel leaned in close on the handmaiden's right side, as the queen did the left. She peered where Flumere's finger rested, on the "package" column of the very first entry.

"Tuleris," it read.

"What's that?" Tassariel asked.

Arivana had gone pale. "A common Panisian surname."

Tassariel felt a cold grip her, one that had nothing to do with her god's calculations. "What else does it say?"

They studied the lines together. Next to Tuleris was a kind of shorthand that was easily worked out. "M–34" translated to a thirty-four-year-old male, probably the father of the family, shipped to a noble household in Fasheshe.

"It doesn't say why, though," Arivana said. "What would they send him there for?"

"If they're treating people like cargo, can it be anything good?" Tassariel stated.

No one seemed in the mood to answer.

Skimming down, the next four entries also had the main package title of Tuleris. By translating the markings, they discerned that a woman, age thirty-one, and three girls—eleven, ten, and eight—were also moved, though none to the same place. The picture that formed presented a startling parallel to Arivana's trip to the lower parts of her city.

And then they read the year of shipment.

It was 11,079, AF.

The queen hissed. "This is over seven hundred years old!"

"That only means this has been going on for a long time," Tassariel said. She sat back, rubbing her temples. "And that the consulate has had a hand in it."

"Can we know for sure what any of this means?" Flumere asked. "I can't help shake the feeling that all this is just speculation run wild."

"I know someone who could tell us for certain," Arivana said.

"Who?" Tassariel asked. "Minister Pashams?"

The queen scoffed. "He's too busy trying to get me to open up my legs to the prettiest boy in the land to give me a straight answer."

"Then . . . ?"

"Claris."

Flumere shook her head at Arivana. "Out of the question."

"Claris," Tassariel said. "Your aunt. The one who tried to kill you."

"And nearly succeeded, I might add," Flumere said. "It's foolishness to expect any straight answers from her. And impossible besides."

"It might have been both except for two key facts." Arivana held up a finger. "One. We have dire need of her knowledge, and she's in no position to deny us answers. Two." She held up another, wiggling it towards Tassariel. "We have you."

"Me?"

"Yes. Flumere's charm might be enough to get us into the dungeons, but not enough to get us out undetected. With your aid, I'm confident we can do both."

"I've never broken into a prison before. What makes you think I'll be any use?"

The queen smiled. "You're older than my grandmother, you know. Lots of people have heard of you. It didn't take much asking around to find out about your Calling."

Tassariel raised an eyebrow. "What does that have to do with anything?"

"If the accounts are true, you're well versed in all manner of martial arts. Including Phelupari stalking and subduction techniques. I've every confidence that, coupled with detailed information about guard locations, patrols, and schedules, you can get us into and out of the dungeon without doing any permanent harm to my dutiful jailers. And, failing that, there's always your magic."

Tassariel sighed. She let her eyes glaze over, looking inwards. *If you've got any wisdom for me, Elos, now would be a good time to impart it.*

But her god kept his lips shut, churning with frosty fury. She knew he couldn't hear her thoughts, but it still irked her to have to make this decision on her own.

Peering at the girl across from her, it wasn't hard

to see how great a woman—and queen—she would someday become.

The ice inside seemed to spike as she spoke. "Well, I *did* promise you my aid, did I not? I can't very well back out now."

Arivana smiled. Flumere threw her hands into the air.

CHAPTER 17

"Where did it go?"

Mevon lifted his head at the question, blinking quickly to adjust his view outwards to the bare hillside they trekked. He'd been staring at his feet again. Their quarry had scarcely veered from the trail the entire time they'd been following it. Draevenus had far better skills at tracking and was far more motivated. Mevon hadn't done much the past week except drag himself along.

The scene from the village in the trees kept repeating over and over in his mind.

"I can't find it anywhere," Draevenus said, insistently. "Did you see where the abyss-taken thing got to?"

"Sorry," Mevon said. "Wasn't paying much attention."

"Of course you weren't. It's not like this is the most important thing I've ever done in my considerably long life."

"Sorry," Mevon repeated.

The mierothi released an exasperated sigh. "Forget it. Just help me find the trail, would you? It has to be around here somewhere."

Mevon didn't even know where to start. The dark creature had stopped bleeding from its wound days past, and they'd been forced to use more subtle markers to guide their path. More accurately, Draevenus had. Mevon wandered in a rough arc opposite the assassin, eyes darting along the ground as if he knew what he was looking for.

The soft soil was indeed pitted by myriad tracks, from beasts in every shape imaginable. Some very well might have belonged to the one they hunted, but he could barely tell talons from claws, much less which were fresh.

Mevon sighed, trying to pretend competence while his mind kept drifting to memories. They'd passed three more villages nearly identical to the first one, and each time had witnessed the same gut-wrenching scene. The enormous pack always seemed a step ahead of them, migrating from place to place to collect their grisly tithes. He wouldn't call it luck that they'd avoided direct contact; despite his vows to abstain from homicide, Mevon kept wishing for the chance to unleash the storm against them.

"I think I found something," Draevenus called. "Come take a look."

Mevon gazed over at his friend, who was crouched, peering into a deep cleft beneath the roots of a gnarled, ancient tree. He began shuffling towards the assassin. Only a few steps in, however, a shadow caught his eye.

A familiar shape, falling in an awkward spiral from the naked branches.

One good wing, and a single remaining talon, were all the beast needed to enact its revenge.

Draevenus fell, spraying black blood from a cut across his back.

The bird-thing screeched in triumph.

Mevon sprang forward, all lethargy forgotten as he raced to his companion's defense, finding—at last—a reason to unleash the storm. The distance between them closed like a falling wave, but the creature merely craned its head sideways, loosing a mocking twitter, then darted into the cleft. It disappeared in a beat.

Mevon skidded to a halt, blades now in hand, regretting that he didn't have a chance to finish off the wretched thing. He looked down at his friend. Draevenus struggled to lift himself, groaning with each twitch. The wound on his back just oozed for now but still looked deep enough to need stitches. Lots of them.

Mevon knew his way around a thread and needle. But this?

This is gonna take a while.

He didn't bother asking how Draevenus felt, for at that moment the mierothi slumped, exhaling heavily, and closed his eyes. Mevon knelt, checking pulse and breathing, and pressed a spare rag to the wound. Setting down his pack, he yanked open the flap with his free hand and rummaged around for the sewing kit, which, of course, was buried somewhere near the bottom.

"Hang on, my friend. I'll have you fixed up in no time."

He had the thing half unpacked when he heard the first howl.

East. Ahead of their direction of travel. Half a klick away at best.

Gotta hurry.

Just as Mevon finally laid fingers on the object of his search, echoing cries rang out from the north, and again from the south. A mark later, all three repeated, obviously much closer this time.

The only clear direction was west. Back the way they'd come. Fighting the creatures off would be one thing, but trying to do it while keeping them away from his companion would be impossible. That left but one choice, even though making it grated against his pride.

Mevon restuffed his pack, strapped in . . . then picked up Draevenus and ran.

"**S**o you're saying Ruul *isn't* a god?" Jasside asked.

"No, no," Vashodia said. "Aren't you listening? I'm saying the world's definition of a 'god' is inherently flawed."

"Well, I can't exactly argue with that."

"Of course you can't. You're a convert to that antiquated Ragremon religion."

"How did you know that?"

"I'd not have taken you on as apprentice if I didn't know more about you than you know about yourself. Suffice it to say, I find your beliefs . . . quaint."

"Well, I find them reassuring."

"Faith that disregards the evidence? I don't know what's so reassuring about that."

"Isn't that the whole point of faith? Besides, the evidence is all around us. In the trees and the soil. The sun and the stars. In all living creatures. You, who've seen things few others have, who understands things most can't even fathom—I would've thought you'd be more . . . open-minded."

"To what? A mystical being that controls all destiny? Please. Elos and Ruul may not be gods, but they're closer to it than the one you believe in. Abyss, even you and I are closer."

"How do you—?"

Vashodia raised a hand, silencing her. Jasside lifted her head to peer down the trail.

Their argument, if it could be called that, had stemmed from boredom. They'd been lying in wait nearly half a day now and were soaked to the bone from the incessant rainfall. A crossroads lay farther up the path, and they didn't know which way the convoy would turn. This was the best ambush site for leagues around.

After the capture of Ongshaith, the war had taken a drastic turn. Coalition forces were on the defensive for the first time since the inception of the conflict. The absolute surrender of the Phelupari forces aided things considerably. They'd handled the vast majority of logistics for the Panisians, able to carry small, untraceable loads on their backs over vast distances. Without them, the opposition had been forced to move supplies in more direct manners.

Control spiraled out of enemy hands faster every day, landing neatly in King Chase's lap. His army now burst at the seams with new recruits as more souls were freed from bondage, and those long given over to despair found the spark of hope once more. All thanks to a little mercy, a little kindness, shown to a single Phelupari man.

A fact Vashodia refused to acknowledge.

But that had been another debate, and now was time to focus on the present. "There," Jasside said, as the first scout came into view. His horse plodded along the road, hoof falls muted by the soaked ground and by a million raindrops impacting the trees around them every beat. A whiff of sweat and mildew reached Jasside's nose on the next gust of wind.

"They've been on the trail awhile now," Jasside observed. "Pushing hard to make up for the loss of their Phelupari assets, most likely."

"Or to avoid us," Vashodia said. "How many convoys will this make? Seven? Eight?"

"Nine. You were right about those sensing trinkets. It was a week well spent, laying them along all the major routes. Not a one has slipped through."

"And none will."

"Unless they get smart about our tactics. Look."

A pair of scouts on foot came a hundred paces behind the first. Another hundred behind them, three more mounted men, still with no sign of the caravan.

"They're adjusting to us," Jasside said.

"It figures," Vashodia said with a sigh. "That's what we get when you insist on leaving survivors."

"You also get a cleaner soul. War is an ugly thing already. No need to drag claws through its face after kicking it to the ground."

Surprisingly, Vashodia had no retort to this, appearing almost thoughtful at the remark. Jasside decided to check her food bag later for psychotropic mushrooms because she *knew* she had to be hallucinating.

"We'll have to split up," Vashodia said, as if the sheer inconvenience of the idea were an affront to her character. "I'll corral the front half if you'll be so kind as to assault the back."

Jasside nodded. Without further delay, she melted into the woods, paralleling the road just close enough to keep it in sight. The mist and shadows worked wonders for keeping her concealed, even on the move, and she had enough experience in the woods to avoid cracking branches or rustling bushes. She had little fear of being spotted.

Yet, a tingle of unease managed to worm its way through her anyway. She knew immediately what was causing it: Daye. Or, rather, his absence.

He'd rejoined his brother at Ongshaith, after Vashodia made it clear he would no longer be needed to babysit them. He'd been a comforting presence on their campaign, a stolid, dependable companion. Jasside didn't realize how much she'd missed him until now.

Lost in thoughts of him, it was almost no surprise when she stumbled into someone.

She pressed a hand to her eyebrow, nursing a blaze of pain after hitting something hard. Stars swam in her sight. A figure stood tall before her, murky in the mists. A Panisian woman—a soldier—one hand wrenching her sword free from its sheath.

"You're one of them, aren't you?" the woman said.

Too stunned not to answer, Jasside said, "One of whom?"

"One of them witches we've been hearing about." The woman took a step forward, raising her blade. "They'll give me a tower for killing you."

Jasside staggered backwards. She caught her heel on a root and fell flat, slamming into the damp soil and losing her air. Vision narrowed. All thoughts of energizing vanished as she clawed for mere breath. The soldier lunged at her.

After all I've been through, is this how it ends?

Jasside could only watch as the blade tip cut through the air towards her chest. The woman's face loomed over her in the gloom, painted with an expression of fear mixed with hatred and manic joy. It wasn't a lot to go on, but Jasside decided she didn't much like the woman.

And my death will not *come at her hands.*

Jasside rolled. Sharp steel sliced past her arm, thunking into the ground.

She pushed herself up.

The soldier tugged at the sword.

Jasside stepped back, drawing a breath and energizing. The woman freed her blade, screamed, and swung.

It wasn't hard to make her decision.

Jasside lifted a hand. A black web of energy belched forward, shredding the soldier to ribbons. Steaming chunks ran red as they sloshed into a pile at her feet.

She groaned a sigh of relief.

Shouts rang out behind her, along with spouts of energy both familiar and not.

Jasside raced towards the road, sure that during her skirmish the caravan had come abreast of her position if not farther. She energized to capacity, bursting and ready—this time—for anything. Skidding to a halt at the top of a knoll, she leaned around a tree and peered at the road below.

Though broken by trunks and branches, she could easily make out the scene. A score of wagons stretched out along the slick, muddy path. Figures raced to the front, fifty at least. Beams of pure darkness shot out from ahead of them, pulsing like a staccato drumbeat, each searing a hole into a single man and no more. Vashodia was being precise today.

Enemy soldiers fell before the onslaught of dark energy. One had managed to draw his bow before being caught in a beam. The arrow went wild, flying just over Jasside's head and striking a trunk behind her, exploding in a shower of charred bark and kindling.

Jasside winced, covering her eyes to protect from the flash. Heat singed the edges of her robes, and splinters embedded in her arm and leg. Wincing, she quickly pried half a dozen wooden shards out of her flesh, then turned back to the road.

Just in time, too. Another group rushed Vashodia, whom Jasside could now see strolling up the road in the fog. Six bowmen had charged up the knoll and now took aim for the mierothi. At this range, they could hardly miss.

Jasside swept an arm across. Darkness scythed out, chopping through each archer at the waist. Intestines crackled with shadows, bursting from bodies that tumbled in two different directions and filling the air with a stench that made her gag. Four screams erupted from the enemy soldiers, thankfully short-lived as life and breath expired.

She looked towards the wagons again. Immediately, she noticed something new. Something that had not been present on any other convoy.

Cages.

They were attached to the sides of each wagon. Iron bars barely big enough to fit the man or woman of child tucked inside it, all Sceptrine by the looks of them. Human shields—just like they had used in Ongshaith. A foul way to ward against attack. Jasside's stomach lurched at the sight. They all looked to be in bad shape. Malnourished and dehydrated for sure, and likely tortured; her heart went out to them. At least, with her arrival, their suffering would find an end.

It's a good thing Vashodia is being discreet with her castings. Otherwise—

The caravan exploded.

All twenty wagons erupted at the same moment with a pulse of sorcerous energy. She fell to her knees, red flames filling her eyes. Some wordless cry sprang from her throat. Tears flowed like lava down her cheeks.

Heat welled up inside her, and she stifled her anguish with anger, stalking forward at nearly a run. In beats, she drew close to Vashodia.

"How could you!" Jasside said, pointing a finger at her mistress. "Didn't you see the cages? Those were people in there. People! That has to matter, even to you!"

The mierothi waved smoke out of her eyes and shrugged. "Wasn't me."

"It doesn't ma—" Jasside jerked her head back. "Wait, what do you mean?"

"Weren't you paying attention? The energy that caused this—what was its source? Certainly not darkness."

"If not us, then . . ." Jasside spun questing out with her senses. It took only a beat to find the other caster.

She aimed towards the trace and shadow-dashed forward. A wide-eyed man greeted her landing, cowering as she approached. He threw up a shield of light. Jasside swept it aside with a blast of her own energy, too angry for a subtle untangling. The caster plopped face-first into the mud. He lifted his head.

Jasside punched it.

"Why?" she said.

"Orders!" he cried.

"From who?"

"From Panisahldron. Can't let you witches capture any more cargo. Better to destroy it than let it fall into enemy hands."

"And your prisoners along with it?"

His eyes flared with fear. "Collateral damage."

She screamed, punching his head again.

And again.

He started to energize, and she smothered him with a blanket of darkness, blotting out his light like snuffing a candle. Strange sounds emanated from his throat.

Vashodia came up behind her. "Well, well. It seems we found our culprit. A rather wretched creature, wouldn't you say? You will, of course, end his life in the most painful way possible."

Jasside took a deep breath, willing herself to calmness, to sanity. In a way, she had Vashodia's demand to thank for that. She shook her head. "No."

"No?" Vashodia giggled. "Why not? If ever a man could be found guilty of crimes in war, surely this pathetic mess before us qualifies."

"Exactly. Which is why we're taking him to Chase." Jasside gazed down at the man, raindrops dripping from her nose. "He'll get a king's justice."

Still, she punched him one last time.

Just in case.

Arivana pressed her face to the corner, one eye glued down the dim stone hall. She hated waiting. Hated being useless. They were only here because she had insisted, yet she had the smallest part to play in their success. Really, no part at all. She punched the wall in frustration.

"Worried?" Tassariel said from just behind her.

Arivana sighed. "About many things."

"Such as?"

"What we're doing here, to start."

The valynkar patted her shoulder. "Your handmaiden may not be the most beautiful or charming woman around, but she has a certain . . . force, I guess you could say. And she's also quite the actress. She'll do just fine with her task."

"Yes, but once we are inside . . ."

"Then *my* skills will come into play. And trust me, there are few alive in the world who are my equal."

"I know. I mean, we're *counting* on that, after all. But—"

"You're still worried."

"Yes."

"About what you're going to say."

"Yes. That, and Tior."

"Your minister? What about him?"

"He's been acting strange lately. Angry. Almost uncontrollably so. I've never seen him like this before."

"Did he say what it was about?"

Arivana shrugged. "Something about the war, maybe. He's hidden the details from me, but recent developments have worried him. I don't think it's going very well."

Tassariel did not answer for a time. Arivana eventually felt the need to stop staring down the hall and turned her head to peer up at the valynkar. The woman's eyes seemed glazed over, yet she held a thoughtful, intense expression on her face. Almost as if she were wrestling with her own mind.

"Are you well?" Arivana asked.

Tassariel shivered, shaking her head as her eyes came into focus. "What? No, I'm fine. Let's just keep watch, all right?"

"Of course."

Arivana returned to her lookout. She didn't have long to wait before a silk scarf sailed into the hall, falling into a patch of light cast by one of the few lightglobes present.

"There's the signal," she said.

"About time." Tassariel stepped past her. "Stay behind me. And keep your feet light!"

Arivana obeyed as well as she could. Even though she moved as quietly as possible at the valynkar's heels, she couldn't help feeling clumsy behind the woman's balance and poise. As they approached the opening where the scarf came from, she started to hear soft chatter and smelled the savory aroma of freshly baked peach pie. It was the keeper's favorite. Flumere blocked the doorway to the guard shack, her merry voice encouraging the occupants inside to eat up. Behind her back she held a key.

Tassariel snatched it without slowing. Arivana's heart thrummed as they passed the light spilling out from the shack, but no cries of alarm chased them down the remainder of the hall. She had no time to calm as they drew up before a surprisingly nondescript metal door.

Arivana had expected the entrance to the black dungeons to be, somehow, more menacing.

"Here we go," whispered Tassariel.

She placed the key in the lock and began to rotate it, a full breath taken between each quarter turn. The creak of the lock mechanism seemed barely louder than a mouse's footfalls, but Arivana cringed all the same. She didn't have a plan in case they got caught other than saying, "I'm the queen."

She wasn't certain that would mean a whole lot considering she was technically breaking the law.

At last, the lock clicked open. Tassariel pulled on the handle, and the door swung with only the faintest squeal. *Thank goodness they stay diligent enough to oil the hinges.*

They slipped inside. Arivana pulled a strip of leather and wedged it between the door and the frame behind her, keeping it barely open. Flumere had suggested it, figuring they'd likely need a hasty exit and wouldn't have to time to fish for the keys again.

Turning from her task, Arivana was greeted by

near-total darkness. "What the abyss?" she said. "How are we supposed to find our way in this? We'll get lost, trapped down here forever!"

"Calm down," Tassariel said. "Give it a mark, and your eyes will adjust."

"We don't have that kind of time!"

A hand grasped her own in the darkness. Arivana jerked at the touch, but Tassariel's firm grip soon helped to calm her.

"I'll keep hold of you," Tassariel said. "If I let go, I want you to tuck down and make yourself small until I come back for you."

"What if you never do?"

"I will. I promise."

There was a firmness—a confidence—in the valynkar's voice that helped Arivana's resolve. Still, she sighed, trying not to let the fear show in her voice. "Let's go."

Led by the arm, she let herself be dragged through several turns. Hopeless, now, to find her way back out on her own, her panic rose further. The darkness seemed complete. Foul sounds and even worse smells radiated from every cell they passed. Her mind filled in the gaps left by her blindness, surrounding her with nightmares.

They stopped at a corner. Arivana pressed herself against a wall and immediately regretted it. Something slimy coated her back. A whiff of the stuff made her gag.

"Shh," Tassariel whispered.

"Sorry," Arivana replied. "Why did we stop?"

"Roaming guards."

"How can they even see in here? How can *you*?"

"I can't. I memorized the layout of the place last night. And I've trained myself to hear and feel and even taste my way in places where sight fails. I suspect the guards are similarly disciplined. I sense no sorcery at work."

Arivana steeled herself to patience, yet it still took what seemed like tolls before Tassariel tugged her into motion once more.

They turned three more times but encountered no more roamers. Arivana almost let herself relax. Though she still kept expecting her eyes to adjust, the dark remained complete, and the valynkar's sure grasp was the only thing keeping her from screaming.

"If the position I gleaned from commune is accurate," Tassariel said, "the cell is up ahead."

"Good. I don't think I could take much more of this."

"It is rather gloomy, I supp—"

Arivana heard a dull smack and bumped her face into the center of Tassariel's back. The grip on her hand released.

She crouched, then rolled out of the way. Ending up on her side, Arivana balled herself up on the cold, grimy floor, as a struggle broke out all around her. Meaty slaps were followed by sharp grunts of pain—many with a decidedly female timbre. Gasps rang out. Something snapped like branches, once, twice. Wet crunching, and warm fluid splashed across her face.

Arivana wrapped her arms over her head, failing to stifle her whimper.

At last, the noise dwindled until only heavy breathing and muffled thumps remained. The thumps grew weaker, then fell off entirely. A large body slumped to the ground beside her.

Arivana held her breath. She didn't know who—if anyone—was left standing.

The huffing continued nearly half a mark before a rasping voice called out from the darkness, "Are you all right, Arivana?"

She released her breath. "Tassariel! You've no idea how glad I am to hear your voice."

"You're unhurt?"

"Yes. And you?"

The pause nearly broke her heart. "I'll survive."

"What happened?"

"Stationary guards. Didn't move. I had no idea they were here."

Guards. Just men doing their duty. *Her* men. "What about them?"

"They'll live," Tassariel said. "But one will likely wake in the next few marks. Please . . . hurry."

Arivana stood. "Where is it?"

Tassariel grasped her hand and guided it across the hall to a door, to a handle of a pane that slid open at her push. A whisper of air flowed through the gap into the room beyond.

She took a breath. "Claris?"

No response.

"Aunt Claris? It's me. Your niece, Arivana. Are you there?"

She pressed her ear to the opening, and made out the faintest shuffling inside. A labored breath. *Someone* was in there. Were they at the right cell?

Pulling back, she intended to ask Tassariel that very question but was interrupted by a voice from inside. "Arivana?"

She choked. Rasping, slurred, strained, the voice belonged to the woman she once knew, but so deeply deformed as to defy recognition. Everything she had prepared to say leaked out of her mind before the stark madness of her aunt's imprisonment. A sentence Arivana had herself pronounced.

"Yes, Claris. I'm here."

"Why, child? Why the abyss would you come here?"

Arivana had been expecting anger, but the words held none of it. Instead, they were filled with pity.

I can't let myself get distracted.

"I'm here to ask you about statute eighty-seven of the Citizens Refinement Act."

Claris spat. "What about it?"

"We know it's being used to snatch innocent civilians off the street. We know the consulate is helping ship them away discreetly. What we don't know is where and why. We were hoping you could—"

Tassariel coughed.

Arivana set her jaw. "You *will* tell us what you know."

"I will, will I?" Gurgling laughter erupted from the cell. "Why don't you go ask Tior? Swallow whatever lie he decides to fool you with today. Or does he tell you anything at all? It seemed he wore the crown more than you, last time I saw you."

"I'm trying to change that. Why do you think I had to sneak into my own dungeon!"

"Prove it, *your majesty*. Prove you aren't merely a tool, like all your ancestors before you. Prove you actually want change."

Arivana leaned her head against the cell door, gritting her teeth. "Tior told me to have you executed. I should have, after what you'd done, but I couldn't bring myself to murder the closest thing I had to family.

"Why did you do it? Why did you try to kill me? Until you can answer that, I'm not the one who has to prove anything."

Silence descended on the darkness, filled only by the wheezing of the unconscious guards. At last, Claris said, "Oh, child. I could never harm you. I was trying to kill Tior, so you could be free of his manipulations. But he turned everything around. Made me swear not to speak in my own defense, upon threat of the pains he would bring upon you.

"I see now that he wasn't entirely successful. If his claws had been too deep, you'd have never come here."

"No," Arivana said, voice cracking. "But I was close. If Tassariel had not shown up when she did . . ."

"Who's Tassariel?"

"Me," Tassariel said. "A valynkar just released from my city. I speak with the voice of Elos. He brought me here to help Arivana. I'm just glad I wasn't too late."

"That is yet to be seen," Claris said.

"Please," Arivana said, "will you help us?"

Claris laughed again, but this one held the first faint trace of joy. "Of course I will, my queen. On one condition."

"Name it."

"That you first tell me what you're going to do with this information."

"Put a stop to it if we can."

"How, exactly?"

Arivana shrugged, then giggled, feeling silly since no one could see her. "I don't know," she said at last. "But we'll figure something out."

"You must be careful. Tior is far more cunning than you realize. And more dangerous."

"I can handle Tior. Please. Tell me what you know."

Claris sighed. "Statute eighty-seven has long been used to get rid of undesirables among our own citizens. Dissidents. Foreign immigrants. Anyone who spoke out too loudly against the council or the crown. Times were, it only happened a few times a month. People were shipped away as slaves or worse to whoever had money and enough sense to keep their mouths shut.

"Since the war began, the enforcement of the law increased a hundredfold. And most of those taken were sent straight to the front lines. To die."

Arivana cringed, a new wave of grief sweeping over her. "And to think I could have stopped it."

"What, the war? Don't be silly, child. You had no more control over it than I do of my mealtimes in here. And you never will until—"

"Someone's coming," hissed Tassariel. "We need to leave. Now."

"No, wait! I won't leave her here!"

"There's no time. And I don't know how to open this door short of using magic, and in this darkness, I'm not even sure if I can do that. And once I do, every guardsman in the entire tower will come crashing down on our heads."

"But—!"

"Go, child," Claris said. "My freedom doesn't matter right now. You must carry on."

Arivana hesitated.

"Go!"

Tassariel grabbed her elbow and dragged her away from the cell. She wanted to shout that she'd find a way to get Claris free, but the need for quiet stilled her lips. Besides, the sentiment was nothing more than a child's yearning. No need to give her aunt false hope before she was sure she could deliver. And more and more, she was realizing that to be an effective leader, sometimes hard decisions had to be made.

For the time being, Claris would have to stay put.

CHAPTER 18

The forest itself seemed a thing alive as the pack surrounded him again. Mevon could hear their breaths, feel the thump of their footfalls, see their red eyes moving among the shadows.

The carcasses at his feet would soon have new company. He only hoped it wasn't his own corpse joining them.

Mevon tensed, sensing arrows in the air.

He swung up his makeshift shield—layers of wrapped bark strapped to his forearm—just in time to intercept a trio of hissing missiles. The impact sent ripples up to his shoulder, exacerbating the wounds still lingering from the last assault. His blessings had been working ceaselessly to heal him since he'd brought Draevenus to the villagers above, and hadn't quite had time to catch up. That, and the two days he'd spent standing guard, had taxed his reserves of energy.

Good thing there's no lack of fresh meat.

The small fire he kept alive even now snapped and crackled with the roasting flesh of his beastly assailants, the savory aroma masking the stench of death around him. The villagers had been dropping him things to eat: nuts, mostly, with other dried fruits and vegetables.

Talk with them had been tricky. Their words were almost intelligible, but not quite. As if they'd once known how to speak but in the decades—or centuries—of their isolation, their speech had devolved into only the most rudimentary form of communication. It had taken a long time to convince them that Draevenus wasn't an enemy. Even longer to prove that Mevon wasn't insane for wanting to defend them.

No one denied the packs their tithe. No one even tried.

Mevon was starting to see why.

Branches rustled. Mevon spun, checking for approaching threats. He'd chosen his position with care. The tree behind him was as thick as he was tall, its trunk pegged with a horizontal lattice of logs in a rudimentary ladder: the lone entrance to the elevated village. One side of him fell away to a short but effective cliff, while on the other two sides he'd erected spiked barriers, firmly entrenched and pointing their wooden teeth outwards. The pack couldn't assault him en masse.

And he'd proven more than a match for what few they could bring at once.

Another arrow. He remained still while it snapped past his ear. As he knew it would. Mevon was ready this time. He snatched a javelin—really just a sharpened stone tied to a stick—from a pile at his side and hurled it on an opposite trajectory as the latest attack. He heard it impact wetly, and a scream sounded in the night.

Mevon smiled. As much for the accuracy of the throw as for realizing that he didn't need to feel any shame.

Power was at work in this place: rampant, unnatural, without reason or conscience. As was so often the case, those who'd stumbled upon it did not understand what a burden it was. What a burden it *should* have been. Beasts were beasts, even those corrupted by a god's errant power. But men? Men always had a choice.

These had chosen . . . poorly.

When people gave themselves over to such a foul instinct, to prey on the powerless for nothing more than their own abhorrent gains, justice need not wait on procedure. When no other law existed, Mevon now trusted that his own hand would do.

And, moreover, he didn't have to feel guilty about enjoying it.

During the battle for Mecrithos, he'd come to realize beyond all doubt that his abilities as a void were no accident. Whatever mechanism had created magic must have known it would need an opposing force to balance it and created his kind for that purpose.

In the same manner, all men had a natural affinity for violence that could only be by design. That he embodied that truth to the most extreme measure was no coincidence. He *had* to believe that his captivation with blood was intentional, that it had some meaning beyond his own sordid satisfaction. If what he'd found here wasn't proof enough, he didn't know if anything could be. And what greater satisfaction could there be in life than finding the reason for your existence and fulfilling it?

Look, Father, I've finally found a purpose for my . . . predilections. I think you might even be proud.

Then again, Yandumar had never shown anything *but* pride for all that Mevon had become. Maybe this whole journey hadn't been about impressing his father, or Draevenus, or Jasside, or anyone else for that matter.

Maybe it had been about proving his own worth to himself.

The brush around him thrashed with a mass of approaching bodies, a promise of menace played out in bared fangs and claws and hatchets. Black fur shimmered in the moonlight.

Mevon lifted his daggers.

Another battle approached. Many had come before, and many would again, but he didn't have to be ashamed of that fact anymore. Draevenus needed time to heal. The people in this and other nearby villages needed someone to be their champion, to deliver them out of the hand of their brutal, hungry masters.

Mevon was done denying who he was meant to be.

It's time to embrace it.

"Come, then," he whispered to the angry night. "Your judgment . . . awaits."

"**S**hould we kill them?" Vashodia said.

"What," Jasside said, "*all* of them?" She looked over the mass of people, tens of thousands strong, rushing down the valley. "That's a tall order. Even for you."

"But not impossible, else I'd not have bothered to ask. I do not remember including the word *could* in my question. Do you?"

Jasside shifted the reins to one hand, then lifted the other to shield her gaze from dawn's scathing rays. The horse shifted beneath her, scraping the stony path with its hooves and sending pebbles cascading down the ridge on her left. They'd acquired the animals from the last convoy they'd attacked, the only four still in good enough condition to travel after the short but violent skirmish. Their prisoner sat atop the one behind her, bound and gagged. Neither of which was necessary to subdue his pitiful sorcery. She and her mistress had both just tired of his venomous babble after the first half day on the path.

The sight before her was another story altogether. "A welcome surprise," Jasside said. "No need to spoil it with undue bloodshed."

"They're our enemy. Is that not cause enough for, shall we say, an aggressive stance?"

"Not when they're fleeing. It's considered ill form to strike a man in the back."

"Even when they're headed straight for us?"

Jasside shrugged. "Our fault for being behind enemy lines. Whatever part in the war they played, it's over now."

Vashodia remained silent for the longest time, merely watching the horde draw nearer with impassive eyes. At last she said, "Good."

"Good? Never thought I'd see the day you passed up the chance for mass slaughter with a smile on your face."

"I guess it's time I grew up." Vashodia wrenched her head around, branding Jasside with her glare. "Or maybe I've grown weary of trying to convince you to slit our prisoner's throat so we can be getting on to more important work. Maybe taking time to *slaughter*, as you say, would be time better spent elsewhere. Maybe I'm not sure I even *want* these people dead."

"Then why ask at all?"

In response, Vashodia turned away, urging her horse into motion.

Jasside groaned. *Back to being cryptic again. Oh joy.*

She followed after her mistress, and the other two horses, bearing both packs and prisoner, jostled down the trail behind her, tethered by ropes to her mount's saddle. They paralleled the retreating crowd, keeping to the paths along the ridge so as to avoid confrontation.

"You know what this means, don't you?" Jasside said.

"Yes," Vashodia replied. "Chase is moving even faster than we anticipated."

"Much faster. The whole northern front must have collapsed by now."

Vashodia shook her head. "The entire coalition presence in Sceptre has. Do you not feel them? Like a tidal wave sweeping down, leaving this land bereft of life and conflict. Chase is good—maybe even a genius—but his strategies and tactics shouldn't have been enough to cause all this. Not so soon."

"Having doubts about the king you practically appointed?"

"He appointed himself. And yes, I have my doubts. About him. About all mankind."

"So you feel the need to guide us to our destiny, is that it? Didn't Yandumar teach you anything? People don't like being manipulated. Not even for their own good."

"They won't mind if they don't know. Besides, you act as if I'm some outside influence. I'm not. What I *am* is concerned with the bigger picture. The petty politics of nations and so-called people groups has always been beneath me."

"Didn't seem that way back in the Veiled Empire."

"Then you weren't paying close enough attention."

Jasside practically growled in frustration. "Look, I know we've never quite operated on the same plane of existence—we have vastly different histories, after all—but I don't know how to help you if you won't, you know, fill me in from time to time. Why can't you at least tell me why you keep me around?"

"Because," Vashodia said, "you've been doing it already. If I tell you, I'm afraid you won't be able to anymore. I'm afraid you won't want to."

Jasside stared at the mierothi, realizing after a mark that she was holding her breath. She couldn't recall a time her mistress had admitted to any kind of fear. She'd never seen Vashodia so vulnerable.

Some sick part of her wanted to exploit that. To twist a soul so long a mystery until all the secrets came tumbling out. But she didn't. She couldn't. *What kind of person would I be if I betrayed such depthless confidence? Not the kind of person who is worthy of trust, that's for sure. Not the me I want to be.*

"Well, then," Jasside said at last, "you keep on doing great things, and I'll keep on keeping your greatness from burning the world."

It was slight—almost a phantom image in her mind—but Jasside swore that Vashodia flinched at the words.

She tore her gaze away, feeling as if her mere perception was an invasion of the mierothi's privacy. Jasside looked instead towards the crowds.

"So," she said. "Our part in this war begins and ends the same way: with refugees."

"Ends?" Vashodia giggled, shattering whatever supposed vulnerability Jasside thought might be there. "My dear apprentice, this war is far from over. And I've a feeling our role in it has only just begun."

Tassariel sat with arms folded in her lap, watching Arivana and Flumere with a mix of disbelief and awe.

They'd been going back and forth for tolls over stacks of books and scrolls, seeking any way they could find to depose Tior or get Claris free or put an end to the war once and for all. She wasn't sure if they'd ever give it up.

The main thing hindering any possible action came down to the fact that Arivana didn't know what power she actually possessed. Even acting within her rights by law, they weren't sure how much she could get away with. And, when in doubt, the laws always defaulted decisions to the council. Days of this, and they seemed no closer to a solution than when they'd begun. If anything, their hope had regressed past despair and well into futility.

Tassariel leaned her head back and groaned. "Abyss take us now."

"No. Not now, but soon," Elos said. "Yes, very soon indeed."

She nearly fell out of her seat. Springing up, she covered her flub by grabbing a book from the table beside her and shoving it back onto a nearby shelf. Flumere and Arivana didn't even notice, still too mired in their debate.

Tassariel feigned searching for another book, keeping her body turned away from her companions. "What are you talking about?" she asked.

"They're coming. Can't you feel it? Like a scar on the heavens, a shadow of the void growing nearer by the day. A force I cannot stop any more than I can cease trying. We are all of us—gods included—ever slaves to our own natures."

"What does that have anything to do with our problem here?"

"Maybe nothing. Maybe everything."

"Enough with the riddles!"

"Not a riddle. Some things can never be calculated. Logic is quantifiable, after all. Passion is not."

"Whose passion? What the abyss are you even trying to say?"

He answered with silence, as usual. But something was different this time. After a moment, Tassariel realized the ice no longer churned. The revelation took her breath away. Warm for the first time since losing her wings, Tassariel sighed in ecstasy. Still, she couldn't help but worry. If Elos had finished his predictions, it could only mean one thing.

They'd reached a crossroads, and the bridge behind them had collapsed. There would be no going back.

She only prayed they hadn't chosen the road bound for doom.

A book slammed down onto the shelf next to her, and Tassariel jumped.

"Did you say something?" Flumere asked.

A flare went up within her at the sudden sight of the woman, but it quickly died out to a mere crackle of flame. Not the raging torrent of lava she'd come to expect. Elos, it seemed, no longer had the passion required for hate. If she were to label the jumbled alien presence inside her, she'd have to call it *resigned*.

"No," Tassariel said. "Just muttering to myself is all. You find anything?"

"Nothing useful."

"Yes we did!" called Arivana.

Tassariel turned to face the queen. "How so?"

Flumere folded her arms. "She wants to take her grievances against Tior to the other ministers. She seems to think they'll take her side in all this."

"They'll at least have to *listen* to me," Arivana said. "The law is clear on that."

Flumere raised an eyebrow. "But what do you think they'll do after you've spoken?"

"I don't know. I guess we'll find out, won't we?"

"It's not worth the risk. Challenging Tior's authority is the same as challenging theirs. I can't imagine they'd respond well."

"I think I'm with Flumere on this," Tassariel said. "I didn't trust him the moment I set eyes on him, and nothing I've learned since has made me change my mind. And what your aunt said—"

"He and Claris have always been at odds. Their opposite stance on the war just brought things to a head."

"That's putting it mildly. I've plenty of people in my life I'm 'at odds' with, Arivana. None of us have ever tried to kill each other."

The queen bowed her head. "She only did what she thought was right."

"So you're defending her now? I thought you'd taken Tior's side?"

"I don't want to take *anyone's* side!"

Arivana's lip trembled, and Tassariel realized she was on the verge of tears. Flumere rushed to her queen's side, producing a silk handkerchief just as the first sobs began wracking the tiny frame. Tassariel had never seen the queen looking so frail, so vulnerable, so alone. It was probably there all along. Arivana must have been adept at hiding it.

Tassariel sat next to the queen and hugged her close. "I understand," she said.

They embraced for a while, rocking gently back and forth. Tassariel hummed some wordless tune, a melody remembered from her childhood. It seemed to work, as Arivana soon steadied her breathing, and all tension leaked from the form between her arms.

The queen lifted her head. "Thanks."

Tassariel only smiled.

"Tassariel?" a voice called from somewhere nearby. "Tassariel, are you in here?"

She released Arivana and stood, recognizing the voice. She wasn't sure if she was happy to hear it. "I'm here, Lerathus."

A few beats later, he came into view and spread his arms out wide. "Ah, there you are," he said. "I was hoping to find you here."

"And so I am."

He drew up short, obviously second-guessing his decision to try embracing her. Maybe *she* wasn't sure about him, but her body language must have held no uncertainty.

Lerathus sighed. "You probably want to know why I'm here."

"Yes."

"I came to apologize."

"Really?"

He nodded. "You haven't been treated like an honored kinsman. And you"—he gestured towards Arivana—"haven't been given the respect due a queen."

"Do you speak for every consular official in this?"

"Unfortunately, no. Things in the consulate aren't . . ."

"Aren't what?"

He drew in close to her and lowered his voice. "I can't really explain it here. Please, join me for dinner tomorrow night. I'll tell you all I can."

Tassariel pondered the invitation. They had been good friends, once, even if from afar. She at least owed him the chance to redeem himself. "Very well. I'll be there."

"Good. Thank you." He smiled, laughing boisterously. "I'll look forward to seeing you then."

Tassariel managed a smile as he retreated. "Things might be looking up after all," she said.

"Don't count on it," Elos said. "Dark days are yet to come. For all of us here. The darkest days indeed."

Tassariel shivered.

CHAPTER 19

Draevenus awoke to the sounds of fighting, determined not to let the tiny old woman wrestle him back into bed again.

It had been annoying the first time, and an embarrassment the second. He wouldn't allow a third. He *couldn't*. Not when he knew how long Mevon had been standing guard, alone, against far too many enemies. It was a suicidal task, even for one of his considerable talents.

Draevenus managed, after several grunting tries, to sit up on the feather-filled sack that the villagers used as a mattress. He paused, hugging his knees as he caught his breath.

It's sad that I actually consider this a good start.

His back still burned with agony, but the stitches seemed to be holding. Draevenus probed what parts of the wound he could reach, thankful that his fingers came back free of his own fresh blood. Another good sign.

Soft as he could, Draevenus rolled over onto his hands and knees. Then, with a slowness made necessary as much for the need to remain quiet as it was for the limit of his own muscles to make haste, he lifted himself to a standing position.

Head spinning, he lost his balance and stumbled forward. He crashed to his knees, grabbing desperately at the thick, round branches that made up the hut's wall in order to avoid a full return to the floor.

Mevon needs me!

The thought grounded him, focusing his effort. With another grunt, he pushed aside the pain and weakness and pulled himself back to his feet.

The old woman who'd been caring for him barreled through the entrance a beat later.

She jabbered in that almost-speech these villagers used, gesturing wildly towards the mattress as she drew close. Grabbing his shoulder, she tried to pull him to it. He resisted. *Finally.* She reached for him again, but he snatched her wrist out of the air and gently pushed it away. Her eyes widened at this; he'd barely been able to hold his own cup just a day ago. Draevenus tried not to show how much effort it took, but unable to see his own face, had no idea how far he'd succeeded.

She stepped back, cooing softly like a hen in a roost as she examined him from head to foot. At last, she shook her head.

Draevenus let go of the wall and straightened. "I'm fine," he said, tapping a hand to his chest. "Well, not *fine*, I guess, but well enough to do what needs to be done."

She crossed her arms, raising an eyebrow. Some gestures, it seemed, needed no translation.

He sighed. "Look, that's my friend down there. Or, he was once. I can't imagine, after the way I've treated him, that he'd still want anything to do with me. I let this quest overwhelm my reason. I put him in danger needlessly, over and over again, never thinking how it might affect him. I even mocked his own efforts to find meaning within himself just because I couldn't fathom the logic behind his methods. Maybe I didn't want to. Maybe I recognized that his struggle was my own and that I wasn't ready to face it. That I didn't have his courage.

"I know you can't really understand me right now, but I have to help him. Can't you hear what going on down there? If I held back even one morsel of strength, and the worst came to pass, I'd never be able to forgive myself. He doesn't deserve that. Especially not for my sake. Please . . . help me."

The old woman sniffed loudly, pursing her lips, and tugged on her greying braid for several long moments. At last, though, her features softened. Whether she understood him or not, the pleading in his tone must have crossed the barrier separating them still. She called out, and a moment later, two young men came in. Draevenus gratefully draped his arms over their shoulders and let them assist him out the door.

The village wasn't large. Still, it took several marks to maneuver over suspended walkways meant for more nimble feet. At last, they came to the edge. Draevenus extricated himself from his helpers and leaned on the wooden railing atop the thick tree that served as the village's lone point of entry.

Bracing himself, Draevenus looked below.

What he saw at first was chaos to his eyes, a tangled mess, indiscernible in the murky, predawn light. One thing quickly became clear, however: Mevon was nowhere in sight.

He widened his gaze in an attempt to establish context for the confused images. At the farthest edges of the field, dark men circled with arrows held to strings, twitching their heads at phantom sounds. Closer in, beasts roamed with noses to the ground.

They were searching.

It was a small thing, but it gave him hope. If Mevon had fallen, there'd be no need to continue their hunt.

Draevenus let his eyes spiral back towards the center. Around two sides were littered the remains of what looked like wooden barriers, nearly a dozen beasts impaled upon the spikes. And now, directly beneath him, he finally understood what he was seeing.

Bodies. Three dozen at least.

Piled almost two paces high, the twisted mass of fur and flesh seemed to ripple as breezes washed past. Slash marks across throats, puncture wounds in hearts, severed limbs and torn heads—the causes of death were apparent and precise.

Mevon had been busy.

How the abyss have you kept it up this long?

Five days of ceaseless combat would weaken any man to the point of death. Hardohl were not exempt from the need for rest. Even if Mevon was still alive, Draevenus couldn't imagine there was any fight left in him.

Taking a deep breath, Draevenus began reaching for his power.

A half dozen of the sniffing creatures drew close together, just below his position, stepping onto the bodies of their peers. Harsh growls passed between them, as if they were coordinating their efforts, closing in on their target. Draevenus didn't know if it was possible, but he couldn't discount it. He strained ever harder to energize.

Between one breath and the next, the mass of dark flesh exploded, dead beasts flying through the air.

A monstrous form emerged from below the pile.

The two closest beasts received daggers through their eyes before the others pounced. The next few moments became a flurry of black forms writhing in furious contest. Angry barks and howls and screeches were cut short, one at a time, as the smell of fresh blood splashed across that of the old.

Then, as quickly as it began . . . stillness.

Draevenus could barely recognize the man left standing. His clothes were torn to ribbons or less, and new scars carved maps across skin drowning in black seas. His chest heaved, the shrill wheezes as loud as dying birds. The whites of the man's eyes were as red as mierothi irises, darting around as if seeing ghosts in every shadow. His muscles seemed to quiver but no longer in rage.

Draevenus felt as if punched in the gut as he saw what Mevon had gone through on his behalf.

The darkness at work here should have drawn his full attention, but he'd been so focused on his goal that he'd been blind to the danger until it was too late. Someone else had had to confront it, suffering for the effort.

A situation that sounded far too familiar.

Draevenus shook loose his melancholic thoughts, realizing their futility. Dealing with Ruul would have to wait. For now, a friend needed his help.

You've done more than enough, Mevon. Let me do the rest.

Draevenus found his power at last.

He began acquiring targets. From this vantage point, none of them could hide from his gaze. Conjuring scores of sorcerous arrows, Draevenus shot them forward, taking out dark men and beasts by small groups. They fled, and he picked them off one by one.

By the time he lowered his hands, exhausted by his efforts, Draevenus couldn't see a single thing moving in the surrounding woods.

Mevon looked up at him and smiled . . .

. . . before falling unconscious atop the pile of his foes.

Ongshaith looked different this time.

Banners hung from every window, displaying the

bear symbol of Sceptre. The damage from the battle was mostly repaired, a fast feat in the two months they'd been gone, and smiling citizens were sweeping up what remained. People moved about as if life were back to normal. As if no occupying army had ever been present.

Jasside almost felt the need to chastise them for their lack of caution but realized there was no need. Panisahldron and its allies had retreated. And every set of lips in the city sang of the praises of King Chase, who had banished the foreign terrors, once and for all.

The only problem was, she and Vashodia couldn't find the target of that adulation.

A skeleton crew remained in the city. A few companies at most, augmented by civilian volunteers to help keep order. And that meant there was a vacuum of power. So when they questioned every soldier who could be found, none had the authority to take the prisoner. Worse, none could tell them where either Chase or Daye had gone, which worried her.

The practical part of her hoped they and their army hadn't run into any unexpected trouble. Another part just wanted to see Daye's face again.

There was only one place left to check.

"That must be it," Jasside said, pointing down the avenue.

Vashodia shrugged. She'd been unusually quiet since they'd left the fleeing mass of coalition forces. Something was unsettling her, but Jasside could not figure out what. And she knew the futility of pressing for answers. Vashodia's lips could be tighter than casket lids, two paces underground, if she wasn't ready to share.

The road split around a large square directly ahead of them, now a hive of activity. Thousands worked to repair the structure there, but this was different than the rest. The building had been destroyed almost a year and a half ago, falling prey to the first wave of the Panisian offensive, and had stood empty and cold. A reminder to the people of Ongshaith about the price of resistance.

The Sceptrines were rebuilding their palace.

They drew to a halt just inside the construction zone and waited. Jasside eyed the passing soldiers until she spotted one who—finally—had sufficient rank on his uniform. "You!" She aimed her hand towards him, then curled up a finger. "Come here."

The man nearly tripped in his effort to run to them. He skidded to a halt and bowed low at the waist. "Great ladies," he said. "It is an honor."

Jasside returned the bow, though not nearly so low—she wasn't flexible enough, and she was fairly sure it would be considered some kind of insult anyway. "We have a prisoner to drop off." She flexed her eyes towards the bound man standing with head down behind her.

Vashodia tugged on his chain. He lurched forward a step but made no other motion or sound. He'd been broken of defiance on the trip. Jasside's mistress had made sure of that.

"We were told," Jasside continued, "that someone here knows where the city prison is. Might you be able to help us?"

"Might I?" The officer bowed again. "I'd cut off my hand before denying you the slightest whim. Your desire is mine."

He turned and began shouting for help, and scores came running at his call—nearly every soul in hearing range. Jasside felt more than a little uncomfortable at the reception. *It's nice to be appreciated, but this feels more like worship.* Earning rabid followers might have been Vashodia's idea of a good time, but it certainly wasn't hers.

The assembled company took charge of their prisoner and led him away. The officer remained behind, waiting expectantly.

"Anything else you wish," he said, "hesitate not to ask."

"You can start by telling us where Chase is," Vashodia said.

The man's exuberance deflated. "The king is . . . not here."

Vashodia nearly growled. "Where else could he be? Drunk in some brothel?"

To his credit, the man hid his shock well. "Not to my knowledge . . ."

"Then where is he?"

"South."

"We came into the city from the south," Jasside said, "and saw no sign of him. All our queries led here."

"And it is to here that the king will return. Once, that is, he has achieved his victory."

"The enemy is reeling, gone from your borders or on the way out," Vashodia said. "What other victory does he seek?"

"The Panisians are fleeing, that is true. King Chase went south to ensure they never come back."

"Fool!" cried Vashodia.

"What?" Jasside said. "Seems a sound plan to me."

"Then you're just as big a fool as he."

Jasside glowered down at the mierothi. "Enlighten us with your wisdom, then."

"Didn't I tell you? The coalition pulled out too quickly. Too easily. I knew there had to be a reason, but I didn't count on their strategist to be so shrewd."

"What are you babbling about?"

"Chase and his army. They're being drawn into a trap. A trap that would only work if they were separated from their greatest asset."

Realization struck Jasside like the incoming tide. "Us."

"Ah, the girl sees at last. I was beginning to worry that all our effortless battles had dulled your wits."

Jasside decided to let the insult go. She had more pressing concerns. "Prince Daye," she said, turning to the officer, "did he go with his brother?"

"Yes. He wanted to stay, to wait for you, my lady, but the king insisted."

"How long ago did they leave?" Vashodia asked.

"Six weeks."

The mierothi grunted. "Barely left time for the rubble to settle before prancing off to his doom." She sighed. "Come, apprentice. We have to save another fool king from his own idiocy."

Vashodia turned to go. Jasside grabbed her arm, wrenching the small figure around. "Why do you even care?"

Eyes like naked spheres peered up at her. For the first time she could recall, her mistress was rendered speechless.

"This obviously means a great deal to you," Jasside continued. "I've held off asking why, but I can't any longer. I *must* know your plan for them."

Vashodia pulled her arm free from Jasside's grasp. "First off—*never* grab me like that again. Second, are you asking for the benefit of *all* the Sceptrines? Or, perhaps, only one?" She smirked. "Has a certain prince caught your fancy?"

Jasside felt a lump in her throat and found it was she who could now find nothing to say. She stepped back, turning her head away.

"I thought as much," Vashodia said. "Stop trying to hold me hostage with accusations of impure motives. No such thing as altruism exists. Not in you or me. Not in any soul under this or foreign suns."

Jasside lowered her eyes to the ground, fighting the longing inside her. A longing she didn't know how to comprehend, much less act upon. "What are we to do, then?"

"Persevere."

Jasside nodded. Sometimes, things needed to be made simple. This was clearly one of those times.

"Let's go."

Together, she and her mistress turned south. They energized, casting their gazes down to the farthest end of the street they could perceive, and began shadow-dashing.

Tassariel lifted the spoon to her mouth, savoring the mouthful of soup. Curried squash with peppers and garlic, and other flavors she didn't even recognize. A veritable rainbow of tastes exploding in her mouth.

"Did you make this yourself?" she asked after swallowing.

Lerathus smiled. "I'm a man of many talents, Tass. You may even be lucky enough to see them all one day."

She took another spoonful, fighting the urge to lift the bowl to her lips and start slurping. "You should consider a Calling as a chef. Or have you done that already?"

He waved a hand. "Oh, nothing so formal as that. It doesn't take a single-minded devotion to become good at something."

"Not a popular opinion among the leaders of our people."

"Bah. Old fools set in their ways never like it when the young talk sense."

Tassariel laughed. "Oh, stop it! No wonder you like

it here. All the consular officials I've met seem to have a certain, shall we say, *rebellious* attitude. I'm surprised they haven't put you in charge."

"One day, perhaps. Ready for the main course?"

She glanced down at her empty bowl. "Um, yes. Please."

Lerathus stood and removed the dishes, retreating to his kitchen to snatch the next part of the meal. Tassariel used the opportunity to study his home.

Rich tapestries lined the walls, and pedestals, placed in strategic locations, held carvings in every shape and material imaginable. Candles in ivory holders danced light across dark wood furnishings edged in gold. A layer of some scent suffused the airy chamber, an aroma that drove her mad with . . . something. A feeling she'd never experienced before. All she knew was that the strong lines of Lerathus's jaw and the hard muscles bunching under his robes drew far more of her attention than normal.

He returned a moment later, placing a plate piled artistically with seared meat. Something dark, drizzled with a fragrant sauce. She leaned into it. Her deep sniff made her dizzy with delight.

"Dig in," Lerathus said. "It may look fancy, but I can tell you're famished. No need to act all proper in *my* presence." He stabbed his own food with a fork and brought the entire pile of meat to his lips, biting off a chunk to emphasize his point.

Tassariel followed his lead.

It wasn't until she'd sat back in her seat before a

plate licked clean that she regained awareness of the world around her. With both belly and palate satisfied to an unheard of degree, her eyelids threatened to fall closed for good.

"Dessert?" Lerathus asked.

"Oh, gods," she replied. "I'm not sure I have room for it."

"We'll wait a bit, then." He leaned forward and re-filled her wineglass. "It's better to milk the anticipation anyway. Makes the dish taste even more exquisite once it comes."

She lifted her glass to him and took a sip. "If it's anything like the rest of your food, I'll have to replace my overstimulated taste buds when we're done."

"You're too kind, Tass. Too kind by far. It's almost a shame."

"What makes you say that?"

"It would have been nice if you could stay here at the consulate. It would give us more time to . . . get to know each other. Alas, they don't allow women in foreign posts. Not in any official capacity anyway."

Tassariel scoffed into her glass, taking a deep gulp of her wine. "A stupid policy."

"I agree."

"I mean, I understand the reasoning behind it. Our people have grown thin as it is, but I don't plan on ever having children, pureblood or otherwise. My parents convinced me it wasn't a good idea. Not for me."

"You may change your mind someday."

"Oh, please, not you, too. Half the reason I sought

so desperately to leave my domicile was to escape the plans men had for my life. Plans they didn't bother consulting *me* about."

Lerathus laughed. "Oh, don't worry yourself in that regard. I'd sooner try to wrestle a crocodile with my bare hands than try to tell *you* what to do. I'm not trying to change your mind."

"Then what?"

He shrugged. "Never discount a possibility, Tass, no matter how far-fetched it may seem at the time. Even if you have no intention of stepping through it, some doors, once closed, stay that way for good."

"Sounds like you're talking from experience."

He cast his eyes down and sighed. "All too much of it."

She reached across the table to pat his arm. Halfway there, a wave of dizziness struck her, and she thought better of it, instead leaning on her elbows and rubbing her forehead.

"Something the matter?" Lerathus said.

"I . . . don't know. Too much wine, maybe? But I've only had the one glass." She studied his face as it began to blur. It seemed sad for some reason—and a little angry. "Weren't we going to discuss something?" she asked.

"We were," he said, sounding far away. "But you've been a naughty girl, Tassariel, with all your snooping around. And we just can't have that around here."

"What're you talking about?"

"Agreements are in place between us and the Panisians. Your every move seems to threaten them."

"I don't . . ." *know what I'm trying to say. I don't know why I'm even trying to speak at all. It's so . . . tiresome.* She shook her head, but it only made the dizziness worse, and she slumped forward, slack-jawed, onto the table. Drool dribbled from her mouth. It would take too much effort to close it.

"Help me," she whispered, but not to Lerathus.

"I'm afraid I can do nothing, my child," Elos said. "The dark days are upon us, and sooner than I had come to expect. I wonder what else I got wrong. I wonder if I haven't doomed us all."

As darkness took her, Tassariel could only marvel at the fact that the god inside her had, somehow, made it all about himself once again.

"**W**here is she?" Arivana asked, pacing nervously in her bedchamber. "It's been two days, and no sign of Tassariel. What could have happened to her?"

"I don't know," Flumere said, sitting calmly. "But working yourself into a panic won't help matters any."

"I know. It's just . . . I don't . . . Abyss! What are we going to do?"

"You're the queen, are you not? How about you remember to act like it?"

"Which version? The ones in all the stories, who were brave and wise and respected? Who had true power and only used it for the good of their nation? Or should I be the queen my council expects me to be? A pretty face to parade before her people? Barely even a symbol? One that gets lied to and kept in the dark on any matter of importance?"

"That, I cannot say. You must decide for yourself."

Arivana huffed and threw herself down into the chair opposite her handmaiden, an untouched dinner cooling on the table between them. "I know what I want to be. But achieving it is another matter altogether."

"Are you going to give up, then?"

Arivana couldn't help but think of Claris, locked away in a nightmare. Her own family butchered and the war to avenge them now in shambles. *If only I'd been strong enough . . .*

"Never," Arivana said. "I won't rest until everything is made right. Not even if it kills me."

Flumere smiled though tears were forming in the deepness of her eyes. "I know. Somehow, I've always known. You prove the worth of my faith in you time and time again, and I will never regret serving you with all my heart. Thank you, my queen . . . and my friend."

Arivana brought her hands to her trembling lips, feeling her own tears beginning to brim at the sentiment. "Oh, Flumere! What would I do without you?" She dashed over and clutched the woman's hands, hugging them to her breast.

"You would have found your way just fine, Arivana. I believe that, truly. I'm just glad I get to be a part of it."

Arivana beamed in delight, but still something nagged at her conscience, a bitterness sapping her joy.

"This will all be meaningless if we don't find Tassariel soon. If something has happened to her . . ."

"I'm sure she's fine. Why don't we take a sky carriage to the consulate? If nothing else, they'll be able to tell us where she is through communion."

Arivana nodded. "As good a plan as any. Lead the way."

They left the bedchamber and made their way through the halls. There was no need to take the lift; a berth was on the same level for conveniently catering to royal whims. Emerging into the broad, airy chamber, Arivana was pleased to see a ship moored and ready for flight.

"Honored as ever by your presence, your majesty," said the attendant, bowing low. "Where would you like to go this evening?"

"The consulate, please."

"Very good." The woman scribbled in her ledger, then lifted her gaze with a smile. She gestured towards the entrance ramp. "Right this way please."

Arivana boarded, with Flumere right behind, and within a mark, the carriage was under way. The pilot remained invisible belowdecks.

Halfway to the consulate, Arivana was leaning on the railing and had just begun to enjoy the breeze through her hair when she noticed something peculiar below her.

"What's that?" she asked.

Flumere squinted. "I'm . . . not sure. Isn't that the barracks over there?"

"Yes. If I didn't know any better, I'd almost say it looked like . . ."

No. It can't be.

Her handmaiden finished the thought for her, out loud. "Soldiers on the march."

Arivana gulped. Her mind seemed unable to keep up with what her eyes were seeing. "There are too many of them. Thousands upon thousands. It must be the entire garrison. Where could they be going?"

"Where else does an army go but to war?"

"We're already at war. One I thought we were winning. Why would we . . . ?"

She spun, dashing towards the ladder and bending down. "Pilot!" she called.

"Yes?" came the tepid reply.

"We need to change course."

"I'm afraid I can't do that. Your majesty."

"Why not?"

"Regulations. Once a destination is logged, no deviations are allowed. I'd lose my job if I did."

"I'm the abyss-taken queen! You'll lose far more than that if you don't—"

Flumere laid a hand on her arm. Arivana forced herself to take a deep breath. *Now I know why the great people in all the stories need someone levelheaded at their side. Flexing their power—no matter its source—never made the situation any better. It only led to grief.*

"Listen" she said, "it is of the utmost importance that I make it to the royal barracks as soon as possible. I understand about regulations—I'm as subject to them as you are. But some situations require our ability to reason, to use judgment. Otherwise, we're a nation of laws, not of people. Look below—doesn't that concern you?"

For almost an entire mark, the pilot made no response, and Arivana thought for sure he was done talking. When she next heard his voice, it was with the greatest relief.

"Yes, your majesty. It concerns me. I've a niece in the army, wrath-bow corps. Not a very good shot, but then again, you don't have to be with those things. We're not the closest of relatives, but I'm sure I would've heard something about her marching out. This all seems . . . odd."

"Odd indeed," Arivana said. "And I plan to get to the bottom of it. To do that, I need you to change course now."

He thought for a spell. Then the pilot said, "Yes, your majesty."

Arivana smiled as the ship lurched beneath her, changing course and heading straight towards the barracks.

It seemed like only moments later they were disembarking. Arivana thanked the pilot before he took off. She didn't know his name and had never seen his face, but she wondered if he hadn't been the first true citizen to wholeheartedly serve his queen. She wondered if this is what it meant to rule.

A few quick queries directed them down a hall past

the uncountable throngs still making their way out of the barracks. Three turns brought them to their destination. Four sentries stood guard outside the thick metal doors, but they saluted at her approach and pulled them open without a word. She stepped past them, fear climbing up her throat as her imagination conjured the worst possible version of what she might find inside.

The sight that greeted her was stranger than she had thought possible.

Arivana blinked several times, squinting to make sure her sight did not deceive. Her mind kept telling her that she'd walked into the council chambers, for every member was present, standing roughly in a circle. But nothing else was the same. Instead of their traditional robes, they were all dressed in golden plate mail marked with glowing, magic-forged crests of their station. Commander's swords, gemmed and glittering in globelight, sat unsurely in each sheath. Between them floated an image of light cast into the shape of the known world. Tiny red and blue markers dotted the surface. Allied and enemy troop locations, she guessed.

A long, thick line of blue inched away from Panisahldron, crashing north to meet a descending wall of red.

"What is going *on* here?" she demanded.

All the councilors turned at her outburst, and she knew immediately that she'd made a mistake. Tior sighed, raising his hands towards the others in a placating gesture. They faced the map once more, ignoring her presence completely. Tior folded his hands and slowly walked towards her.

He stopped a pace away, careful to block as much of her view as possible. "What are you doing here?" he said.

Though every fiber of her being wanted to fly into a rage, she knew that would achieve only the opposite of her desire. Shaking with the effort to control her emotions, Arivana said, "I asked a question, Minister. I believe a queen, at the very least, should have the courtesy of being answered first."

The corner of Tior's eye twitched. "Very well. Your *majesty*. You wish to know what we're doing here? I'll tell you. We're marching off to fight your war."

"*My* war, is it now? Seems to me you've taken considerable liberties in its execution."

"You would chastise me? For seeking to shield you from the realities—the horrors—inherent in such an endeavor?"

"Spare me," she said, holding up a hand. "I'm done with your manipulations. I'm done with the lies. And I want this war to end. Now."

Tior's shoulders slumped, and the strength seemed to fade from his normally rigid posture. It was only an instant, though, before he returned to his normal posture. "You've grown bold lately, and that valynkar girl is to blame I think. It's my fault for not removing her sooner."

"Removing her? What are you talking about?"

"But her touch remains on your soul regardless," he continued, as if she'd never spoken. "I was hoping to avoid this."

Arivana felt a chill travel up her spine. She stepped back from him. She'd never exactly been comfortable around the man, and at times he made her feel downright awkward. But now, with his eyes looking like they'd been released from bondage, gleeful and malicious in their release, she felt only fear.

He raised a hand, sorcerous light crackling at his fingertips.

You wouldn't . . .

Flumere rushed past her. Fist clenched, she swung towards Tior's face.

A sheet sprang up just in time. Her punch shattered it on contact, and both figures reeled backwards. The minister, unfortunately, was the first to recover.

Twirling a finger towards the handmaiden, ropes of light spiraled out and around her. She tried to spin and bat them away, but they tightened in an instant, pinning her limbs and drawing a sharp gasp from her. Tior gestured dismissively, and Flumere, bound beyond hope of escape, crashed sideways to the ground.

Tior paused to draw a single breath before twisting his gaze towards Arivana.

She called for the guards.

None of them even twitched.

PART IV

PART IV

CHAPTER 20

Mevon crouched beneath the ancient tree where Drae-venus had sustained his wound and pulled back the skein of thorned vines covering the cavern entrance. The wind that blew through his ragged hair lacked teeth, boding well for the coming of spring. Mevon was glad. Cold seemed the one thing against which he had no defense, affecting him as much if not more than normal men. And after his time on the plateau, he wasn't sure if he'd ever be warm again. He welcomed the season of blooming with open arms.

He just hoped he lived to see the next one.

We've no idea what awaits us down there in the dark. Whatever it is, I've a feeling we'll be completely at its mercy.

With the way nearly clear, Mevon yanked on the last stubborn vines. Thorns dug into his flesh in a dozen places, but the pain only made him pull all the harder. With a final grunt of effort, he revealed the hole at last.

He straightened and wiped the blood from his arms. He didn't mind doing all the work, even with the added injuries. The wounds would close in moments, and besides, Draevenus surely had a lot on his mind.

He turned to see the mierothi standing silently behind him, studying the dark entrance with faraway eyes. Mevon left him to it. He gathered up his pack and cinched the straps tight, turning in a circle to make sure nothing had come loose. Finally, he could find no more reason to delay.

Mevon cleared his throat. "Ready?"

Draevenus shook himself out of his reverie. "I suppose so. It's funny, in a way. I've been waiting for this opportunity for hundreds of years, but I never expected to actually make it. And even in my darkest dreams, I hadn't envisioned it like this."

"Envisioned what?"

"Sorrow, Mevon. So much sorrow."

Mevon merely nodded. He understood completely.

"Will you walk with me once more, my friend?" Draevenus asked. "Will you accompany me into darkness?"

In answer, Mevon smiled and hopped down into the shadowed hole.

He landed with a squishing sound, boots imprinting deeply into the damp soil. His companion alighted at his side a moment later in utter silence. An unneeded reminder that they were now in the assassin's element. Mevon let the mierothi stride ahead of him.

In mere beats, the light from outside had faded to memory. If the tunnel were anything but arrow straight, Mevon would have had trouble following his friend's faint footsteps. He'd been expecting twists and turns, cliffs to climb, false paths and dark creatures to bar their way, and yet there were none.

He found the lack of it all disturbing.

The dark and silence stifled reason, making even simple thoughts difficult. Mevon had to lick his lips before he felt able to speak. "Are you *sure* we'll find Ruul here?"

"I'm sure," Draevenus replied. "This place . . . it's like I've been here before. Like I remember it. A memory tainted by my transition from human to what I am now. 'Mierothi' was simply the name of our tribe, once. It was Ruul who changed all that back then, and it was his essence—his flavor, if you will—that will ever live on in all my people's hearts. Here, it suffocates."

"Could this be the same place you first encountered him?"

"Perhaps."

"You don't know?"

"Memories from the days prior to our change, and just after, are hazy at best. Besides, the Cataclysm altered the very landscape of the continent. Even if such recollections were clear, they'd be useless."

They walked without words for a while, and Mevon soon lost track of how long they'd been in there. He'd never been afraid of the dark, but extended stays made him wish for even a glimmer of light. Unease burgeoned within him, growing more acute with each step, until he could take it no more.

"Something is wrong," he said. "Do you feel it?"

"I do," Draevenus said.

"Do you know what it is?"

In the dark, the mierothi emitted a low chuckle. Mevon felt his anxiety begin to drain at the sound.

"We're close. To the source, that is. You'll see soon enough, I'll wager."

A hundred steps later, the assassin's prediction came true. Mevon felt, more than saw, the tunnel open up on the right side into a wide-yet-shallow chamber. The sound of dripping clued him in, and the faint slosh of water told him where they were with certainty.

"So," Mevon said. "This is the source: a pool. It must have leaked out into the surrounding waters and caused whoever or whatever drank of it to transform. I can feel its power."

"Ruul's power."

Mevon stepped closer to the edge, and the unease within him sharpened. Retreating, he sighed in relief. "Aye. But where is the god himself?"

"I don't know. The tunnel branches ahead. Above maybe? It would make sense that the liquid would drip down and collect here."

Mevon, though not in any immediate danger, knew himself to be on the brink of the storm. He needed the heightened senses it would bring. In order to push himself beyond that sweet, cutting edge, he imagined what would happen if they were unable find Ruul.

We'll be stuck down here, wandering impenetrable dark till our water runs dry and we die of thirst. Not the way I want to go.

The storm came easily after that.

Mevon . . . listened.

After a mark, he had the answer he needed. "No," he said. "Not above."

"How can you tell?"

"Bubbles."

"Bubbles?"

"Tiny bubbles. In the pool. Rising up from cracks in the floor. I can hear them. Popping. And each time they do, a miniscule pulse of energy is released into the surrounding fluid. Dark energy. Pure as can be."

"Shade of Elos, you can *hear* that?"

"Yes. Now, can you find the branch that leads down?"

"Easily. And gladly. What would I do without you?"

"Die, probably."

"Thanks, Mevon. Very insightful. You really know how to lighten the mood."

"Happy to be of service."

Mevon followed the sound of his friend's breathing down several forks in the path, each one leading them lower and lower. The air grew colder, staler, with every curved descent, and he couldn't shake the feeling that they were plummeting into the very bowels of the world.

At last the turns ran out, and their steps stayed

straight for what seemed like tolls. The urge to turn back grew greater by the beat. He allowed himself to briefly wonder how these tunnels had been carved but realized it didn't matter. There was too much about gods and magic that could never be understood. Trying led to madness. He had only to look at his companion's sister to prove that point.

Just as sunshine was beginning to seem nothing more than a pleasant dream, something . . . changed. It was so sudden, Mevon had no time to react.

A swarm of darkwisps crowded into the tunnel ahead of them.

The snapping sparks of dark energy nearly suffocated him with their unexpected proximity. And they came in such abundance as to clog the tunnel entirely. He'd never feared the creatures before—they died at his touch—but now, a surge of dread crawled up his spine.

"What's going on?" Mevon asked.

"Sentries, maybe?" Draevenus energized. "Or, perhaps, a welcoming party?"

"*We are a warning,*" the hive hissed.

Mevon jerked backwards in shock.

"What do you mean?" Draevenus said, seemingly undeterred.

"*The void can progress no farther, lest he destroy us.*"

"The void? You mean Mevon here?"

"*Yessss.*"

Mevon rubbed his eyes, fearing they were playing tricks on him. It didn't help. The swarm had indeed formed itself into the likeness of a face. A human face. Or something close to it. Either way, the effect disturbed him more than the darkwisps' ability to imitate speech. More than anything he'd ever seen.

"Who, or what, lies beyond you?" Mevon said.

"*I do,*" the hive replied.

Mevon could only shiver.

Draevenus turned to him. "Mevon. I don't—"

"Go," Mevon said.

"But—"

"Enough, Draevenus. This is why we came here, is it not? Why we struggled across a forgotten land the length of the Veiled Empire. You *must* go on. I will hear no excuse to the contrary."

The mierothi managed a wry smile. "You're a good friend, Mevon. A true friend. What did I do to deserve you?"

"You stood up for what was right when no one else would. That, I think, is enough. I only hope that, one day, I can become as good a man as you are."

The assassin nodded. "You're not as far away as you think. In fact, it is I that should be following *your* example, not the other way around."

"*Leave, now,*" spat the swarm. "*Your very presence threatens usssss.*"

"Should I wait outside?" Mevon asked. "Or . . . ?"

"*No. Your companion will not leave the same way he entered.*"

Mevon pondered the possible implications of the pronouncement and found he didn't like it one bit. He reached out a hand, and Draevenus clutched it, shaking vigorously.

"I guess this is good-bye," Mevon said.

"What will you do?"

Mevon didn't hesitate. "I've hurt too many people. It's time I started learning how to heal." He smiled. "Though, in a more immediate sense, I could use a hand navigating my way out of here."

"*A guide will be dispatched,*" the swarm said. A single darkwisp broke off from the cluster and flew over Mevon, heading back the way they came.

Draevenus left, following the hive into the gloom, and Mevon retreated with the lone darkwisp. He envisioned the road ahead and had but one regret: that he couldn't see this one thing through to the end.

He vowed, right there in the darkness, that he would never leave anything unfinished again. Including the things he had already begun.

It seems I still have work to do. Best get started now.

Breathless, Jasside emerged from yet another of countless shadow-dashes she'd performed in the last few days. This time, however, she had hope of relief.

Through the fog, she could see the mierothi colony.

"Last jump," she said. "And we can finally get some rest."

"Rest?" Vashodia said at her side. "You've quite the imagination."

Jasside groaned.

Energizing again, she sent herself forward, traversing a league in an instant. She didn't even bother trying to beat her mistress this time. She stumbled upon arrival, nearly slipping in a patch of mud between two of the daeloth barracks. Vashodia was already marching away.

Jasside chased after her. Once she caught up, she slowed her steps to match the mierothi's short legs. She had a good idea of where they were going, so she held her tongue instead of asking to make sure. She was too tired to weather an assault upon her intelligence just now. Instead, she let her mistress guide her steps and studied the changes all around her.

Though not worn by any means, the houses had taken on a lived-in look in the half year they'd been away. Patterns had been painted or carved into the walls. Laundry hung out to dry on lines between adjoining homes. Herb or flower gardens pushed up bursts of color and splashes of scent from nearly half the yards she could see. Daeloth, mierothi, and even the occasional human—foreign traders from the looks of them—bustled about avenues now lined with smooth stones.

All it needs is children. Then, it might almost pass for a real city.

Vashodia led them to Angla's door and entered without knocking.

A kettle stewed over a wood fire, filling the space with the smell of smoke and brewing tea leaves. Jasside almost felt like she was home.

"Oh, Mother?" sang Vashodia. "Mother dearest? Please tell me you're in. We've important business to discuss and not a moment to lose."

A door swung in silently, and a sweaty woman entered, wiping her greasy hands on a cloth. "Six months," Angla said, "and that's the best greeting you can come up with?"

"So good to see you, too," Vashodia said. "You're not busy."

"Shouldn't that be stated as a question?"

Vashodia smirked. "Look, my apprentice. You're not the only one prone to flights of fancy."

Jasside only had the strength to roll her eyes.

Angla tucked the cloth into her belt. "Since you've arrived so unexpectedly and discourteously, I can only assume my life is about to be severely disrupted. What emergency is it this time?"

"Glad to see you appreciate the direness of the situation."

Angla scowled.

"What she means to say," Jasside said, "is that we're going to need—that is, we could really use your help."

"Doing what?"

"Saving the world," Vashodia said. "Do you think I respect you so little as to bother your for anything less?"

Angla's jaw opened wide, but no sound seemed capable of coming out.

Jasside raised an eyebrow at her mistress. "Look, I know that the Sceptrines are walking into a trap and need all the help they can get. But . . . saving the world? *Really?*"

Vashodia ignored her. "Well, Mother? Can we count on your aid or not?"

Angla managed to close her mouth, shaking her head in disbelief. "You've done fine managing this planet without me for the last few millennia. Why the sudden change?"

"Because," Vashodia said, "it's the last thing the gods would expect."

"Going up against *them* now, are you? If such an admission is supposed to sway me, I'm afraid it's done quite the opposite. The gods can sleep in the beds they've made. I want nothing to do with it."

"No?" Vashodia smiled, strolling closer to her mother. "Perhaps not. But I know one thing you *do* want. More than anything in the world."

She curled a finger. Angla reluctantly bent down her ear. Jasside couldn't hear what words were shared between child and mother, but the older woman's eyes grew wider, and sadder, with each whispered syllable.

The sound of whistling reached her from behind, and Jasside turned in time to see Harridan Chant enter with an armful of fresh vegetables from the fields. He stopped short after seeing what awaited him, the tune from his lips dwindling to a discordant hum.

Jasside didn't even have time to greet him before Angla rushed into his arms. He gasped in surprise at the assault, but grinned ear to ear just the same.

"Oh, Harridan!" Angla said, still hugging him tightly around the neck. "It's so good to see you."

"Likewise, love," Chant said. "Ever and always. I see your scions have made it back safe and sound."

"For the moment," Vashodia said. "However—"

"We'll help you," Angla said. She released Harridan from her grip and locked eyes with him. "Won't we, dear?"

"Anything for you," he replied, then cleared his throat. "Might I ask—what help are we giving?"

"All the mierothi," Vashodia said. "And as many daeloth as you can spare. No humans, I'm afraid. You'll need to move fast."

"I'll coordinate it," Angla said. "Tell me where to go."

"East, into Fasheshe," Jasside said. "Then south."

"Can't you get any more specific than that?"

Jasside shook her head. "We don't know exactly where it's going to take place."

" 'It' what?"

"The battle," Vashodia said. "Not the first one, and certainly not the last, but upon its outcome rests the fate of our world."

Jasside scoffed. "You and your grandiose designs again. Is Panisahldron truly so great a threat as that?"

"Panisahldron?" Vashodia giggled. "Who said anything about them?"

The creak of the wheels belonging to the wagon they'd stuffed her in was the only sound Arivana could hear.

Day after day, the low, grinding squeal had become as familiar as the sound of her own breathing, something she only noticed when it stopped.

Arivana pitched forward in her seat, smacking her forehead into something hard. The pitch-black interior of the wagon made it hard to distinguish what she'd collided with. Her only consolation, as she brought a hand to the site of injury, was that she felt no trickle of blood between her fingers. She'd almost be glad, though, if there were. That sharp, coppery scent would be a welcome change from the bland sterility that brushed her nose with every breath.

Three clicks like twisted metal. Arivana shielded her eyes from what she knew came next.

The door swung open, blasting her with starlight. *Must be night again. Funny how little that matters anymore.* A figure stepped up into threshold, his body outlined against pinpricks of brilliant light. Arivana let her hand down from in front of her eyes, then held out both arms to accept her meal.

"Expecting dinner, my queen?" said a familiar voice. "I'm sorry to disappoint."

Arivana wrenched her hands back, shrinking into the hardwood wall of the wagon. "Go away, Tior."

"I think not." The minister stepped closer, further cramping the space. "I've been away from you too long as it is. What good is an advisor, after all, if he does not tell his charge what she needs to hear?"

"I won't listen to any more of your lies."

"The time for deception is over. You've proven

too intractable for that. You will get the harsh truth, whether you're ready for it or not. I suspect the latter."

Light burst forth. Arivana cried out, curling up to hide from the eye-scorching illumination. Fire seemed to burn the back of her closed eyelids, and it took a few dozen beats before she could sit up and face the man again. It seemed the most difficult movement of her life.

A ball of light hovered over his wrinkled hand, bathing the wagon's interior in lurid, flickering radiance. There wasn't much to see. Sharp shadows crossed Tior's face from below, making him seem a stranger. Well, even more of one anyway. His eyes still danced with malevolence. Appearing normal, kind even, had been the act. She knew she now saw his true self, unrestrained by the need to appease her. Or appear sane. He seemed more animal, now, than man.

"Child," he said, "you are indeed the queen. But you haven't been raised to understand the true meaning of your title. I sought to ease you into it, to show you the truth slowly so that you would come to accept it. Gradually. Without discomfort. Your impatience and impulsiveness are what led to these . . . growing pains."

Arivana gulped. "I'm nothing more than a figurehead."

"Indeed. All your predecessors understood their role from the very beginning, but being fourth in line to inherit the crown, your parents sought to shield you from such an unpleasant notion. They filled your head with fables and fairy tales, making you think the life of a royal was a charmed one. That you could be beautiful and intelligent and inspirational and powerful, all at the same time."

"You're as much to blame for planting that idea in my head as my parents. More so. Did you even shed a tear when they died?"

"I did. They were beautiful people. Your siblings as well. The people loved them, and thus had little reason to complain. Or, at least, they found their gripes easier to overlook. Use of statute eighty-seven fell dramatically under their reign."

Arivana almost screamed. "Next you'll be telling me this is all for the good of our nation. Our people."

"Ah, but it is. Don't you see? How else can you lift something up than by cutting away that which drags it down? Cater to the useless, the lazy, the deadweight, and all of society will eventually be sucked, strangling, to their level."

"They're still *people*, though. They still matter. Why can't we make them better? Why can't we even try?"

"It *has* been tried. But the thing you don't understand is that they're *not* people—they're parasites. They want the world handed to them on a silver platter, expecting not to have to lift a finger to have their every need and want and whim met by the sweat of others. These people are a disease, Arivana. An infection, spreading. There is no accepting them. There is only . . . excision."

She turned away from him, unable even to look

upon his face. Her stomach tightened and curdled. *This isn't how it's supposed to be!*

"What am I supposed to do, then?" Arivana said, mustering all her strength to turn back to him. "Accept something I can never agree with? Play along for the rest of my life?"

"That's exactly what you'll do," Tior said. "There is no choice in the matter. The only choice is how long that life will be."

Arivana shuddered, barely able to contain her fury. Such blatant threats might have unnerved her once, but with what she now knew to be happening to her country, the possibility for harm didn't seem to matter much anymore.

"Think on this, my queen," Tior said, backing out of the wagon. "Think long and hard about how best you can serve your people. How little good cold corpses lying in tombs can do."

The door slammed shut upon his exit, and Arivana was once again left alone in the darkness. She thought she might be starting to prefer it.

Voices.

Tassariel heard voices.

Blurred and distant, she couldn't make out words. Couldn't identify who they belonged to. But the tone was easy enough to read, even in her . . . condition.

They were arguing.

She couldn't move nor open her eyes. Speech was out of the question. *If I could only clear the fog from my ears, I could tell what they are saying.* Concentrating, she focused every ounce of effort into working her jaw around. It was several marks before she succeeded in the slightest budge.

A smile formed in her mind at the victory.

"Don't strain yourself," Elos said. "It'll undo all I've been trying to accomplish."

It was a good thing she couldn't speak at the moment. The words that came to her mind upon hearing his voice fell far short of kind and verged on blasphemous. She ignored his advice, continuing to clench what muscles she could, as much now in protest to him as in determination.

"Right. I guess you've given up taking my instructions on faith alone." Elos paused. "I'm sorry I can't be the god you deserve."

Now it was Tassariel's turn to pause. She willed herself to relax, signaling, as best she could, that she was willing to listen. *I can do that much for you, at least.*

"Good. Now, if you didn't know already, you've been drugged."

Thanks. Couldn't figure that one out on my own. Next you'll explain to me how this is a bad thing.

"This is a bad thing."

Tassariel rolled her metaphysical eyes.

"But I have a plan."

You'd better.

"They've been timing their doses from when you

begin to stir. I've been keeping you still a little longer every day—don't ask how—and they've been adjusting their administration accordingly.

"Today, you're finally cognizant enough to hear my voice. And theirs, I think, though not distinctly. As long as you follow my instructions, you'll soon have a chance to break free."

Tassariel couldn't help but get excited at the prospect. A surge of energy coursed through her.

The fingers of her left hand twitched.

"Quick, she's waking up," said a voice close and suddenly clear. Hot breath on her cheek let her know why.

"Fine," said another, "but this isn't over."

"Yes. It is."

Lerathus?

"Why are you defending her?" a third man said. "The consul passed his judgment. She'll never see a free sky again. I don't see why we can't have a little fun?"

"Go play with the daughters of light," Lerathus said. "That's why they're here, is it not? Tassariel is our kin. That should still mean something, even now."

"Never done a valynkar woman. Prissy bitches never even looked at me twice."

"Oh, save your sad story. Lerathus doesn't look like he's going to budge. Besides, she's not *that* pretty."

"In the dark, all that matters is the feel of them. And she's got a lean hardness to her I'd just love to break."

She started to struggle at that.

"Stop that! They're not going to touch you—I promise."

And for the first time in a long time, she believed her god.

"Enough," Lerathus said. "Give me that. Now go."

"What? So you can have her all to yourself?"

"Go!"

Tassariel felt a thumb on her jaw, pulling down, then something smooth and hard pressed to her lips. Panic set in, and she writhed against what was about to happen, furious that she could do little more than tremble.

"Easy, now," Lerathus said. "I'm sorry about this, really I am."

His sincerity meant nothing at the moment.

Cool liquid began trickling into her mouth. The same aromatic wine he'd served at their dinner by the taste of it. She berated herself for not being more careful. It was dangerous business stirring up the establishment. And those with the most to lose would go to the greatest lengths to ensure their continued dominance of others. It was a lesson she'd learned long ago, but never the hard way until now. *This time, it might actually stick.*

Her mouth filled with the vile concoction, but she had enough strength to resist swallowing. Lerathus sighed, then pinched her nose. "No use struggling, Tass. It'll only make things more unpleasant. Be comforted. I *could* just let my companions have their way with you. The more trouble you give me, the less inclined I'll be to keep defending you so arduously."

Her resolve wavered, under both the need for air and the unveiled threat of his words.

She swallowed.

He released her, standing and shuffling away. His footsteps slowly faded out of range.

Tassariel didn't feel any effects of the drug yet, but she knew they were coming. She couldn't stand the thought of being helpless a single beat longer, of being at the mercy of men whose minds were filled with vile thoughts.

"Settle down," Elos said. "Another few days—a week at most—and we'll have our opportunity."

I can't wait that long!

Fighting with every drop of blood in her veins, Tassariel reached for her power.

To her surprise, it came.

Energy burst into her control. But only the tiniest fraction of her capacity, and even as she struggled to shape it, she could feel that paltry amount start to slip away.

So she did the only thing she could think of . . .

Gilshamed dipped the cloth into the washbasin, squeezed, then dabbed it across Lashriel's forehead. The movement had become routine. As had everything else about the time he spent with her. Nothing ever changed. Not even the hair-width strand of hope that stubbornly refused to die.

He'd brought her out of the temple of healing months ago and cared for her himself in their home. The place had been decrepit, lived in barely a handful of years in the past two millennia, but he'd cleaned it up as best he could and hired a caretaker to look after the house and his wife while he was at council. She seemed to do better here. Or maybe that was just his imagination. Maybe it was only better for *him*.

Her brow thus cooled against the afternoon's warmth, he set the cloth aside and sat back. Every day, he asked himself how much longer he would continue this act. And every day, he told himself *just a little bit longer*. He didn't know if what he did was a kindness. By sustaining her empty body, was he keeping her soul from paradise? Was this an act of selflessness or selfishness? Such questions no longer plagued his conscience. It all simply *was*. He'd given up trying to change things more than need be. *Let the good I accomplish as a member of the council stand on its own. Let that be . . . enough.*

Gilshamed stood and strode out onto his open balcony. He peered down the steep edge of Halumyr Domicile to the dancing surface of the sea endless fathoms below. For a time, he lost himself in those distant waves.

A sound from behind interrupted his reverie and made him turn.

Lashriel sat up in the bed, eyes shining like stars.

Gilshamed tried to take a step towards her, but all the strength seeped from his limbs, and he fell to the floor. "My love . . ."

She gasped. The glow faded as her eyes returned to normal. Open. Aware. She blinked rapidly, her gaze flitting around like a hummingbird until finally coming to a rest on Gilshamed.

Heart pounding in his chest, he couldn't think of a single thing to say.

Lips cracked open, and she tried to speak but only succeeded in coughing. Gilshamed broke free of the invisible bonds that held him and rushed to her side.

"Lashriel," he said. "Don't try to speak. Just look at me. Just let me know you're really here."

A smile tugged at the edge of her mouth. She nodded.

Gilshamed's heart burst. Tears dripped down his cheeks as he embraced her. A hope thought lost. A love that could never fade. He let the sorrows of his soul seep away to make way for the joy he'd never thought to see.

Lashriel coughed again, then cleared her throat. "There is no time," she said.

Gilshamed pulled back, cupping her face with his hands. "Oh, my love, now that you're back, we have all the time in the world."

She shook her head.

Gilshamed felt a tiny twinge of fear echo through his delirious happiness. A fear that he was only dreaming and soon would wake. *If so, let me sleep alongside her forever and never know the nightmare that is reality.*

"Tassariel is in trouble," Lashriel said.

"Our niece?"

"She needs help. She needs *you*. This cannot wait."

"How do you know this?"

"She came to me in communion. She was desperate, and empowered by . . . something. But her message was clear. You must go to her."

Gilshamed ran fingers through her violet hair. Lashriel closed her eyes, moaning softly at the gesture. She hadn't forgotten after all.

His fingers slipped free as she slumped back onto the bed.

"Go to her," she said, eyes fluttering. "Promise me you'll go to her?"

Heart broken in half, Gilshamed uttered, "I promise."

Lashriel fell asleep once more.

Gilshamed screamed.

CHAPTER 21

Draevenus crept along darkened paths that seemed somehow familiar. The darkwisp hive undulated a dozen paces ahead, morphing in and out of the shape of a giant face, guiding him towards an encounter he'd long yearned for but never actually expected to have. As the moment drew near, every nerve seemed to fray into senselessness, pushing out all reason and enveloping his mind in a cloud of surreality.

The tunnel opened up into a chamber not quite as large as he had expected. The swarm dissipated to its edges, and he took the shape of the space to be similar to the throne room at Mecrithos: large and rectangular but far short of vast. A quick glance made it almost seem a natural cavern, bedecked in dripping stone and fungus, but his keen senses allowed him to see another layer most men would miss.

Scattered lumps could easily be the decrepit remains of chairs or desks. Too-regular clusters around the perimeter might be shelves or cabinets of some kind. The occasional flicker of something perfectly flat and metallic poked through the ancient flow of rock, indicating something not naturally occurring. Something *made*.

And the contraption at the far end put any doubts to rest.

Draevenus shuffled forward. A faint-yet-steady glow rose from what he could only describe as a sarcophagus. Dozens of tubes stretched from it, sagging with the weight of ages as they disappeared into hidden crevices in the wall behind. He could feel the energy gathered there, like a web of power, every strand in the world flowing into and through it. Sweet and soothing, it welcomed with familiar darkness yet stung with painful potency. Like pulling off a scab. Whatever he had come to find, Draevenus had no doubt it rested inside the rectangular box against which his hips now rested.

This is it . . .

Gulping, he leaned over the coffin-like object and pressed down a palm. He swiped, surprised to find his hand still clean of dust and grime. Whatever mechanism or magic sustained his god had worked wonders in this one space alone. Draevenus was not surprised. Expectation itself had fled. The shutters of his mind were flung wide open.

So he wasn't surprised when, from out of the darkness, a voice spoke.

"Have you come to kill me?"

"Yes," Draevenus replied. "I have."

The mierothi shook with the power of his own pronouncement. Even in the most shadowed corners of his soul, he had never admitted to such a purpose. His own skill with subtlety and deception, unparalleled among either the living or dead, had worked to hide it from him until now. He'd always told Mevon he planned to make Ruul answer for his crimes. To pay for them. Never had he spoken—or even thought—the word kill. *It seems the time for lies is over. Especially those told to myself.*

Again, the incorporeal voice sounded, seeming to come from everywhere and nowhere, from both inside his head and outside of time simultaneously, each syllable surging like a vast shore of waning tides.

"I see. Know, then, that I have little defense against you. Were even the opposite true, I would not strike down one of my own children to save what little remains of my life. Do what you must."

"What I must?" Draevenus clacked his claws in rhythm atop the coffin's lid while his other hand stroked a dagger hilt. "I don't think I believe in 'must.' All men have a choice in all things. Those who claim otherwise merely seek to pass off the burden of their sins to fate."

"Ah, the fickle mistress. Ever blamed for failures yet rarely credited with success."

Draevenus sighed. "I suppose you'd know."

"Yes. It was a hard lesson to learn."

He stepped back, drawing a cold, damp breath. Knees buckling under the weight of all he'd been through, both in the last two years and the last two thousand, Draevenus came to kneel before the sarcophagus. Because before he could kill Ruul, he needed to know one thing.

"Why?" he asked, the words that followed flowing like stones out of his throat. "Why did you create us?"

"I created nothing. That power is beyond me, beyond anything in this universe. I merely . . . transformed."

"Don't avoid the question."

"What kind of answer are you looking for?"

"The truth. All of it."

"That may take some time."

Draevenus shrugged. "There's nowhere else I need to be."

The darkwisps around the room fluttered, shimmering with shadows, and the air around the coffin seemed to constrict. For some reason, it made him think of a sigh.

"The easy answer would be to say that I took pity upon you. Seeing your plight, I knew I had the power to offer succor, a way to turn your fortunes around. While there is no falsehood in this statement, it does not encompass the full scope of my motivation.

"I made your tribe into what you are now because I needed a strong right arm to enact my will."

"So we were tools after all."

"Yes. But it was not I who ended up wielding you."

Draevenus growled. "Rekaj."

"Your third emperor was a shrewd and jealous man, and, unfortunately, clever enough to figure out how to sever the link I shared with all your people, hoarding all knowledge of my will to ensure his own stranglehold on dominance. That it also affected his own ability to contact me was unintended. I think, in the end, he came to regret it."

"A pity you couldn't have done anything to stop him."

"Pity? Pity is reserved for the misguided, and there were none more so than Rekaj. None *less* so than your sister."

Draevenus grunted. "I take it she was not kind to you during her visit?"

"Hardly. But I care little what is done to me. My only concerns are for the people of this world. For it was my own folly, so long ago, that set in motion events that are now coming to pass. I *must* make it right. I tried to impart upon Vashodia the importance of such a task, but I fear I have failed."

"She's not very good at taking orders."

"No indeed. But now that you're here, perhaps hope is not lost after all."

Groaning with the seemingly monumental effort, Draevenus lurched to his feet. He leaned over the sarcophagus, feeling a burden settle on his shoulders that he was not ready to accept. "Please, don't ask. I can't be your champion in this. I'm a broken man, good at only one thing despite centuries I could have spent better-ing myself. I'm not worthy of your trust."

"There are none worthier for the task I have prepared for you. Devalue yourself not. I could love you no less even were you to fulfill your original purpose in coming here."

"You're so sure I've changed my mind?"

"No. I simply have faith."

Draevenus let out a short laugh. The absolute absurdity of the situation demanded no less. *This is not at all how I envisioned this encounter going.*

"Tell me something," Draevenus said.

"Yes?"

"Why do you even care what happens to this world?"

"To explain that would be to tell the tale of the ages. The recitation will not be over quickly."

Draevenus turned and slid down, pressing his back against the smooth side of his god's living tomb. The ground just around it was clean and dry, yet soft, a fact for which the assassin was grateful. He had a feeling his backside would become intimately familiar with it.

"Then tell me. Maybe afterward—if you're lucky—I won't still feel the need to kill you."

Jasside wiped sweat from her brow, freeing her forehead from the hair matted across her face. They'd been tracking the Sceptrine army, having crossed the southern border into Fasheshe days ago. The trail was not hard to follow.

The remnants of the coalition forces retreated south, while Fasheshish horsemen harried Chase's host every step of the way. Signs of their clashes, brief yet violent, marked a straight line across the country, a land that dried out and flattened more with every passing league. Both she and Vashodia wore only loose black dresses, having packed away their cloaks sometime ago. Jasside didn't miss hers in the least.

"Those vultures are a good sign," Vashodia said, pointing over the next hill. A flock thick as a storm cloud hovered on the horizon.

"Ah, yes," Jasside replied. "Flying harbingers of death. How lovely."

"You might *actually* think so if you stopped to ponder the implications of their presence."

"We've been dashing nonstop for over a week now. Pardon me for my lack of preternatural insight."

Vashodia sighed. "If I must spell it out for you then. Does Sceptre make it a practice to bury their dead?"

"Yes."

"And Fasheshe?"

"I don't think so."

"Then those vultures . . . ?"

"Aren't feasting on our allies' flesh."

"See? Lovely indeed."

Jasside scoffed. "Not the word I'd use to describe carrion ripping apart corpses with their beaks."

"Then you show your lack of imagination once again."

"At least I don't mistake imagination for reality."

"My dear apprentice, don't you understand? There

is no mistake when our will can recraft the world around us to our liking."

"Just because we have the ability to do something doesn't mean we should."

"Why not?"

Jasside took a deep breath to calm herself before continuing. "Innocents always pay the price when the powerful fail to contemplate the repercussions of their actions. No matter what good you think you're trying to do, some losses can never be justified."

For a time, Vashodia remained silent. Jasside almost believed that the mierothi was actually considering her words. She supposed there might have been bigger miracles, just none *she'd* ever seen.

"Come," her mistress said at last. "I do believe the chase is almost up."

They shadow-dashed to the next hill and looked down upon the sight of slaughter. A single glance confirmed their suspicions. Jasside tried not to study the mass of bloody flesh and squawking feathers too closely. She'd witnessed the aftermath of enough battles to know she'd never grow used to the sight.

"Chase never stopped to engage these raiders the whole way down," Vashodia said. "I wonder what changed?"

Jasside lifted her eyes over the carnage. "I think that might explain it."

Across a flat expanse of brown only rarely broken by strangled shrubs and pillars of spinning dust, two great stains smeared the horizon. The space separating them seemed pitifully, dangerously slim.

The two armies, in the fullness of their force, were about to meet at last.

At this distance, and with no terrain barring her view, Jasside was able to estimate a count of their numbers. The result staggered her.

"Something troubling you, apprentice?"

Jasside licked lips rendered dry by harsh, incessant winds. "There are so many of them. Even the battle for Mecrithos, with both sides combined, had fewer than each army here. Bloodshed is coming on a scale this world has never seen and should never have to witness."

"Well, then. I suppose we'll have to put a stop to it, now won't we?"

Jasside turned to question her mistress, but before she could, the mierothi vanished in a streak of darkness. With what seemed the last ember of her reserves, Jasside followed.

Sceptrine soldiers were already bowing to Vashodia by the time she arrived.

"Oh, enough with the honorifics," Vashodia was saying. "Just tell me where the king is already."

A guide volunteered from among the crowd, and their trek began.

Navigating the massive camp took nearly two tolls. The delay would have driven her mad if she hadn't seen the reason for it. Chase kept his headquarters in constant motion, never settling down in one place for long to make it harder for enemy war engines to strike at his location. Even their guide had to ask around, changing directions more than once.

By the time they reached the royal tent—which looked no different than any other—Jasside didn't even have the patience to protest when Vashodia flung the guards out of the way with a wave of power. They marched in without further challenge.

"What the bloody abyss are you doing?" said Vashodia.

Chase sat on a cot, oiling his sword. "Preparing for battle. Nice to see you, too, by the way."

"It was folly to come here."

"I appreciate all the help you've given me and my people, but that does not give you the right to dictate our fate."

"We agreed that I would help you. Yet what's the first thing you do once my back is turned? Throw all I have accomplished on your behalf to the wolves."

Chase stood now, sword gripped tightly under white knuckles, a dangerous look in his eye. "We had our enemy on the run, and I, for one, would like to ensure they never return."

"Oh, and I suppose it was your brilliant strategies that led to all your victories?"

"In part. Though I could not have done it without your assistance. If you think I seek to diminish the scope of your aid—"

"I know very well the depth of my aid. I hardly need the approval of a suckling king to know my worth. What I do need is for you to listen. Because I've weighed the impact of my actions against the capabilities of you and the coalition. Do you know what I found?"

"I'm sure you'll tell me whether I want to hear it or not."

"Only a fool spurns the words of those wiser than himself. And you're no fool. I'd have not let you take the crown otherwise."

"*Let* me? How dare you!"

"Yes. I *do* dare. Because, *king*, the coalition forces left your land far too easily and quickly. You've led your army into a trap."

Chase shook his head. "They're well entrenched, but we have them outnumbered and have captured enough of their weapons to negate any advantage."

"What about the war engines?" Jasside asked.

"That will soon no longer be a factor."

Vashodia clenched her fists. "What have you done?"

"Our enemy thought that keeping those monstrosities to the rear of their position would keep them safe. They are too arrogant to think we'd have the courage or the skill to assault it from behind."

"When is the attack to take place?"

"As we speak."

"Then your soldiers are either dead or captured already."

"You can't possibly know that!"

"Yes, I can. Just as I know the reason for their doom. And soon, yours."

"Which is?"

"Reinforcements, come up from the south."

"Impossible. My scouts would have seen—"

"What? Dust clouds behind a marching army?"

"Yes."

"That would help if they were all coming by land. But what if the bulk of them came in the night by air?"

Chase's mouth dropped open. "No. No it can't be. They never used their sky carriages in Sceptre."

"For fear they might be captured, and your casters would be able to reverse-engineer their construction. But where are we, right now?"

"Fasheshe."

"Indeed. And they have both the plan and the power to annihilate every last one of you. They've no fear of their little toys falling into the wrong hands."

Chase slumped back onto his cot, the sword falling from limp fingers. "What have I done?"

Jasside now realized what she should have immediately. What the king's strong reactions had been indicating all along.

"Daye," Jasside said. "He's leading the sneak attack."

The king's slight nod was almost unnecessary. "What can we do now?"

"Whatever you do," Vashodia said, "do not attack."

"We've come too far to retreat now."

"Do your best to avoid engagement, at the least. You've been aggressive thus far, so if nothing else, the tactic will give them pause."

"We will defend ourselves if necessary. I can promise nothing beyond that."

Vashodia scowled but said nothing else as she spun on her heels.

"Where are we going?" Jasside asked.

"To keep all these fools from killing each other. We can't afford any more deaths on either side. Every last body will be needed."

"For what?"

Vashodia only shook her head. And Jasside couldn't help but wonder what could be worse than the bloodshed about to take place.

Arivana felt guilty for enjoying the wind. After so long stuffed inside that wagon, though, the pleasure of fresh air and light seemed almost overwhelming. The deck of the sky carriage, converted to purposes of war, hummed beneath her, swaying mere paces above the crest of a dune. Her guilt stemmed from many places, it seemed. From the sight of all the fighting men and women arrayed across the dry land before her. From Flumere, broken of will and voice, chained up and bruised at her side. From accepting the grace of a man she'd once looked up to but now only despised.

"Look, Arivana," Tior said, perched against the oiled-wood railing. "Look upon the realities of war."

And so she did.

Even through the clouds of dust, she could easily

make out ranks of the fabled Panisian war engines, lined up like the hedgerows in the royal gardens. And closer, climbing up a ridge behind them, a cluster of dark-clad soldiers.

Sceptrines.

It was, she realized, the first time she had actually set eyes on the people she'd declared an enemy. That the war was never truly her doing was little comfort. She'd gone along with it willingly for far too long. That she'd even sat among the councilors and *encouraged* it.

Such was inexcusable.

At a gesture from Tior, four smaller ships sprang forward. Arivana studied their decks, filled with wrath-bowmen by the scores and over a dozen robed casters. Had the Sceptrines been alerted to the threat ahead of time, it might have been an even match. As it was . . .

She turned her head away as the slaughter began.

"I think not, my queen," Tior said. "If you wish an end to your ignorance, you must watch and watch closely. *This* is truth. I will never withhold it from you again."

He gripped her chin with wrinkled fingers and began pulling. She resisted at first, mostly out of reflex, but soon gave up. She could hear the screams, smell the fire and blood. There was no use trying to salvage the innocence of her eyes.

To her surprise, the battle was far from over. Two of the ships burned on the ground, and the other two had landed to unload their troops. The Sceptrines must have had wrath-bows or sorcerers of their own. The fighting devolved into a close frenzy of flashing steel as the enemy soldiers counterattacked. No spells flew. Had they already killed all the casters?

She could not find it in herself to cheer on those combatants in Panisian uniforms. They were not *her* soldiers even though they were still her countrymen. That their true leaders worked through deception, and stood for no good thing, did not detract from their loyal, brave service. But that didn't mean she wished ill of the Sceptrines. Not anymore.

Why can't we all live in peace?

She knew immediately it was a stupid, childish thought and hated herself for even thinking it. As long as things like greed and domination were allowed to run rampant—to even be called virtues—there would always be those who didn't know the meaning of *enough* and would burn down the world just to have a little more. Too many people had died in service to vile callings already. *As long as I draw breath, I will never stop fighting to end it.*

Tior shifted at her side. His hand relaxed, and she quickly jerked her head out of his grasp. Not to look away, though. Instead, she glanced up, and saw a concerned look on his face, replacing the arrogant confidence from before. A more focused scan of the battle revealed why. The Sceptrines had nearly succeeded in driving back their attackers. She could make out a single swordsman cutting through Tior's men like a whirlwind and his allies rallying everywhere he went. Unless something changed drastically in the next mark or so, Tior's trap would fail.

"Ah," Tior said, his grimace reversing, "so the message got through at last. It's about time."

Arivana followed his gaze. Upon the ridge that the Sceptrines had recently abandoned climbing, a fresh wave of Panisian soldiers appeared. Reinforcements from the artillery companies, no doubt. They aimed crossbows down the steep incline and began loosing bolts in perfunctory waves, cutting down the Sceptrines from behind.

The remaining enemy scattered, but Fasheshish horsemen raced out from adjacent ravines, eclipsing any hope of escape. Hands rose in surrender everywhere she looked.

Tior gestured behind him, and their ship lurched forward. "Let's go take a look at our new prisoners, shall we? I think I recognized one of them. If I'm right, we'll have made quite the catch before battle has even begun in earnest. Tell me, my queen, are you enjoying your new education yet?"

She was almost numb. And yet, she found it wasn't from shock but from anger. Anger at her lack of control. Anger at the unnecessary slaughter.

She said nothing, though. She simply stood there, refusing to give the minister even a drop of satisfaction.

At the moment, it was the only victory available to her.

"Is she still asleep?"

"Her dose isn't due for another two tolls. You've seen how she is. Won't stir a bit."

"What about Lerathus?"

"Out cold."

"You sure?"

"A jug of wine to warm his belly and a daughter of light to warm his bed. He won't be waking anytime soon."

"Yes, but—"

"All the rest of consular staff went north with the army. It's just us here. No one will stop us. No one will ever find out."

"I don't know . . ."

"Look, she's a threat to our operation here. If the council found out, they'd have us strung up and gutted. No way Ulayenos will ever let her go. Do you want to go back to the way things were? When no woman—human or valynkar—would let you even touch her if she hadn't been convinced it was her sacred duty?"

Tassariel struggled to keep her breathing steady, her muscles still, as the conversation paused. She didn't know if she was ready. And Elos had grown quiet again of late.

"No. I don't want to go back to that. Not ever."

The lock on her door clicked open, and the hinges squealed in protest. Her heart rate began to rise. A pair of sandaled feet shuffled close, stopping next to the bed that had become her prison.

"Do we kill her first? Or . . . ?"

"No. I want to feel her squirm."

A cold hand fell upon her exposed thigh. It took all of her will not to flinch.

With Elos's help, she'd been keeping still after the wine began wearing off a little bit longer every time. She knew she could move right now if she wanted but was unsure how much control over her body she would actually have. She feared it wouldn't be enough.

"Are you ready?" Elos said.

The hand on her leg was joined by another on the opposite side of her. Together, they began sliding up, lifting the hem of her loose robe.

"Yes," she said.

"Huh? Did she just—"

Energy surged through her, like a bolt of lightning. It felt the same as when Elos first came to inhabit her. The day she had lost her wings.

This time, however, she welcomed it.

Fire raged through her veins, obliterating the lingering effects of the poison. She clenched every muscle. Flexed. Stretched. It felt good to be whole, in control of her own body once more.

"Something is very wr—"

He never finished the statement.

Tassariel grabbed the hair of the man hovering over her and wrenched down as she brought her knee up. It slammed with a satisfying crunch into his nose, and he reeled back, blood spraying from a ruined face.

A knife flashed down from above. She jerked to the side, avoiding impalement by a hair. The blade scraped the edge of her breast and ribs, sinking into the mattress beneath her. The pain and the blood gushing from her wound only served to waken her further.

She rolled, trapping the man's wrist and forcing them both to the floor. She landed atop him, her legs straddling his neck and chest, his arm hugged close. All she had to do was lean back. She felt his elbow snap against the hard base of her abdomen, and he screamed.

Tassariel caught the knife as it fell from his fingers. Without thinking, she flipped it around, catching the tip of the blade, and flung it across the small room. The other man's raging advance stopped short as sharp steel punctured his chest. He took one step, one breath, and gave one look of disbelief before crumpling to the floor, dead.

She flipped backwards, springing to her feet. One glance revealed that further vigilance was unnecessary. The man writhed on the floor, whimpering and hissing through clenched teeth as he cradled his shattered arm. Tassariel worked to calm her breath and pulse, which had soared during the struggle.

"P-please," the man said. "I didn't want to. He made me do it!"

"Save your pathetic excuse for someone who cares," Tassariel said. "I assure you, I do not."

"What will you do with me?"

Tassariel sighed, looking away. He was out of the fight now. As much as she wanted to, she couldn't bring herself to kill him.

"**Look out!**" Elos said.

She felt it before seeing it. Energy gathering in the man's good hand. He roared in fury, punching towards her.

Not out of the fight after all.

She dodged. Not back to full form after weeks in captivity, she couldn't quite get out of the way. A beam shot out from his hand, scorching across her shoulder. The room filled with the stench of cooked meat. The remainder of the spell careened into the ceiling, erupting in a blast of molten stone.

Blinded by pain, Tassariel fell, stiffening one hand. She chopped across the man's throat just before hitting the ground. A sound like seashells under a boot accompanied the collapse of flesh beneath the edge of her rigid palm.

She rolled onto her back, panting. The man at her side gasped out his last few moments of life, then went still. When silence fell at last, and the room stopped spinning, the darkness beckoned to her sweetly.

"**No! Stay awake!**" Elos said, strangely distant.

"Why . . . should I?"

"You've got to get out of here. The other one is still around. No doubt he's heard the commotion and is on his way."

"Lerathus." Her fists clenched at the thought of his face. True, he might have taken measures to protect her dignity, but he was the reason she was in this mess in the first place. She shook herself, blinking away the shadows, and slowly clambered to her feet. "I need to make him pay."

"Not in your condition. Do you honestly think you can handle much more exertion at this point?"

As if to prove his point, a wave of nausea slammed into her as the pain from her injuries combined with the weakness from her imprisonment. She leaned back and took stock of herself. Her burnt shoulder throbbed, and the arm below it was useless. The cut on her breast and rib bled freely. Holding her head up for more than a few beats made her vision go blurry. And to top it all off, she felt hungry enough to strip an entire kitchen bare.

"All right," she said. "You win. I'll try to avoid any more exercise."

"Good. Now, through the door. Let's get out of here."

Tassariel stumbled out into the passageway and down the deserted corridors of the consulate. It took all her concentration just to keep one foot in front of the other as she followed Elos's directions. Eventually, she rounded a corner and came in sight of the exit.

And there stood Lerathus, energized and waiting.

She ducked back, unsure if he'd seen her or not. Holding her breath, she strained her ears for any indication of his awareness.

"There's no use staying here," Elos said. "You won't get any stronger, and he won't give up his post."

"What do I do, then?"

"Talk to him."

"I don't want to."

"I know."

"Can't you just, I don't know, give me another burst of energy, like you did back there?"

"I cannot. I'm sorry. It was a risk doing so the first time, and I have been severely diminished. Another attempt will surely kill me."

Tassariel was once again struck by how faint his voice sounded, like it was far away and drowned out by the noise of breaking waves. Her god, it seemed, had at last sacrificed something for her. The sentiment brought tears to her eyes.

"**Go**," he said, firmly yet gently. Sniffing, she obeyed.

Lerathus stiffened at her arrival, raising his energy-soaked hands. A moment later, he narrowed his eyes, studying her appearance with scrutiny.

"What happened to you, Tass?"

"Your friends did. What's left of them, anyway."

"They were no friends of mine," he said, shaking his head. "How did you do it, anyway? How did you break free?"

"Elos gave me strength."

He grunted derisively. "Save it for those with wool firmly tied around their eyes. Elos is a myth."

Tassariel couldn't help but chuckle at the absurdity of it all, a reflex that quickly shifted into hysteria.

"What's so funny?"

She steadied herself with a few deep breaths. "Your disbelief."

He shrugged. "Many of us are convinced he's just a

construct of the council, an enigma wrapped in mysticism as a way of controlling our people."

"Sadly, he's not far off. I'm more a tool of the council than they are of me."

"Well," she said, "you've got it half-right, at least."

"What do you mean?"

"The council no longer enacts his will. Not truly. But that does not mean Elos doesn't exist. Just that our definition of a god isn't quite what it should be."

Lerathus sighed, nearly rolling his eyes at her. She could tell there was nothing she could say to convince him. Whispering, she said, "Why did you think this would work? He's not budging."

"Precisely."

"How does that h—"

Then, she felt it.

Lerathus must have as well, a moment later, for his eyes went wide, and he turned.

But not in time.

Gilshamed plunged out of the sky, a meteor of fury rimmed in light. He smashed feetfirst into Lerathus and sent him sprawling. The green-haired valynkar grunted, in pain this time, curling up into a ball as the energy he'd gathered spun away uselessly. He did not try to collect any more.

The relief at seeing Gilshamed was so great that Tassariel collapsed to her knees.

"Niece!"

Gilshamed was at her side before she could blink. His golden eyes seem to take in her condition at a glance, and he laid hands on her, injecting her body with warm, healing light. She jerked as the energy seared her cut closed, and again as it chilled away her burn. She took a breath—her first in what seemed like ages—that was completely free of pain.

Tassariel smiled.

"I got your message," Gilshamed said.

"But I didn't send it to you."

"I know. Lashriel was able to deliver it for you."

"Truly?"

Gilshamed nodded. "How was that even possible?"

"I don't know. But I think our mutual acquaintance had something to do with it."

"If so," he paused, a tear dripping down his cheek, and took a breath. "If so, then I must thank him. With all the sincerity that is in me. It was only a few moments, but it was time I thought I'd never get with her. If he is still with you, please, give him my thanks."

Though Elos did not respond, she felt a warmth blossom inside her that had nothing to do with her uncle's healing. "He can hear you," she said. "And he wants you to know that he's sorry."

Gilshamed shook his head. "I think, now, I understand him a little better. No apologies are necessary."

"Enough of this," Elos told her finally. "We must go north, and fast. There may still be time."

Tassariel sighed, not bothering to ask 'for what?'

"Very well." Fixing her eyes on Gilshamed, she added, "I find myself in need of transportation. Mind if I borrow your wings?"

CHAPTER 22

"Alas," Ruul said, "we must bring our reminiscing to a close. Time grows short."

Draevenus stirred, as if waking from a dream. Ruul had been speaking at length—for tolls or days or weeks, he did not know—explaining the history of the world, a time line he could scarcely fathom, and events that made little sense to his small mind. He knew his sister had him soundly beaten in intellect. He doubted any living thing besides her could comprehend a problem so vast as this.

Yet, at the words of his god, the entire conversation flitted away like butterflies. He remembered what they had been discussing but couldn't, at the moment, recall a single specific detail of what he'd learned. It was as if the account had been committed directly to long-term memory. He knew the information was in there somewhere, but he hadn't the faintest idea where to look.

Shivering, he stood, cramped muscles protesting every twitch. "I've only just gotten here. Haven't I? And . . ." Draevenus paused, confused by his own thoughts. Somehow, the desire to kill his god seemed the most ludicrous thing imaginable, yet he couldn't recall when exactly he'd changed his mind.

He cleared his throat, then reached for the waterskin at his belt.

It was empty.

"Where has all the time gone?"

"You'll find out eventually. But for now, events move more quickly than I can account for. You must make haste."

"To what?"

"Has your sister not been keeping you informed?"

"Last I heard from her, she was working to settle the border of our people's new colony. Why?"

Ruul chuckled. A strange effect, especially as it was mirrored by the hovering swarm of darkwisps. "Only Vashodia could take on the responsibility of saving the world yet still leave this one burden to me."

"What burden?" Then, he realized what it was. "You mean . . . me."

"Yes. But do not think it such a disparaging term. The duty to family often weighs heaviest of all. We can, I think, forgive her such a weakness."

"Not like she'd give us much choice in the matter."

"Indeed."

Draevenus allowed himself a secret smile. Of all the things he imagined doing upon his arrival here, complaining about his sister to Ruul had never even crossed his mind.

"Well, what is it, then? What's the big rush about?"

"War," Ruul said. "War that must be avoided at all cost. She knows the right of this, I'm sure, but her efforts may very well fall short. And beyond this one task, she can foresee nothing."

Draevenus closed his eyes, surprised—though, perhaps he shouldn't be—that he was prepared to accept whatever Ruul might ask of him. "What must I do?"

"I have a gift for you. For all of your people. I need you to deliver it for me."

"Seems simple enough."

"I hope so, my son. I truly hope so."

"May I ask what it is?"

"I began a work in your tribe, long ago, but I was constricted at the time and could not finish it. This . . ."

The wall opened up, and a box floated towards Draevenus. It seemed plain, made of some dark metal, its lid held closed by a single sturdy clasp.

"This is my gift. The completion of a promise. Please, take it. Take it with my words of apology for making you wait this long. Take it that I may be absolved before the end."

Draevenus clutched the box. Though it seemed to weigh nothing at all, he felt its burden all the same. Like the weight of a soul held in his hands. Like destiny.

"If it's forgiveness you're looking for," Draevenus said, "know that I give it freely."

Ruul took a long time in answering. **"Perhaps that is all I need."**

"Perhaps. But something tells me it won't be all you get."

"I can only pray you are right."

The cavern began shaking. Draevenus turned and witnessed the floor parting to admit a strange platform. A few short steps led up to a hollow metal circle, standing upright. Indecipherable glyphs adorned the circumference.

As he watched, the circle began spinning. Faster and faster it spun, until the edges blurred, and sparks of black energy shot out towards the center. They met, forming a sheet of pure darkness. It hummed with virulence. Draevenus felt sweat squeeze out between his scales.

"What is it?" he asked.

"The way," Ruul replied, "to make up for lost time."

Draevenus swallowed down the lump in his throat. "Yes, but what does it do?"

"It is an artifact designed with one purpose: to aid in teleportation."

"Tele-what?"

"Ah, yes. I believe your people colloquially refer to it as 'shadow-dashing.'"

"I see. How do I make it work?"

"I have set the location, which will likely be accurate enough for our purposes."

"Likely?"

"Be gracious. It *is* rather old."

"That doesn't inspire much confidence."

"Then perhaps the result will. When you're ready, simply step into the centrifuge and . . . dash."

With a great sigh, Draevenus placed his foot on the first step, then followed onto the second. He energized, cringing. "Here goes noth—"

Jasside knew before they'd even reached the front lines that she'd failed. That they'd been too late.

The Panisian war engines were firing. For effect.

Explosions of energy, both magical and mundane, crashed into her ears every beat, but she knew she was in little danger herself. The enemy was too smart for that. Instead of targeting the front of the Sceptrine formation, the massive projectiles landed right across the center.

Her allies were effectively cut in two.

The rear half retreated. The front had nowhere else to go but forward.

"Hurry," Vashodia called. "Once the lines converge, there will be no stopping the bloodshed." She pointed a clawed finger at Chase. "And most of it will belong to *your* soldiers."

"There's still a chance to save Daye," he said. "Please, can't you—"

"I've more important things to worry about than one man. Like saving your *entire* army."

"But he might still be alive. His sneak attack failed, but that hardly means he's dead. He's too good a soldier, and makes too good a hostage, to fall so easily as that."

"He's right," Jasside added. "Let me go and find him. I'll be quick. Invisible. In and out before they know what hit them."

"Neither of you are seeing things clearly. Am I the only one around here who still thinks with her head?"

"Maybe," Jasside said. "But if we don't listen to our hearts, at least once in a while, what's the point of even living?"

"Insufferable girl. This is not the time to debate philosophies."

"Is that *really* why you're opposed? Or do you simply think I can't do it? Lack of faith in your pupil, after all, equates to lack of faith in your own teaching."

Vashodia gave her an exasperated look.

Jasside leaned into her mistress, pulling the small figure close. "*You're* the one who said how important it is that Chase be a king to his people. Look at him! He's a mess. How can he lead properly when there's a chance he might still save his brother, and he doesn't take it?"

The mierothi's face turned utterly blank.

Jasside sighed. "I know you don't understand how strong the bonds of blood can be, but I do. If you ever trusted me, even in the slightest, you'll listen to me on this."

It was three full breaths before Vashodia responded. "Fine. But *I* will be the one to try to find him."

"You?"

"Yes. I need you for something else. Something more suited to your . . . moral afflictions."

"Oh, please. I—"

Vashodia held up a hand, cutting her off, and locked her crimson eyes on Chase. "I'm going to take out the war engines. If Daye is alive—"

"Thank—" Chase said.

"*If* he's alive," Vashodia continued. "And *if* it's not too much of a hassle, I will see about setting him free."

"Thank you," he finished. "Even for the effort, you'll have the eternal gratitude of me and my nation."

"Right. Whatever. Does that set your mind at ease enough for you to actually lead your people?"

Chase looked around, as if seeing the carnage and chaos for the first time. He gritted his teeth. "Yes," he said. "Yes it does."

"Good. Come along then, apprentice."

Jasside chased after her sprinting mistress as the shouted commands of the Sceptrine king faded into the distance. Before she had time to register where they were headed, they broke free of the foremost advancing ranks.

Vashodia only accelerated.

Out of breath by the time she caught up, Jasside belatedly realized how quiet it had become. They were exactly halfway between the opposing armies. Alone. A land in which no one would ever want to find himself.

"What are we doing here?" Jasside asked between heaves of her lungs.

"Hmmm? Oh, I'm just resting a spell. Gathering my energy, so to speak."

No 'so to speak' about it. Vashodia loosed a sphere from her hand, releasing a buzzing cloud of dark-wisps. The mierothi energized, pulling from the latent power of the hovering, snapping creatures. In moments, she held more than any being should be allowed to possess.

"Is that really necessary?" Jasside said, trying not to cringe before the display.

"Probably not," Vashodia said. "But there are too many unknown powers opposing us today. I'd rather not take the risk."

"What am I supposed to be doing?"

Vashodia pointed to the coalition front lines. "See them?"

"Yes?"

The mierothi pointed back towards the Sceptrines. "And you see them?"

"Of course. What is—?"

"Stop them from killing each other."

Jasside jerked her head back. "How am I supposed to do that?"

"Use your imagination. I have faith in my teaching, after all. You care so much about human life? Prove it. I'm sure you'll figure something out."

Leaving only the afterimage of a sharp-toothed smile, Vashodia shadow-dashed towards the Panisian lines, disappearing into the dust.

Jasside scratched her head. "How the abyss am I going to keep them from fighting?"

She didn't have the strength to literally hold them back. Erecting a wall large enough to span the massive front lines would take everything she had and would only last a few marks at best. Less, if the coalition casters started battering away at it with their own spells.

I need something simple yet effective. What could make them hesitate to advance?

The answer, when it came to her a moment later, seemed so obvious she berated herself for not seeing it sooner. *People always shy away from the things they fear, and all men remember a time when they were afraid of the dark.*

Arivana felt her eyes go wide as a cloud as black as midnight erupted between the armies. Roiling like flameless smoke, it rose a thousand paces into the sky. Sparks of energy arced within it, sucking the very light out of the air with each snapping strike. She had seen awesome displays of sorcery before but never anything like this.

"What *is* that?" she asked of no one in particular.

"Our friends," said the captured prince. "The ones who made your invasion turn tail and run."

She glanced down at him. Bound hand and foot, secured to a post and surrounded by half a dozen guards with bared steel, the prince still appeared defiant. Even a little bit hopeful. He was either foolishly brave, or his friends were a threat to be reckoned with.

She couldn't help but think it was probably both.

"Good," Tior said. "I had hoped they would join our little party. I wanted to see the faces of those responsible for giving us so much trouble. Before I kill them, that is."

"You'll regret those words before the day is out," the prince said.

Tior let loose a throaty, rasping chuckle. "My good prince, do you not realize the scale of our response?" He pointed south. "See what measure your friends have called down upon their heads and yours."

Arivana looked back over her shoulder. A gasp seized her at the sight.

An army hundreds wide and thousands deep marched across the flat desert plain. The cloud of dust kicked up at their advance was enough to rival a hurricane. Yet it was not they who drew her eye the most.

Suspended by magical energies in the air above the host floated half a dozen ships. *Ship*, however, didn't seem quite the right term. They were gargantuan monoliths, vertical in design. Six immense towers flying through the sky. Each one was painted in the unique crest of the house to which it belonged.

The great families of Panisahldron had come to war.

"Accounts never quite agreed," Tior said, "but even the most generous estimate puts the number of your friends at around fifty. Tell me, can they contend with three thousand casters, each near to the strength of a full valynkar?"

The prince laughed. "Fifty? You honestly thought there were fifty?"

"As I said, reports varied. How many were there in truth? One hundred?"

"Two."

"Two hundred? That is surprising, but not—"

"No, you fool. Not two *hundred*. Just *two*."

Arivana felt indefinable joy at seeing the shock that crossed Tior's face.

He spun away and raced to the crest of a hill twenty paces away, where a command center of sorts had been established. All the prime councilors were there, along with their usual aides, and the valynkar consul as well. Arivana left the prince behind and sauntered over. She didn't want to miss whatever would be said. Flumere plodded along behind her, still silent, the fading bruises from her failed attack on Tior marring any expression. The four guards set over them stayed content to simply herd them.

The other five family heads gathered close to Tior, but before he could start giving instructions, the explosions began.

Arivana whirled as a series of concussive blasts tore across the battlefield. She looked up, squinting through the dust, and realized whence they had originated. Smoke billowed on the horizon as dark flames consumed every last one of her army's war engines.

Tior growled, then ripped his gaze away from the

sight. The other councilors seemed to wilt as his attention turned to them. "Get your families into position and start full-scale harmonization at once." A series of quick nods was all the response he received. Tior shot a glance at the consul. "We need you to stall them, Ulayenos. Can we count on your aid?"

"I don't know," the grey-haired valynkar said.

"What! Need I remind you again of our agreement? About the services and protections we provide?"

"No. But I received word that a member of our high council paid a visit to the consulate last night, and two I left behind have now passed onto the abyss. Our secrets are laid bare. Can you protect us against the full fury of valynkar self-righteousness?"

Tior shook his head. "We can still fix this. But I can't do it without your help."

"You misunderstand," Ulayenos said. "I am not withdrawing from your side. But the enemy arrayed against you today is none other than that ancient enemy of the valynkar. The mierothi have returned to the world."

Tior paled. "I thought they were just a myth?"

"I was there, Tior, nearly two thousand years ago. I *fought* them. My people still carry the scars of that war on their hearts. My consular personnel *must* defeat them here. Alone. If we do that, the high council may yet forgive our . . . indiscretions."

Without another word, he unfurled his pale, steely wings and launched himself into the air. Arivana watched as he was joined by scores of other valynkar, darting skyward from across the battlefield, and, as a single formation, dove towards the last place whence the dark sorcery had come.

It was strange enough clinging to her uncle's back. Stranger still doing it while half a league up in the air. But strangest of all were his golden wings, flapping straight through her body as they flew. She'd always known valynkar wings were ethereal, not quite anchored in the physical realm, but she'd never had quite so potent a demonstration as this.

"Are you all right back there?" Gilshamed asked, shouting over the wind of their passing.

"Fine. Thanks," Tassariel yelled back. "How much longer?"

"A toll at least. Maybe more. Can't you feel the energies at work?"

"You forget, Uncle. Most of us aren't nearly as strong as you. Frankly, it scares me a bit that you can sense anything when we can't even see the battlefield yet."

"Yes. Speaking of which, are you going to tell me what this is all about?"

"Abyss if I know all the forces at play. The only thing that concerns me is Arivana."

"The Panisian queen?"

"The one and only. I took her under my wing, so to speak, and I've come to care about her a great deal. She's in danger right now because of me. Because I wasn't careful enough. I *have* to get her to safety. It's the only way to make things right."

"I understand completely." Gilshamed turned his head, and she could see the broad smile he cast over his shoulder. "Let's go rescue a queen!"

Jasside remembered the first time she had ever seen a valynkar. Her half brother had introduced her to Gilshamed on a dreary autumn day, but the light ever around him made it seem like spring. For years, the sight of wings brought forth an instinctive response of hope and joy.

Today, however, as nearly a hundred valynkar swooped towards her mistress, all she felt was a niggling worm of fear.

The cloud of darkness she'd conjured had done its work, as both armies remained hesitant to march through it. And with the war engines out of commission, a pall of peace had settled like dust over what otherwise would be a blood-drenched battlefield.

Which meant she could go help her mistress.

She looked towards the smoking ruins of the Panisian war engines. Winged figures began assaulting the ground around the shattered weapons with spells of scorching light. The burnt husks splintered under the assault, shards flying in a shower of sharp wood, and the space around the scene quickly cleared of soldiers. The attack raged on as more valynkar banked down, raking across the line.

No return attack came from below, but Jasside could still taste Vashodia's unique energy trace dashing sideways along the ground and springing clear of the coalition formation. She sighed. *Yes, I really* should *help.*

Still, her feet remained anchored. Part of her didn't want to help, hinging on the excuse that she would only get in the way, that her mistress would berate her for even trying. Even though she hated herself for contemplating it, the thought would not go away.

A moment later, it ceased to matter.

Jasside spun as a fresh wave of power rushed onto the scene. New to the battle, but familiar to her, over six hundred black-clad figures dashed past the Sceptrine flank into the open desert, converging on Vashodia's position.

The mierothi nation had finally arrived.

Just in time, too.

She watched the distant clash as countless tendrils of darkness arced through the sky to meet the flying light. Suddenly outnumbered, the valynkar wisely elected retreat. They formed shields like glowing bubbles about themselves, many of which popped before the valynkar could get out of reach of the lashing darkness.

With all the commotion, it didn't seem likely that anyone would be paying much attention to prisoners thought secure in the rear of a well-fortified position. Now was the best chance she'd likely find to rescue Daye. She *had* to operate on the notion that he'd been captured and not killed outright. She'd lost too much already to believe otherwise.

One more dead soul on my conscience—one more person I cared about lost because I couldn't save him—I'm pretty sure that would break me.

She spared only one half-regretful glance in the direction of her mistress before cloaking herself in shadow and shadow-dashing the other way.

Arivana squinted up at the sky overhead. "It's going to be a slaughter, Flumere. What can we do?"

The six great ships were rolling up the backside of the rearmost dunes and would soon be in position to strike anywhere on the battlefield. Even with no sensitivities of her own, Arivana could still feel the magic thrumming inside each one, as entire houses of casters linked their power together.

"I'm sorry," Flumere said at last, her voice raw and cracked. "I'm afraid it is too late for me to do anything to help. Too late for us all."

"You can't blame yourself. I pulled you into this mess. If anyone should be sorry, it's me."

Flumere slowly shook her head. The chains around her wrists and ankles clanked softly with the motion. "You do not understand. I gave you my aid freely, honestly, and against my . . . better judgment. I will not *ever* regret that I tried. But now, all this pain is coming to a head—pain *I* am responsible for—and I won't get the chance to explain why—"

A figure crashed to the ground just paces away, and Arivana jumped, gasping. The smell of sweat and burnt cloth clogged her nose as the valynkar dismissed his wings and rose shakily to his feet.

"What now, Ulayenos?" Tior said. "Couldn't handle two little girls?"

"We only saw one, at first," Ulayenos replied, huffing for air. "But she is the most devious mierothi to ever live."

"So? You still had her outnumbered a hundred to one. She can't be *that* dangerous."

"She led us into a trap, don't you see? Six hundred more of her abyss-taken kin showed up, just as we had her in our grasp."

"Six *hundred?*"

"Yes. This must be all that's left of their entire species."

Tior gritted his teeth. Arivana saw the cold calculation in his eyes, naked with ambition and deviousness. "We've no quarrel with them. They must only be here because of you."

"Perhaps. Either way, you *must* kill them all."

"You presume to give *me* orders?"

Ulayenos bowed his head. "Forgive me. I spoke out of place. But their destruction is the only way I can see to ensure our continued . . . cooperation."

"In that, my friend, you are wrong."

"What?" the consul asked, clearly confused.

"You and I have grown used to a certain lifestyle, my friend. One predicated on the assurance of no outside influence. The only way to ensure it continues is to permanently end the threat of chastisement."

Ulayenos paled. "You cannot be serious."

"The looming presence of you valynkar has long been a thorn in humanity's side. A thorn that may need to be plucked out, sooner or later. If you'd like to survive the fire that's to come, you'll do exactly as I say."

"Abyss take you, Tior. I'll do nothing of the sort."

"Very well, then. I guess I'll have to have a nice long chat with these mierothi. Given time, and proper incentive, I'm sure we can come to some understanding. Or even an alliance."

"You would dare ally yourself with them? To those who live in darkness?"

The minister shrugged. "Darkness has many uses."

Arivana watched the consul of the valynkar as defiance slowly morphed into resignation on his face. She found her gaze being drawn past him to something that couldn't possibly exist.

A shadow that moved. A shadow belonging to nothing.

She watched, horror and fascination mixing like addiction, as the living blot of darkness darted towards the two men.

"You help me annihilate my ancient foe," Ulayenos said, with all the enthusiasm of a corpse, "and I'll do anything you say."

"Agreed," Tior said. "Now, with all your experience, I'm sure you'll be able to answer this next question."

"Ask it."

"What's the best way to kill a mierothi?"

"As the only one present who has done so," interrupted a new voice, female and confident, "perhaps you'd best include me in the discussion?"

Arivana could scarce contain her laughter as the shadow resolved into the form of a woman dressed in black, with blond hair and tanned skin. Both Tior and Ulayenos staggered back a step in shock.

"Seize her!" Tior shouted, pointing a shaky finger at the intruder. Arivana's guards, the only soldiers in the area, leapt towards the woman.

"Oh, come now," the woman said, as they bound her arms behind her back. "We haven't even been properly introduced."

"Who are you, and why are you here?" Tior demanded.

"Jasside," she said. "Jasside Anglasco. I've come to begin negotiations."

The old man's laugh grated on her nerves, but Jasside forced herself to keep smiling. She was beginning to think it might have been better simply to attack.

No. Not better. Just . . . easier.

She hadn't been planning to talk at all, but after hearing the contention between the two leaders—and what they planned to do—she thought she might be able to drive a wedge through the already apparent rift. At the very least, she had to try.

Besides, there was the girl.

Jasside glanced down at her now. Sad and curious—

yet somehow amused—eyes met her gaze, framed by disheveled orange locks. This was no place for someone so young. Jasside had feared the girl, whoever she might be, would pay the price if she took any direct action. Were she to cause harm to something so innocent in her haste, she would never be able to forgive herself.

Hence letting herself get captured.

"Negotiations?" the man—Tior, she believed he'd been called—said. "We've every advantage here. What reason could we possibly have to relent?"

Jasside faced him, taking a moment to soak in her surroundings. She quickly realized how much attention her arrival had garnered. The six guards around Daye all stared at her, their charge forgotten. The aged valynkar gaped openly. Five others, dressed in similar battle regalia as Tior, and a dozen aides halted all activity to peer in her direction. Power throbbed, flavored of light, from nearly everyone around her, yet it was nearly drowned out by the massive gathering of energy taking place in the floating edifices above her. Strangely, Tior himself was the only one who hadn't energized. That fact only made her more wary of him than the others.

"You speak of advantage," Jasside began, "but even if your assessment of the situation is correct, what's the point of fighting on when your opponent is willing to make peace?"

"To win," Tior said. "To punish the Sceptrines for their crime."

"Stop using my family as an excuse!" the girl cried. "You didn't care about them when they were alive, and I'm certain you didn't shed a single tear after they were assassinated."

"Assassinated?" Jasside said. Then, the puzzle pieces clicked together in her mind. "You were the heir of Panisahldron. That makes you—"

"The queen, yes," Tior said.

Jasside shook her head as tears began rolling down the young queen's cheeks. Something about this was very, very wrong.

"Tior—" the queen began, but the man cut her off.

"Hush now, Arivana. I'm dealing with an adult. Though . . ." Tior swept his eyes across Jasside. " . . . one surprisingly naïve for her age."

Jasside knew, then, that her attempt at negotiation would never have succeeded. Perhaps she *was* a fool for believing such people could ever contemplate peace or that she could be the one to broker it.

Still, she didn't regret trying. She now knew where the *true* threat lay.

Before her stood remorseless men who wielded their power like a hammer over others. And if she had learned one thing from Vashodia, it was this: There was only one way to deal their kind.

Jasside turned to Arivana. "Your majesty, will you answer me one question?"

"Of course."

"If the decision were in your hands, would you still press for war?"

The queen shook her head. "There's been enough bloodshed. If I had the power, we'd all go home."

"Then it is a good thing you do *not* have that power," Tior said. He turned to Jasside. "And I've heard just about enough of your voice. Ulayenos?"

The valynkar jerked, apparently surprised to be called on. "Yes?"

Tior gestured at her. "This one may not be a mierothi herself, but she is their ally and draws power from the same dark source. Their extermination begins with her. Will you do the honors?"

Ulayenos took a deep breath before answering. "So be it."

As he lifted his hand, already sparking with a killing spell, Jasside energized. She didn't need much. Not with all the time they'd given her to prepare.

"Arivana," Jasside said.

"Yes?" the queen replied.

"Run."

Jasside waited a full beat until the woman at Arivana's side grabbed her hand and began racing away.

Then she attacked.

Most people couldn't cast with bound hands, the motions and gestures tied so closely to the act of sorcery that it was impossible to separate the two. Jasside suffered no such impairment. Will controlled her power. Nothing else. Though she rarely used thought alone to form her castings, preferring the extra mechanism of control afforded by her hands—her mistress chided her relentlessly for such gestures—she *had* learned the method for use in emergencies.

And I'm pretty sure this counts.

She would hold back no longer. Jasside formed a sphere among the seventeen Panisians gathered in rough circle a short distance away, then crafted miniscule channels running away from it. With a snap of will, all the air inside the sphere escaped along the channels.

Two things happened.

The first was a great sucking sound, as the surrounding air collapsed in to fill the void she'd left behind. The seventeen people were pulled like metal to a magnet, slamming into each other in a great heap.

The second was the rush of air down the paths she'd made, faster than crossbow bolts and harder than a hammer. Twelve, to be exact. One each to the ten guards, and another for both Tior and Ulayenos. The men all went sprawling from the blast.

The whole thing had taken less than a single beat.

A strand of energy danced from a finger, severing her bonds, even as Jasside raced down the hill towards Daye. A quick glance told her that the queen had gotten out of harm's way.

The prince lifted his head at her approach but looked none too happy. "You shouldn't have come for me. What were you thinking, doing it alone?"

"You're one to talk about making rash decisions." But she said it with a smile, sweeping a hand over the sprawled forms around them. "I was thinking I could win. And a 'thank-you' wouldn't be entirely amiss." She severed his chains, which took a moment—it was difficult finding a spot that wasn't too close to his skin.

Daye sighed as his bonds fell free and immediately began stretching and rubbing his sore wrists. "Thanks."

"There. Was that so hard?"

"No. It's just . . . I couldn't stand the thought of your coming to harm on my account."

"Oh, bother your masculine pride. I know how to take care of myself."

"It's not . . . that."

Jasside saw the look he gave her. A look she had noticed him give before. A look, she now knew, she'd been hoping to see again.

But she wasn't ready to process it. Not now. Maybe not ever. "Please," she said, "we can figure out . . . whatever this is later. I must make sure you get back to your brother in one piece."

"I'm sure he'll be—" Daye's eyes went wide, peering past her. "Look out!"

She felt it then. A surge of energy, just behind her. She formed a shield in an instant, barely erecting it before a stream of livid fire struck. The flame seared against her defense, hissing in virulence. She pushed more energy into her shield, then pulsed it back. The fire dissipated, allowing Jasside to determine who had cast it.

Tior, not quite as defeated as she thought.

Around him, brightwisps swirled.

"Looks like you'll have to find your way back alone," Jasside said to Daye. "I've got one last tyrant to dethrone."

It seemed instantaneous, like every other shadow-dash he'd ever performed, but the landing left Draevenus in a state of extreme disorientation. Where Ruul rested had been damp and dark and chilly. Here, the sun blinded him, and he coughed up hot dust that seemed to have filled his lungs with his first breath. He staggered, barely able to keep his balance, and clutched the strange box to his chest.

Ruul's gift. Whatever it might be, the god had entrusted it to him. Draevenus knew he had to find his people and deliver it. But first, he had to get his bearings. After a moment, his vision adjusted enough that he could see the basic shape of the terrain around him. Spying a rise larger than any others around, he began hiking up it. Sand shifted beneath his feet with each step, threatening to send him sliding, but he resisted the urge to try dashing to the top. He'd had too much of that recently and didn't think he could stomach another trip, however brief.

At last, Draevenus reached the crest and looked down on the landscape before him. What he saw took his breath away.

Two massive armies stood facing each other, separated by a dark, angry cloud along the ground. On the near side, he witnessed scores of bright, flying figures retreat before an onslaught of dark energy. And, below them, the clustered mass of mierothi.

Dread wracked him as memories of that ancient war took hold of his mind.

"No," he said, falling numbly to his knees. "Not again."

He watched, frozen by despair, as the skirmish went on. It wasn't until the last valynkar had retreated out of range that he sighed in relief and felt able to control his limbs again. He lurched to his feet. The distance was too great, and time too short, to let his feet bring him there as he wished. Draevenus energized, then shadow-dashed forward.

Though he landed slightly dizzy, there were no other ill effects.

Unless seeing his sister counted.

"Brother," Vashodia said. "How lovely of you to join us. Did you have fun on your little adventure on the other side of the world?"

"Other side of the . . . What the abyss are we doing here?"

Vashodia lifted her arms. "We're at war. Couldn't you tell?"

"With the valynkar? After all the work I've done to keep peace between us?"

"Relax, dear brother. These ones are all but renegades. And they started it besides."

"Think that will matter to the valynkar high council once they start turning up dead?"

"After what they've done, we'll likely be thanked for wiping them out."

"Out of the question. The fighting stops now."

Vashodia shrugged. "Oh, very well. I suppose even naughty boys like them can be put to good use."

Draevenus stepped back, eying her sternly. "If I know one thing about you, sister, it's that only a miracle could make you change your mind." He shook his head, grunting in mirth as it dawned on him. "You didn't want to kill them in the first place."

"If I had, do you really think there would be any left alive?"

"No. Abyss take me for certainty, but no."

"As long as we understand each other."

Draevenus turned at approaching footsteps, grinning broadly when he saw who it was.

"Mother," he said, rushing forward.

Angla threw out her arms to embrace him. "Oh, my sweet boy. I have missed you so."

"I've missed you too, Mother." He pulled back, holding up the box in one hand.

"What have you got there?" she asked.

"A surprise. Is everyone here?"

Angla gestured to the crowd of their kin behind her. "Every last one of us."

"Good. Gather them up, please. I need to speak to them all at once."

His mother gestured over his shoulder towards an army or three. "This may not be the best time."

"It can't wait. Please."

Sighing, Angla nodded, then moved off and began rounding up the rest of the mierothi. Draevenus turned back to his sister to explain all that had happened. But the look on her face made him pause.

He'd never seen her appear the least bit sad before.

"*He* gave it to you, didn't he?" she said softly.

"Yes," he answered, knowing exactly of whom she spoke.

"And you plan to open it?"

"Of course. Why wouldn't I?"

"Because it will kill you, brother. It will kill you all."

Draevenus shook at the words. "No. No that can't be. Ruul promised, and I believe him."

"Funny. I thought you had gone there to end him."

"I changed my mind."

"No, you didn't. You just don't know that yet."

"What's that supposed to mean?"

"Just that you have no idea what the gift will do. No concept of future ramifications. If you ever loved me, please, do *not* open that box."

Cringing at the words, Draevenus could only look away. "I'm sorry."

Vashodia lowered her head.

Angla returned, smiling somberly. "We're ready, son."

He turned to face the crowd. He decided to keep it simple and merely repeated the words Ruul had spoken to him. The last six hundred mierothi in the world held their breaths as one. Draevenus reached for the clasp.

Out of the corner of his eye, he caught a glimpse of Vashodia dashing over the horizon.

Jasside sprang back, avoiding a hammer of light as it crashed down in the space she'd just vacated. It slammed into the sand and exploded like shattered glass made of fire. The man was strong, besting her in raw power with the aid of his brightwisps, and skilled as well. She kept telling herself she was retreating to get clear of any bystanders, but her singed dress and frantic heartbeat proved such assertions to be a lie.

She didn't know if she could actually beat him.

Jasside dashed backwards again, giving herself room to breathe. Relentless, he came after her.

A giant wave of light rolled towards her. She formed a shield around herself, which held against such a broad dispersal of energy. The spell crashed around her, but she felt little more than a warming of the sand beneath her feet.

She struck back at him with darkness in the shape of razor-sharp discs, dozens shooting forth from her outstretched hand every beat. He waved a hand, conjuring his own shield. The discs deflected off it as he trudged forward, unconcerned.

A thousand missiles of light burst out from him in every direction. Jasside's eyes went wide as they curved in towards her. Her shield would be about as helpful as paper if they all struck at once. She dismissed it, pouring all her gathered power into a nullifying field, cast in a broad net around her. The missiles passed through, unraveling into harmless strands of energy, but ate up most of her remaining reserves in the process.

Her knees buckled under the strain. Will alone kept her standing, kept the field in place. If he knew how weak she was right now, it would likely be over in moments. Thankfully, the deception worked. Tior paused, studying what she'd wrought.

"That's a neat trick," he said. "Mind telling me how it works?"

"I could," Jasside said, "but it would take all day, and you still wouldn't understand."

"You think so little of my intelligence? Have you no idea the skill required to run the world? The insight? Come now, woman, one of us will be dead before nightfall. Don't allow the chance that such knowledge might die as well."

Jasside laughed. "Oh, this isn't even a tenth of my knowledge. And what I know isn't a hundredth that of my mistress. Shall we delay our duel for years, so that I may pass everything on?"

"No," Tior said, a smile slowly spreading across his face. "Just long enough for me to recharge."

Jasside felt the blood drain from her face as Tior gestured forward. A beam of blinding fire shot forth. It struck her net, dissipating as had the other spells, but something was different this time. The beam increased in potency, and she could feel the edges around the point it met her field start to fray. He was burning open a hole.

She dove to the side, giving up the net. The beam scythed across, close enough to singe her exposed skin and turning sand into glass wherever it touched. With her little remaining energy, Jasside disturbed the dirt in a wide circle, raising a cloud of dust to obscure her. She rolled away from the beam and lay still.

Tior's jet of flame winked out, only to re-form a beat later in another direction. Then again a third time, and fourth, and fifth, each lasting less than a breath. He was probing for her.

Jasside began energizing.

A beam landed just a few paces away, spitting molten shards of newly formed glass towards her face. She turned away, clamping down on the urge to scream, to get clear of the danger. Will won out, and she was able to stay unmoving and undetected. She smelled a strange, pungent burning, and swiped a hand behind her to extinguish the flames licking across her hair. Tior sought for her again, but the spell never came any closer.

She reached her capacity and stood.

Tior coughed, a reflex she fought as well, as dust settled thickly towards the ground. "Enough of this!" he said.

A blast of conjured air swept past her. The dust cleared. The side of Tior's face appeared ten paces in front of her.

Jasside pointed a finger. "Gotcha."

A jet of pure darkness lanced out from her hand.

Tior turned. His own beam spun forward.

The two spells met midair between them.

Jasside lurched as the opposing forces collided but kept her balance. Darkness and light warred, spitting and sparking in twisted whorls as they annihilated each other. She focused, pushing forward, and felt her energy slowly gaining the advantage.

When once there were dozens, now only a few brightwisps still spun about her opponent. And while he'd been wasting energy probing for her in the dust, she'd pooled all she had into this one attack. Her power now exceeded his own.

From the frantic look in his eyes, and the scream erupting from his throat, he must have known it, too.

Jasside stepped forward. The darkness gained on the light, now only two paces from Tior. Now one. The energies, locked together, pulled at her as much as she pushed, and she knew the same was true for her enemy. There would be no escaping for either of them. This could only end with one of their deaths.

And it will not.

Be.

Mine!

Tior lifted a fist. In anger, or frustration, she didn't know. But his power waned in that moment. Her darkness broke through his light, slamming into him.

The man turned to ash in an instant.

Jasside hadn't even the time to smile before a crack of lightning struck the ground at her side. She flew, sizzling with pain, and realized what he'd done. A last-ditch spell, coming from a different angle that she wouldn't see coming.

As she tumbled along the sand, breathless and exhausted, she cringed to realize just how close he'd come to succeeding. She came to a stop and closed her eyes.

Before Draevenus had even fully opened the lid, a black mist erupted from the box like breath on a cold day, encompassing every mierothi present. He felt virulent energy, not of his own making, coursing through every vein and cell in his body. His back arched. Limbs splayed out, stiff and out of his control. Fingers and toes tingled with pain.

Though nearly blinded by the darkness, Draevenus looked out among his kin. All were in the exact same state as he.

What . . . is . . . happening?

Cold fire seemed to rage within him. His scales writhed in agony. His back churned.

Were you right, sister? Have I killed us all?

The pain was already as bad as he could possibly imagine. But somehow, it grew worse. He begged within his mind for release, welcoming death even, to end this torture, wondering how he could have so badly misjudged his god.

Ruul's gift is death.

Then something happened.

Draevenus . . . remembered.

That window into his mind swung open, and his ancient memories awakened once more. His consciousness honed in on an instance that he didn't think he ever could have forgotten, and realization struck him in the gut like a hammer.

I've done this before.

The day his tribe had first met Ruul. The day they lost their humanity.

His god's words came back to him. This was to be a completion of the work he'd begun almost two thousand years ago.

They were being transformed.

But into what?

Draevenus didn't know. All he could do was be patient until the pain passed. A task made more difficult by the swarm of glowing wings he glimpsed approaching through the sky.

"**R**emember to breathe," Gilshamed said.

Tassariel let go of the air from her lungs. She hadn't even realized she'd been holding it. But if anything had the right to take her breath away, the sight before her surely qualified.

"Look at all the people," she said. "A million at least. And they all came to kill each other. How is it possible for such hatred to exist?"

Gilshamed shook his head. "I forget how young you are. That you've never seen war."

"Is it always like this?"

"Not always to the same scale, but yes. How it's

fought—the implements, that is—adapt over time, but the nature of war never really changes."

"If that's true, I've had enough of it already."

Gilshamed nodded. "Me too. What's your plan for finding the queen in that mess down below?"

"If she's anywhere, she'll be with that minister of hers. Tior. I caught him in communion once, it'll only take a moment to find him again."

Without waiting for a response, she energized and slipped into that dark place. Once a soul had been touched, finding it once more was only a matter of thinking about the person. She conjured that wrinkled face in her mind and felt herself drifting towards one of many nearby stars.

Just as she drew close, though, it flared, then winked out of existence. She'd never seen anything like it before.

Tassariel popped her consciousness back into her body. "Quick. West side of the field. I think . . ."

"What?"

"I think he just died. If he did, Arivana could be in serious trouble."

Gilshamed banked down, picking up speed as he swept over the Panisian army. Reaching its edge, Tassariel pointed down to a group of figures near a charred stretch of sand. "There," she said. "That was the last place I felt him."

Her uncle landed, and she leapt off at a run. Dust and smoke lay thick in the air, and she couldn't make out who the people were. They seemed to be gathered around something on the ground.

"Arivana?" she called. "Queen Arivana, is that you?"

"Tassariel?" came the reply.

Tassariel held a hand to her heart, relieved beyond measure. "Your majesty! I was so worried." She drew close, and could now make out Arivana and her hand-maiden, and another man she didn't recognize. A woman in black lay in the sand, looking like she'd run through a fire.

"As was I," Arivana replied. "But we'll have to catch up later. Disaster has only barely been avoided today. And it may still claim us yet."

"I only just arrived, so I'll take your word for it." Tassariel gestured at the strangers. "Who are they?"

"I," the man said, "am Prince Daye Harkun, brother to King Chase Harkun of Sceptre." He pointed to the woman. "This is—"

"Jasside," Gilshamed said, coming up on Tassariel's side. "How the abyss did you end up here?"

The woman—Jasside—turned her head but made no move to sit up. "Long story, Gilshamed. It's . . . good to see you."

"You as well. I must admit, I lost track of most members of our revolution. I . . . I couldn't face them after what I'd done."

"It's all right," Jasside said. "It all worked out in the end." She closed her eyes. "Most of it, anyway."

Gilshamed hung his head.

"What about Tior?" Tassariel asked. "Where is he?"

Jasside pointed to a pile of ash not far away.

Tassariel felt her jaw drop open. "You mean . . . ?"

"He was tougher than I expected," Jasside said. She gestured towards her ragged condition. "Hence."

"Good riddance," Tassariel said.

"As much as I agree with you," Arivana said, "we have bigger problems to face. You two are valynkar, right? Surely you can sense what's going on up there."

"They'd better," Daye said. "What they're doing feels . . . wrong. Even from this far away it pulls at me, as if I'm compelled to step in and break up the party."

Tassariel peered up towards the six great ships in the sky. She'd been sensing the goings-on there for a while now but had dismissed the importance in her focus to find Arivana. Now, she could ignore it no longer. "What *are* they doing?"

"Linking their sorcery, however that works," the queen said. "Once they finish, no power in this world can stand against them."

"They will not finish harmonizing for several marks at best," Gilshamed said. "What worries me most is *that*."

They all followed the direction of his pointed finger and saw scores of flying valynkar converging on a point across the battlefield.

"Where are they going?" Tassariel asked.

"Oh, gods," Jasside said. "They're headed for the mierothi."

"The mierothi are here?" Gilshamed asked. "How many of them?"

"All of them," Jasside said. "I can feel them as surely as you feel the casters in those floating fortresses above us. Something is going on, though. Something . . . strange. I think they're vulnerable."

She moved to sit up, as if she were in any state to help, but the prince laid a hand on her shoulder, eliciting a gasp as she nearly flopped back onto the ground.

"Ease your mind, Jasside," Gilshamed said. "I remember the real reason behind the revolution in the Veiled Empire. I know that not all mierothi are monsters."

"The monsters among them are dead," Jasside confirmed. "All but one, at least. And I'm pretty sure I've got her under control."

Tassariel watched her uncle shiver at the words. Saying no more, he spread his wings and launched into the sky. She turned to Jasside. "Let me see what I can do about those wounds."

Gilshamed could not feel his brethren energizing, drowned out by the thousands doing likewise above them, but he knew it all the same by the bright glow that surrounded them. That and the rage writ clearly on all their faces.

He did not recognize most of them. Many were young—relatively speaking—born after the war that saw their kind banished from a continent. They'd never faced mierothi in battle before. So he was at a loss at their motivation. Such angry passion could find no root in ancient animosity. There must be another reason.

What he'd found at the consulate, though, might be more than sufficient cause. And between what his own eyes witnessed and Tassariel's account, he was sure he'd only just brushed the surface of the depravity there. These valynkar before him had been driven to desperation by their own sins.

But desperate men are ever seeking a way out. A release from the chains they've wrapped around themselves. Perhaps I can be the one to show them how to break those bonds.

Glancing down, he saw why he had to try.

His old foe had gathered in a cluster, six hundred strong. All the mierothi left in the world, according to Jasside. Her description of them, though apt, fell far short of the truth.

Vulnerable? They're as helpless as babes!

Caught in the grasp of some strange summons of dark energy, he did not know if they were unaware of the danger above them or simply unable to respond. Either way, his window of opportunity to prevent their annihilation was swiftly drawing to a close. He sped forward through the air, energizing as he dove between them and his kin.

Gilshamed cast a bright aura of light around him, capturing the attention of the hundred other valynkar. Amplifying his voice, he addressed them.

"Consular personnel," he said. "I am Gilshamed, a long-standing member of our people's high council. Take heed of my words!"

All eyes were drawn to him now, yet his kin were still poised to strike with their sorcery. None appeared too happy to see him.

"I do not claim to understand all your reasons for being here nor why you feel compelled to attack a helpless foe. I do, however, see the desperation in your eyes. The guilt and fear driving you to acts you know are unconscionable."

Many of them lowered hands held ready with deadly magics, and a few even hung their heads. Not all, though. Not even most.

Not nearly enough.

"Whatever orders you've been given, whatever promises you've been made, I free you of them all. My brethren, I beg you, please, stand down."

No one moved.

"Hear me! I know about the happenings at the consulate. Do not let your own sins trap you into further misdeeds. There is no escape from that wicked spiral of lies. The only way out is through repentance." He held out a hand. "I offer you forgiveness, freely and without restraint. All you must do . . . is take it."

Gilshamed let his words hang in the air as he met each set of eyes in turn. It seemed to take tolls for him to make a connection with everyone, and he feared there wasn't enough time. That even as he got through to dozens, too many would be left unconvinced, willing to let fly their eldritch violence and succumb to the fear that drove them.

Still, he sought them out one by one, knowing that only a true bond—not the one they felt shackled to at the moment—could divert this disaster. Even then, it felt like an impossible task. *I've done so much to stay out of the affairs of my people, and for far too long. Will they recognize that I'm trying to change that?*

Will they even understand what I'm trying to do?

Almost to tears, he kept up his physical communion with the valynkar before him, and slowly—so slowly—the defiance in every gaze withered away, replaced by a mix of sorrow, shame, and relief. Silently flapping their glowing wings, the consular personnel all discharged their gathered energy.

Gilshamed sighed. He turned, looking down once more upon the mierothi, still writhing in the throes of an unknown ritual. He bowed his head to the man standing before them.

For you, Draevenus. For the kindness you showed me. For leading me to my love. For helping me let go of the past and find the way back to myself. As long as you and I live, let the peace between our peoples stand.

Though he couldn't be sure, Gilshamed thought he saw the old assassin smile. He returned the gesture in kind . . .

. . . only to have that small surge of joy wiped out as he felt a change in the massive conjoining of power in the floating towers above him.

The casters of the first of the houses had completed their harmonization.

The searing heat from Tassariel's casting faded as Jasside inspected her newly healed flesh. Her fatigue had only worsened, as was usually the case, but at least the pain was gone.

"Thank you," Jasside said.

"It was nothing," Tassariel replied. "I'm happy to—gah!"

The valynkar woman gasped, turning her head towards the great ships above them.

"What is it?" Jasside asked.

"The houses. They're . . ." Tassariel gulped, " . . . they're completing their links."

Jasside turned to Arivana. "Who's in charge of them? What are their orders?"

The queen shrugged. "You killed everyone who had the authority to command them. And the last thing I heard Tior say was that they were to take out all enemy casters. I suppose that means—"

"The mierothi," Jasside said. Fear and frustration coursed through her, knowing there was nothing she could do to stop it.

Knowing she had to try anyway.

Energizing, she took a step towards them.

"Hold on," Daye said, standing in her way. She stopped abruptly, afraid to make contact and lose the power she had just drawn in. "You're in no condition for any kind of strain. I know you're skilled, but against these odds? All you'll accomplish is your own death."

"You think I don't know that!"

"Then why go? Abyss take me woman, I will *not* let you throw your life away for nothing!"

"This is not the time to discuss your feelings for me," Jasside said, almost adding, *Or my feelings for you.* "You do not have the right to make decisions for me. Lives are at stake. People I care about. Do you see anyone else able and willing to stop this?"

"Maybe . . ." Tassariel said.

Jasside spun to face her. "What do you mean?"

The valynkar gestured towards the queen. "With all her advisors dead, what's to stop Arivana from handing out new orders?"

"Tior made it very clear to me that I have no actual authority," the queen said. "The prime councilors were the true rulers of Panisahldron." She looked to her handmaiden, as if for comfort or encouragement, but seemed to find neither. Instead, she shook her head. "The crown has long been nothing but a symbol."

"I guessed as much," Tassariel said though she was smiling. "But who else actually *knows* all that?"

"I . . ." A look of wonder came across the queen's face. "I don't think anyone does."

Jasside felt her attention pulled away. Distant, yet drawing closer every beat, something was coming. For once, this day, it was a surprise she welcomed.

She laid a hand on the shoulder of both Tassariel and Arivana, grinning. "Do what you can. I'll see if I can buy you some time."

Turning away, she raised an eyebrow at Daye. Wisely, he kept his mouth shut.

This time, at least.

Jasside shadow-dashed across the battlefield. Once, twice. The mass of mierothi came into view, and she made one more leap to their position. She spared only a glance for their unusual state before sprinting behind their formation.

She held up her hands in greeting as the daeloth arrived in force.

"Quick!" she called, as the blurred streak of their passage came to a halt before her. "There's no time for explanations. Your mother's lives, and countless more, will be forfeit unless you all do exactly as I say!"

Ten thousand daeloth stared at her in confusion, but none raised a voice in challenge. After a moment, a grizzled veteran stepped forward. "We're here to obey, great mistress. Just tell us how we're needed."

She turned, pointing up at the floating fortresses now converging in the sky over the mierothi. "Distract them!"

Though he'd stood witness as Gilshamed managed to save the mierothi from death at the hands of the valynkar, the joy Draevenus felt at being saved in such a fashion, at seeing his reward for past faith paid in full, withered like corpses left out in the sun as chaos broke out on all sides.

Helplessness cut like a knife.

The transformation still raged on, and he'd felt no worse pain in almost two thousand years of existence, yet it still paled before the torment in his soul as his half-blooded kin fought and died on his behalf.

Dark missiles in the thousands streaked skyward, battering the underside of the hulking ships and sending chunks crashing down among the ranks of both armies, while great rays of flame struck from above like the clutch of a six-fingered god, melting flesh and sand and bone—the latter, though, rebuffed by strange fields springing up to block the worst effects and protect those below by a sorceress so powerful and skilled he knew she could be none other than his sister's mysterious protégé.

Ruul's gift kept on giving, now reaching a peak, and Draevenus could feel himself falling like a boulder down the other side, shoving all his will towards holding on for one more beat . . .

One more beat . . .

Arivana felt the weight of each measured step as she ascended the makeshift platform, made from the hastily piled remains of several wrecked war engines. Tears flowed freely down her cheeks. She'd thought to hold them back at first, thinking she must grow used to the sight of bloodshed if she was to be an effective leader. Sometime between the first step and the last, she'd changed her mind.

If ever I get used to death, I'll know then that I've failed.

She reached the summit of her podium and allowed her eyes to take in the full extent of the sorcerous conflagration erupting before her. Breath fled her lungs while heartbeat raced. It seemed the world itself might be torn asunder beneath such magics unleashed.

As if I'm not under enough pressure already.

The eyes of a thousand nearby soldiers pinned her into place, with more joining every beat. More pressure. More possibility for fear. Yet, somehow, she grew calm. Focused. She'd spoken to enough crowds to know how to emphasize for effect. The fact that untold lives were at risk did not make it any more difficult, she found. It only hardened her resolve.

If I'm to be queen, she thought, then stopped herself with a shake of the head.

"Something wrong?" Tassariel asked from behind her.

"Nothing. It's just . . . I *am* the queen. I think it's time the rest of them knew it, too."

"I couldn't agree more."

Arivana nodded. "Let us begin."

Tassariel moved just behind her, so close Arivana could feel the valynkar's breath on her neck, and extended glowing palms past her shoulders. Arivana's next exhale seemed loud enough to shake mountains.

It was time to address her people.

"Fellow Panisians," she said, "and citizens of all other nations present: The queen greets you."

Her voice rumbled with vitality, carrying itself over the heads of a million troops, even reaching the six grand skyships. A hush fell over those below though the sorcerous enfilade continued unabated.

She pressed on. "Circumstances being what they

are, it falls to me to issue orders directly to those claiming allegiance to our coalition. I have spoken to representatives from the opposing faction and discovered that a possibility for peace exists.

"As long as I live and breathe, no one should have to suffer for sins not his own. This war . . . ends . . . now!"

As she'd been speaking, she noticed a curious change in the exchange of sorcery. The dark streaks from below dwindled, then halted altogether. And now, she could see a barrier of some sort erected in the air above the entire Sceptrine front, a patchwork shield reinforced by what seemed many thousands of those masters of darkness. She knew, without doubt, that the change had been Jasside's doing, in response to Arivana's words. She'd only met the woman a toll ago, but she knew a good soul when she saw one.

Unfortunately, the flaming arcs from the flying fortresses did not relent. If anything, they intensified.

My work isn't done yet.

"To you, great houses of Panisahldron, I give this command with no uncertainty: Stand down! Negotiations have already begun. Your vigilance is acknowledged, and your display of power holds us all in awe, but the time has come to let words accomplish what power alone never can."

Arivana inhaled, holding it in as long as she dared. *Still*, the fire fell. Cracks began appearing along the dark barricade. They couldn't maintain it forever.

She pursed her lips and hunched her shoulders. *If logic won't sway you, let's see how you deal with a scolding.*

"The heads of your houses are dead," she said, fiercer than ever. "The old way of doing things is abolished. If you, dear citizens of mine, wish to continue your lives of privilege and luxury under my rule, you *will* obey. Now!"

The spells vanished in an instant.

Arivana sighed in relief. Suddenly exhausted, she sagged backwards, nearly falling into Tassariel's arms.

"Well done," the valynkar said in her ear. "Few people I've met can tolerate a sudden loss of status. Appealing to their baser natures always seems to motivate people even when nothing else will."

"I'm just glad it worked. This time, anyway."

"With the way you handled that, I think you'll have no problems controlling your people from here on out."

"Controlling them? You make me sound like Tior. Like a tyrant."

"Let me rephrase, then. You'll have no problem helping them see the right course of action."

Arivana felt herself smiling. "Maybe. But one little chastisement isn't going to make these people forget the power they wield. Or how little real respect they ever gave the throne." She stared out over the countless ranks of people for whom she now had responsibility. "Let's hope I can tell what the right way is myself."

"You will," Tassariel said.

"How do you know?"

The woman grinned. "Let's just say I have faith."

Draevenus felt himself surging, not to the bottom, as he expected, but to the top of something wholly new. Pain dwindled in an instant. In its place came relief so great he wept freely, unconcerned with appearances. His world of a moment before, of unparalleled torment, differed so greatly than the now, he scarce believed either could be real.

With hurricane force, the dark mist sucked back towards the box, which shut closed with a hiss. It all ended so fast, Draevenus barely had the presence of mind to catch himself on hands and knees as he fell.

With eyes closed, he inhaled.

The breath was the sweetest thing he'd ever tasted. Despite the arid atmosphere, his lungs filled with air more pure than babies' laughter, more refreshing than hot springs in winter. His clawless fingers pressed against sand, for once the less coarse of the two. Within, deep within, warmth blossomed like a flower on the first day of spring, permeating his body with every pulse. A warmth he'd not even known had been missing. But now that it was there, he couldn't imagine how he had lived so long without it.

Exhaling, he opened his eyes.

Angla stood before him. Draevenus could see the changes he'd felt reflected in her and others he had yet to notice. A full-faced smile revealed straight, flat teeth. Her obsidian skin shone smooth and glossy in the waning light. The edges of her eyes were ivory white, and the irises were . . .

"Brown," Draevenus said. "I'd forgotten that your eyes were brown."

"A hereditary trait, it seems," his mother replied.

She ran fingers through the brand-new hair running down over her shoulder, shimmering black locks with the faintest streaks of grey. Angla had not been a young woman—though not yet old either—when she'd first changed. Draevenus wondered what that meant about their life spans in this new state.

Then he realized what Vashodia had been trying to say.

And why she had fled.

He lowered his head and cried silently. This was the greatest gift Ruul could ever had given them. And his sister had missed out. Yet for all his sorrow, he understood instinctively why she had wished it that way.

"Do you feel it, son?" Angla asked. "In your back. It's so . . . so . . . I don't know how to describe it. Just let go. Let go, and you'll see what I mean."

Draevenus felt it. A knot of something clenched within the upper part of his back. Despite his conflicted emotions, he did as his mother asked.

He let go.

And from his spine sprouted black wings.

CHAPTER 23

Arms crossed, Vashodia tapped her foot against the frigid apex of the mountain as night began to fall. Facing south, the lands split three ways. Directly ahead, a few dozen lesser peaks of the Nether Mountains faded into the distance, shadows chopping them into pieces as the day's light waned. To their left, the land rolled up and away, gradually growing greener as the Fasheshish desert gave way to the fertile plains of Panisahldron. To the right, it twisted and curled down into the foggy bogs of Weskara. Far beyond them all, at the farthest visible edge before the world curved away, sparkled a slice of the ocean the mierothi had crossed during their exodus from the Veiled Empire.

The expanse of land before her might have been breathtaking, but she could not appreciate the beauty through a vision stained by red. Things had not gone to plan thus far. Not perfectly, anyway. Which, to her, was all that mattered.

Vashodia sighed. *Enough of the pieces have fallen into place. Things may still work out as I envisioned. Shall I become the child I seem because of a few minor setbacks?*

But "minor" didn't really cover it. She'd let that girl get to her.

Abyss take you, Jasside.

Her apprentice had taken to her task admirably, even without being explicitly instructed. She'd been there to temper Vashodia. To stand in the place of a conscience she knew had long since vanished. Fled, or chased away, the difference mattered naught. For the last nineteen hundred years and counting, Vashodia had been studying the effects of greatness combined with power and left unchecked. She'd be a fool to let such a fate befall her.

No, the problem hadn't been with Jasside's *fulfilling* her role. It had been with her doing it *exceedingly* well.

Vashodia knew the value of detraction, of opposing viewpoints. Every step of the path she walked needed that voice of reason asking if that was truly the best place for each foot to fall. Jasside had done all that . . . and more. Now Vashodia was beginning to question everything. The rightness of her cause. The justifications. Whether she could actually save the world.

Whether the world was even worth saving.

Vashodia shook her head. *No. That, at least, she made abundantly clear.*

Still, she worried, for the first time, about the possibility of defeat. And about the price she was willing to pay to give victory a fighting chance. Neither concern had crossed her mind for more than a few fleeting moments, and rarely at that, since she had embarked on this campaign all those centuries ago. But if she'd learned anything in that time, it was that nothing could ever be completely accounted for. Societies changed in subtle ways she hadn't expected, and even Ruul and Elos, those two claimants to godhood, had managed to surprise her.

And, of course, there was no predicting the heart.

Vashodia kicked in frustration, dislodging a small shower of stones down the snowy slope. She giggled as she watched them tumble.

"A pebble rolls down a mountain," she said to herself, "and the world's very turning changes. Or . . . it doesn't."

She used to be so good at predicting which it would be. But no longer. Now she found herself, more and more, playing a reactive role, a task ill suited to her temperament and expertise. Doable, of course—few things weren't—but far less comfortable than she would have liked.

But comfort, she knew, would soon be a luxury few on this planet could afford.

Vashodia turned north as she felt a familiar energy

signature dashing leagues closer by the beat. The apprentice returning, for the last time, to the mistress.

"What a shame that I have no more lessons to give."

Jasside shivered the moment she landed out of her final dash. Each breath filled her lungs with ice and little else, a stark indication of their elevation. She pulled her cloak close, glad she'd thought to don it again before leaving the battlefield. Vashodia, of course, didn't seem the least bit affected.

"What are you doing up here?" Jasside asked. "This must be the highest peak in the world."

"Outside of our old empire, there are only two higher, but both are too distant for my purposes."

"Which are?"

"You'll soon see."

Jasside scoffed. "Cryptic as ever. Can't you just this once deliver a straight answer?"

Vashodia waved dismissively. "By the time I explain, it will already be over. Patience, Jasside. This time, I only ask for a drop of it."

Jasside clenched her fists, forgetting the cold for the moment. "Will it be worth having left all your kin unprotected when they were at their most vulnerable? Will it be worth nearly killing us all?"

"I was sure you and the daeloth would be sufficient to protect them. As it was, I barely managed to escape."

"Escape? Abyss, Vashodia, don't you realize what you missed?"

As she turned her back, the mierothi looked less like a little girl than Jasside had ever seen. "I realize all too well."

Jasside jerked her head back, seeing the woman as if for the first time. The burden she'd been carrying. The responsibility. The pain and fear held hidden so long beneath a mask of absolute confidence. Jasside almost felt a voyeur as she spied all this and more in the slightly drooped shoulders of her mistress.

The anger she'd thought righteous vanished faster than the mist of her exhalation.

"What's going on?" Jasside said. "Something is happening. I can feel it. You can't afford to keep me in ignorance any longer. Please, I *must* know."

Vashodia only shook her head as she pointed to the sky.

Tassariel smiled as Arivana began giving orders like the queen she always could have been, but she felt little joy. Commanders, newly ascended heads of the great families, and foreign dignitaries all came to the girl, who handled them all deftly and fairly, with the grim determination of one only recently raised to authority and eager to get it right. The girl was a natural.

Tassariel wished she could be happy for her. It was everything they'd both wanted, after all, but now that they'd achieved it, she couldn't help but feel out of place. *I hadn't even been the one to save her. Some stranger did. It took me months to realize what needed to happen, yet Jasside arrived at the same conclusion in mere moments. And she had the talent to make it happen just as quick. What did I even do to help?*

"I'm . . . pointless."

The words came out at less than a whisper, and no one standing nearby could have possibly heard.

But someone still did.

"You are not pointless," Elos said. "You're exactly where you need to be at exactly the right time."

Tassariel shook her head. "I don't know how you can say that. I was supposed to be your chosen one, but chosen for what? I—we—did nothing here that made any difference."

"Not yet."

"The fighting is over, and it looks like Arivana will be able to handle herself from here on out. What else is left?"

"Oh, child. Did you really think helping secure a queen's throne was vital enough to be worthy of my descension?"

Tassariel scratched her elbow. "Wasn't it?"

"Hardly."

"But it was more than that. Look around us. Look at all the lives that were saved."

"As you have said, that had little to do with us."

"Then why the abyss are we here!"

"Players," Elos said. "So many different players

in this game. We all had to show up to throw in our hands. The cards have now been revealed, and I am proven to be the least of them."

"But . . . you're a god."

"What difference does that make?"

Tassariel sighed. "Less, apparently, than I had come to expect. Care to fill me in on the big secret?"

"Yes."

"Really?"

"Yes."

"That's . . . I mean . . . wow."

"I haven't even said anything yet."

"No, but you're willing to. That's saying something, coming from you. Should I be worried?"

"Yes."

Tassariel felt a chill run up her spine and realized she hadn't felt the icy churning of Elos's calculations in tolls. The physical aspect offered no relief before the growing dread of its absence.

"What is it? What's wrong?"

"I lied about my hand. I have one or two more cards to throw in. With luck, they will be enough to prepare you for what soon will come. Either way, they'll be the last I ever play."

"Last? What happened to all your calculations? I thought you could practically see the future."

"There are some things no one can see beyond."

"Like what?"

"Death, for one."

"And for another?"

Elos paused, whether searching for words or deciding how to respond, she didn't know, yet for some reason she felt herself growing more and more sad for each beat the silence stretched.

"Perhaps some other time," Elos said at last. "Tell me something, child. Do you trust me?"

"Yes," Tassariel said, surprised by how easily the assertion came to her. Her blind faith had been shaken, but something else had taken its place. A faith born of promises kept and character unveiled. A faith that lived.

"That is good to hear. There's something I need you to do, but I have no means to show you how. The only way is for you to . . . surrender."

Tassariel gulped. "You need to take control."

"Yes. I am sorry."

"Will it be like last time?"

"I have no plans to kill anyone if that's what you're asking."

"Good to know. So, how do I . . . ?"

"Just let go."

She nodded. "All right. Do it, then."

The force of his presence surged forward into her mind, neither ice nor lava this time but something solid, sturdy. Elos tingled throughout her muscles, dancing across her skin. Rather than fight him, she did as he had asked.

She surrendered.

Her body lurched forward, awkwardly. "First steps," her lips said with strange inflection, "are always the hardest."

Panic rose as control of her own body fell away. She fought the urge to claw her way back into the saddle of her being. *I told him I trusted him. Will I go back on my word so soon?*

The next few steps saw them both slowly ease into their new roles. Thankfully, Elos didn't have far to go.

He stopped her body a few paces away from Arivana. "My queen?"

She turned. "Tassariel? Yes, what is it?"

"I came to ask you a favor."

The girl smiled broadly. "Name it, and it's yours."

"I need your handmaiden."

"Flumere? Whatever for?"

Elos lifted Tassariel's hand, which brimmed with familiar energy shaped in an unfamiliar way. The handmaiden's eyes flared like falling stars. "The world needs to know who she is," Elos said through Tassariel's lips, "and why she, and her kind, are here."

Tassariel only wished she could ask herself what that meant.

"What *is* that?"

Jasside craned her neck, staring up at what appeared to be a crack in the sky. Its edges flailed like tattered cloth ravaged by gale-force winds. It looked to be getting wider.

"I knew, even before I met Ruul, that the world wasn't as simple as most people assumed," Vashodia said, ignoring the question. "And his very nature not only confirmed my suspicions but urged me to probe even deeper for the truth."

"And what truth would that be?"

Vashodia giggled. "We weren't the first species to lay claim to this world."

"We? You mean humans? I thought the valynkar were the first to settle here?"

"Think, girl. What did you just witness on that battlefield? What became of the rest of my kin?"

Jasside thought back, remembering the new shape Angla and the others had taken. Dark clones of the valynkar. *And if they were once human, transformed by their god into their current form, then* . . . "The valynkar were once human as well."

Vashodia snorted. "A fact those still living have forgotten."

"But who was here before us, then? And how the abyss do you know all this for certain?"

"As I said, my visit to Ruul prompted further investigation. He revealed the existence of the threat but had no way to ascertain its scope. Since his knowledge was as ancient as it came, I had to search even farther into the past. On my own."

Jasside gasped. "You peered through time."

Vashodia nodded.

"But that's dangerous! Gilshamed told me—"

"He filled your head with his own fears born of a limited mind. Justifiable, but ultimately pointless. The light illuminates too much, overwhelming the seer, but darkness hides the extraneous. We only see that which matters most."

"Exactly what we seek."

"Precisely."

"What did you find?"

"I found a people decimated by the arrival of our twin gods, their remnants flung to the farthest reaches of the void in a desperate escape. More importantly, I gazed into the very heart of their society and saw an enemy that would never forget. One that would never let go of revenge."

"Enemy? *What enemy?*"

Arivana winced as a surge of light danced from Tassariel's fingertips and slammed into her handmaiden. Flumere jolted. Her eyes and lips cut towards the valynkar like knives dipped in poison. Elos wove the spell around her, making it spin ever closer with each breath. Layer by layer, the caustic light seemed to strip away the woman Arivana thought she knew.

What remained was something unrecognizable.

Something . . . inhuman.

Tears streamed down cheeks that seemed hard and yellow, like candle wax if it were made of stone and sunken like a corpse yet, somehow, still vibrant, still alive. Two tall, thin slits stood in place of nostrils. Flumere's mouth protruded, almost beak-like but soft, and her jaw and neck slanted towards her chest as if a single piece of ridged flesh. Her exposed body bore all the same signs of her sex, but the positions of each joint and muscle were distorted enough to render hopeless any attempt at identification.

Arivana forgot how to breathe.

All the eyes once glued to her found a new place to rest. There would be no containing this. No trying to keep it a secret. Something momentous was being revealed, and she doubted anything short of divine intervention could stop the whole world from learning of it.

For one fleeting moment, Arivana wished it could all just go away. Her crown. The pain of her loss. The mountainous task ahead of her. The unpleasant secrets soon to be unveiled.

The moment passed. *I have work to do.*

Taking a deep breath, she folded her hands neatly together, taking the dancer's stance that Claris had taught her so many years ago. She became the very image of repose.

"Flumere," she said, forcing her gaze to remain steady upon the creature crouching naked before her. "Please, tell me what is going on."

The crack widened, radiating outwards like pain from a knife wound. Pressure assaulted her mind as it flashed open, and unknown power flooded from the breach. It was like nothing she'd ever felt before. Neither light nor dark, it was something else entirely. Something unholy.

Chaos.

The crack snapped shut. Its energy fizzled away, frayed strands wobbling throughout existence in no pattern she could discern. Jasside hazarded another glance skyward.

There were . . . things . . . blocking out the stars.

"Does that answer your question?" Vashodia asked.

Jasside forgot what she had asked.

"I don't understand."

"And I don't have time to explain. Please, Jasside, I need your help."

She felt a physical jolt at the words. "Come again?"

"You heard me. And you know I don't like repeating myself."

"Yes, but . . . you asked for help. It even sounded sincere. I'd almost say—"

"Abyss take me, girl, will you shut your mouth for once and just listen! There is a task I must perform, but I cannot do it alone. I. Need. Your. Help."

Jasside peered coolly into the last crimson eyes in the world. "What task?"

"Giving humanity a fighting chance to avoid our own genocide." Vashodia pointed towards the sky once more as the objects blocking the stars burst into flame. "Stopping the first wave of this invasion before they wipe out the bulk of our fighting force."

It was the word *invasion* that triggered it. Jasside felt the puzzle pieces snap cleanly into place. She knew, now, that she was right where she needed to be. She had been all along. There was no decision to be made.

"I'm yours to command," Jasside said.

Vashodia flicked her wrists. "Take these."

Jasside lifted her hands just in time to catch two metallic spheres. She smiled.

Ruul's light, it's about time I got to use these.

"**M**y name is Sem Aira Grusot. I am a spy. And . . . an assassin."

Though she didn't know how, Arivana managed to hold back the tears. It was, perhaps, that they'd all been shed, but young as she was, she knew no tragedy ever released its grip upon a grieving soul. Not entirely, at least. And with the eyes of the world all pointed in her direction, there was no room for error. Especially the error of weakness.

"Assassin," Arivana said. "Do you mean to say . . . ?"

"That I had a part in your family's death? Yes. My team was responsible for the fire that claimed their lives."

"Your *team*. I see."

Arivana did *not* see. But she knew she must appear to be in control. "Why did you do it?"

"To sow chaos among your kind and destabilize your greatest threats. It worked, for a time. But now that you're all here together—making peace, it seems—I see that our mission has failed."

"How many of you are there?"

"Enough." Flumere—no, Sem Aira Grusot—shook her head. "But don't expect me to be giving up any names. I won't betray my own."

"Just me."

It was a small voice, Arivana knew, and she hated herself for it. But the idea struck her to her core, and it was impossible to shake. Especially because . . .

"You helped me," Arivana said. "You went well beyond the duty of your position. You were . . . my friend."

"I was. I am. I . . ." Sem Aira hung her head. "I do not have to explain myself to you. I *will* not."

Elos pushed Tassariel's body forward, locking eyes with the queen. "Her reticence will be dealt with in time, your majesty. We have more pressing matters to address."

"What could be more pressing"—Arivana snapped a hand towards the thing standing where her hand-maiden had been—"than this?"

"The consequences of her failure." Tassariel sighed. "The punishment will not be endured by her, however, but by us."

"I don't understand!"

"You will." A sad smile spread across the valynkar's face. "It has been an honor to meet you, young queen. I have faith that you will lead humanity well."

Arivana felt a lump forming in her throat. "Tassariel? Why does it sound like you're saying good-bye?"

"Don't be absurd, my child. I am merely saying . . . hello."

"**S**hall we harmonize?" Jasside asked.

"No. Our tasks will intertwine but must be kept

separate. Link with your darkwisps"—Vashodia removed another pair of spheres from the folds of her robe—"and I will with mine. It should be sufficient for our purposes."

Jasside obeyed within the beat. She energized, flicking open the clasps on the metal balls with each thumb. Dense swarms surged skyward, crackling with black static. She directed her energy among them, imposing her will with ease, and soon found a few hundred new signatures aligning with hers in moments. The rush of amplified power pulled at her like a waterfall, and she gasped in ecstasy.

"Sweet blessed creator, I could get used to this."

"Another time, perhaps. We'll need to act quickly yet precisely. The margin for error is so insignificant, it might as well not exist."

"No time. Impossible odds. The world at stake. Am I forgetting anything?"

"People will hate us for what we do here today."

"Lovely."

"You've no issues with that?"

"Why should I? Just because people don't recognize their gifts doesn't mean we should stop giving them."

Vashodia's lips slowly twisted into something resembling a smile.

"Something funny?" Jasside asked.

"Just that we finally found something to agree on."

Jasside mirrored the expression. "Good. Our task?"

The mierothi lifted her gaze towards the sky. "To simply reach my target over such a vast distance will take up all my energy. I'll need you to be the bridge. Or, more accurately, the river."

"I create the current, and you swim it?" Jasside said, catching on immediately.

Vashodia nodded. She cracked open her spheres, and swarms of darkwisps—thicker, Jasside noted, than her own—buzzed around the small figure. Her mistress lifted a hand, manipulating matter into the shape of a disc no larger than her hand. Dragging a claw along the opposite palm, Vashodia drew her own blood, then smeared it across the disc she'd just created.

"Making an extension of yourself?"

In answer, Vashodia flicked the disc into the air. Jasside caught it on a thin wave of energy, holding it in place. Drawing a steady stream of power through her linked darkwisps, she lifted a hand towards the flaming objects in the sky and readied herself for a long push.

"No," Vashodia said. "Not that way."

Jasside raised an eyebrow. "In case you missed it, oh mistress of mine, there're some big scary . . . things . . . falling out of the void that we need to deal with."

"And we will. But not directly."

"Care to explain why not?"

"I do not know our enemy's capabilities, but Ruul hinted that he was all but helpless when he first encountered them. Until we know more, the only sure way is to hit them in a way they cannot deflect."

Vashodia pointed towards an empty spot in the sky.

Jasside squinted, trying to read what few stars

were already visible. Then she realized where she was staring.

"You . . . you can't mean to . . ."

"I can. And I *will*." Vashodia giggled. "Haven't you ever dreamed about killing a god?"

Though the celebration among the mierothi continued, Draevenus could not join in. Something was wrong. Not with their new bodies—he'd never felt better in his life!—but in the world at large. Something that had always been there, even if never consciously recognized, had now gone missing. Like floating on a sea, only to have the boat beneath him vanish.

His eyes drifted down past the jubilant faces of his kin, to a ground cloaked in dust kicked up by their dancing feet. An object lay there, small and forgotten.

The box that had contained the very gift they all now embraced.

Draevenus shuffled towards it, gently pushing through the crowd. No one paid him any heed as he knelt and, like a sickly infant, cradled the metallic container to his chest. It was empty now. Hollow. Just the like the unseen presence of his god. And knew what was missing.

Ruul.

Ruul was dead.

"He will not be forgotten," a woman said from behind him.

Draevenus turned to see a young valynkar with

lavender hair approaching. Other mierothi gave her a wide berth, gazes narrowed with distrust, but she seemed to be ignoring them.

"What would a valynkar know about Ruul?" Draevenus asked.

"Nothing, and less," came her reply. "But *I* happen to know a great deal." She stopped a few paces away, peering down on him with eyes that seemed more ancient than her age suggested.

Though he didn't know why, Draevenus felt humbled in her presence. He took hold of the sensation, turning it over and analyzing it, until he realized that he'd felt something similar before. Once. Very recently.

"What *are* you?" he said.

"A friend," she said. "Despite what history might suggest."

"It can't be. You're—"

"What? A *woman*?"

"I was going to say *here*. Down here. On the surface. I always thought you stayed . . . you know . . . up above?"

"The time for that will soon be gone. As will you if you don't heed my instructions carefully, and quickly."

"I'm supposed to just take your word, am I?"

"You will. Unless, of course, you wish to throw away the dying gift of the being you claimed to serve."

Logic told him to laugh in her face, but instinct screamed the opposite. He'd never had much success, throughout the ages, listening to the former.

"Very well," Draevenus said. "What would you have us do . . . Elos?"

"Survive," she said. "As long as you can. Fight on until your final breath. Do not lie down and rest as annihilation comes calling."

"Will it?"

Shaking her head, she pivoted and pointed towards the horizon. "It already has."

"**P**ush, girl."

"I am."

"Not hard enough."

"I must be nearly there by now."

"You're not even halfway."

Jasside felt her breath catch at the statement. Her appreciation for how vast this world and all of creation were grew tenfold in that moment. And with it, dread. "I don't think I can make it."

"You'll be fine. Just flare your darkwisps."

"Flare?"

"Pull all the remaining energy from them at once. It will destroy them but grant you a sizable increase to your capacity. Pace yourself, though. Burn through them too quickly, and this will all be for naught."

Jasside did as instructed. She singled out one of her harmonized darkwisps and snatched everything from it she could in a single beat. It fell to the ground, a scattered heap like flakes of spent ash, but she could feel the increase to her own power instantly. She pushed Vashodia's disc even farther into the sky.

After half a mark, she felt the boost of power begin

to fade, so she flared another darkwisp. The bonus power lasted just as long this time, but the energy required to move an object over so great a distance grew more demanding the farther away it traveled. She flared the next one sooner, and the next sooner than that. It became a race between the distance still to go and the darkwisps she had left under her control.

Sweat poured down her brow despite the freezing temperature as she maneuvered the disc with exponentially increasing amounts of effort. At last, with only three darkwisps remaining, her mistress cracked a brief smile. "Close enough. Hold it there and do not let it waver."

Shaking to obey, Jasside didn't have enough mental capacity to reply.

"Now, old man," Vashodia said, "let's see what you have to work with."

A growing sense of disembodiment fell over Jasside as both she and her mistress, at each other's side manipulated energies whose effect took place leagues and leagues away. The unease only grew as Vashodia probed an edifice more ancient than Jasside could fathom. A monolith in the sky she'd seen almost every night of her life.

The Timid Moon. Or, as the valynkar called it, the Eye of Elos.

Its bright circle blossomed into sight, illuminating the world below with pale light several tolls ahead of schedule.

"What did you do?" Jasside asked.

"Just maneuvering for an approach vector," Vashodia said. "Got to get the angle just right."

"Huh?"

"Enough questions. I need to concentrate."

Jasside relented—not understanding the answers anyway—and angled her glance sideways towards the cluster of flaming objects. Only they were flaming no longer. Closer now, they streaked across the sky perpendicular to the summit upon which they stood, and Jasside was able to get her first clear look at them.

Her first thought was of elongated boulders, impossibly huge and falling from a great height, but that conception soon faded before the truth. They were not falling—they were flying. Banking and swooping, they arranged themselves into what could be called, with no uncertainty, a formation.

And they were slowing down.

Though they still appeared as great lumps of rough stone, she now knew them for what they were.

"Skyships," Jasside said.

Vashodia, lost in her own working of power, merely grunted in reply.

"But who are they? And where did they come from? And what the abyss are we trying to accomplish here?"

Jasside turned back only to find the Timid Moon twice as large as she remembered and with its edges now ringed by flames.

The Eye of Elos was on the move.

"Keep pace with it," Vashodia demanded. "I'm not done yet."

Jasside once more complied. Out of the corner of her eyes, she witnessed the front edge of each skyship begin to glow with lurid, colorless light.

"**W**e come," Sem Aira Grusot said.

Arivana followed the trail of the woman's eyes and squinted towards a darkening horizon. Through the shimmer of the desert heat, she saw no more than shadows, faint specks against a sky caught midway between day and night.

"That was . . . quicker than I expected," Sem Aira continued. "That can only mean—"

"What?" Arivana asked.

But the creature clamped her oddly curled lips shut and shook her head.

Arivana knew she would need to press her for answers, but the thought of interrogating the woman who had once been her closest confidante drove hollow spikes through her gut. *Someday soon, I'll get answers from you. But not today. Today, I can only mourn for the friend I lost and the trust broken so completely by this hurtful truth.*

The young queen vowed never again to let herself become so vulnerable. Never to let herself be duped or betrayed. She gritted her teeth as the last remnants of the child inside her died. A necessary sacrifice, she deemed, if she was to hold together the broken pieces of her people through the trial to come.

She glanced back towards the horizon, which

seemed to have captured Sem Aira's gaze. A sound of surprise escaped her throat.

Those specks she'd so easily dismissed had morphed into boulders in the sky, growing larger—and closer—by the beat. Their front edges began glowing with malevolence, and her throat closed up.

"What are they?" Arivana asked. "Why are they here?"

"Punishment," Sem Aira said.

"For what?"

The strange grey-yellow lips curled up in a sad smile. "For the sins of your kind against ours. Sins, it seems, you have forgotten in the eons that have passed. I see that now."

"Then *do* something! Tell them to stop! Tell them it wasn't our fault!"

Sem Aira sighed. "I doubt they would listen to me. None of this was according to plan." She chirped with what Arivana could only assume was laughter. "But if there's one word that could adequately describe my people, it would be . . . *uncertainty*. It quite literally empowers us."

"Empowers?"

The woman shook her head again. "I've said too much. You'll see what I mean soon enough."

Arivana knew that issues of power had never been her forte. Claris and Tior had been experts in the field, and lately, in their absence, Tassariel had been whom she'd turned to for advice.

She spun, seeking to locate the woman, even knowing the valynkar was not . . . herself.

What she saw, instead, was a sky filled with figures who were the very embodiment of both light and dark. The valynkar she recognized, but the others . . .

"Those must be mierothi," she said to herself. "I didn't know they, too, could fly."

The two races, once the most bitter of enemies, sailed through the air, weaving among each other in a display that would have left her breathless on any other day. With the impending threat, Arivana was only glad they weren't at each other's throats. A toll ago, the story had been different.

It was amazing what could change in so short a time.

She hoped that the change would have an effect on whatever was occurring now.

Valynkar and mierothi alike swept through the dusty air above her, arranging themselves into two massive blankets of cloth and flesh. The valynkar led. The mierothi formed up fifty or so paces behind them. She could see Tassariel issuing orders from the ground, flanked by a mierothi male just as youthful and confident in appearance as she.

Arivana's eyes were drawn sideways as the gathered glow from the distant objects shot forward like hungry vipers.

"I'm well clamped now," Vashodia said. "I don't need you anymore."

It was not a moment too soon. Jasside collapsed.

Her power fled, and any hope of retrieving it vanished, along with her sense of balance. A lone darkwisp limped free of her control and skated down the mountainside, soon lost in drifts of shadowed snow. Jasside barely had the strength left to angle her head and eyes towards the conclusion of all she'd worked for.

The skyships raced sideways across her line of vision, strange energy beaming forward from their hulls. But the Timid Moon approached them faster still.

"Just a matter of time, now," Vashodia said. "Let's hope my brother is cognizant enough to heed to the last testament of our supposedly rival god."

Jasside could barely comprehend the words, much less make sense of them. It was all she could do to keep her gaze locked upon the clash soon to come. But even that effort proved futile as both the cluster of skyships and the Timid Moon dashed away, becoming mere dots on the horizon opposite whence they came. Her neck could only bend so far.

Shaking, Vashodia sat down at her side and sighed in obvious relief. "There. All I can do, for now. In less than a mark, it will be finished."

"What will be?"

"The first skirmish of the war to come."

"You call this a skirmish?"

"Yes. Unfortunately. Things will only escalate from here. We're going to need help."

"Nearly every nation in the world is already gathered. Who else can we call upon?"

"Old friends." Vashodia smiled, then a sly look came

across her face. "And speaking of which, did I mention that Mevon Daere is still alive?"

"What!"

Tassariel watched from the background of her own mind and body as Elos directed her people, in concert with the mierothi, in a desperate defense of life itself.

Energy beams raked towards them from an enemy as ancient as history itself. The valynkar formed a wall, erecting their patchwork shield just paces away.

The beams vanished just outside.

Behind them, the virulent rays re-formed, having somehow skipped across the ensuing space. But now, a wall of darkness met them. The strange beams, which seemed a different color every time her eyes grazed across them, met their match in the even more massive barrier of shadows.

Energy exploded across the sky, careening every which way in chaotic patterns. But no one that she could see was harmed.

Elos directed her eyes once more towards the approaching skyships. Tassariel could see them gathering energy for another attack. But she saw something else as well. Behind them, closing fast, came a disc of pale, reflected light.

Is that the Eye of Elos?

"Yes," Elos whispered in her voice. "I'm afraid my calculations were correct on this point. My time draws to a close."

What do you mean?

"Take care, Tassariel. I couldn't have asked for a more faithful or capable servant."

I'm not even sure what I did.

"You helped me experience my people again. To understand what they've become. To love them even if they can't or won't return it. The abyss will soon take me, but this close to the end, there's no reason to hold back what little there is left of me. You've convinced me, by your very nature, that I should use myself to help those in need."

Tassariel felt power flow out of her, but it was not the simple energy she was used to manipulating. It was greater, more complete. Like a woven wool robe compared to an unshaven sheep. It was the same power she'd felt coursing through her the day of her hundredth birthday. Yet she could see no effects around her. The power manifested far, far away, touching those lost souls lying dormant in the temple of healing.

Awakening them.

"Tell Gilshamed, you're wel—"

The flaming orb that housed her god's body, almost forgotten by her in the distance, intruded into the middle of the enemy skyship formation . . .

. . . and detonated.

She lost and regained all sense of herself and her surroundings in the next moment. Surging forward once more into the forefront of her own body, Tassariel gasped in a breath fully under her own control for the first time in a toll.

It felt glorious and horrible all at once.

She flexed every muscle in her body, only barely aware of the debris falling to the ground a few leagues away. Lifeless scrap and nothing more. She was too busy exalting in the fact that she was herself again. Whole.

Elos was gone. And in his place came something she'd had her whole life, and whose absence she'd only grown used to in recent months. Tears flowed freely down her face as she flexed her back, and her wings sprang forth once more.

At last . . . I'm whole.

"Is it over?" Arivana asked, watching pieces of the attacking skyships fall scattered and flaming to the ground.

"No," Sem Aira Grusot said. "That was only one fleet. We have many.

"I'm afraid this war has only just begun."

EPILOGUE

Yandumar swept a cloth-covered finger along the display case, which was lit from behind by discreetly placed lightglobes. He ran his hand along the length of his personal shrine, then raised the pearl-colored cloth to his eyes. Faint grey specks screamed at his sight. Dust.

Once again, my vigilance falls short. Will my failures never end?

"We have servants for that, you know."

The emperor of the once-veiled empire turned to face his best friend and greatest adversary.

His wife.

"I know, Ren," Yandumar said. "You don't need to remind me every day."

"Apparently I do." Slick Ren approach his side and rubbed a hand down his arm. She perched her chin on his shoulder, and a lock of red hair fell into his peripheral vision. "And you have more important things to concern yourself with."

"What? Like running this abyss-taken empire?"

"It will only become that way if you stop ruling it. No one else can do the job half as well as you can. I thought we'd exhausted this particular subject of discussion?"

Yandumar shrugged her off. "Don't you have some dissidents to intimidate?"

She let loose a throaty laugh. "There haven't been any of those in a year at least, my sweetness. Word got round of how the last bunch were dealt with."

"With the tips of your blades, you mean."

"Why, dearest, you wound me!"

"Just as you wounded them," he said wryly.

"But it was my brother's silver tongue that made them see reason," she protested.

"That would almost be convincing," Yandumar said, "if Derthon still had one."

Slick Ren laughed again, nestling her cheek deeper into his neck. She tried to grab at the cloth covering his hand, but he jerked it out of reach. She should know better.

"Come to bed, Yanny?" she asked. "I'd like to entertain the notion that I'm still a young woman, from time to time. Please don't make me suffer."

The edge of pleading in her tone was not lost on him, but it moved him not. He hardened his gaze on the display case. "I made a vow—"

"Abyss take your vows!" she said, tensing. "What good have they ever done?"

He opened his mouth to retort but found no words that could adequately describe the conviction inside him. He shook his head instead. "It's just who I am, Ren. I thought you'd realized that by now."

Though some part of him expected, or even *wanted* her to blow up at him, she merely sighed and withdrew from his touch. "Don't stay up too late this time," she said. "There's only so much you can do to fight the dust."

No matter how much I do, it will never be enough. "Sure."

Her sigh seemed to suck the air from room as she departed. Each footstep echoed across the empty expanse of the receiving chamber, and the musky scent of her lingered long after she'd gone. Even the smell of sawdust and mortar, which permeated the palace as the repairs finished up, were nothing compared to the enticing aroma of his wife of these past two years. Yandumar knew he'd not been the best of husbands to her, but knowing didn't necessarily make it any easier to improve. He'd long been devoid of any motivation to make things better.

Why even try when I've already lost my best reason to live on?

The door clicked closed at the far end of the drafty, rectangular room. Yandumar resumed his cleaning.

Scrubbing from one end to the other, back and back again, he set about ensuring that not a single smudge or speck of dust remained on the glass front of the display. He had to replace the cloth three times. And though he knew not how long it took, eventually he'd cleaned it well enough to satisfy his . . . .

Obsession. No use calling it anything other than what it was.

Yandumar pressed his forehead into the cold stone just fingers away from the illuminated glass though careful not to mar it with impressions from his skin. He let loose a long-held breath.

"Oh, son," he said, "why did I have to lose sight of what was most important? Why did I let my focus stray to things that mattered so little when compared to family?"

"Do not blame yourself," called a deep voice from far behind him. "The chaos of such times as we went through made many things difficult to discern. What truly counted chief among them."

Yandumar squeezed his eyes shut, unable to face even the specter of his son. Such visitations were frequent in the past few years but never brought any comfort. A small surge of joy, perhaps, before reason kicked in. But after that, only regret. Only pain.

A few words of logic usually sufficed to banish the illusion.

"There are no excuses for what I did," Yandumar said. "I can only hope for some small measure of atonement. But that will not come for a long time yet. It may not *ever* come. And certainly not if I stray from my own vows."

"What vows would that be?" the ghost of his son asked.

"To never forget who I lost. To never let this empire forget who saved them."

The ghost sighed. "My part was never significant, in the grand scheme of things. I killed the emperor, yes, but I saw that he was a man long wearied of the life he'd been dealt. In the end, I saved no one but myself."

Yandumar sagged deeper against the wall. The specter had never been quite so eloquent as this. Nor so wrong. "But you didn't manage that. I should have been there to protect you . . . to watch your back at least . . . but I was too busy playing general for the revolution instead of paying attention to the whole reason I got involved with it in the first place."

"You did a duty no one else could have when you had it thrust upon you. I'd be a fool to blame you for what any sane man would call heroism."

"Don't say that," Yandumar spat, fighting the urge to whirl around and force the ghost gone with a fist. *I've even started to hallucinate the sound of his footsteps. How long until sanity slips away entirely?* "I'm no hero. I never was. Even a memory has no right to mock me."

The ghost laughed. "You've grown old, Father. But not *that* old. Can't you—won't you—see what's right in front of you?"

"I see a wish," Yandumar said, tears shaking loose from trembling eyes. "Nothing more. One I don't deserve to have come true."

"I see one as well. And not long ago, I thought as you did."

Yandumar grunted. Much as he wished the ghost to fade, as it always had before, he was unable to resist playing along. "What changed?"

"I realized," his son's ghost said, "that I must forgive myself. If I don't, I can't expect anyone else to do it for me. And I certainly won't find any meaning with the life I've been given."

Yandumar couldn't take it anymore. The specter had never lingered so long. Had never spoken with such force or surety.

With such truth.

He fell to his knees. "Please, spirit, leave me be. Haven't I suffered enough for my sins?"

"Too much." Heavy footfalls rang out, coming closer. "Perhaps it's time to put our self-inflicted pain to rest?"

Yandumar could only wonder, frozen by disbelief, as a waft of warm breath fell across the back of his head. A moment later, a palm as large as his own came to rest on his shoulder.

"It . . . it *can't* be . . ."

"It is, Father," Mevon said. "I'm home."

Yandumar jumped to his feet, uncertainty fleeing. Energy blazed through his limbs. Without hesitation, he formed a fist and slammed it through the display case. Glass shattered, cutting his knuckles, but he barely paid heed to the blood or pain. He reached in and snatched the object contained within.

"I kept it safe for you son," he said, "for some reason

I couldn't explain. I think some part of me hoped that it would someday come in handy. That it would have another chance to live up to its namesake."

Yandumar dropped the metallic object into his son's outstretched hand.

Mevon twirled Justice a few times for good measure.

And smiled.

Here ends book II

ACKNOWLEDGMENTS

Once again, I have to thank my agent, Nicole Resciniti, and my editor, David Pomerico. Getting a book published was a dream come true. Being asked to continue writing? Well, it doesn't get much better than that. I'm grateful for your willingness to work around the difficulties that stem from my military service, especially that one time I had to—REDACTED FOR REASONS OF NATIONAL SECURITY—man, that was wild.

To my parents and sisters: Thanks for all the endless support and encouragement and feedback. You guys have always rocked, and you always shall.

To my favorite alpha-reader (who also happens to be my wife): Sorry about all the nights you spent staring at the back of my head while I typed and/or stared at the blank screen in defeat. I know you'd have rather snuggled up on the couch and watched TV, or anything else really, but I couldn't have done any of this without you.

To my boys: Thank you for constantly reminding me about the need for imagination.

And to my readers: What is a story without someone to share it with? You make all of this worthwhile. Seriously.

ABOUT THE AUTHOR

Born in 1983, **NATHAN GARRISON** has been writing stories since his dad bought their first family computer. He grew up on tales of the fantastic. From Narnia and Middle-Earth to a galaxy far, far away, he has always harbored a love for things only imagination can conjure up. He counts it among the greatest joys of his life to be able to share the stories within him. He has two great boys and an awesome wife who is way more supportive of his writing efforts than he thinks he deserves. Besides writing, he loves playing guitar (the louder the better), cooking (the more bacon-y the better), playing board/video/card games with friends and family, and reveling in unadulterated geekery.

www.nathangarrison.com
@NR_Garrison